TEMPTED BY FOLLY

BOOK ONE
THE ELLSWORTH ASSORTMENT

CHRISTINA DUDLEY

WILLIAM ELLSWORTH = (1) HENRIETTA BALDRIC   CHARLES ELLSWORTH = JEANNE MARTINEAU
                  = (2) CATHERINE CATCHWAY
                  = (3) ANNE FIELDING

(1) FLORENCE

(1) LILY

(2) TYRONE

(2) ARAMINTA

(3) BEATRICE

BENJAMIN   AUSTIN

THE
Ellsworth Assortment

CHAPTER ONE

My honour in the honour of my family is bound.
— Fanny Burney, *Cecelia* (1782)

O h, heavens, no," muttered Lily Ellsworth, peering through a gap in the window coverings into the tidy garden of Hollowgate. "Minta—stop bouncing that ball—and Tyrone, go and see what Beatrice is crying about."

With a sigh, her younger sister Araminta stuffed her India rubber ball into the Derby porcelain vase and flung herself across the sofa, but Minta's twin Tyrone did not bother to glance up from his book, and little Beatrice carried on wailing upstairs.

"Why are you imprisoning us here?" asked Minta. "Aggie is waiting for me at Oram's Arbour, and she'll wonder where I've got to."

"Shhhh!" Lily held up an imperious hand, only to ball it in a fist the next moment and shake it vigorously. "Oh—no! She's done it! I know she's done it! Here they come! Sit up, Minta. Tyrone, for pity's sake, close that book and go and shut Bea up. Stow her in a closet, if need be."

Tyrone groaned but forsook Defoe's *A General History of the Pyrates* and dragged himself off, just as the back door opened and closed, and Florence Ellsworth glided into the sitting room, trailed by the Dreadful Mr. Gregory. She was a tall, pale young lady with dark hair and grey eyes who would have been singularly pretty if she smiled.

"You must congratulate us, Lily," said Florence serenely. "Where is Papa?"

"Where he always is," answered Lily, her tone decidedly cross. "In the library."

The Dreadful Mr. Gregory murmured something to Florence and then excused himself, leaving her to face her sisters. "Lily, that was very rude of you. Why did you not congratulate us?"

"Oh, Florence, forgive me, but I couldn't! Because I think it's *horrible*. I would as soon see you marry a post as Mr. Gregory, and if you do marry him, I think you will regret it your whole life."

"Are you indeed going to marry Dreadful Mr. Gregory, Flossie?" asked Minta, fishing her ball out of the vase and tossing it in the air to catch behind her back.

"Don't call him that. And what have I said about throwing your ball in the house, Minta?"

"Not to do it," Minta replied, giving it another toss. This time she missed the catch and the ball rolled away under the sofa. Though she had reached the mature age of fourteen, she dived to retrieve it, heedless of her dress riding up to reveal the voile trim of her pantaloons.

Before Florence could reprimand her, Tyrone reappeared with little Beatrice in tow. "She managed to lock herself in Wilcomb's room," he explained, pushing his youngest sister toward his oldest, that he might return to his book.

"Whatever were you doing in the cook's room, dearest?" asked Florence, smoothing Beatrice's rumpled brown hair. "Remember you mustn't enter people's private quarters unless you are invited."

"I heard Wilcomb tell Boots that she was cutting out illustrations from Papa's old copies of *The Gentleman's Magazine* to paste up in her room, and I wanted to see them, and then I couldn't—I couldn't get the door to open again." The memory made sobs break out anew. "And I thought she would find me there and be angry!"

"*I* would be angry, you prying little creature," said Lily, as Florence tried to hush and soothe the little girl.

"Lily," chided Florence, "you're not helping."

"How can you expect me to help?" cried Lily, throwing herself to her knees to fling her arms about both Florence's legs and all of Beatrice. "When you have decided to do something absolutely, utterly foolhardy?"

"Nonsense," said Florence, trying without success to wriggle from Lily's grasp. "I am doing the wisest thing. Let go of us. And do get up. Mr. Gregory will be back any minute with Papa."

But Lily only clutched them harder, making Beatrice start to giggle and Minta grin and Tyrone even look up from his book. "I won't. I won't let you go, Florence, until you promise me you won't do it. Promise me you won't marry that block! That rectorly, prebendarical, clerical *Androides*—"

"Pardon my interruption, Miss Lily," came Mr. Gregory's robust voice from the doorway. "You were saying?"

He was not an unattractive man, but his burly chest and silver-streaked hair always put the younger Ellsworths in mind of a woodpigeon. Behind the rector stood their father Mr. William Ellsworth, tall and bald, and affecting not to have heard or seen anything amiss.

Lily had the grace to turn crimson, and she stood up, making her curtsey, smoothing her frock, and taking a seat beside Minta. "It was nothing."

Florence hastily put Beatrice aside and went to stand beside her betrothed.

"Florence, Mr. Gregory, I congratulate you," said William Ellsworth in his best beneficent-patriarch voice, taking each of their hands in his to form one single chain of blessedness. "May you enjoy, in future, such happiness as I have ever found in the married state."

"Thank you, Papa."

"Thank you, Mr. Ellsworth."

The patriarch then turned his radiant gaze on his other offspring. "My children, I hope you will not be behindhand in welcoming Mr. Gregory as a new brother."

One by one, the latter Ellsworths approached the clergyman, Lily pale and martyred, leading Beatrice as if to the scaffold. Araminta whistled cheerfully, transferring her ball from one hand to the other that she might shake with the rector, and favoring him with a grin.

As for Tyrone, he carefully slipped a pen knife between the pages of his book to mark his place before coming forward.

"I will tell your stepmama the good news, Florence," Mr. Ellsworth continued. "I know she will be delighted, and you must go up to her room later to receive her felicitations." Turning to his future son-in-law he added, "Mrs. Ellsworth will share our universal joy, I am certain, but you must excuse her, Mr. Gregory. Her health does not allow her to participate in our frequently rumbustious family life, and she has been particularly weak of late."

Mr. Gregory bowed his acknowledgment. "I hope she feels better soon."

Continuing to beam upon the lovers, Mr. Ellsworth raised two fingers in blessing, as if he were the bishop, and withdrew.

And that, thought Florence, *is that.*

No sooner was their father gone than Araminta took advantage of her older sisters' distraction to escape, ball in hand, but none of the others showed any sign of yielding the sitting room to Florence and her new intended. Tyrone's continued presence was not malicious—he merely opened his book again—and Beatrice preferred Florence above all her other half-siblings, so her remaining behind was to be expected. She even imitated Lily's example and took up her sewing, a clumsy little sampler of which she was proud. No, Florence had no objection to Tyrone and Beatrice being there to hear her first official conversation with Mr. Gregory as her accepted lover, but she did very much mind Lily. Lily, who dug in her workbasket as if it had done her an injury, and whose intermittent throat-clearings and humming made Florence want to toss a pillow at her.

"How beautiful the Easter service was," Florence said to Mr. Gregory.

"You and my sister did commendable work with the flowers in the church," he replied. He had a large voice to correspond with his large chest, and therefore his speeches tended to emerge as Pronouncements.

"Has Miss Gregory enjoyed the hyacinths she took home after the service?"

"She has, and the dean's wife called and remarked on their beauty." (Here Lily gave an audible yawn, holding the back of her hand to her mouth.)

"I hope you will dine with us soon," Florence said in a louder voice. "You and Miss Gregory."

"It would be a pleasure," Mr. Gregory replied. "Between my duties at the cathedral and St. Eadburh's there are many claims upon my time, but you, my dear Miss Ellsworth, will always be accounted a happy interruption."

(Scoffing sound from Lily, which she made a half-hearted attempt to disguise by blowing her nose in her handkerchief.)

Mr. Gregory turned a questioning eye on his almost-sister-in-law, one brow raised. When Lily did not receive the look, he regarded Florence again. "And of course there will be the wedding itself. I am anxious for you to name the date."

He might speak of anxiety, but he did not look at all anxious, and Florence was reminded of one of his more frequent sermon points: in all things moderation. Even Mr. Gregory's emotions were moderate, and she hoped soon to learn to moderate her own. She might not wear her heart always on her sleeve as Lily did, but Florence feared she still did feel some things altogether too strongly.

She hesitated before replying, not wanting him to know how much thought she had already given to this question, as if she had expected his offer. "What would you say to later in the summer, Mr. Gregory, after the Races and Election Week and such?"

Lily gasped then, abandoning her pretense of not listening. "But Florence, that would be July, and it is already April!"

Now it was Mr. Gregory's turn to affect deafness. "I think there is merit in the idea. We will consult your father and my sister before we decide. I will also confer with the dean regarding my prebendal duties."

"Of course." Even as she said it, Florence was aware of a twinge of disappointment that his sister's opinion entered into the matter. And another twinge that, considering how Mr. Gregory's plodding courtship had taken a year to bear fruit, he still had these matters left to do.

More murmured conversation followed, which made Lily fidget with impatience and Tyrone leave the room to seek quiet. Unfathomably dull topics (to Lily's mind) were canvassed, including improvements to be made at the rectory, what Miss Gregory intended to plant in the garden, a remark of the archdeacon's recently overheard and what it might mean, etc. etc. At length, however, Mr. Gregory rose to take his leave, pressing Florence's hand and bowing to the remaining sisters.

When the door shut behind him, Lily counted to ten, to give him time to get away, but it was Florence who spoke first.

"Lily Ellsworth, you made that as mortifying for me as possible," Florence accused. "How could you have been so discourteous?"

"How?" echoed Lily, ready for the fight. "How could I *not* be discourteous if I love you? Florence, you cannot expect me to be glad, to learn you are going to marry such a person. Such an—insufferable, dreadful person!"

"You speak of your own rector thus?"

"I don't speak of him as my rector when I call him names," countered Lily. "I have no objections to the man as a clergyman—apart from thinking his sermons are ten minutes too long and that he has no poetry in his soul. I only object to Mr. Gregory as your husband."

"And why would that be?" Florence demanded, her grey eyes glowing like shards of ice. "He is an honorable, intelligent, sensible man."

"Yes, and he's old and serious and wooden as well! And he speaks at the same volume, whether he is in the pulpit or out of it. Oh, darling Florence! Imagine your life! Imagine every day, every hour, having conversations such as you just participated in. Only worse, because your other companion will be Miss Gregory, who is old before her time from keeping house for him. Do you not see that will be your fate as well, if you don't die of boredom within a year?"

"Our conversation did not bore me," declared Florence. "I happen to find those subjects interesting—indeed, I do. You, of all people, should understand how sweet a calm and orderly life sounds to me. Have we not had enough of upheaval and notoriety in our family?"

"I suppose you mean because of Papa."

"Of *course* I mean because of Papa."

"What has Papa done?" asked Beatrice.

"Nothing, poppet," said Florence, while Lily said, "What has Papa *not* done, rather?"

Florence favored Lily with a reproachful look and then took little Beatrice's hand. "Papa has married several times, and people like to talk about such things."

"Never mind that," Lily waved this off. "I will explain to you later, Bea. But Florence, if you want to marry a man simply because he is not Papa, then there are thousands of other gentlemen you might consider. Why did you so rashly snatch at the first one?"

Florence swelled with indignation. "I did not 'snatch' at him, Lily. And it was not rash at all, on my part. It has been at least a year since you told me you thought Mr. Gregory was sweet on me—"

"I said it as a warning, Floss, not as an encouragement!"

"—And I have given it much consideration in that time. He will make a good and steady husband, just as he has been a good and steady rector and brother."

"I will try to love him," vowed Beatrice, coming to perch on Florence's lap. "If you do."

"Thank you, sweeting."

"But *do* you love him, Floss?" questioned Lily. "Because if you really, truly do, I may marvel at it, but I will try my very best to hold my tongue and conquer my aversion."

Color rose to Florence's pale cheeks. "I am—quite fond of him. Of course I am, or I should never have accepted him. And I expect, with time, I will come to love him. Dearly."

"Ardor indeed," said Lily dryly. She pressed her lips together, shaking her head.

"I know you don't remember Mama much at all—you were so very young when she died in her carriage accident, but she said to me more than once that a woman must choose a husband for sensible reasons if she hopes to live a contented and blameless life. She said we must not be confused by dashing looks or heart flutterings or such like because they don't last."

"That's because *she* was confused by dashing looks and heart flutterings!" retorted Lily. "That's what got her Papa. And how contented could her life have been, if she was saying such things to her little girl?" Snapping the fabric flat of the shirt she was mending, she stabbed the needle through the material as if each tiny stitch were an enemy.

"If you marry Mr. Gregory, does that mean you will not live at Hollowgate any longer, Florence?" Beatrice asked, her blue eyes filling.

"For mercy's sake," groaned Lily, "don't start crying again, Bea. I can't bear it."

"I'm not crying," Beatrice uttered, frowning at Lily. Of all the family, Lily and Beatrice bickered the most, largely because, of all the family, Lily made no special allowances for Beatrice being the Baby.

"Not yet, you aren't."

"But who will teach me my lessons?" Beatrice pressed. "If you are gone, Florence? You said you would do it. My mama is too sick to and Lily is too—Lily."

"You'll have go to school in town with Minta, of course," said Lily.

Beatrice shook her head with decision. "I don't want to go to school in town. Minta says it's dull and the girls are silly."

"That's because Minta only cares for games and sport," Florence reasoned. "I think you would like it."

"Why can't I have a governess, if I can't have you?"

The two older sisters looked at each other. To them it was obvious enough. With a father who had married the two previous governesses, it would be folly indeed to bring another one to Hollowgate, even if the third Mrs. Ellsworth's continued existence prevented history repeating itself.

"We'll see," answered Florence vaguely, adding *Persuade Beatrice that school is lovely* to her mental list. An antenuptial list which included other daunting tasks such as training Lily to keep house and manage the servants; encouraging Minta to begin behaving like a young lady; ensuring Tyrone did not spend his entire vacation sitting indoors reading; teaching one of the servants—probably Monk—to keep track of Mrs. Ellsworth's medicines and tinctures and whatnot; and, perhaps most difficult of all, keeping an eye on her father.

There was one more item on her list, but it was one Florence Ellsworth would not acknowledge, much less admit. It was that she wanted her intended husband to love her. Not just be fond of her but *love* her. Florence might speak of love as folly when it applied to her father; she might tell herself that it was wisest and best, as her mother counseled, to choose with one's mind and let love follow, but in her heart of hearts there was a hard little fear, a thorn among the roses: what if fondness always remained fondness?

And what if, if she would only dare to confess it, love might be the food of her soul?

CHAPTER TWO

Manners makyth man.

— Motto of William of Wykeham, founder of Winchester College and New College, Oxford (14th c.)

A funeral procession blocked the path of the coach.

"It must be for the third Mrs. Ellsworth," gasped the matronly woman opposite Robert Fairchild to her sister. "She's gone off at last."

"Third Mrs. Who? How can you tell?" asked the other eagerly, pressing her nose to the glass, her boot sliding against Fairchild's. He shifted his foot away.

"William Ellsworth's third wife. Have I never told you about the Ellsworth Assortment?"

"Ellsworth Assortment, Letitia? What on earth?"

"One husband, three wives, five children. And two of the children might not even belong to him! It's a scandal, that family! That William Ellsworth, I should say. I know no harm of his younger brother. But surely this must be the third Mrs. Ellsworth's funeral because—see—there are all the children. That's Miss Ellsworth and Miss Lily from the first Mrs. Ellsworth, you know—" pointing a plump finger. "Miss Ellsworth is the tall, pale one—engaged to the rector of St. Eadburh's—"

"Is that the rector? The stocky one in the robes?"

"Yes—Mr. Gregory. Quite a distinguished fellow, I hear. But see next to Miss Ellsworth? That is Miss Lily. Isn't she lovely? Even mourning clothes couldn't make that girl look plain! And then behind them are the twins, Master Tyrone and Miss Araminta. They are from the second Mrs. Ellsworth, and you can see they don't look a thing like the first two…"

"Not a thing," agreed her sister eagerly, "for they are both fair, and the older sisters are brunette. Are the twins the ones that…?"

"Yes, rumor did say that the second Mrs. Ellsworth—caught more than William Ellsworth when she married him."

"No, sister!"

"Yes, Adelaide, people whispered that…" cupping a hand to her sister's ear, she supplied more information, to that one's repeated squeaks and exclamations.

Fairchild shook out his newspaper and held it up, as if he could block both the sound and sight of his fellow passengers.

"And then that little one holding Miss Ellsworth's hand is Miss Beatrice, daughter of the third Mrs. Ellsworth, Miss Fielding that was." She clicked her tongue in sympathy. "Poor child. So young to lose her mother. But I suppose that was the fate of all of them, only with different mothers. Both the third and the second Mrs. Ellsworths began as the children's governesses, but you know how it is, when a young lady is employed by a rich widower."

"I do indeed," said Adelaide. The sisters shared a significant look. "Is Mr. Ellsworth handsome, then, as well as rich?"

"Oh, he once was handsome, others have told me. Mrs. Fellowes the dean's wife, who is nearly seventy, says he and his brother were devilishly attractive in their youth, else how would a penniless William Ellsworth have won his first wife, Miss Baldric of Hollowgate? The Ellsworth brothers hadn't a groat, you see, after their father gambled away the family fortune. But, despite his poverty, Miss Baldric accepted William Ellsworth! *That* was how handsome he was. Some ladies do lose their heads over attractive men, I'm afraid. Miss Baldric wasn't the first, and she won't be the last."

Both women glanced toward the gentleman walled behind his newspaper, for their fellow passenger was undoubtedly handsome enough to make young ladies irrational and older women wistful.

When he continued to ignore them, they went on.

"Sister, which one in the procession is William Ellsworth? Point him out to me. *Him*? But he—oh, dear. I pictured something quite different."

"I told you he had lost his looks. He *is* in his late fifties now," the first answered, with a note of defensiveness.

"Yes, but he's quite bald and looks even older." Adelaide sat back with a sigh, as the procession turned down the lane toward the church, and the coach creaked into motion again. "Imagine him surviving three young wives! What became of them all, Letitia?"

"Let me see...the first Mrs. Ellsworth died in a carriage accident. Tragic. The second of a fever. And the third..." Letitia gave a little shrug. "Who can say? She took her time about it. She was an invalid ever since little Miss Beatrice was born, and the girl is now six, perhaps."

"How old does that make Miss Ellsworth, then?"

Letitia considered. "Why, she must be nearly three and twenty or thereabouts."

"What a good catch she is for the rector! Hollowgate is a prosperous estate, is it not? She must have a goodly portion."

"Oh, indeed it is, and she does. Despite their chequered history, the Ellsworths are among the most prominent families in the district, and you see the clerical families do not hesitate to ally themselves. It is too bad Miss Ellsworth will need to postpone her wedding now. The entire time the third Mrs. Ellsworth lay abed, poor Miss Ellsworth has been keeping house for her father and mothering her half-siblings, and she would probably like to escape by now. Not only that, but she is everywhere overshadowed by Miss Lily, the beauty of the family, whom I suspect will make the more brilliant match. You wait and see."

"Well, the beautiful Miss Lily will likewise find her plans altered, if her stepmother has just died. How inconvenient mourning is, when one is that precarious age! They will have to miss the Races and the Domum Ball and the music meetings this year..."

By the time the flyer coach deposited Fairchild and his traveling companions at the George Inn in the High Street, his ears were ringing from their prattle, and though he gave the two women a courteous bow, he never wanted to hear the name of Ellsworth again.

A painted banner draped the entrance of the inn, proclaiming, "Welcome, Old Wykehamists," and then Fairchild grinned to hear a familiar voice call through one of the open windows, "Rob! Old Fairchild himself! How long he's stayed away."

Entering the coffee house, he found it full of schoolmates from his years at Winchester, former boys now grown to (nearly) unrecognizable men. It was Kemp who had announced his arrival and who strode forward to seize him by the hand. Kemp, who used to be a small, scruffy lad in Fourth Book when Fairchild was Senior Part, the Fifth, but who now towered over him by a head.

"What lured you back?" drawled Partridge, the former Præfect of Tub. Fairchild perfectly remembered Partridge conning him with a trencher in Hall, when Fairchild had been in his first year and accidentally spilled the older boy's tea. "We thought New College swallowed you forever."

"Just for an epoch," he answered mildly. "I was articled to an attorney in Oxford after leaving university, but when the time expired I decided to join a practice here, and my new senior asked me to arrive in time for the quarter sessions and assizes."

"It's a madhouse, isn't it?" Kemp asked. "I'm staying in Stockbridge because there wasn't a room to be had within a mile of here. All overrun with old Woks and would-be Wykehamists and their families."

"Speaking of would-be Wykehamists, my nephew Paul is a candidate this year," Fairchild said. "He comes tomorrow with my sister and her husband."

"Never say! Are you here as an Elector then, to nominate him?"

"Not I, but I've done my duty, I hope, currying favor with the New College fellows that are."

"Twelve spaces this year in College," another schoolmate Lincoln said. "Competition will be fierce. Ever since Goddard took the school in hand..."

Reminiscences of their own more chaotic days under Headmaster Warton followed, including a thorough rehearsal of the ill-fated "Rebellion of 1793," which Fairchild had missed, having matriculated at Oxford that year.

Interesting as the subject was, his mind went back to his nephew Paul and Paul's chances. He shuddered to imagine his sister and brother-in-law's response if their son were not enrolled. Circumstances being as straitened with Fanny and James as they were with himself, a scholarship would make all the difference. Fanny pictured her son following in his uncle's footsteps, from Winchester to New College to a career in law or the church, and she had talked of little else since she formed the idea, to the point that her husband James could likewise imagine no other destiny for little Paul. In an attempt to hedge his nephew's bets, Fairchild tried to persuade them that countless other schools would serve, or that the College's reputation had suffered in recent years, or that Paul might learn from a local clergyman—all true—but he had wasted his breath. In the Tillwoods' minds, it was either Winchester or utter defeat.

"Are you staying here at the George, Fairchild?" Kemp was asking.

"Yes, until after Election Week, when my lodgings become available."

"Lodgings? Are you at Mrs. Barnstable's or Cloak's?"

"Neither. My landlady is Mrs. Archibald. Do you remember her? We used to send the choristers to fetch us her Sally Lunns on an afternoon."

A chorus of appreciative groans met this, as well as regrets that now Mrs. Archibald was too elderly to continue her baking business. "But if you are her tenant, Fairchild, she may still bake a batch for you, and then you might sell them on the side. Any local Old Woks would be glad to take them off your hands."

"Where does good old Mrs. Archibald live?"

"In St. Thomas Street still. At Number 26."

"Why, you will be next door, then, to Ellsworth and his wife," exclaimed Boggs.

Fairchild blinked at the name. "Ellsworth? The coach passed the funeral procession of a Mrs. Ellsworth as we entered town."

"No, no. You're referring to a different Ellsworth, father of the so-called 'Ellsworth Assortment.' *That* Ellsworth lives outside of town, and the fact that he's buried three wives gives him the reputation of Bluebeard! No, no—it's his harmless brother who lives in St. Thomas Street. A Mr. Charles Ellsworth. Assistant Master at the College. Married to a Frenchwoman—just the one wife for him—who bakes in the tradition of Mrs. Archibald, I hear, and who helps the boys with theatricals."

Partridge gave a leering grin. "Lucky Fairchild. Living next to the Ellsworths, you may catch glimpses of the lovely Miss Lily, if she comes to call on her aunt and uncle. It's beastly selfish of the third Mrs. Ellsworth to pop off just now, for it means Miss Lily won't be at the ball or indeed any of the Election Week events."

"You haven't a chance with her anyhow, Partridge," Boggs mocked. "Now that handsome Fairchild has returned. The old days have gone, when you were Præfect of Tub and Fairchild a lowly inferior. Now he's too big and important to clean your butter or make your tea, and if you were to clow him as you used to all the juniors, he's likely to box your ears in return."

Fairchild laughed along with the others, but he thought ruefully that, while time might level the temporary differences in school rank, the permanent strata of money and family remained. Partridge, despite his awkward build and mottled complexion, hailed from a prosperous, landed Hampshire family, whereas Fairchild, having been a scholarship boy all his years at College and a fellowship man at Oxford, had only the modest salary offered by his new employer Mr. Darby to his name. But who knew? He felt a grin tugging at the corners of his mouth when he remembered the women who shared his coach: maybe this Miss Lily Ellsworth might prove as foolish as her mother, the former Miss Baldric. Maybe she too would choose a man solely for his handsome person, and to the devil with prudence.

Whatever the case, barring a wealthy young lady losing her fool head over him, it would be Fairchild's lot in life to serve the rich and great, so he might as well get on with it. Get on with ingratiating himself generally. Which meant meeting each man in the way he would best be won. Therefore he raised his ale and nodded at Partridge, adopting the group's rallying tone. "Though I quake in my high-lows to defy you, Partridge, I had better say straight off that, if I am so fortunate as to catch this Miss Lily's fancy, I will try as hard as the next Old Wok to win her. I am beginning the world now, and a beautiful bride never hurts."

"A beautiful bride with a generous portion," Lincoln observed, when he had lowered his tankard again. "Her family may have an unfortunate sobriquet and her father questionable judgment, but there is no denying the William Ellsworths' prosperity."

"To prosperity!" Kemp offered a second toast.

"Hear! Hear!" cried the former schoolmates, thumping their hands on the board.

"With England at war, let peace reign among Old Wykehamists," declared Boggs. Raising his hands, he made as if to conduct them. "Now who will join me in singing the Election grace?"

CHAPTER THREE

The Characters are affecting, as they may be every Man's Lot who runs his Neck into the Marriage Noose.
— Henry Fielding, *The Welsh Opera* (1731)

I had better advertise for a governess for Beatrice," said William Ellsworth to his oldest daughter.

Florence regarded him solemnly. He was seated in his favorite chair beside the window in his library, the morning sun unflattering on his bald, spotted pate and the hairs growing from his ears. The sight was especially jarring because a portrait of him and his younger brother in their youth hung just to the right of the window, and Florence thought two handsomer young gentlemen could hardly have been found in Hampshire. While her uncle Charles had lost his hair as well, he had the better shape of head for baldness, now that wigs were no longer the fashion.

She had been expecting this announcement—dreading it, from the moment her second stepmother died at the end of June. She knew William Ellsworth was not the sort of man who could carry on alone. She knew the funeral-baked meats would hardly be set out before he would be thinking of a new wife, but it did not make the moment any more welcome.

"Papa, I have been thinking about this," she answered, "and I have already told Mr. Gregory that he and I must postpone our marriage until next spring."

"Next spring? Whatever for? Nonsense. There is mourning, and then there is mourning, Florence. No, no. You must not sacrifice your plans for us, my dear."

"Thank you, Papa, but I think it best to...arrange matters here at Hollowgate before I go. You know I have been teaching Lily about housekeeping responsibilities and how best to work with the servants—" (her father gave a derisive snort here, and Florence could hardly blame him, the lessons had been so fruitless) "—and I have talked to Beatrice about attending school in town with Minta this autumn."

"No, no, Flossie. It had better be a new governess," Mr. Ellsworth replied. "One preferably with some housekeeping skills herself. I shudder to think of Lily running Hollowgate. And as for little Beatrice going to school—I should not like that at all. I will want my family about me when you are gone. It is bad enough to have Tyrone at Winchester, and I only make the concession for Araminta to go to school because the girl cannot be made to stay within doors unless it is raining buckets or hailing, so it hardly matters if she be here or there during the day. But Beatrice—no, little Bea will have a governess."

"But Papa, to be very honest, you spend much of your day either closeted here in your library or riding the rounds of the estate with Mr. Falk the steward. You might not even notice if Beatrice spent a few hours every day in town."

For the first time, his unruffled countenance ruffled. "I would notice," he said. "I want Beatrice here, and that is an end of it."

Thus the first round of the contest went to Mr. Ellsworth.

Slowly, that she might have time to gather her thoughts, Florence made a stack of the *Hampshire Chronicles*, idly fluttering the pages. She had not expected to carry that particular point, despite hopes that, with advancing age and three wives predeceasing him, her father might have had enough of marriage.

Well, then.

"What would you say, then, Papa, to letting me interview the candidates?" was her next attempt. "You have much on your mind, and I would like to be of help." As she asked, she pictured choosing the oldest, plainest, lumpiest, most taciturn woman who applied.

Clearly her father made the same calculation, for he replied hastily, "Of course not. What would you know of children's education? You should be turning your attention to the home you will make with Mr. Gregory. When you have children of your own, that will be time enough for you to assume a parent's duties."

Florence stifled a protest. Was there any point in saying that she had already half assumed a mother's duties to her siblings, ever since Beatrice had been born and her late stepmother took to her bed?

"And I need distraction," he continued, "lest grief overtake me."

As her father's favorite method for out-running grief was to take a new wife, Florence could not prevent her skepticism showing.

But she was bitter, she supposed.

Though Mr. Ellsworth had long forgotten his first wife Henrietta, Florence had been very attached to her mother, and the loss of her still stung at times. Mama might not have loved Papa violently, but she was a calm, amiable woman who made the best of things, including her marriage. Florence had been seven when she lost her, and Lily only five, and sometimes Florence thought she was the only one who remembered the first Mrs. Ellsworth.

After her mother died, the appearance of the governess Miss Catchway marked a new, unhappy chapter in Florence's life. Miss Catchway was neither calm nor amiable and had not seemed pleased to become either a governess or, later, Papa's second wife. She tolerated Florence and Lily crossly enough, disliking Florence more than Lily because Florence tried to speak for both the sisters. And then, after Tyrone and Araminta were born, she dropped any pretense of interest in her stepchildren, for fear they would outshine her twins. Poor Florence and Lily learned that even a cross stepmother was preferable to one who looked right through them, but they found consolation in their new little siblings and in their father's continued affection. For, to his credit, William Ellsworth bestowed equally upon all his children the same mild regard, and by blithely ignoring everything which might disturb his peace, he plumed himself on modeling for them the ability to be content in all circumstances.

When her first stepmother died, Florence felt only sweet relief, to be very, very honest. In penance for which, she assigned herself the task of completing the complicated embroidered seat cushion her stepmother had been working on before the fatal fever struck, a cushion which now served as a bed for the family terrier Snap.

But no sooner was the former Miss Catchway laid to rest than Papa insisted on a new governess for Florence and Lily, as well as a nursemaid for Tyrone and Minta, that he might choose a new bride from between two candidates, as it were. Florence would have preferred the jolly, affectionate nursemaid for a new stepmother, but the woman was neither as youthful nor as pretty as the governess, and William Ellsworth predictably chose Miss Fielding. Pretty, delicate Miss Fielding, who no sooner became the third Mrs. Ellsworth than she got with child; and she no sooner bore Beatrice than she took to her bed and stayed there ever after, leaving her oldest stepdaughter to take up lady-of-the-house duties. Not that Florence minded terribly. Her second stepmother was kind, if frail, and maternal kindness had been in short supply.

And now, after twenty-odd years, three wives, and five children, when his oldest was two-and-twenty and on the brink of marriage and his youngest school-age, Papa wanted to put his head into the noose again? Did the man never learn?

He was already mending his pen, preparatory to drafting his advertisement, his daughter's admonitions neatly swept aside.

There was a knock, and Lily appeared.

"Are you coming, Floss? You said we might walk into town."

"In a minute, yes. When Papa and I have finished speaking."

"I think we have finished," he smiled brightly.

"Papa is going to advertise for a new governess," Florence supplied.

"New governess?" echoed Lily, her smooth brow furrowing in alarm. "You can't mean it, Papa!"

"Not for you and Florence, naturally," he soothed, "but for Beatrice. And Minta, if she would rather not attend the school in town. And the governess might also chaperone you, Lily (and Flossie, for as long as she is unmarried). It is time you were able to do what other young ladies do: dance and go to assemblies and parties, not stay always at Hollowgate. Your stepmama's health did not permit her to accompany you, but a governess might."

"You need not trouble on our account, Papa," interposed Florence yet once more, "for Lily and I cannot do any of those things anyway. Not until we are out of mourning. Besides which, I am already engaged, and I suspect Mr. Gregory is not much for dancing."

Lily said nothing, but her expression said plainly, *Is Mr. Gregory much for* anything?

"Nevertheless, the search must begin now," said Mr. Ellsworth, his pleasantness unrelenting. "These things take time. Now run along with you both." His two oldest exchanged glances which, in his most Papa-ish way, he pretended not to see.

"I don't know why you bother," said Lily, when the sisters were walking along Cock Lane toward the West Gate. "Have you not noticed Papa always does precisely what he pleases? Always, and with a smile. All you did was make him more determined. We will probably return home this afternoon to find the woman already installed in one of the bedrooms."

"But Lily, he cannot marry *again*!" protested Florence. "You know people are already calling him Bluebeard and Henry VIII. It will be so humiliating!"

Lily kicked at a stone. "Well, this one would only be his fourth wife, not his sixth. She would be his Anne of Cleves, as it were. And Anne of Cleves outlived Henry VIII, you know, and did not do so badly for herself. Once the embarrassment of having Papa marry the governess *again* has passed, it would be rather nice to go to balls and assemblies, even if your dull Mr. Gregory does not dance. Whoever Papa chooses cannot be worse than our first stepmother and will likely enjoy better health than our second."

"But suppose she is young and there is another child? We are already the Ellsworth Assortment."

Lily shrugged this off as well. "One more child will not make any difference. An assortment is an assortment." Taking her sister's arm as they passed the barracks, Lily gave it a squeeze. "Foolish Florence! What difference does it make if Papa takes one more wife or fifteen more wives? You won't be at home much longer. You could even marry the Dreadful Mr. Gregory straight off, if you liked, though it pains me to say it. You might do it quietly, and I suspect no one would even notice because they would be too busy gossiping about Papa." Peeking over her sister's shoulder, she hid a smile from the admiring sergeant on duty near the entrance.

Florence frowned. "Get married straight off? Nonsense. How could I leave you all now? It's all very well to speak of me not being around. I know you can hold your own, but don't you care what happens to Tyrone and Minta and Beatrice? Supposing Papa chooses another Catherine Catchway?"

"Well, Tyrone will be at the College most of the time now," Lily answered evenly, "and if you give Minta a bat or a ball or a bow, she might not even notice a new stepmother. It will only be little Beatrice." She grimaced at this because Beatrice could not be dismissed so easily. "Perhaps Bea could live with you. Or me, when I marry. Or Uncle Charles."

"Hmm." It was Florence's turn for the noncommittal sound as they passed through the West Gate into the High Street. "If Papa will not let Beatrice go so far as school, he would never let her live elsewhere altogether. But speaking of Uncle Charles, let us call on him and Aunt Jeanne. They may advise us."

"But I wanted to see the new items at the draper's. You wouldn't let me go into town during Election Week."

"What is the use of seeing new items there? We can only wear black in any event. Come."

But the siren call of the draper's was too alluring for Lily. "You go along, Floss. I don't want to talk about Papa anymore. Call for me when you are done."

"My aunt and uncle will be sorry to miss you, Lily."

"Oh, don't be so stiff! I saw them last week. If one can't neglect an aunt and uncle one sees at least every fortnight, what hope is there?"

So Florence sighed and left her in the High Street.

CHAPTER FOUR

Love in a Cottage contentedly flows,
And e'ery dear Minute is blest.
— Charles Coffey, *Devil Upon Two Sticks* (1745)

Twenty-four St. Thomas Street was a plain, three-storey gray cottage with a tile roof, white window trim, and a vine coaxed to grow around the front door. Florence loved it for its coziness and better yet for its inhabitants. Her own father might have had three wives, but her uncle Charles only one: the French maidservant he met in Paris when he was marooned in France on his Grand Tour, decades earlier.

"Flossie, *ma chère,*" murmured her pretty aunt Jeanne, opening the door herself. Her black hair was streaked with white now, but it still curled charmingly, and her blue eyes were dancing. "What a pleasure. We have another caller, but you must come in."

When Florence drew back, Jeanne took hold of her hand and tugged. "*Ne t'inquiète pas.* It is just the neighbor."

"Mrs. Archibald?"

It was not Mrs. Archibald. Instead of an elderly lady whose stooped form made her head level with Florence's shoulder, Florence found a straight and hale and handsome dark-haired *man*, whose equally dark eyes took her in with one swift glance.

"Mr. Fairchild, may I present my niece? Miss—"

"Miss Lily Ellsworth," he interrupted, still looking at Florence as he made his bow. Then he seemed to remember himself and made an apologetic sound to his hostess. "Pardon me."

"But Mr. Fairchild, you mistake yourself," Jeanne Ellsworth laughed. "This is not my niece Miss Lily. This is her elder sister. Miss Ellsworth of Hollowgate."

"Oh—but surely—" he broke off again and made a second bow. The color which rose to his face only heightened his striking looks, and Florence was aware of her own countenance growing warm.

"They do look alike," Florence's uncle Charles spoke up, gesturing for them all to be seated. "Both brunette and of a height."

Yes, and there the resemblance ended, in Florence's opinion. For she was paler both in complexion and eye color, and Lily's person was the more rounded. Moreover, Lily had lips so red one would think she painted them and dimples that flashed when she smiled. Their first stepmother had once said, "Look at the two of you. It's as if God made Lily on a sunny day and you on a rainy one, Flo."

Therefore Florence was quick to demur. "When you meet my sister, sir, you will never mistake us again."

By heaven, thought Fairchild, *they say the sister is even prettier?*

Florence was pensive. It was not only the usual embarrassment she felt, when she knew she was being compared to Lily. In this instance, personal vanity gave place to embarrassment for her family. How could it be that this person, but newly arrived in Winchester, whom she had never before seen nor heard of, already knew something of her family? If he knew there was a Lily Ellsworth, he likely knew the entire Ellsworth saga. As who did not? That was precisely the problem. And to think, her father wanted to add a new chapter to the sorry, sorry tale. It was possible, of course, that her aunt and uncle had mentioned the William Ellsworths, though they were not the sort to rattle on about their connections, and they knew how much Florence disliked idle talk about the family. Fervently she hoped this Mr. Fairchild was nearing the end of his visit, that she might discuss the impending crisis with them.

"Mr. Fairchild is recently returned to town," her uncle explained. "He was a pupil at the College once and then a fellow of New College, Oxford."

"And now I am an attorney with Darby and West."

"Darby and West! Why, Mr. Darby is my father's attorney," said Florence more smilingly. Perhaps Mr. Fairchild knew of her family not through gossip, but rather through his employer! That would not be so very bad. "I am very well acquainted with him." Between all her father's marriages, the births of new heirs, and the estate business, Mr. Darby came to Hollowgate several times per month and always stayed to dine. "I hope he is well," she added.

"Generally. Though I regret to say his gout has flared up."

Florence murmured her regret, not the least surprised. She had seen ample evidence of Mr. Darby's love for plenteous meat, puddings and wine. It would be a shame if young Mr. Fairchild shared his employer's tendencies and also came to develop a red nose, jowls, and spreading midsection. "Please pass on our best wishes for his recovery."

With a nod, Mr. Fairchild rejoined, "Before you arrived, Miss Ellsworth, I was saying to your aunt and uncle that I was sorry to hear of the loss of your stepmother."

Which one? she would have liked to ask. Florence's mouth twisted wryly. So he did know all about the Ellsworths!

"Thank you," she answered. "She had been unwell for quite some time." Wanting to lead the conversation away from her family, she ventured, "I see you may be new, but you are already caught up on the news of the town. Is it—strange to return to a place so familiar, Mr. Fairchild? Or do you find it comforting?"

"A little of both, Miss Ellsworth. I have fond memories of my time here in school, where, incidentally, my nephew Paul will enroll this autumn."

"Ah! Perhaps my uncle or Mr. Darby told you that my brother Tyrone is a pupil at Winchester as well. He is fourteen now, so entering his third year. Still a junior, but he hopes the worst of the mistreatment is behind him."

Mr. Fairchild's dark eyes gleamed. "Do you call it mistreatment, Miss Ellsworth?"

"I don't know what else it might be called," she returned. "I am certain Tyrone didn't tell us the half of it, but I could see the bruises and the—burns, even, that one time!—on him, when he visited home. All that 'fagging' the poor little juniors do for the older boys! Fetching tea and cleaning butter and toasting bread and carrying books and building fires and—and doing for some bully everything which that bully ought very well to do for himself. And then there was the 'watching out' at cricket and 'kicking in' at football—Mr. Fairchild, if you knew my daydreaming brother, and how easily distracted he is, you might begin to imagine the tortures his wandering thoughts put him to—"

By this point Mr. Fairchild was laughing, holding up his hands in surrender. "You win, you win, Miss Ellsworth. Let us call it mistreatment. I do not think you would find one single new boy who would argue with you. And there certainly are bullies to be found in every gathering of men, so why would a school be any different? But I would assert that, in the main, when the first year has passed and the 'duties' grow lighter, the young men of Winchester learn camaraderie and responsibility, and they even come to regard the early hardships in the soft light of nostalgia. At least I have."

Florence raised a skeptical brow. "I suppose that is an oblique way of saying you eventually became a prefect and gained the whip hand?"

"Florence," reproved her uncle, but their guest only grinned.

"She's too much for me, Ellsworth. I did indeed become a prefect, so you are justified in questioning my testimony, Miss Ellsworth. I tip my hat to you metaphorically."

Florence gave a rueful smile and sat back, abashed. "Pardon me, Mr. Fairchild. I don't even know you. But I am rather protective of my siblings."

"It does you credit. Never mind. I will tell my nephew Paul that, if he runs into difficulties, I know where he might find a champion."

"I give you credit for a keen understanding, Mr. Fairchild," interjected Jeanne Ellsworth. "So quickly you have discovered that my oldest niece is a friend to the young people—her siblings, my own two boys who are at Oxford now…They can always be sure of sympathy and protection from our Florence."

"Excellent qualities in a clergyman's wife," her uncle put in, reaching to pat Florence's arm.

Instead of appearing pleased at her husband's concurrence, Jeanne gave an audible sniff. Then she began to stir the sugar into her tea more decisively than the action warranted.

Fairchild was aware of his own surprise and annoyance. Of course. He had forgotten. Miss Ellsworth was engaged to be married. The busybodies who shared his flyer coach in late June had said as much. What had the one woman remarked? Ah, yes—the lucky man was the rector of St. Eadburh's. Fairchild wished now he had got a look at the fellow.

"Florence is to be married shortly," Charles Ellsworth was saying, giving his wife's arm a playful tap. "How old we are growing, my love. I remember little Flossie in her long clothes, with her brown curls and eyes like pools of winter water."

"My poetic husband," Jeanne smiled at him.

"Oh—uh—in fact the marriage will not take place so very soon after all," spoke up Florence with another blush. "Mr. Gregory and I have decided—with the recent loss of my stepmother—that we will postpone it a while."

"Postpone it?" echoed her aunt, with a lift to her voice.

"Yes. Till spring, perhaps."

"Oh. Yes, yes, I see." Jeanne beamed upon her niece. "There is no hurry. Despite what your uncle says, you are still very young. A mere infant. Take your time."

"Thank you." Florence was not slow of understanding, and she knew very well her aunt was hardly fonder of Mr. Gregory than Lily was. But it was not practical of Jeanne Ellsworth to expect every girl to meet and love and marry in the dramatic way she and her husband had. If Florence had asked, her aunt's counsel regarding marriage would have completely contradicted Florence's mother's, just as Jeanne Ellsworth's love match turned out so very differently. But, for all that Florence loved and respected her aunt, she was her mother's girl. Aunt Jeanne would just have to pin her expectations of a Belle-Passion on Lily and let Florence go her own way.

"Whenever the happy event takes place, I wish you both joy," said Fairchild conventionally. Conventions were convenient at times like these, when one might say exactly the right thing without troubling overmuch to sound sincere. Not that he wasn't sincere. What was Miss Ellsworth to him, anyway, that he should care whether she lived or died, married or didn't marry? She was merely an acquaintance made in the last half hour. Nobody.

A nobody with waving dark hair and eyes of winter water (would he ever forget that description now?) that shone as she spoke. A nobody who expressed herself with heart and intelligence—

He was suddenly impatient to go, and when Florence politely asked him more questions about his work and his family, he answered precisely, almost curtly, before rising as soon as he was able and taking his leave.

"You must call again," said Jeanne. "There are many more Ellsworths for you to meet."

To this he only bowed, and then he was gone.

Jeanne grinned roguishly at Florence. "An interesting gentleman, I think. But new young men are always interesting. Lily will be sorry to have missed such a handsome one, will she not?"

"She will," answered Florence absently, her thoughts hurrying back to her own predicament. "But for my part I am glad he has gone because I must speak to you both. Oh, Uncle Charles—Aunt Jeanne—Papa told me this morning that he is going to advertise for another governess!" Both her relations inhaled sharply, exchanging a glance as Florence rushed on. "With my stepmother hardly cold! I tried to say he could send Beatrice to school with Minta, but he wouldn't even listen to me because he has already made his plans. He is going to marry again, I know it! For the fourth time! Isn't it dreadful?"

Jeanne clicked her tongue while her husband frowned.

"Uncle Charles, please—do you think you could speak to him?" pleaded Florence.

"My dear Florence, for your sake I will make the attempt, but when has my brother ever listened to me, regarding his amorous entanglements?"

"Never," said Jeanne. "William will do exactly as he pleases, *comme toujours*. Though his handsomeness is long gone—pouf!—there is still Hollowgate and his fortune. Which means there will never be any shortage of women eager to assume the role of Mrs. William Ellsworth."

"You see—this is why I told Mr. Gregory I couldn't marry him yet—it isn't only about being in mourning, it's that I am so—so mortified—"

Jeanne made some characteristically Gallic sound and wrapped her niece in her arms, as Charles rose and began to pace.

"I must overcome it," Florence went on. "Mr. Gregory assures me that it does not make him feel differently about marrying me—though how can it not? Would anyone welcome such a connection? I know his sister Miss Gregory will be shocked, only she will be too courteous to say so."

"Your father is your father, and you are you, Florence," said her aunt firmly. "If Mr. or Miss Gregory respect you the less for the actions of your father, then—pfff!—I will respect *them* the less."

Florence managed a shaky smile. "But it is not only that, you see. How could I possibly marry now and abandon my siblings at such a time? Suppose Papa should choose another Miss Catchway, who would be unkind to Beatrice?"

"My love, I do not suppose your father will consult you in choosing his wife," observed Charles.

"I know. Though I did try asking if I might choose the governess, which amounts to the same thing, and that went as well as you might imagine. But at least, if Papa chooses someone who will—not care for Beatrice very much, I could work harder to convince him to let her go to school. And then Lily suggested—if we could ever persuade Papa—that Bea could come and live with me, or with her when she marries..."

"Or with us," Jeanne cried, hugging her again.

Florence felt tears threaten. "Oh, thank you, Aunt Jeanne, Uncle Charles. I feel better just to have shared my fears with you both. And who knows? Perhaps somebody kind and respectable will apply for the position. Somebody who will love little Bea, as well as being a good stepmother to Tyrone and Minta when they are at home, and Lily, until she marries. Lily is so lovely it can't be long."

"We will hope for that outcome," Charles agreed, "but in the meantime I will make the attempt to advise my brother, futile though it might prove. And perhaps you might call on Mr. Darby at his office, my dear? You are of age, and, on the pretense of discussing the postponement of your marriage, you might share some of your concerns with him. Your father might listen to his attorney where he is deaf to us."

"Yes. Yes, what a good idea! I will try that," she answered, hope dawning. "I never thought to speak to him before. When Papa married Miss Fielding, I was only fifteen or sixteen and would never have taken it upon myself to speak. But Mr. Darby has served him faithfully, and he will surely see the sense in Papa—refraining from

marrying a fourth time. Yes. Thank you, Uncle Charles! I will call at
his office next week, to give him a few days for his gout to improve."

CHAPTER FIVE

Because I am a stranger in this land, & but here lately
arived, they wil hold me as an upstart.
— Robert Greene, *A quip for an upstart courtier*
(1592)

There was someone sitting in the Whisps' pew.

The diminutive congregation of St. Eadburh's was accustomed to the righthand front pew standing empty, the Whisps having long been absent in Weymouth, claiming the value of sea-bathing for Mrs. Whisp's health. As the Whisp family had produced generations of Winchester clergymen, the latest Mr. Whisp had been duly appointed a prebendary of the cathedral, which duty he took so seriously that he had not been seen in the cathedral close for at least eight years. Mrs. Whisp and the four Whisp offspring had been gone even longer. Florence had only cloudy memories of three boys and a girl—near in age to Lily and herself.

The stranger sitting in the Whisps' pew was a woman, but Florence thought it could not be Mrs. Whisp, unless Mrs. Whisp's circumference had dwindled by half. Nor could it be Miss Whisp—who must be at least twenty by now—for why would she attend church alone?

The Ellsworths filed into their lefthand front pew, Mr. Ellsworth leading the way and Florence bringing up the rear, which gave her the best view of the person every head was turned toward. Even Mr. Gregory paused in rising to begin the service, his attention caught.

The woman bore her head high, her features and hair color hidden by the brim of her bonnet from all save the rector, but Florence could see she had a noble figure, encased in a gown striped black and olive, and black lace gloves on the long white hands folded in her lap. A widow, then?

There were no answers to be had until the service concluded, and the combination of Mr. Gregory's dry, long-ish sermon and curiosity regarding the newcomer ensured that not a single person present derived spiritual benefit that day.

When the parishioners rose at the conclusion, Florence turned toward the aisle, her gaze meeting that of the woman. She was golden-haired, Florence saw, her tresses perhaps two shades darker than Araminta's, with round blue eyes, a small mouth, and a sharp little nose and chin, and she looked at Florence as if she would take the measure of her.

Florence found herself yielding the right of first egress, and every Ellsworth behind her fanned out to either side to peer around her for a glimpse of both the stranger and the cause of delay.

At the door of the church all present massed and lingered, that they might overhear the woman saying to Mr. Gregory in a high, lilting voice, "Good morning to you. My father-in-law Mr. Whisp will be greatly pleased to hear how well St. Eadburh's fares in his absence."

Quiet Miss Gregory bristled beside her brother, thinking the opinion of a negligent, long-absent prebendary was neither here nor there. Within the walls of St. Eadburh's—should Mr. Whisp ever deign to show his face there again—he would find he was just another parishioner, and thus not in a position to pronounce opinions on how her brother handled his duties.

Mr. Gregory only bowed politely, tenting his fingers together. "Thank you...Mrs. Whisp. In return we are pleased to have you in attendance today. Pray, are all your family returned?"

Mrs. Whisp ducked her head. "I'm afraid not. Only I. For that reason I have not opened the Great House and will be living in Whisp Cottage."

"How delightful," said Miss Gregory, flatly. "I hope you left the other Whisps well."

"My father- and mother-in-law were both well when I left them in Weymouth, as were Mr. Richard, Mr. Blaise, and Miss Whisp."

"Oh, but—" Mr. Gregory frowned. "Then your husband must be Mr. Thomas Whisp, the—is he the second son?"

Mrs. Whisp raised a handkerchief to dab at her dry eyes. "My husband was indeed Mr. Thomas Whisp, but he is unfortunately no more. The grippe, a fever—no avail—"

Miss Gregory unbent fractionally. "We are sorry to hear of it."

"I thank you. He was a good husband. A model husband. We had not been married more than two years."

The rector turned then to acknowledge a select portion of his dawdling flock. "Would you do me the honor, Mrs. Whisp, of allowing me to introduce you to my intended and her family? Mrs. Thomas Whisp, this is Mr. William Ellsworth of Hollowgate. And Mr. Ellsworth's children: my dear Miss Ellsworth, Miss Lily, Mr. Tyrone, Miss Araminta, and Miss Beatrice Ellsworth."

In making her curtsey, Florence noted that Mrs. Whisp's round blue eyes betrayed no knowledge of local gossip, and Florence was pleased, for once, that the Ellsworths might make their own first impression. They were a presentable family, after all, if you knew none of their history. Especially in church on a Sunday, when even Minta was neat as a pin and Tyrone didn't have his nose in a book and Beatrice could be counted on not to cry. Moreover, a beaver hat hid Mr. Ellsworth's spotted bald head (though likely Mrs. Whisp saw his pate when he uncovered on entering the church). Lily, of course, looked well any day of the week, and Florence saw Mrs. Whisp's gaze linger on her sister.

"I see you are in mourning as well," she murmured, her gaze returning to Florence.

"Yes. My...stepmother." Florence left it at that.

"Ah. I am sorry." Mrs. Whisp pressed her lips together. Her eyes flicked to Mr. Ellsworth and then back to Florence. "Family must be such a comfort. My home is very quiet. Just three servants and me. How I would like to be a good neighbor and invite you all for dinner, but—I am not yet prepared to act the hostess, and the cottage needs ordering..."

"No, indeed," agreed Florence because she could not do otherwise. "It would not do, in any case. You are the newcomer, and we must invite *you* to Hollowgate."

Mrs. Whisp's face lit up, and she clapped her black-laced hands together. "But how delightful! I am pleased to accept. Thank you."

"What were you thinking?" demanded Lily, cornering Florence in the kitchen, where she had been informing Wilcomb of the preparations to be made. "Why would you ever invite an unmarried woman to Hollowgate? I thought you were in dread lest Papa make a fool of himself again!"

"I am in dread," Florence sighed. "But I asked her because I could not help it. She almost begged for an invitation, and it would have been unneighborly to pretend I did not understand. All we can do is try to dilute her presence. We will have the Gregorys to dine as well—"

"Oh, be joyful," muttered Lily.

"And Mr. Darby," Florence added, in a fit of inspiration. "That will put her on notice, if Papa's attorney is also present. Especially if I have already spoken to him and let him know my concerns."

Lily shook her head. "Mr. Darby always does whatever Papa asks. It is his job. If Papa tells him, 'I want to take a fourth wife,' Mr. Darby will declare it a capital idea. You will see. When you go to see him, he will pat you on the head and beg you to run along."

"In any event, perhaps we are fretting for nothing, Lily. Just because Papa might take an interest in Mrs. Whisp, it does not necessarily follow that Mrs. Whisp will take an interest in Papa. Look how she moved away from the rest of the Whisps! Why should she leave one large family, only to join another?"

"Because Papa is rich, and if she married him, she would be Mrs. Ellsworth of Hollowgate, and not merely some displaced widow of a younger family member whom perhaps nobody wanted around."

There was enough plausibility in what Lily said to make Florence lose sleep that night, but in the morning she put those thoughts aside, for there was her visit to Mr. Darby to face first. As Charles Ellsworth had predicted, his interview with his brother yielded nothing, William brushing off all fraternal advice like so much lint from his sleeve, so Florence's last hope lay in the attorney.

This time Lily accompanied her into town in order to call on her aunt and uncle, and after separating at the head of St. Thomas Street, Florence continued on to Mr. Darby's office in Parchment Street. Darby and West occupied a modest brick building squeezed between shops and presenting a freshly-painted green door to the street. It was a hot, dusty day in late July, and though Florence was dressed in fine lawn, her frock was nevertheless black, and the walk had brought color to her normally pale countenance. She wished she could remove her bonnet and wave it as a fan, as she supposed Lily was doing at the Charles Ellsworths', but it would never do in this setting.

The clerk, a long bony young man with flaming red hair, bolted up at the sight of her, knocking over the stool on which he had been sitting. It gave a great clatter in the small space, and he darted a look at the door at the other end of the room, which stood ajar. "Good—afternoon, miss."

"Good afternoon." Florence gave him a tentative smile, and the stool he had just set upright tumbled over again with, if possible, even more noise. She waited for him to restore it, which he did, but then he straightened and rested an elbow on his desk in an attempt at nonchalance, causing the sheet of foolscap he had been working on to sail off the surface and zigzag toward the floor as he swiped and lunged for it.

Florence bit her lip.

But when the foolscap was replaced and the now-scarlet clerk holding perfectly still, she said gravely, "I wondered if I might see Mr. Darby. I am Miss Ellsworth, and he is our family attorney."

"Miss Ellsworth! Of course I know the Ellsworths. Plenty of work from the Ellsworths, if you don't mind me saying. Don't see Mr. Ellsworth in here very often, however, and you—well—you, never."

"Yes. Well, Mr. Darby usually comes to Hollowgate, though it has been some weeks since we've seen him," she replied. "I hoped I might catch him today. Is he within?" She glanced toward the partially open door.

"Oh, no, miss! Miss Ellsworth, that is. He isn't here. Gout, you know. His gout. Gout."

Her shoulders drooped, but it was no more than she had feared. "I am sorry to hear it still pains him then, Mr.—"

"Hence!"

She blinked at his rudeness, backing up a step. "Oh—I do apologize for intruding—" Flustered, she turned back toward the entrance, wondering if the strange clerk would bark at her again if she asked to leave a note. But the next instant the inner door swept open, and there stood Mr. Robert Fairchild.

"Miss Ellsworth," he addressed her calmly. "I see you have met our clerk Mr. Hents."

"Oh." She blushed at her mistake, and then the giggle repressed earlier at Mr. Hents' antics escaped her. "Yes, I have. Thank you. I was just telling...Mr. Hents that I hoped to speak with Mr. Darby."

"Gout," blurted Mr. Hents. "Gout."

Fairchild grinned. "If you didn't catch that, I'm afraid Mr. Darby has not yet recovered sufficiently to come in. But perhaps I might help...?"

Florence's mirth evaporated quickly enough. It was one thing to spill her woes before Mr. Darby, whom she had known from childhood, and quite another to say anything to the handsome young stranger.

He seemed to read her thoughts. "Miss Ellsworth, I may as well tell you that I called on Mr. Darby yesterday to acquaint him with Darby and West's most recent affairs, and he expressed to me that he has decided to retire from employment. His age, his health...Hents here was making a list of all the clients who will need to be informed."

The clerk tapped the sheet of foolscap and bobbed his head. "Don't you fret, miss," he said. "Don't fret. Mr. Fairchild here will see to things."

But Florence was already fretting. Mr. Darby retiring? How could he, when the Ellsworths needed him so? Mr. Darby retiring, who knew the Ellsworth affairs inside and out, backwards and forwards! Wringing her hands, she cried, "Oh, but he can't! I know he isn't feeling well—the gout—but perhaps he might be persuaded to stay on just a little longer? Or perhaps I might call on him—at home?"

Darby, as Fairchild had last seen him, flashed into the young attorney's mind: cross and heavy and unkempt, his red, shiny, swollen limb propped on an ottoman, foot bare, plump toes wriggling. No—Darby would not thank him for sending Miss Ellsworth to call.

"I understand this is very sudden, Miss Ellsworth," he soothed. "And perhaps you would prefer to speak with his partner Mr. West when he returns from London—"

But Florence was already shaking her head. She had one memory of Mr. West from several years earlier, when he called at Hollowgate in place of Mr. Darby for some reason. He had made both Florence and Lily quite uncomfortable with his half-closed eyes and his habit of hissing through his teeth in agreement, rubbing his hands together as if he were warming himself at a fire. No. Speaking to Mr. West would be quite impossible.

"No, thank you," she breathed. She ought to give a reason, but she could hardly add, "Lily says Mr. West is like a sinister grasshopper."

Fairchild held up his hands, uncertain how else to advise her. He did not blame her for hesitating to accept him in the place of the family stalwart, but if neither would she agree to Mr. West, he did not know what more could be done.

That Florence came to the same conclusion was clear when she ceased to wring her hands and instead clenched them in fists by her side. She took a deep breath. "Very well. Mr. Fairchild. If—you are to be our new attorney, I—will talk to you, if I may."

Wordlessly, he gestured her toward the inner office, and the tall pale girl marched in as if ordered to walk the plank. For propriety's sake, Fairchild left the door entirely open, and it was Florence who said, "Oh, Mr. Fairchild, would you mind terribly if—we spoke in confidence?"

No ready response came to mind. He hesitated, lips parted, but then Miss Ellsworth's ready blush returned, and she put her hands to her face. "Oh, never mind. I wasn't thinking. Of course we can't shut the door. And what is the use anyway? If you haven't learned yet, Mr. Fairchild, you soon shall—my family is a favorite topic of gossip in Winchester. I am certain there is nothing I can tell you which will not soon be widely known."

She turned her clear grey eyes on him, her expression a mix of chagrin and defiance, and he heard himself say, "Nevertheless, as your attorneys, no gossip will begin with us, Miss Ellsworth. Whatever we are told by our clients is held in total confidence."

"Thank you." Waiting until Mr. Fairchild indicated which of the massive walnut desks belonged to him, she perched on the purple-upholstered chair that faced it. He took his own seat opposite, busying himself retying the string around a bundle of papers. Indeed, when Florence troubled to look around, she saw they must spend a great deal of time at Darby and West keeping papers in order. There was a wall of shelves, some fitted with small drawers and others open and stacked with deed boxes; various bulging blue pouches hanging from hooks; several pegs from which hung documents strung together; and still more hooks on which papers were skewered. When Mr. Fairchild finished tying up the ones at hand, he deposited the bundle in one of the pouches.

"You are very busy," she began apologetically. "I will not take much of your time."

"Please," he returned. "I am at your service." Then, with a glint of mischief: "After all, the Ellsworths have long been one of Darby and West's most valuable clients."

"I don't doubt it," sighed Florence. She nodded toward the deed boxes on their shelves. "How many of those, for instance, are filled with Ellsworth marriage settlements and wills and affidavits?"

"Don't forget Baldric papers," said Fairchild. "Darby and West advised the Baldrics of Hollowgate as well, and you and your sister Miss Lily are all that remain of that ancient family."

She bowed her head a moment and then gathered herself to look him in the eye. "Yes, I see you know of my family history. I need not think I am revealing any secrets when I tell you that my father has been married several times. Miss Baldric of Hollowgate—my mother and Lily's—she was the first."

"Yes. And it was your *second* stepmother that you lost recently." He saw the effort it required from her to rehearse the Ellsworth story and hastened to skip to its conclusion.

"That's right," agreed Florence, relieved. "Therefore you know that Lily is my sister and that the younger children are half-siblings to us and to each other. Well—Tyrone and Araminta are fully related to each other, of course—"

"I am well acquainted with your family tree, Miss Ellsworth," he interposed gently. "Why don't you tell me what concerns you this afternoon?"

Absently Florence did remove her bonnet then and began to fan herself with it, and Fairchild found himself admiring her dramatic coloring, only enhanced by the flush of the day's warmth and her discomfiture. He remembered the women in the flyer coach saying how well Miss Lily Ellsworth's mourning weeds became her, but Fairchild thought the same could easily be said of Miss Ellsworth. The dark lawn of her gown matched her dark brown hair and made her creamy skin glow by contrast. And her eyes, those eyes of winter water—well, he supposed any color in the world would set them off.

"It is this," uttered Florence, interrupting his thoughts. "My father thinks to marry again."

"Again?" Fairchild was startled into asking.

She nodded, accepting his astonishment as due penalty. "And as Mr. Darby is—as Darby and West have always been Papa's legal advisors, I wondered if you might—if you might...dissuade him from such a course."

He sat back in his chair, exhaling thoughtfully.

"I was going to invite Mr. Darby to dinner at Hollowgate Monday next," she hurried on, when the attorney said nothing. "So I may as well invite you in his place, because I fear Papa will...take steps...without first consulting—Mr. Darby. Indeed, that he would prefer to take steps, without Mr. Darby even knowing, if you understand me. Therefore, won't you please come? I know you and Papa have not yet been introduced, but, as you are now Mr. Darby's employee and trusted representative, perhaps Papa might listen to you. Take a liking to you, even. You seem a—pleasant—young man. Perhaps over port you might be so cunning as to raise the subject and sound him, and then, if he admits to wanting to marry again, you might—might—might give him some reasons why it would be unwise."

"Miss Ellsworth—"

"Oh, please, Mr. Fairchild!" She clasped her hands together in entreaty. "Please say you will come."

"Certainly I will come. I would be glad of the invitation." *If not of the task assigned to me*, he added inwardly. "But Miss Ellsworth, Mr. Darby has been candid enough, in his discussion of the Darby and West clients, to inform me that your father Mr. Ellsworth is more the sort of man who—forgive me—more the sort of man who consults his attorney to 'lift him out of the mess,' as it were, than one who asks for guidance before the fact."

She sighed again. "There is no need to beg my pardon, Mr. Fairchild, for the mere statement of fact. But, please—I am not asking you to work miracles. I am only asking you to try. I have tried, without success, and I thought maybe such a suggestion, not coming from a child, a daughter, might be received more readily."

Sitting forward again, Fairchild took up a loose file, and he rolled the metal points of the string between thumb and forefingers. "Miss Ellsworth, before I make such an attempt, I think it worth saying that, although Mr. Ellsworth's several marriages have led to comment, which I am sure is unpleasant for you all, his...actions...have not—er—damaged the respectability of—uh—his children's reputations."

Her only response was a grimace, and Fairchild cursed himself. He was not persuaded he would have taken much comfort from that either. It was like saying she carried a cloud everywhere with her but had not yet been unduly rained upon.

"Do you mean, sir, because I am already engaged?" Florence asked. "Yes—it will be too late in honor for Mr. Gregory to have second thoughts. But can the same be said for my siblings' prospects? For Lily and Minta and Tyrone? Heavens—by the time Beatrice is of age, who know how many wives Papa might have outlived?"

"Miss Ellsworth, I understand your concern. Perhaps I was thoughtless to say such a thing. I meant only that, whatever your father's actions, you yourself are sure to command respect and admiration."

Her lips parted, and she felt a queer tightness in her throat. Did he mean it? Or was it mere politeness and flattery? She only knew that she very much wanted to believe he meant it. That he found her worthy of respect and even admiration. Despite her name. Despite her father. Despite all.

"Furthermore," Fairchild tried again, anxious to fill the pause because he did not know how Miss Ellsworth was construing his words, "I am pleased to be able to say that, through the work of Mr. Darby, you and your siblings will be altogether cared for, in terms of marriage settlements and inheritances, no matter how many times Mr. Ellsworth might marry."

It was the wrong thing to say.

Poor Mr. Fairchild had no way of knowing Florence had trembled at the thought of general respect and admiration, and this appeal to prudence dashed her like a bucket of icy water. Her grey eyes sparked in anger at him and at herself, and she pressed a palm flat upon his desk. "Mr. Fairchild. I did not come today out of any fear for *money*. There is money from my mother, and my father's money is precisely that—*his* money, to do with as he pleases. I have no need of it. Again, I am to be married soon, and Mr. Gregory is well able to support me. Besides which, he is an honorable man who would take me without a farthing, I daresay."

"Of course he would, of course," Fairchild fumbled. "I only meant—"

But she had risen and was tying on her bonnet with quick, jerking movements. "I came out of concern for my father's reputation and the future of my siblings. A stepmother—is not always the easiest person to introduce to a family, especially if she is young and may have children of her own—"

"Miss Ellsworth, allow me to explain—"

"There is nothing to explain," Florence shook this off. "It doesn't matter. It only matters that, for whatever reasons you see fit to raise, you at least *try* to speak to my father—if Mr. Darby cannot come. I still hope Mr. Darby might. If you would please let him know about it, and if his gout permits. You may both come, if you like. But either Mr. Darby or you or both of you must advise him. Please! May I ask that much?"

She was at the doorway now, her hand on the jamb, Hents having already sprung up to open the outer door for her.

Fairchild bowed. "Yes. You may depend upon it."

"Then good day to you."

"Good day, Miss Ellsworth."

When she was gone, Fairchild returned to the inner office and shut the door, resting his head against it.

What had he done? What had just happened?

He had never met anyone like her. She was fire and ice. She was a prickly blend of pride and mortification, beauty and passion. He gave a rueful chuckle. After the fierce way she had attacked the Winchester system of prefects and juniors, with its attendant abuses, he had dared to hint she was fearful of losing her marriage portion?

Not my most brilliant deduction, he said to himself. And yet, in ninety-nine cases out of a hundred, it would have been a valid one. But in this hundredth case—

And now she probably thought him calculating, if not mercenary and weak. Whereas he—

Oh, yes, and there was the little detail of her being already engaged to the respectable rector who would take her "without a farthing." Apparently St. Eadburh's provided an income comfortable enough for the confounded Gregory to ignore such petty matters as marriage portions and a wife's inheritance, whereas he, Robert Fairchild, would never have that freedom—

No. That freedom to give his heart wherever he pleased, heedless of petty financial considerations.

But it wasn't the thought of not having the penniless bride of his choice that troubled him at present. In fact, he had a sinking feeling that all these points he was rehearsing to himself were actually of no consequence.

None at all.

For the sinking feeling told him that, somewhere between Miss Ellsworth discomposing Mr. Hents and Fairchild himself discomposing *her*, Miss Florence Ellsworth had slipped under his guard. And this heart of his, which could not be handed out willy-nilly because of his modest means—some piece of it might already have walked out of the door in her possession.

CHAPTER SIX

She says her spirits are so damped and her nerves so bad,
she must...endeavour to soothe her mind by change of
scene and country.
— Isabella Pigot, Letter to the Prince of Wales (c.1792)

Hollowgate, long the seat of the ancient Baldric family and now the property of the Ellsworths, consisted of a fine, square, two-storey Jacobean house faced in red brick, with symmetrical gabled bay windows and octagonal chimneys, surrounding an open courtyard. Florence and Lily's grandfather had remade the interior for elegance and comfort and brought in Capability Brown himself to design the park, while the girls' grandmother reigned supreme over the formal walled garden beside the house. Within Hollowgate were still found both a great hall and a long gallery, but the convenience of smaller drawing rooms and parlors for the family's daily use had been added, as well as a second staircase and a screens passage to hide the servants' comings and goings.

There were larger, grander houses in the county, but none so near Winchester and none whose history was so long entwined with the town. It was Hollowgate's setting, nestled in a shallow basin between West Hill and Sleepers Hill that gave the estate its name, not the brick-and-iron arched gateway fronting the Romsey Road at which Robert Fairchild paused to brush the dust from his clothing. It was late afternoon, and he had walked from Parchment Street. Mr. Darby had declined the invitation with a groan, saying, "Regretful as I am to miss a meal from their excellent cook, I fear it is overindulgence which landed me in my painful predicament. No, Fairchild, now is as good a time as any to make Ellsworth's acquaintance. Mind you, he's a pleasant enough man on the surface because he positively refuses to consider anyone's opinion or well-being but his own. Don't cross him and he'll like you as well as he ever liked me."

Hardly reassuring advice for Fairchild, considering Miss Ellsworth's request, and it was to the father rather than the daughter that Darby and West owed its fiduciary duty, so it was altogether too bad that Fairchild had determined to try to help her. Suppose he were to anger Ellsworth, and the man withdrew his business? That might very well result in Fairchild's own dismissal, and what would become of him then was anyone's guess.

I might need to take a leaf from William Ellsworth's own book, in that event, he thought wryly, *and trade on my looks to secure a wealthy bride.* He remembered the jokes of his fellow Wykehamists when he first returned to Winchester—how they bandied Miss

Lily Ellsworth's name about. He had laughed with them then. But though the scheme sounded plausible enough, common enough, at the time, he suspected he would find such a course of action impossible to carry out, even if he had not discovered his new fondness for the elder Miss Ellsworth. He had never been any good at pretending.

"Good afternoon."

A loud and solemn voice broke into his thoughts, and he glanced up to see a burly gentleman with silver-streaked hair, accompanied by a faded, too-slender, younger woman.

"Good afternoon," he replied, bowing.

"If you are going to Hollowgate, you must be Mr. Robert Fairchild. I am Mr. Clifford Gregory of St. Eadburh's, and this is my sister Miss Gregory."

Ah, the celebrated Mr. Gregory, chosen one of Miss Ellsworth. The man was not bad looking; nor did he lack for dignity (some might say self-importance), but he was older than Fairchild expected. Older and—more wooden.

He was conscious of a desire to dislike the man, but his innate sense of justice cautioned him to reserve judgment. After all, the rector of St. Eadburh's had not only won Miss Ellsworth's regard but had also had the good sense to notice her charms.

As for Miss Gregory, Fairchild could only guess that she had been born much later than her brother, or that she hid her age more successfully. She was not a plain woman, but she gave the impression of one, fading into nothingness beside her large, distinguished, clerical sibling.

The introductions accomplished, they turned in at the gate to walk the few furlongs to the house.

"Miss Ellsworth tells me you are employed by Mr. Darby, the family attorney," began the rector.

"I am. Unfortunately, his health did not permit him to come, so I represent us both."

"Are you new to Winchester?"

"By no means. I was at the College in my youth. But I have been gone nearly ten years in Oxford."

"Do you find the town much changed?" asked Miss Gregory quietly.

"Not on the surface. But, of course, as a boy, my experience was more gown than town," he explained. "Therefore I am best prepared to tell you that the *school* is not much changed, except that all the pupils seem half the size they were when I was there and the place much more orderly."

"Yes, a capable man, Mr. Goddard, the headmaster," pronounced Mr. Gregory.

"So I hear."

They tramped along some ways in silence, but then Fairchild bestirred himself. "And you, Mr. Gregory, I believe you are to be congratulated?"

The man's broad chest swelled even larger, and he intoned, "I thank you, Mr. Fairchild. Yes. I have the great good fortune to be engaged to Miss Ellsworth."

"I—made her acquaintance when I was calling on my neighbors the Charles Ellsworths," Fairchild said. "An estimable young lady."

He thought that, if Mr. Gregory's chest swelled any further, he would burst his waistcoat buttons. But perhaps that was sour grapes. If Fairchild had won the hand of so admirable a young lady as Miss Ellsworth, he supposed his own waistcoat buttons would be in equal danger.

Upon arriving at the house, they were admitted and announced by one of the footmen.

"Ah, Mr. Gregory, Miss Gregory," beamed William Ellsworth, coming to clasp their hands, "and you must be Mr. Fairchild—Darby sent a note with his apologies. May I introduce my children? My eldest, Miss Ellsworth. Miss Lily. Master Tyrone. Miss Araminta. Miss Beatrice. Children, this is Mr. Darby's new young man, Mr. Fairchild."

"He is a Winchester boy," declared Mr. Gregory. "Like you, Tyrone."

Tyrone, like most fourteen-year-olds, had nothing to say to this, though he gave Fairchild a good stare, as did the rest of the Ellsworth Assortment, apart from Miss Ellsworth, who was pointing Miss Gregory to a comfortable chair.

Fairchild decided the description of Miss Lily as the family beauty had not been exaggerated. She was indeed beautiful, sharing her older sister's dark hair and flawless complexion, but there the resemblance ended. Instead of eyes of winter water, Miss Lily's were decidedly blue and, if Fairchild had not known better, he would have thought she colored her cheeks and lips, so rosy were they. She had the more generous figure as well and did not seem burdened by Miss Ellsworth's reserve. Yes, indeed. If Fairchild had seen Miss

Lily before he saw Miss Ellsworth, he would have said there was no comparison.

But he had not seen Miss Lily before he saw Miss Ellsworth. And his few minutes in the latter's company had been enough to do their work. Therefore, he was able to withdraw his gaze from the fabled Miss Lily in a surprisingly short space and turn it upon the other Ellsworths.

Master Tyrone was well-grown for his age, though still a stripling. He and his twin Araminta were both golden-haired with unusual dark eyes. And while Araminta was decidedly tanned and restless, Tyrone sat pale and abstracted. Fairchild hid a grin. Whatever their differences, it was clear both twins wished they might be spared the gathering.

The youngest, Miss Beatrice, hovered at Miss Ellsworth's side, only emerging to make her curtsey when prompted. He had a glimpse of curling light brown hair and no more. Mr. Gregory bent his bulky self to boom something at the girl, but she shrank away, and Fairchild saw Miss Ellsworth give her intended an apologetic smile. She looked very well that afternoon—neat and fresh and collected. Only a telltale wash of pink across her cheeks hinted at her nerves. When her eyes flicked over to his, he felt his own face heat, as if he had been caught doing something wrong, and he turned abruptly away.

It was to Mr. Ellsworth he must direct his attention, of course. To Mr. Ellsworth, who gazed upon the gathering as a sovereign might his tidy little sunlit kingdom.

"Sir," Fairchild addressed him. "I am pleased to make your acquaintance. Mr. Darby has told me of his long service to the family."

"Oh, yes," replied Mr. Ellsworth graciously. "He has been a faithful retainer. I regret to hear he continues unwell."

"I too. But I hope I may prove as useful a person in the interim and in future. Do allow me, sir, to express my condolences on the recent loss of Mrs. Ellsworth."

The bereaved clicked his tongue and sighed appropriately, but the effect was ruined the next moment when the footman opened the door again and heralded, "Mrs. Thomas Whisp." At once, Mr. Ellsworth brightened and straightened, and the metamorphosis was not lost on Fairchild.

Nor was he alone in his dismay. Although Florence did not observe the abrupt change in her father, she was alarmed enough on her own.

Because Mrs. Whisp did not appear as she had in church.

She still wore half-mourning, to be sure—a lavender gown trimmed in black, but the quiet grief and demureness that marked her at St. Eadburh's were vanished, gone the way of the lace tucker she had worn in her neckline then for modesty. Without her bonnet, her dark golden hair was swirled atop her head in curls and coils, held by a ribbon headband, and Florence would have wagered the woman was even wearing scent.

Oh, dear.

And then Lily was at her side, whispering, "Is this the same Mrs. Whisp? We are doomed."

"Mrs. Whisp," cried Mr. Ellsworth, striding forward to welcome her. "What a pleasure. You are very welcome at Hollowgate."

"Mr. Ellsworth," she replied in her high voice, curtseying gracefully. "A pleasure."

"You know the Gregorys, of course, and my children, but I believe you have not yet met Mr. Robert Fairchild? Attorney with Darby and West. Mr. Darby has long been a trusted advisor, but sadly he was not well enough to join us."

"What a shame," she murmured, her eyes widening for a moment as they lingered on the handsome Mr. Fairchild.

"Perhaps our fine new attorney can distract her," hissed Lily.

And though Florence should have been glad Mr. Fairchild was there to outshine her father, instead she felt a prickle of annoyance. Good heavens! Was it not only William Ellsworth who would need a wary eye kept upon him? Of course, it was no business of Florence's if Mrs. Whisp should choose to operate on Mr. Fairchild. Mr. Fairchild must look out for himself. Still, she hoped he would not be diverted from his mission. *He must use this time to ingratiate himself with Papa*, she thought, *not to flirt with some strange person.*

Her brow knitting, Florence shook her sister off. It should not matter a bit what Mrs. Whisp did, as long as it did not involve William Ellsworth. Without the appearance of haste, she crossed to stand beside her father, winding her arm through his. "Papa, now that we are all gathered, will you lead us to dinner?" And to the room at large she added, "Please forgive me for hurrying us to table, but our cook Wilcomb has certain special creations in store, and she begged me not to dally long."

Mr. Ellsworth frowned when he saw he would not be able to offer his arm to Mrs. Whisp, but he comforted himself that they would only be ten at table, and she could not be seated at any great distance.

At a raised eyebrow from his intended, Mr. Gregory extended an arm toward the woman. "Madam?"

That left Mr. Fairchild to take Miss Gregory and the other Ellsworths to follow how they might.

Before taking the chair to Florence's right, Mr. Gregory obligingly seated Mrs. Whisp at Florence's left hand, at the farthest diagonal from Mr. Ellsworth. Indeed, Mr. Ellsworth ended in being flanked by Mr. Fairchild and Minta, and Florence was pleased to see the two gentlemen conversing as the footmen laid the first course.

"Mr. Gregory, I found your sermon yesterday both edifying and poignant," Mrs. Whisp told the parson after some minutes. "When you spoke of the foolish man who built his house on sand, I found myself nostalgic for home. Weymouth has beautiful sand."

"But I hope not its fair number of fools," interjected Lily.

A little silence met this, but then Mr. Gregory asked in his usual pulpit voice, "Did you live long in Weymouth, Mrs. Whisp?"

The widow laid down her spoon with a little sigh. "Ah, mine is a sad story, Mr. Gregory. I hesitate to bore the company with it." Her round blue eyes looked up and down the table, and it was Mr. Ellsworth who obliged by assuring her that they would dearly like to hear it, if she was willing to share with them.

"Well, then—I am not a native of Weymouth, but rather of Gloucestershire, where my father was a clergyman. When I was not very old, I am sorry to say he agreed to sign a bill for a young nobleman of his parish, the son of the family to whom my father owed his living. When the bill came due, there was no money for it. The young nobleman fled abroad, out of reach of his creditors, leaving the bailiffs to fall upon us."

"Oh, Mrs. Whisp," breathed Miss Gregory, a hand to her throat. "Was there no help to be had from the lord and lady of the family?"

"I'm afraid they blamed my father for not preventing their son falling in with bad company—you see, the two of them had been at university together. In any event, ruined as we were, we removed to Weymouth, where my father had still an aunt living, and he opened a small school there. It was a shocking change in circumstances, but we were grateful to have some means of support."

Florence could see from the compression of Mr. Gregory's lips that he was torn between deploring youthful foolishness and deploring the injustice of a clergyman paying for the sins of his friend. She herself felt a stirring of sympathy for their guest. After all, Florence knew what it was like, to feel burdened by a father's mistakes.

"Were the Whisp sons some of your father's pupils?" she asked.

"Nearly. They were friends of pupils," Mrs. Whisp answered with a smile and a vague wave. "So kind to me. So good, the Whisps. There was good fortune! To be blessed with the affections of such a man as Thomas Whisp. After he—well—after I lost him, the Whisps insisted I was part of the family and might stay with them always, but I—needed a change of scene. I could not continue in a place where every happy memory was turned to—" Here her handkerchief emerged, and she gave a dab to each eye.

"Do you think the Whisps will ever return to Winchester?" Miss Gregory asked after a proper interval, when the handkerchief was stowed again.

The company sat forward, as clerical comings and goings are always of deep interest to a cathedral town. Mrs. Whisp drew herself up. "Much as I would love to be surrounded by them again—my great-aunt and father are no more, you understand, and the Whisps are my only remaining connections—my mother-in-law Mrs. Whisp continues to suffer from her cruel rheumatism, and only sea bathing affords her relief."

"Let them stay in Weymouth, then, say I," Mr. Ellsworth said from his end of the table. "After so many years' absence, what are a few more? We must be grateful for what we are given, and I speak for all, Mrs. Whisp, when I say your coming to Whisp Cottage will prove an ample recompense."

Florence and Lily were separated by too great a space to kick each other beneath the table, but they had no need of it. Perhaps their fear of a new governess was premature, if the candidate for the fourth Mrs. Ellsworth presented herself so conveniently! It took all of Florence's self-control to keep her expression neutral, and she could not help throwing one glance at Mr. Fairchild. Did he see what was happening under his nose? It all depended on him now—and if he were unsuccessful?

He caught the glance, and the flash of anxiety in it made him want to reassure her, though he had little enough confidence in what he might accomplish with such a man as Ellsworth. But he bent his head in acknowledgement of her unspoken plea, and Florence felt an unexpected surge of relief, as if she had thrown a rope from her end of the table to his, and he had tugged on it to make it fast. He would try to help her. And, despite the eager interest her own father might show in their new neighbor, Mr. Fairchild did not seem to share it beyond what politeness demanded.

The dinner conversation turned to other topics, and presently Florence rose to excuse the ladies and children, leaving the men to their port and Mr. Fairchild to make a beginning.

By prearrangement, Florence had set Lily to play on the pianoforte and Tyrone on his violin while Minta turned the music for them, a common grouping when there were guests at Hollowgate. Beatrice, as ever, snuggled next to Florence, whose mind was occupied with praying that her father would take a liking to Mr. Fairchild. Of course Mr. Fairchild could not accost him on the subject of remarriage with Mr. Gregory present, but if Mr. Ellsworth approved of Mr. Fairchild, Mr. Fairchild could ask for a private interview later in the week.

As hostess she could not ignore Miss Gregory and Mrs. Whisp, however. They took seats to either side of her and Beatrice, and Florence wished Boots would hurry and bring in the tea things, that the ladies would have some natural occupation.

They could and did stare at Lily and Tyrone as they played, of course, but the interval before the gentlemen joined them could not be passed with no conversation at all.

When the first piece finished and the next began, Florence pinned on a smile and faced the widow. "Mrs. Whisp, I did wonder, when you told your sad history, whatever became of your father's friend."

"Friend?" Mrs. Whisp repeated, blinking.

"Yes. The nobleman for whom your father signed the bill. The one who had to flee abroad," Florence prompted. "Did he return to England once war broke out?"

"Oh! I'm sure he must have, Miss Ellsworth. But you understand—so painful—my father did not maintain contact with him. After we left Gloucestershire, all relationship with that family was necessarily at an end."

"How unfortunate! Perhaps the friend might have repented and sought him. I know if I had done an innocent person such a wrong, I would have no peace until I could make some amends. Or at least beg his pardon."

"Hmm. Yes, very unfortunate," said Mrs. Whisp. She snapped open her fan and began to wave it briskly. "But I insist on learning more about *you*, Miss Ellsworth. Come—you are to be married. Tell me about your *amour* with the sturdy clergyman. When did he first steal your heart?"

"Oh!" The directness of the question took Florence aback, and her eye involuntarily caught Miss Gregory's. They both looked away. "Oh—well—I..."

"It must have been his eloquence that won you," Mrs. Whisp suggested mischievously. "I can tell from his sermons that he has a way with words. You were probably helpless when he turned the force of that persuasiveness on you."

With a telltale blush Florence tried to recall Mr. Gregory's declaration. It had been sensible, loud, certain. His exact words were lost now—swept away by the stronger memory of Lily's disgust.

"He—is persuasive," she agreed, aware of how lame this sounded. She hoped Mrs. Whisp would think she was blushing because the recollection was so flattering and delightful. And how she wished Miss Gregory had been out of earshot! Miss Gregory knew better than anyone what her brother's proposal must have been like and that she, Florence, would not have been in any danger of being carried away by his fervor. Or her own fervor, for that matter.

She was never so thankful as when the door opened at that moment to admit both the gentlemen and Boots with the tea. Instantly Mrs. Whisp's attention was removed from her, which was a very good thing because Florence's first glance went not to her intended but to Mr. Fairchild. How had his time with her father gone?

The attorney did not return her look but at least she could see he had not made himself *persona non grata*, for Mr. Ellsworth was saying, "Ah! I see the children have been playing for our guests. Fairchild, you must bear with my overweening pride and hear them perform."

"Gladly, sir," he replied.

Other than handing the man some tea, Florence had no opportunity to take Mr. Fairchild aside, and even then he happened to be seated beside Miss Gregory, so she could not even venture a questioning look.

No, it took until the guests were departing, in the bustle of finding various wraps and making various parting remarks and determining who was walking with whom which direction, for Florence to steal an eyeblink of a moment.

"I hope you had a pleasant evening," she blurted.

"Very much so," he replied. "I enjoyed both the setting and the company."

"And—my father?"

"Smiled graciously throughout and asked me to return."

"I am so glad!" she answered, with a smile of her own. She would have liked to hear more, but Mr. Gregory stalked over to take his loud leave, and with that she must be satisfied.

CHAPTER SEVEN

A garden inclosed is my sister, my spouse;
a spring shut up, a fountain sealed.
—Song of Solomon 4:12, *The Authorized Version*
(1611)

The walled garden at Hollowgate reminded Florence of her mother, and often when she called upon those misty memories of the first Mrs. Ellsworth, she saw her encompassed by climbing roses and ivy, espaliers and brambles. It was here, on the stone bench, that her mother instructed her not to let her heart rule her head when it came to marriage—it must have been shortly before Mrs. Ellsworth died, or Florence would not have been able to remember it. But now the spot was sacred to her. The enclosed space was a connection not only to her lost mother, but also to her extinct Baldric forbears. It had originally been the creation of Florence's Baldric grandmother, and it would not have surprised Florence to learn that her mother loved the place in turn, because she too associated it with her mother.

Whenever the weather permitted, and even more when the constraints of mourning limited the Ellsworths' public activities, those who knew her understood that if Florence was not to be found within, she would usually be in her garden. Therefore Mr. Gregory bent his steps there a few days after the dinner without troubling to call at the house. (Though he did not admit it to himself, he also preferred to avoid Miss Lily's scowls and remarks.)

The lower door to the garden was shut, and as Mr. Gregory paused to reach over and unlatch it, he was in time to make his bow to the departing Mrs. Whisp. At the sight of her, he became his most woodpigeon, Lily Ellsworth would have said, for his head bobbed back in surprise, and his chest swelled before he made his bow.

Mrs. Whisp was demure again; the lace tucker restored to her neckline and a plain chip bonnet hiding much of her burnished hair. Making her curtsey, she merely smiled and passed on, leaving the rector to emit a series of preliminary sounds that failed to develop into coherent speech. That must wait for when the half-door was shut behind her and he watched her down the path. Then he sought out Florence's favorite stone bench, where his intended sat with folded hands, her eyes troubled.

"My dear," he accosted her, "I am not convinced that Mrs. Whisp is the sort of companion I would choose for you. As a young lady, you must be particularly careful of your friends."

If there existed young ladies who enjoyed being greeted by a lover with suspicions and reproaches, Florence was not one of them. Which accounted for her uncharacteristically snappish reply. "But Mr. Gregory, I did not seek her company. She called upon *me*."

Instead of being chastened by this correction and immediately reversing his course, he swelled further. "And yet you invited her to walk in your garden with you?"

"*Invited*?" cried Florence, rising to her feet in indignation. "Indeed I did not. The woman called at the house, and Bobbins directed her out here, as has happened to you, sir, numerous times, I may point out."

"Ah," he said. Which was not the same as an apology.

Therefore, she felt a perverse desire to needle him in return. "You did not object to meeting her at Hollowgate the other day."

"How could I object to any guest your family chooses to invite?"

"Exactly! And if I had indeed invited her to call again today, which I did not, I do not see why such an invitation must only be issued subject to your approval."

"Now, now, Miss Ellsworth," he said, holding up placating hands. "I did not say you require my approval in such matters, but...I daresay I supposed you would welcome my opinion."

Her nostrils flared, and she found herself pressing her lips together. What possessed her today? It was not so irrational a belief on his part. She ought to welcome his opinion on any and all subjects, and when they were married she would be expected to consult him in all things. Yet she felt a most Lily-like desire to give her displeasure its head.

While she was still struggling to master her temper, he then compounded matters by gesturing at the bench behind her, as if bidding her to sit again.

"No, thank you, I will stand," Florence declared, vexed anew. This was *her* garden, and as the mistress of it, she was the one to offer seats or not offer seats on her mother's bench.

"I fear you are overexcited this morning," he sighed.

Worse and worse.

Her own breast swelled. "I assure you, I am quite mistress of myself. If I show any tendencies to excitement, it would not be without cause, as this is the second interruption within the space of an hour."

Mr. Gregory raised his eyebrows and blinked several times in wonder at this behavior, which Florence chose not to notice, even as she inwardly censured it. Why was he to come stomping into her private retreat to berate her, after she had already been disturbed by Mrs. Whisp? And why should she be made to feel defensive, when she had done nothing wrong? They might be engaged to be married, but she could dispense with his lord-of-the-manor airs until the deed was done.

If he had understood her better, he would have known Florence had not been the least bit pleased to find Mrs. Whisp joining her; nor had matters improved when the woman spent her fifteen-minute call seeming to press Florence for more information on her father. "How well Miss Lily and Master Tyrone played! Mr. William Ellsworth must be very fond of music, that he ensured his children would be so skilled. Were those some of his favorite songs and pieces?" "What well-mannered children the younger Ellsworths were. Were they tutored at home, or did they attend school? Oh, Miss Beatrice did not go to school? What did Mr. Ellsworth propose to do with her, then?" And so forth.

"You need not fear that I sought out Mrs. Whisp," Florence said now through gritted teeth, yanking off a faded aster bloom and chucking it over the wall. "It was she, rather, who sought me out. I suppose as an intermediate step to seeking out my father." Another shriveled aster followed the first. "I don't blame her for not wanting to call upon Lily this morning. Lily would likely have told her *it was no use making up to us, for Papa was going to marry the next governess who came along*, or something of that sort."

"My dear!" said Mr. Gregory again, as taken aback by his intended's manner as by her words. Not knowing where to begin, he began with the last. "Do you mean to say you think Mr. Ellsworth might—remarry?"

She fixed him with her cool grey eyes. Well, why should she not tell him? She had told Mr. Fairchild, after all. "I do, Mr. Gregory. I not only think it, I would stake my life on it. Unless Papa can be prevented. But I do not know if he can be prevented."

"I see."

Her chin came up. She would have liked him to say something like, "Never mind. What has that to do with us, Miss Ellsworth? You will still be the same charming girl, and it changes nothing about my determination to make you my bride." But he did not.

To be fair to Mr. Gregory, he had already resigned himself to Mr. Ellsworth's spotty history and the ill-assorted nature of his chosen bride's family. But it would be asking too much for him to swallow this news with a smile. How many wives had Bluebeard had, after all?

Noting Miss Ellsworth's continued displeasure—good heavens, he had never seen her look that way! The resemblance to her sister Miss Lily was far more obvious when she was cross—Mr. Gregory hastened to say, "Would you like me to speak to him on the matter, my dear?"

Florence started. Why, it had never even occurred to her to ask Mr. Gregory to speak to her father. For one thing, she suspected her papa would too easily dismiss and ignore whatever the rector had to say. Even asking Mr. Darby (and hence Mr. Fairchild) to approach William Ellsworth had been a stretch. But that was because, she realized, she put more faith in the attorneys being heard than in Mr. Gregory. And that was not right, was it? Shouldn't she trust her own intended husband's judgment and discretion more than that of her father's paid advisors?

The insight did not improve her mood.

"What would you say to him?" she countered. "I have already spoken to him, to no avail. Papa will do what Papa will do, I'm afraid. But now you understand why I wanted to postpone our wedding."

This declaration staggered him. "I—I thought you wanted to postpone it because of your stepmother's death."

"Well, obviously, that too," Florence said impatiently, and though she did not stamp her foot like a child, her slipper scraped on the gravel. "But more because I need to ensure I leave my siblings as best cared for as I am able."

"My dear, why did you not say so before?"

"Because—" Florence broke off abruptly. *Because you are not the sort of person I am comfortable confiding in*, she had been on the point of saying. Her mouth popped open in surprise. Of course she should be comfortable confiding in him! She was going to marry the man, for heaven's sake, and how could she marry someone she was not comfortable confiding in?

It was just that it would be a new habit. Yes, that was it. A new habit that must be encouraged, until it became habit indeed.

"Because I did not," she finished awkwardly. And then some truth slipped out before she could stop it. "You are not the sort of person easily confided in."

"How could I not be, in your case?" he protested, with some justification. "I know we have not yet grown to know each other as well as we will in the days to come, but could you not take my interest in these matters on credit? What could interest me more, my dear, than your nearest concerns?"

And now Florence knew she was being unjust, because the "my dears" were grating on her nerves.

"I do not doubt your interest," she retorted, striving without great success not to sound peevish. "And I thank you for saying my concerns are important to you. But you will pardon me if I say I seem to be a person who requires that confidence to be in place *before* I confide."

She no sooner spoke the words than scarlet washed over her face. Because hard upon her speech followed the realization that she had just lied to her betrothed. Lied! After all, had she not confided in Mr.

Fairchild, hardly knowing the man? What pre-existing confidence had she had in him?

But that is different, she argued with herself. *Mr. Fairchild is Papa's man of business. Or will be. He needed to be told—these things—so that he might give Papa the best advice.*

"Mm," grunted her betrothed. He began to pace back and forth before her, nodding thoughtfully, his hands clasped behind his back.

Florence waited, shutting her eyes briefly, as if doing so might ring down the curtain on this unpleasant scene and raise it again with all the players restored to their previous positions. Mr. Gregory would assume the role once more of her admired, respected betrothed, who promised her a future of peaceful uneventfulness. And she would be once more his unquestioning admirer who gave all future decisions into his capable hands. *This* person, this undeputed deputy Florence who was delivering her lines today, seemed to prefer trusting her own judgment and making her own future decisions. But that couldn't be right, could it? How could she trust herself? Suppose she were to have more of her father in her than she liked? What a mull that would make of things, if Miss Florence Ellsworth proved as folly-prone as he! And how disappointed her mother would be, looking down from heaven—if mothers indeed could look down from heaven. This would be a question well-suited to pose to Mr. Gregory, and yet she could not manage it.

With an effort and a balling of her fists, Florence prepared to apologize for her pique. But she was forestalled by Mr. Gregory stopping directly in front of her, puffing himself up again to his maximum chest circumference, and saying, "I did have a reason for calling today."

And somehow this harmless beginning set Florence off anew. "Mr. Gregory, we are engaged. Is that not reason enough to call?"

"I—"

"If I were to look in at the parsonage," she persisted, "would you then ask my purpose in doing so?"

"I would welcome—"

Florence's fingertips flew to her temples. "Everything is a muddle," she muttered. "That woman has muddled me. Mrs. Whisp had no qualms about calling, and yet *you*—"

"I did not say I had qualms!" bellowed Mr. Gregory, provoked at last. He delivered this sentence in a thundering tone not heard in the pulpit of St. Eadburh's since Russia abandoned Britain and the Second Coalition. And, instead of shrinking back in dread, cowed, Florence looked almost relieved to find there was a point past which she could not push him.

"I—did—not—say—I—had—qualms," her intended repeated, flustered to have lost his temper. He began smoothing his lapels like a ruffled woodpigeon, and Florence had a terrible urge to giggle. She did not have to struggle to repress this urge long, however, for his next remark distracted her. "You understand, my dear—" (she twitched at the endearment) "—that I am not a man in his first youth, who may hang about his beloved's neck without becoming an object of ridicule. Moreover, as the rector of St. Eadburh's—well—let that rest. What I mean to say is my sister Miss Gregory begs that you take tea with us this evening. She was going to send a note, but I offered to walk over. And—er—Miss Lily may come if she likes."

"Thank you," said Florence humbly. She tried not to picture Lily's distaste when the invitation should be issued. "I would be glad to."

"Very well." He took a deep breath. Seeing her calm again, he pulled out his handkerchief and pressed it to his brow in relief.

She waited for him to replace the handkerchief in his pocket before venturing, "I—and what *I* mean to say, Mr. Gregory, is that I hope you will not stand on ceremony and require an excuse to come to Hollowgate." She wondered if she should ask if he meant it, calling her his 'beloved,' or if that were merely a figure of speech. Somehow she did not dare.

Then Mr. Gregory did a bold thing. He reached out and patted her once—twice—on the forearm. It seemed like they both waited, then, to see how such an action would be received.

Florence did not protest, but neither did she rush into his arms. She merely stood.

He withdrew his hand. "Ahem. How kind of you. I will tell Miranda to expect you. Perhaps you had better rest before then, my dear. You are not yourself today."

The grey eyes turned on him then. "Not myself, Mr. Gregory?" she asked. "But if I am I, and I say and do such things as I have just said and done, how can I not be myself?"

But this was one conundrum too many for the put-upon parson to un-knot in one morning, and he only bowed to her with a mumbled something-or-other and took a hasty leave.

CHAPTER EIGHT

You do not counsel well:
You speak it out of fear and cold heart.
—Shakespeare, *Henry IV, Part I,* **IV.iii.2461 (c.1597)**

A week passed before William Ellsworth bothered to reply to Robert Fairchild's note, asking for a convenient time to visit Hollowgate and discuss affairs. Again Fairchild refrained from mentioning Mr. Darby's decision to retire—that had better be announced in person—but he did cite his principal's continuing ill health.

If Mr. Ellsworth's answer had not come when it did, Fairchild would have called at Hollowgate uninvited because that morning Mr. West slapped the *Hampshire Chronicle* upon his desk and jabbed a finger at one of the advertisements. "Have you seen this? The man is mad!"

With misgivings, Fairchild bent his head to read:

Governess — Wanted, an accomplished woman, in the above capacity, who can have the most respectable references, and not younger than five-and-twenty; she must be complete mistress of the French Language, and it is much wished that she be able to give some instruction in Italian, Music, &c., &c. As it is to form the education of a young Lady, none need apply who are not properly qualified. — Letters with particulars addressed to W.E. at Hollowgate, Winchester, will be answered.

"He means to marry again, you may depend on it," Mr. West declared with a disgusted hiss. "'Not younger than five-and-twenty,' indeed! Ellsworth is five-and-fifty, if he's a day. He should be ashamed of himself. Some men never have so much as one wife, and that man thinks himself entitled to a fourth!"

Panic rippled through Fairchild. He should not have let so many days pass. He should have *insisted* that Ellsworth meet with him. Imagine having to face Miss Ellsworth without having lifted one little finger to assist her—!

"Though why I should complain, I don't know," Mr. West was saying. "One man's folly is another man's fortune. The prosperity of this firm owes much to Ellsworth's carryings-on."

"I will go out to Hollowgate immediately," said Fairchild, rising and reaching for his hat.

"Then you'd be a fool yourself," grimaced Mr. West. "Didn't Darby warn you? Ellsworth needs fine handling. If you go flying out there unbidden, the man will balk like a horse at a leap."

"Note, sir," said Hents, appearing in the doorway. West held out a hand for it, but Hents made an apologetic scrape and thrust it at Fairchild.

"It's from Hollowgate," he muttered. He ran a quick finger under the seal and unfolded it.

Perching on the edge of his desk, West regarded the young man through lowered eyelids. "Well? Does he summon you to draw up the marriage settlement?"

"I hope not," he replied honestly. "But he says I am welcome to call this afternoon."

"Better go at two o'clock, then," advised his partner. "Nice intermediate time between breakfast and dinner. Then at least Ellsworth won't think you're presuming on old Darby's rights and privileges to dine with the family."

Though Fairchild had, of course, already dined with the family, he saw no need to belabor the point and merely nodded, thanking West and instructing Hents to reply.

At fifteen minutes to two o'clock, he made his way along the Romsey Road to Hollowgate. The August day was warm, and he was glad of the excuse to be out of doors. Darby and West was a flourishing concern in a flourishing town, and while Fairchild appreciated the work and the promise of steady, increasing earnings, he had much less free time than of yore.

The first Ellsworths he encountered were just within the gate: Miss Araminta and Miss Beatrice, joined by Miss Araminta's friend and the little terrier, who was running in circles around them.

"Hold still, Bea," ordered Araminta, nocking an arrow. "I'll only hit you if you wriggle."

"I'm scared," whimpered her little sister. "Why can't you shoot at Aggie?"

Hurrying forward, he stretched out a hand. "Miss Araminta—!"

"Oh—good afternoon, Mr. Fairchild," she said pleasantly, lowering her bow. "Are you here to see Papa?"

Her aplomb made him laugh in spite of himself. "I am, but do I dare to pass on? Are you really going to shoot an arrow anywhere in the vicinity of Miss Beatrice?"

"Well...yes," she admitted, "but she was going to stand behind the tree and just hold the apple out, so really the chances of my hitting her were quite limited."

Beatrice did not seem to agree because she dropped the apple in the grass and scurried over to him, taking hold of his sleeve.

Araminta's friend Aggie, a maypole of a girl with whitish hair bound in a tight crown of braids, gave a groan and flopped down on the lawn, snatching up the apple and taking a bite of it. "I'm not being the target anymore," she declared. "Minta already shot a hole in my skirt that I'll be made to sew up myself."

"Get up, Aggie, or how will I introduce you to Mr. Fairchild? Mr. Fairchild, this is Miss Agatha Weeks."

"Charmed," said Fairchild to the toppled maypole, who merely rolled onto her stomach and waved at him. Turning back to Araminta, he asked, "Will I find Mr. Ellsworth within doors?"

"Of course. He rarely goes out." She was already nocking her arrow again, this time aiming for the branches above Aggie's head.

He bent to remove the dog from where it sat on his foot, giving Snap a friendly pat for consolation. "Off I go, then."

Beatrice released his sleeve but clung closer than his shadow until they reached the flight of steps leading to the front door. Then she darted ahead, flinging it wide and disappearing within.

Fairchild hesitated. The door was now open and not a servant in sight, but it hardly seemed fitting for him to saunter in unannounced.

His fist was lifted to knock on the open door when he saw the lad Tyrone descending the staircase, one hand skimming along the handrail while the other held an open book. His eyes flicked up and noticed Fairchild on the step, and, without a pause in his descent, his gaze returned to his reading and he hollered, "Floss! Visitor!"

Fairchild held his breath without realizing, and the next instant both a maid and Miss Ellsworth appeared in opposite doorways, the latter hurrying to remove her apron.

"It's Mr. Fairchild, miss," said the maid.

"Thank you," said Miss Ellsworth dryly. "I see that."

"I'm here to call on your father. He sent for me. Earlier. In a note. And I wrote a note giving this time." Aware he was bumbling, Fairchild shut up.

"Yes, of course." She gave him a brief smile and gestured toward a parlor across from the main drawing room where they had gathered for the dinner. "Boots, would you call Mr. Ellsworth, please? He is in his library, I believe, and—he may be—er—napping."

She followed him into the parlor and pulled the door shut behind her, leaning against it. "Oh, Mr. Fairchild, I began to worry you would never come."

"I did not forget your request, Miss Ellsworth, but in so delicate a matter as this, I did not think I should force my way."

She was biting her lip, her grey eyes wide. "It may already be too late. He has *placed an advertisement* for a governess in the *Chronicle*!"

"Yes, I saw it."

"And heaven only knows who will answer it," she fretted. "He already told me I may not help him choose the person, and short of stealing the replies before he sees them, and burning the ones which sound the worst, I cannot think what to do!"

"Miss Ellsworth—" He was still standing, as she was, and he came a step nearer. "I hate to say this, but there may not be a great deal you can do. Legally or morally, I mean. I still intend to try speaking to him," he added quickly, seeing her carriage droop, "but I would not want to give you false hope."

Wordlessly, she nodded, and then she drifted over to a worn pink chair, plumply upholstered, and sank into it.

"Perhaps no one will apply," Fairchild suggested, selecting a chair opposite hers. "And you will find you have only borrowed trouble."

She looked her skepticism, and he felt the inadequacy of this remark. Whatever it was about Miss Florence Ellsworth, she seemed to bring out his inadequacies. Or at least his self-doubt. He wondered if she thought him a blunderer.

He was both relieved and disappointed to find she wasn't thinking of him at all.

"There is more, Mr. Fairchild," she said, sitting forward and throwing a glance at the door.

"Yes?"

Her voice lowered to a whisper. "Mrs. Whisp called again. After the dinner, I mean." When his brows rose inquiringly, she added, "I think she is interested in—knowing Papa better." Her pretty face distorted in a grimace. "I know it sounds like gossip, Mr. Fairchild. Like—paranoia and pettiness. But if you had heard the questions she put to me..."

The door opened, and there was Boots with Mr. Ellsworth in tow.

Miss Ellsworth sprang up, as did Fairchild. "Papa. Here is Mr. Fairchild for his appointment. I will leave you both." And she did, though at the doorway she turned and, behind her father, clasped her hands together and gave Fairchild one last anxious look. He gave an infinitesimal nod.

He would try.

If he angered their most profitable client, Mr. West might have his head on a platter for it, but he would try.

"Come, come, sit down," said Mr. Ellsworth, with his most benignant smile. "We will become quite familiar with each other, so let us not stand on ceremony now. Though I begin to think my dear Mr. Darby will never come again. What do you think, Mr. Fairchild?"

"Mr. Ellsworth," Fairchild began, after clearing his throat, "both Mr. Darby and I are sorry to inform you that we think it unlikely he will ever return to full employment. The doctor Mr. Fisher has given his opinion that only prolonged rest and a somewhat stricter diet will relieve Mr. Darby's symptoms. But I would like to assure you that Mr. Darby and I have been in constant communication, and I am fully acquainted with your history and situation." He colored as he mentioned Mr. Ellsworth's "history," but the man himself did not appear to share his embarrassment.

Ellsworth heaved a sigh, clicking his tongue regretfully. "I see. Ah, too bad, too bad. Too bad for my friend Darby. I will have Florence send some of her raspberry cordial to him. It always helps me when I am not quite the thing. Alas. But Mr. Fairchild, you seem an intelligent and well-spoken young man, and you're long familiar with Winchester and an alumnus of the College, to boot! If we cannot have good old Darby, we will be happy to work with Mr. Darby's protégé."

Fairchild exhaled in relief. One obstacle overcome. Now it remained to be seen how far he might prod Mr. Ellsworth before the man lost his goodwill. Patting his pocket, in which he carried some notes, he said, "There were a few items I thought we might discuss today, sir, but before we get to those, we should start with questions or concerns you have. Would you allow me—?" Rising, he removed to the desk against the wall, where he examined the condition of the pen and ink bottle.

"To be sure, Fairchild," agreed Ellsworth, following him and setting a chair for himself closer to the desk. "Let's attend to business first. You will stay for dinner, won't you? Darby always did."

"I would be glad to, sir," he answered, adding to himself, *If I am still welcome then*. Taking the pen and dipping it, he wrote the date at the top of a fresh sheet of draft paper.

Popping up, Ellsworth wandered away, humming tunelessly. Then he strode back and leaned with his hands on the back of the chair. "Very well, very well. Let me see...the first reason I summoned you was to make sure of my late wife's settlement. She hadn't much to bring to the marriage, poor Mary Fielding that was, but there was a tiny income—some fifty pounds per annum—from her own mother that I believe now becomes the property of Beatrice."

Should she live to enjoy it, thought Fairchild, remembering Miss Araminta's archery practice. He smothered a grin. Aloud he said, "Yes, sir. Fifty pounds per annum. Now the property of Miss Beatrice."

"It's more than my second wife could call her own when I met her," Ellsworth continued, sounding rather smug. "When Catherine departed this world, she had nothing at all to leave Tyrone and Minta. All those two will have derives from me."

And all you *have derives from your first wife Henrietta Baldric.* As he scratched down this information he already knew, Fairchild marveled as many had on William Ellsworth's good fortune. If the Ellsworth sons had truly been as penniless as Fairchild had been told, William Ellsworth had certainly made the most of a difficult hand. While his younger brother Charles seemed happy enough, the latter's choice to marry a French servantwoman had done neither him nor his sons any financial favors. But the varied children of

William Ellsworth all stood to inherit handsomely, especially Miss Ellsworth, to whom would eventually pass Hollowgate.

"Your children will be well provided for—all of them," agreed Fairchild. He lay the pen down. This seemed the moment to sound him, when the man was thinking of his offspring. "Sir, I did see in the *Chronicle* today that you have advertised for a governess."

"I have." Ellsworth took a seat, crossing his legs and smiling. "My little Beatrice has just lost her mother and does not wish to attend school as her sister Minta does. Therefore, a governess."

"Who taught Miss Beatrice when your wife was still living?"

"Taught her? Beatrice is but six. She may have learned the alphabet and some numbers from Florence, but that would be all. And Florence will marry shortly and leave us for the rectory, so a governess it must be."

Fairchild gave a brief nod. As he had suspected, he had no reasonable argument to dissuade Ellsworth from hiring a governess. If the man chose not to send his youngest child to school, Fairchild could hardly insist on it. No—all he could attempt on Miss Ellsworth's behalf, would be to prevent the man using the position to find a new wife, or, alternately, to make the possibility of marrying Ellsworth as unappealing as he might. Dangers lurked for him in either case.

"In your advertisement, sir," he began delicately, "you make no mention of the terms to be offered the applicant."

"I did not."

"Then perhaps I might offer some suggestions on that head?" When Ellsworth did not immediately reply, Fairchild took up his pen to give his hands something to do and pressed on. "According to our records, the last time you employed a governess, you paid her thirty pounds per annum, in addition to board and lodging. A generous sum. Although that was eleven years ago, Mr. West counsels that twenty should be more than adequate in this instance. Unlike the previous governess—er—this one will only have the teaching of one child, rather than four."

Ellsworth's mouth thinned. He lay one arm along the desk and began to drum his fingertips on its surface.

Fairchild felt perspiration start. He knew the man was thinking, as they had, that the lower salary might reduce the number of interested parties.

Dipping the pen in the inkpot, he wrote, "Salary of £20," only to have Ellsworth flatten his hand on the paper.

"No," he mused, "let it stay at thirty pounds. She may only have the teaching of one child, but she will still have the managing of all of them."

Fairchild swallowed. "Yes...but as you point out, Miss Ellsworth will soon be gone, and Miss Lily is of an age to require little. Not to mention Master Tyrone being at the College many months of the year."

"No, no," rejoined Ellsworth, his tone lighter as he insisted. "Thirty pounds. I have already told Lily that the governess can chaperone her to assemblies and such. The woman must also be recompensed for this work as a companion."

"You didn't mention such companion duties in your advertisement, sir."

"But I will, when I meet with the applicants. Some things are better proposed in person."

Like marriage, Fairchild thought. He repressed a sigh.

Very well. There was still the second strategy.

Drawing a line through "Salary of £20," he wrote, "Salary of £30 to include companion duties." Then he looked up, trying to mirror Ellsworth's beneficent expression.

"Very thoughtful of you, sir, to think of *all* your children at such a time," he said. "All five of your children. And now would be the ideal time to tidy up your plans for them. Your existing will, of course, made provision for the last Mrs. Ellsworth, in the event she were to survive you. That not being the case, however, you would do well to execute a new will."

"Oh?"

"Yes. A new will in which we would only concern ourselves with the three possible situations remaining. One: your children—all five of them—survive you, and the Ellsworth estate is divided among them. Two: only some of the five children survive you, and the estate is then divided among those still living. And three: if you happened to survive all five of the children."

There was a flash of calculation in the older man's eyes, but it vanished before Fairchild could read it.

"I do hate talking about death," sighed Mr. Ellsworth, shaking his head. "This will be the—what—fourth or fifth will Darby and West executes for me? Is there so much to be settled? How much, say, would my last will have bequeathed the late Mrs. Ellsworth, upon my demise—?"

Fairchild drew his notes from his pocket and smoothed the sheets on the desk. "She was accorded twenty thousand pounds and a life-right to remain at Hollowgate. Very generous terms indeed."

Shrugging, Ellsworth affected to stifle a yawn. "There you have it, then. In the event of my death, Hollowgate will pass immediately to Florence, and the twenty thousand pounds formerly accorded my third wife may be divided evenly among the five children. That will do for now. Should any of them die before I do, that child's portion will be divided evenly among the remaining ones. Simple."

"Yes, sir." For a minute there was silence as Fairchild's pen scratched along the paper. But he was thinking hard. If a governess candidate came along with an eye to the main chance, the knowledge that William Ellsworth's money was locked up for his children might not be enough. She must be made to understand that, even if the lord of the manor offered marriage, the man was only growing older, and there would be no future guarantees.

Replacing the pen in its stand, he blotted his notes, saying in the most offhand manner he could produce, "That should settle it. Perhaps we might add one more provision, stating that, in the event of your marrying again, if the woman were to be widowed, she would be pensioned off with the minimum disturbance to the estate. An equal, modest sum, garnished from each of the children's inheritances. Say, a thousand apiece and £5,000 in total? And without the life estate in Hollowgate, naturally."

There was no reply, and he could only blot so long. Steeling himself, he looked up to find his client's face red, the paleness of his bald pate standing out alarmingly, like when one picked a promising strawberry and discovered its shoulders under the leaves were still white. Moreover, Ellsworth's nostrils were wide and his hands clenched. Fairchild thought for one bad instant that the older man was going to have a fit.

But then the door to the drawing room opened to admit a footman with the tea things, Snap the terrier darting at the man's ankles. This interruption served to restore Ellsworth's pose of equanimity. He sat back once more in his chair, his angry flush receding and his hands now folded quietly. In another moment, a bland smile reappeared.

"If such is Darby and West's advice," he said evenly, "have it drawn up."

Only with a herculean effort did Fairchild resist jumping up to punch the air in triumph. Had he succeeded? If he had, it was only a partial success—any truly penniless gentlewoman would still likely take her chances on five thousand pounds in a lump sum—but it was more than he thought he would come away with. And with no guaranteed life interest in Hollowgate, at least the interloper would take her tidy bequest and remove herself to Ramsgate or some such place, never to bother the family again.

On the other hand, the new will would not neutralize the danger posed by Mrs. Whisp—five thousand pounds would be nothing to sniff at, with the convenient Whisp Cottage still at her disposal—but perhaps the woman could be encouraged to keep other irons in the fire. Irons who were neither clients of Darby and West nor objects of Miss Ellsworth's concern.

No, let Mrs. Whisp be trouble for another day—this was a beginning and more success than he had hoped for, and Fairchild longed to go in search of Miss Ellsworth.

Much, much too soon, however, his urge to celebrate was checked.

For under the clatter of Bobbins nearly dropping the entire tray when his boot clipped Snap's paw and the dog let out a piercing yip, Fairchild heard Ellsworth mutter to himself, "Let it be, let it be. One afternoon's work. With as little effort it can all be changed back again."

CHAPTER NINE

Sirs, those provisos will not serve the turn.
—John Marston, *Histrio-mastix; or, the player whipt*
(1599)

When Florence left Mr. Fairchild to his interview with her father, she was tempted to press her ear to the door and might even have given in to this reprehensible urge if Lily had not appeared at the other end of the passage.

"What is it, Flossie?" asked Lily in her naughtiest tone. "You look distressed. Has Mr. Gregory advanced the wedding date?"

Scowling at her sister, Florence took her hand and marched her away to the gallery on the opposite side of the entrance hall. "Mr. Fairchild is here. He says Papa summoned him to talk business. And he has seen the advertisement Papa placed for a governess."

"Ooh! I hope Papa invites him to dinner. Mr. Fairchild is a great deal more pleasant to look at than Mr. Darby ever was."

"Lily, do be serious! I told you how I asked Mr. Fairchild to help me persuade Papa not to marry again."

Lily put her arm through her sister's, that they might pace the familiar length of the echoing passage. "You did. As if it weren't bad enough, you nursing these improbable wishes! Now you go and involve other people, including someone obligated to pretend interest."

"You think he only pretends?" asked Florence. The thought gave her a little stab.

"Florence—honestly! He knows on which side his bread is buttered. Would it be better for him to disappoint you or to disappoint Papa? Naturally he cannot wish to disappoint Papa, if he wants to continue long at Darby and West. And *I* think it was dreadful of you to put him in that position, no matter what Uncle Charles advises. Uncle Charles is so used to being poor that he doesn't even notice any longer! But for Mr. Fairchild, if Mr. Darby dismisses him, poverty might come as a shocking novelty."

"I don't want him discharged, of course," began Florence, alarmed.

"And for nothing!" Lily went on, unheeding. "For while Mr. Fairchild seems a talented young man, as well as a handsome one, there has never been anyone who has succeeded in managing Papa, or making him do or not do what he does not want to do or not do."

"I know it," said Florence, remembering she had said much the same thing to Mr. Gregory during their argument.

Lily went to the mirror that hung between the portraits of their great-grandfather Silas Baldric and their great-uncle Cleveland Baldric. Peering into its spotted surface, she began to repair the damage done to her coiffure by her bonnet. "You distracted me, Flossie," she told her sister's reflection. "I was going to tell you that when I was walking, I went up Sleepers Hill, and who should I see in the road below but Miss Gregory and Mrs. Whisp! Together at the rectory gate. Do you not think that an odd conjunction?"

Florence only shrugged, still preoccupied with how she might have endangered Mr. Fairchild's future. "What of it?"

Lily shrugged in return. "Nothing, I suppose. Only I hardly think that would be a friendship Miss Gregory sought. You know how retiring she is, and Mrs. Whisp is so...colorful. Therefore I think Mrs. Whisp must have initiated."

"Well, and why not? She must make friends, I suppose. Or perhaps she was only passing by. Do you really think Papa might dismiss Mr. Fairchild?"

There was no more time to consider the matter, however, for a racket arose of running steps and Minta and Aggie shouting and Snap barking. Florence and Lily hurried out to find Aggie presenting a bloody ankle and slipper, but Florence had been sister of Minta long enough not to panic at the sight, and she soon had the girl bandaged and dispatched home with a note of explanation and apology. Then there was a reproving lecture to deliver on proper and improper targets for weaponry, a lecture which glanced off Minta, much as Minta's arrow had glanced off Aggie's ankle.

No sooner was all this accomplished than Florence and Lily withdrew to the small parlor, where Wilcomb the cook soon found them. "Miss Ellsworth, if you please, what else should be put on the table, if Mr. Fairchild is staying for dinner? Mr. Darby always liked roast beef and a great deal of wine, you know, but Mr. Ellsworth didn't tell me there would be a guest and there's no beef ready..."

"Papa might toss Mr. Fairchild out and hurl a crust of dry bread after him," said Lily, taking up a book and then putting it down again when it turned out to be Tyrone's pirate volume.

"I am certain that, even if beef is Mr. Fairchild's favorite as well, he can survive one meal without it," Florence assured the cook. "And I don't remember him drinking much wine when he was here before."

"He hadn't to face Papa on that occasion," muttered Lily.

So it was decided to leave the menu as it was, and not a moment too soon, for both girls heard the drawing room door open. Bobbins rattled his way out with the tea things, followed by Mr. Ellsworth's carrying voice. Something about partridge season.

"Partridges! I think either Papa took things well," whispered Lily, "or else Mr. Fairchild's courage failed him, and he has not yet broached the matter."

Relief flooding her, Florence rose and hastened to the doorway. "Shall we dine, Papa?" She would tell Mr. Fairchild at the first opportunity that he need not honor her request—that she withdrew it! But had he spoken yet or not?

Her father's countenance told her nothing—it was as frustratingly serene as ever. Her eyes flicked past him to Mr. Fairchild, and she felt anxiety bubble up anew. He was meditative, uncertain. But at least he had not been dismissed. He would not stay to eat if he were dismissed.

His eyes met hers briefly, and Florence hardly knew what to make of it all. She must steal a moment aside with him, if she was to learn anything.

When guests were not present, dinners at Hollowgate were simpler affairs. Wilcomb was always sure to prepare a soup, roast meat, vegetables, and a savory pudding, but selections were fewer and tended to be trusted family favorites, to limit complaints from the younger children.

To Florence that day, everything might as well have been sawdust, though she mechanically partook of it all. Each bite seemed to require more and more chewing to make it palatable, and each swallow required greater and greater effort around the increasing lump in her throat. For she was increasingly convinced she had behaved selfishly. Lily was right: she had asked Mr. Fairchild for his help, with no thought to the consequences! She had asked him to jeopardize his own livelihood—had strolled into his office and placed such demands on him. Had played upon a gentleman's chivalric desire to assist a lady in distress, even. And if Mr. Fairchild had managed to speak against remarriage to his client without losing the Ellsworth custom on the spot, it was no thanks to her own thoughtlessness.

Even Lily realized what helping me would entail, Florence upbraided herself. *Lily, who is not precisely the soul of consideration.*

Too busy concocting an excuse to pull the attorney aside, Florence could not say afterward that she attended to any of the conversation, which was general and harmless, in any case. Mr. Fairchild said something to great amusement about a squirming between his ankles, followed by sudden weight and warmth across his feet, when Snap took his own "seat" at the table. Beatrice complained to her father about Minta using her as an archery target, to which Mr. Ellsworth responded with his usual beatific unconcern, saying only, "Ah, the recklessness of youth."

The one thing which finally penetrated Florence's abstraction was an awareness that, though William Ellsworth might be behaving in his customary manner, Lily was not. Lily was—there was no other word for it—Lily was *flirting*.

"When Mr. Gregory is with us, we must always have a plain broth," Lily declared to their guest. "Because Mr. Gregory prefers plainness in all things."

"Indeed?" asked Mr. Fairchild dispassionately.

"I myself prefer a soup with something in it," Lily went on, smiling, her head tilted and lashes fluttering. "Spice, I mean to say. Which do you prefer, Mr. Fairchild?"

"At my lodgings, Mrs. Archibald prepares a delicious oxtail soup with turnips that has already become a favorite of mine."

"Dear Mrs. Archibald," cried Lily, as if the elderly woman was a favorite. "She lives beside my aunt and uncle."

"Yes, I am aware."

"Lily," asked Beatrice, "have you got something in your eye? Why do you keep winking and blinking?"

"Perhaps she's trying not to cry," spoke up Minta, "because her favorite, Mr. Gregory, isn't here." That caused the younger

Ellsworths to laugh (even Tyrone snorted), and Lily's eyes were miraculously healed of their ailment for the remainder of the meal.

For her part, Florence simultaneously wanted to throw her napkin across the table at Lily and sink under that same table, to have Mr. Fairchild witness how little her family cared for her intended husband. She said nothing, however, and at last the dinner concluded, with the younger Ellsworths scattering in every direction and Mr. Ellsworth retreating to his library with a "Good to see you, Fairchild. Let me know when you have anything to show me."

"But you need not wait for Papa's summons, Mr. Fairchild," put in Lily, extending her hand to him. "We would be glad of you calling whenever you liked."

With his same calm, Mr. Fairchild took the young lady's hand, bowing over it and releasing it, and then he bowed in turn to Florence.

"Oh, Mr. Fairchild," she burst out, coloring. "I wonder if I might detain you one second and ask a favor of you. I have some—some damsons I know my aunt will enjoy, if you will be so good as to bring them to her. And—you may have some for Mrs. Archibald as well."

"Of course."

"Aunt Jeanne has her own damson tree," pointed out the troublesome Lily.

"Not like my damsons," said Florence with determined sweetness. "Come, Lily, and help me choose them." Stabbing an arm through her sister's, she marched her off to the kitchens.

"My, how forceful of you," Lily grinned.

"Whatever are you about, behaving in that way toward Mr. Fairchild?" demanded her sister, thumping a basket of the fruit down upon the table. Seizing a brown Holland sack, she began to toss the plums in at random.

"Behaving in what way?" asked Lily, all innocence.

"Winking and blinking and simpering and I know not what else!" Several damsons bounced onto the floor, but Florence scooped them up and hurled them in, undeterred.

"And why shouldn't I?" Lily countered. "He is a handsome, eligible young man, and I am a single young lady constrained by the conventions of mourning to stay mostly at home seeing nobody at all. If I can't go to any assemblies or parties this autumn and winter, I must practice my wiles on whomever comes my way. It is easy enough for you to criticize me—you already have someone to marry—such as he is."

Nothing in this reply smoothed Florence's ruffled feathers, and she flung two more pieces of fruit in the sack before spinning the neck to tie it.

"Better let me make up the next bag for Mrs. Archibald," observed Lily, "if you are going to be so violent. We don't want the fruit made into jam before it even reaches her."

Trying to slow her rapid breathing, Florence faced her sister. "Are you saying, Lily, that you would like to charm Mr. Fairchild?"

Lily hid a smile, taking her time selecting just the right damsons and then measuring twine to secure Mrs. Archibald's sack. "I am saying, why should I not?" She pushed the bag across the table at Florence.

"After all—nobody else seems to want him."

When Florence went to rejoin Mr. Fairchild, she found he had left the entry hall and was standing at the bottom of the front steps, hat in hand, the sunshine gleaming on his dark hair.

"Pardon me for keeping you waiting," she said, hurrying down to him.

"It is no trouble at all." He replaced his hat and reached for the two Holland sacks. "Goodness. Will you have any left for yourself?"

She blushed. "They are rather heavy, aren't they? I'm sorry to make you walk back to town so burdened. Maybe I should remove some."

"Don't do it on my account, Miss Ellsworth. Imagine how everyone would mock me, if I couldn't walk under a mile carrying two extra pounds. I have a reputation to uphold in town, you know." He gave a quick grin, thinking to himself that he would gladly carry two hundred pounds back to St. Thomas Street, if it meant he could stand alone with her in the late summer sunshine a few more minutes, her grey eyes fixed on him.

His teasing relieved her embarrassment and emboldened her to speak of what was most on her mind. "Mr. Fairchild," she began gravely, "I am grateful for this opportunity to speak to you again because I feel I owe you an apology."

"Another one?" he chuckled, his tone light. "That will make three, in the short time since you emerged from the house."

"I am in earnest! Please—" With a glance behind her, she beckoned him further down the drive. After a careful survey of the front of the house to ensure she saw no open windows or twitching draperies, Florence smoothed her gown to quiet her hands and said, "I must apologize to you because, when I asked you to speak to my father and to try to dissuade him from marrying again, I'm afraid I was thinking only of myself and not of the position that put you in."

He was silent a moment, not wanting to reply too quickly, lest she think he was dismissing her concern.

"And—and—if you have not yet spoken to him about it," Florence rushed on, "you need not. I would not have you imperil your standing at Darby and West. That is—Papa is your client, not I, and therefore I understand your loyalty must be to him."

"But Miss Ellsworth, suppose you were to become my client in future?" he smiled. "Unless Mr. Gregory already has a man of business..."

"Mr. Gregory?" she repeated blankly. "Oh—I don't know, to be honest. We have never discussed it. Perhaps Papa knows, if they talked about it when he asked my father's permission—"

He held up a hand to stop her. "Now you must forgive me, Miss Ellsworth. I was just rallying you again. You are so in earnest that I find I want to ease your mind a little. It so happens I agree with you—that your father marrying for a fourth time at his age would not be advisable. Therefore, while I knew the subject to be sensitive, I did not have to contravene my own judgment in raising the matter."

"Then you *did* raise the matter?" breathed Florence.

"I did. And met with both more and less success than I hoped. That is, he agreed rather easily to the execution of a new will—which needed to be done in any case because of Mrs. Ellsworth's death.

This one will contain a proviso that, if he marries again, the new wife's settlement will be more modest than that of the third Mrs. Ellsworth. But I cannot promise you, Miss Ellsworth, that such a proviso will deter a determined or determinedly impoverished woman, or that your father will not insist on executing still another will if the fourth Mrs. Ellsworth comes into being."

"Ah." Florence absorbed this information. It was not worse than she expected, and she realized she had already begun resigning herself. It had always been a long shot, and she must have unwittingly given it up as lost when she told Mr. Gregory that her father would do what her father would do.

No, at present she found her relief was entirely for Mr. Fairchild. Then she had not damaged his prospects after all! It was a great burden lifted from her conscience. And with that burden lifted she was able to see he had been so good, so kind as to help her, to take that risk! Brave as well—Florence knew what courage it required to cross her father, and, unlike Mr. Fairchild, she had her father's love to guarantee some measure of pardon. Oh, yes—at this moment she was so flooded with relief and gratitude and appreciation that she hardly cared what folly her father would pursue. Let him do what he might, only let Mr. Fairchild continue to be a friend to them!

Looking up at him, these were the thoughts that brought a fervent glow to her eyes and a slow, heartfelt smile to her lips.

Not being privy to her thoughts, her unwonted radiance caught Fairchild completely off guard. He hardly knew what to make of it, though he felt his breath catch and his carriage stiffen. It was as if a curtain had been drawn back and a treasure revealed. Good Lord.

Why was it that all Miss Lily's cooing and fluttering at dinner had not had this effect on him?

Without thought, half in self-defense, he retreated a step, almost losing his grip on one of the sacks of damsons, and the next instant Florence was backing up herself. She, too, thought of Lily's conduct at the table and how she had rebuked her for it. Did Mr. Fairchild now shrink from her, Florence, because he thought she was flirting with him as well? Oh, no! Horrible notion! After Lily's behavior and now her own, he would think the entire family afflicted. He would go away believing that, if Mr. Ellsworth married too much and his daughters flirted so shamelessly, this must be a case of *like father, like daughter*, the whole lot of them upon the prowl for anyone who came their way.

Mortified, she whipped the figurative curtain shut and drew herself up with unwonted coldness. "I thank you again, Mr. Fairchild. You have done more than was required of you, and the result has been as much as can be expected. Thank you as well for delivering the damsons. I wish you good afternoon."

Her icy speech ended on a just-audible quaver, and, with that, she almost fled into the house.

CHAPTER TEN

Forthwith the Devil did appear,
(For name him, and he's always near).
—Matthew Prior, *"Hans Carvel"* **(1702)**

Early September brought the beginning of the autumn term at Winchester College and a tidy stack of replies to Mr. Ellsworth's governess advertisement. Of the two, preparing Tyrone for another year fell to Florence's lot, though she would gladly have taken the replies off her father's hands as well.

"How is it possible you have grown three inches since July?" she asked of her younger brother. "We will have to sew you longer trousers and a new serge gown."

"At least his waistcoats still fit," Minta pointed out, "for he is still wiry as a whippet."

"And how fortunate that juniors always wear black," Lily said, ruffling his golden hair. "For then you can still be in mourning for Stepmama."

Wordlessly he nudged her hand away. But he didn't much mind being fussed over by his sisters, perhaps because, away at school, tenderness would be a rarity.

Minta was never required to contribute her needle because her stitchery was execrable—"She does it on purpose," insisted Lily, "in order to be excused!"—nor was Beatrice, because she did not yet produce wearable items. Therefore Florence and Lily and the maid Boots had their hands full with black wool, in addition to white linen for neckcloths and bands and Tyrone's chapel surplice.

On this particular day after breakfast, after submitting to be measured, Tyrone retreated with a book to the window seat to read while they worked, and, as Minta had vanished with Aggie somewhere, and Beatrice sat curled by Florence, brushing Snap, all was peaceful until Bobbins the footman appeared.

In the uneventful life of Snap the terrier, the footman played the role of villain, and the dog instantly sprang from Beatrice's side to lunge for Bobbins' stockinged ankle.

"It's Miss Gregory, if you please," he announced, trying unobtrusively to shake Snap off while maintaining a blank expression.

"Please send her in," murmured Florence around the pins in her mouth.

"I am positive Bobbins kicks poor Snap when we are not around," Lily declared, when the servant was gone, "or why would Snappy hate him so?" She cupped the pet's furry little face in her hands and cooed at him. "Poor puppykins! Is that dreadful old Bobbins mean to you?"

"That's a question of the hen and the egg," spoke up Tyrone. "For Snap does take up certain inexplicable likes and dislikes to people, and perhaps Bobbins only hates him because Snap hated him first."

In any event, the terrier liked Miss Gregory very much, and he forgot all about harassing the footman when the rector's quiet, faded sister appeared.

"Good morning, Miss Gregory. What a pleasure." Florence tried to inject said pleasure into her voice, but she was uncomfortably aware of a sensation of guilt. Guilt because, Miss Gregory's tea evening aside, Florence had not called at the rectory even once since her garden argument with Mr. Gregory. Not once, and yet she had somehow found no shortage of time in which to regret her treatment of Mr. Fairchild and to wonder what he thought of her and when she would see him again. Such thoughts had been stuffed down dutifully, but they had recurred just the same.

"I see you are busy, and I am interrupting," their visitor said in her even voice as she bent to pet Snap. Miss Gregory's voice was perhaps the most attractive thing about her because, instead of being listless and mumbling, as one expected from so unprepossessing a mouthpiece, it had life and warmth and music.

"It's not that she's *un*attractive," Lily had explained once. "Because, if you take each of her features separately, each one is perfectly acceptable. But the sum of the parts—! It's as if she *tries* to be a nonentity! Or as if, living with Mr. Gregory as she does, he has sucked all the vitality out of the parsonage and left none for her."

Florence remembered this opinion now as she studied her intended's sister (all the while keeping her eyes lowered to her work). Would it happen to her, after she married Mr. Gregory? Would she fade like Miss Gregory into insignificance? What if Lily's theory proved correct, and she and Miss Gregory must divide what remained of the diminished, remnant vitality between them?

She roused herself now to answer her future sister-in-law. "Of course you are not interrupting. We—are family now. Or will be soon. You are always welcome."

"As are you," returned Miss Gregory with surprising earnestness. Her gaze held Florence's. "You are always welcome at the rectory, Miss Ellsworth. I know I speak for both myself and my brother when I say that. We *could never see enough of you.*"

Florence had no idea what to make of this odd interchange and was glad when Lily interposed.

"Miss Gregory, I quite admire what you have done with your flowerpots at the rectory gate," Lily said, threading her needle expertly. "Are those cyclamen?"

"Yes, and violas."

"And of course the hollyhocks along the fence. I have begged Florence to plant more hollyhocks in her garden, but she uses most of the wall space for fruit trees." Carefully aligning the pieces of cut linen, she began to stitch. "You must have many passersby who stop to enjoy your charming display."

"I suppose." Snap had leaped into Miss Gregory's lap by this point and would have purred, had he been a cat. Miss Gregory rubbed his head and scratched under his chin.

"As a matter of fact, did I not see our new neighbor Mrs. Whisp doing so the other day?" Lily persisted. "Delightful Mrs. Whisp."

Florence had no clear idea why Lily was nattering on about Mrs. Whisp, but she ventured a peek at her future sister-in-law and saw Miss Gregory turn a faint rose. Miss Gregory, blushing? It was a distinctly flattering look for her, for it lent much-needed color to her face. "She did stop, yes." As soon as she said it, she looked at Florence again, a faint crease to her brow, and Florence felt another flutter of guilt. Was Miss Gregory reproaching her, for paying them less attention than even Mrs. Whisp?

"She's called on us as well, since our dinner," continued Lily. "Such a conversationist! One need never fear silence with her—she always has another question at the ready."

"Yes."

"When really the one who ought to answer all the questions is she herself!" Lily held up her work to the light, frowned, and set to again.

"Oh? And what would you ask her, Miss Lily?" prompted Miss Gregory.

"Why, everything! Am I the only one who suffers from curiosity? I would love to ask why she chose to come to Winchester, for instance—a place she has never been—when she might have remained in Weymouth, among those familiar and dear to her. Is it really just so she might have the cottage to herself? Moreover, I wonder what she proposes to do, now that she is here. And finally, I would dearly like to ask more about whatever became of the young lord who wronged her father."

"As to the last question, I already told you she said she didn't know," Florence rejoined. "And as to the former, since we are so little acquainted with her, indulging our curiosity in that manner would hardly be courteous. We would do better to wait and see if she tells us any of those things herself."

Before Miss Gregory could give her opinion, Snap's ears snapped up, and he hurled himself off her lap to greet with a volley of barks Bobbins opening the door.

"Mrs. Whisp, miss," said Bobbins, looking daggers at the dog.

"Oh!" Lily and Florence exchanged stricken looks, hoping that Hollowgate's thick, ancient walls had prevented them being overheard by their new caller. Tyrone gave a snort at his older sisters' embarrassment, but when Florence frowned in his direction, he quickly returned his attention to *Horrid Mysteries*.

"Mrs. Whisp," Florence welcomed her, clutching her sewing to her so she could stand and curtsey. (Lily's curtsey was suspiciously exaggerated, but thankfully Mrs. Whisp did not appear to notice.)

"My, my, what a gathering! It seems I picked the right time to call. Such a family! Everyone here—even Miss Gregory. Everyone here except—Mr. Ellsworth."

"And Minta," whispered Beatrice.

"Papa prefers his library most times," explained Florence. "Likely he is meeting with his steward Mr. Falk."

"Actually, miss, it's Mr. Fairchild in there with him right now," put in Bobbins, one finger looped under Snap's leather collar to keep him off his ankles. "And he's asked me to bring the tea things, for they will join you shortly."

"Oh!" said Florence.

"Oh!" said Mrs. Whisp.

"Ah," said Lily.

Bobbins' announcement had a curious effect on the group. Florence, for one, went scarlet, but she continued to sew steadily. The news energized Mrs. Whisp, who gave a little shiver of eagerness. Turning to Miss Gregory, she asked, "And how is Mr. Gregory today? Did he not want to call with you?"

"He had an appointment with the bishop." Miss Gregory was clipped in her reply. Almost curt.

"The bishop? But what is a bishop," cried Mrs. Whisp, "compared to a beloved?" Here she smiled at Florence who, instead of feeling pleased by the reference to her engagement, felt rather vexed. Because there was some truth in her words. Why should she, Florence, be the only one to feel guilty for not calling? Half the fault lay with Mr. Gregory, surely. Shouldn't *he* have called on her at some point after their argument? Not when he had to meet with the bishop, of course, but at any other time. There had been a dozen other opportunities. They had greeted each other at church, of course, but that was all.

And she had something of an excuse for her neglect. She had been preoccupied, confused and embarrassed by her last meeting with Mr. Fairchild—not that Mr. Fairchild had anything at all to do with her engagement to Mr. Gregory. Not a thing. And the fact that she felt fluttery of a sudden, to hear he was at Hollowgate, had nothing to do with anything either.

"Bishops are very important to a clergyman, Mrs. Whisp," she returned, relieved that her voice sounded so calm. Her remark was inane, but at least it was a reply.

It did not mend matters when Miss Gregory added, "But Clifford said it would not take long. Some cathedral business concerning Michaelmas, it was. Perhaps he will come by on his way home."

And now if he does not, Mrs. Whisp might remark on that too, thought Florence.

Snapping off her thread, Lily said, "Speaking of home, Mrs. Whisp, have you heard much from the other Whisps? I hope they are all well in Weymouth?"

The widow's mouth thinned as she considered the beautiful girl for a moment. Then she said answered, "Their health is good. I suppose they continue to grieve my lost Thomas as I do, but we must carry on."

"Too true. But don't you miss them, Mrs. Whisp? Would it not be a greater comfort to be together?"

Florence widened her eyes at her sister. Had she not just said it would be discourteous to interrogate the woman upon so brief an acquaintance?

"We grieve each in our different ways" was Mrs. Whisp's stiff response. Recovering, she added, "As I'm sure your family has discovered, after the loss of Mrs. Ellsworth..." With deliberation she rose from her chair to stalk up and down the room. She gave Snap a pat (he growled). She tipped Tyrone's book cover to see what he was reading (he would have growled too, if it were permitted). She stopped beside Florence's seat. "What fine stitches you make, Miss Ellsworth!"

"Not that we regret you coming into our midst—new people are always so exciting," continued Lily blithely, as if Mrs. Whisp had not clearly signaled her desire to quit the subject. "Take Mr. Fairchild. I deem Mr. Fairchild quite exciting. So handsome and all."

Florence signaled her sister more strongly with a scowl. What on earth was the girl stirring up? Was she trying to redirect Mrs. Whisp's attentions to another eligible party? Not that Mr. Fairchild was nearly as eligible as William Ellsworth. For all his youth and handsomeness, Mr. Fairchild lived in lodgings, with few pennies to call his own.

Could it be Lily was sweet on Mr. Fairchild? Had her flirting when he stayed to dinner been more than mischief?

Lily's blue eyes blinked in mock innocence.

"He is indeed quite handsome," agreed Miss Gregory, when it seemed no one was going to answer this comment at all. "And seems a very good sort of young man."

No further reply was possible because once more the door opened, this time to admit Mr. Ellsworth, accompanied by the very good sort of young man.

"Ah, Fairchild! Look at this garden of beauty we have stumbled into," beamed Mr. Ellsworth. He bent over Florence to kiss her hair and laid a fond hand on Beatrice beside her.

"Indeed, sir," answered Fairchild, though he could hardly say otherwise, Florence supposed.

When she made her curtsey, Tyrone's trousers slipped from her hands and spilled to the floor, and there was Mr. Fairchild, bending to retrieve them and hand them back to her before he took his seat. She managed some peep of acknowledgement and was vexed again to find Mrs. Whisp's eyes upon her, with that same knowing look she had when she made the remark on bishops and beloveds. *Mind your own business!* she told the woman in her head. One thing was certain: Mrs. Whisp or no Mrs. Whisp, Lily flirting or Lily behaving, Florence was determined to be her usual self and to do and say nothing to Mr. Fairchild that might be construed as setting her cap for him.

"How lovely that you and Mr. Fairchild could join us, Mr. Ellsworth," said Mrs. Whisp. "An estate as vast as Hollowgate must require much work to maintain."

Mr. Ellsworth gave another bow. "So it does, madam, and I am pleased to report Mr. Fairchild is an able assistant."

"Have you received any responses to your governess advertisement yet, sir?" asked Miss Gregory, and Florence could have kissed her for raising the subject.

"Indeed we did," replied Mr. Ellsworth. "Several. Fairchild looked them over with me."

"And—what did you decide, Papa?" asked Florence.

It was Mr. Fairchild who answered her. "We wrote to three of them to come to Hollowgate to meet the family and be further considered. The final decision will lie with Mr. Ellsworth, of course, but I recommended Miss Beatrice and Miss Lily be present. If this person is to take on the roles of teaching and chaperonage, it would be best for all involved." In the same mild tone he added, "And I wonder if you might be willing to meet the candidates, Miss Ellsworth. You will be marrying shortly and leaving Hollowgate, but I am certain your family values your opinion."

As Fairchild had not made this suggestion in his time with Mr. Ellsworth, the latter's eyes and mouth both popped open in surprise, but Lily said quickly, "When will they come, do you suppose?"

"We have set the interviews for Monday next."

"I will only meet them if Papa thinks it helpful," Florence spoke up. In addition to being thoroughly unflirtatious with Mr. Fairchild, she wanted to show him that she had repented putting his work in jeopardy. Not that she looked at him. Or any higher than his chest since he entered the room. But her heart warmed to have him remember she had desired to meet the candidates. "As you say, I will be gone soon, and it is Papa and Lily and Beatrice who will be most—taxed—with this person."

His daughter's concession, so changed from their earlier discussion of the matter, had the perverse effect of filling Mr. Ellsworth with magnanimity. He did, after all, think of himself as a generous and beneficent head of house, especially when those under him proved compliant. Raising both palms like an alms-giving king welcoming a contingent of beggars, he declared, "You will meet them, Florence."

She knew better than to let her surprise and delight be seen, only murmuring her agreement and continuing to sew. But then Boots entered with the tea things, and she must lay down her work to pour the tea, beginning with Mrs. Whisp and Miss Gregory. Mrs. Whisp, after requesting two lumps of sugar and just a little milk, swished about the drawing room, admiring in turn Lily's needlework, the view over the drive from the windows, the pictures over the mantel, and how Miss Gregory took her tea, and ending her journey beside Mr. Ellsworth's seat, as if she drifted into the chair beside him by pure chance.

Florence fidgeted at the sight, but she could hardly ask the woman to remove herself.

When Miss Gregory approached to accept her cup she said under her breath, "Miss Ellsworth, I am sorry my brother did not come today."

"But—he has much to occupy him," said Florence, startled. "The bishop."

"Yes, the bishop," agreed Miss Gregory. "But still—I hope you won't think him neglectful. He might not be the most ardent of suitors, but he—"

But he what? Florence waited, regarding her steadily, but apparently Miss Gregory could not supply a virtue to make up for her brother's lack of ardor. Instead she added inadequately, "But I hope you will call at the rectory again soon. You might see my flowers."

Florence gave an awkward nod and rose to bring her father his tea.

"Marvelous!" he was saying to Mrs. Whisp. "And did you make frequent use of these bathing machines?"

"You naughty man!" she teased, laughing melodiously and being joined by Mr. Ellsworth's appreciative ho-ho-ho.

"Papa, your tea," muttered Florence.

"Thank you, my dear," he said, still chuckling and not even looking at her as he reached for it. Then there was nothing to do but return to the urn, where she found Mr. Fairchild serving himself. Miss Gregory had gone to help Lily hold the surplice up to Tyrone, who obediently held his arms out, his shaggy golden hair falling in his eyes.

"I was going to serve you next," Florence uttered, taking hold of the sugar tongs, which promptly squirted through her fingers and dropped with a clatter on the tray. Reddening, she picked them up again, but he murmured, "Never mind the sugar."

Not knowing how long they would have to speak, she hastened to say, "Mr. Fairchild, I thank you for suggesting I meet the possible governesses."

A brief bow. "I think it merely good sense, Miss Ellsworth."

Florence reddened further. Oh, dear. Had she inadvertently done it again? Did he think she implied that he had done it to please her? If he did, he seemed to imply in return that, on the contrary, she had not even entered his mind. "Yes, of course. Good sense. I didn't mean—that is—I know you didn't—"

He could not answer because he had taken a hasty, overlarge sip of his tea. Something was necessary to stifle the inadvisable confession threatening to be voiced. Because he had been on the point of saying, "But of course I suggested it to your father. I asked him because I knew you wished it. What more may I do for you?"

"Were the...three applicants...well qualified?" she ventured, after another moment.

"On paper, yes. French, Italian, music, drawing, needlework, arithmetic, geography, and so forth." He gave her a measured look. "I...tried to guess, from the length of experience listed, their approximate ages."

She held her breath. "...And?"

He set his teacup back on its saucer. "While I recommended two of them with...much longer tenures at their current posts, he...preferred the opposite, saying whoever was selected would then be 'better able to conform herself to the habits and interests of the family.'"

"Ah."

"And, Miss Ellsworth—I—see your concerns in other areas." His dark eyes flicked toward where her father and Mrs. Whisp continued in lively conversation.

Somehow this observation flooded Florence with both pleasure (she wasn't imagining things!) and distress (she wasn't imagining things!). And to her wonder, the pleasure prevailed, because Mr. Fairchild's confirmation felt like an affirmation. It made her think he had decided to forget her seeming forwardness the other day. That his respect had returned. This possibility made her want to smile at him from ear to ear, only she mustn't, or all the progress would be undone.

With a nod, she poured herself more tea, despite her cup being hardly touched.

A great bang interrupted their *tête-à-tête*, as Araminta and Aggie flung open the door and burst into the room, bringing a wave of fresh air and setting Snap yapping and leaping.

The spell was broken.

The little groupings of the room became one general gathering again, and Florence comforted herself that, if no more could be said between her and Mr. Fairchild before he took his leave, at least the same was also true for Mr. Ellsworth and Mrs. Whisp.

CHAPTER ELEVEN

"Will you ever preserve me your affection?" "By Heaven, for ever!" "Then come to my heart, my brother, and receive from me the same vow."
—Carl Grosse, trans. Peter Will, *The Horrid Mysteries* (1796)

H onestly, Fanny. You had better let James and me deliver Paul to school," Robert Fairchild told his sister as she fussed over her son in the coffee room of the Chequers Inn. "If his mother brings him, it will only get him off on the wrong foot." By which he meant, *get him bullied by the other boys.*

Fanny Tillwood was near tears, alternately smoothing her boy's hair and cupping his round cheek. Both she and little Paul had the Fairchild look about them, handsome and dark of hair and eye, but in Fanny's case the darkness extended beneath her eyes, for she had slept poorly the past few nights.

"Oh, Robert—perhaps I might accompany you all as far as the gate? I promise not to cry, and Pauly, I won't even hug you there. I will do all my hugging here." And she proceeded to do just that until even Paul, who was rigid with fear and excitement, pushed her away.

"What will happen today, Uncle Robert?" he piped. "A-after you leave me, I mean."

With a grin, Fairchild thought back to his own arrival as a trembling lad years and years earlier, but time had blurred the rougher edges. There had been the trepidation, yes, but also the leaping anticipation.

"Let me see...firstly you'll be allotted to a prefect—an older boy in charge, called your 'tutor.' You know the motto of the school: 'Manners makyth man'? It will be that tutor's task to superintend your morals and manners and—er—purge you of your grosser faults."

"'Purge' him?" squeaked Fanny. As the start of term had drawn nearer, her zeal for sending Paul to Winchester had flagged.

"But he'll also protect you from unjust treatment at the hands of other boys," Fairchild added quickly.

"'Protect?'" yelped Fanny, in an even higher register. "He will need protection?"

Little Paul paled, and his uncle put a bracing hand on his narrow shoulder.

"They call it 'teejaying' you. From *proteger*. Come along, we'd better make a start."

The streets were crowded as they proceeded down Little Minster and Symond's Street toward where the South Ditch and embankment marked the line of the former city wall. Fairchild and his nephew led the way, followed by Fanny clinging to her husband's arm, and a porter from the inn with Paul's trunk.

"Now, boys will play some jokes on the greenhorns, Paul," his uncle told him, under cover of the general noise around them. "They might send you for a *pempe*—an imaginary item, like a book with a Greek-sounding title. '*Pempe*' is Greek for 'send,' as in, 'send the fool further.' I was taken in that way, at your age. I ran from pillar to post, asking first one person and the next and then the next for this nonexistent book, until a Master took pity on me! Oh—and if another boy asks you if you're 'Founder's kin,' steel yourself, for he's likely going to knock you over the head with a plate. If the plate breaks first, it's supposed to mean you're hard-headed and definitely Founder's kin."

Though he chuckled in relating these things, he wanted to bite his tongue when they passed through Kingsgate into College Street and he saw Paul looking greenish. *Lord,* he thought, *I'm the greenhorn, where children are concerned.* Perhaps the memories were more pleasant in retrospect. Paul's mouth was working, and his small feet began to drag, leading Fairchild to think Miss Ellsworth might have some justification in criticizing treatment of the lowly juniors in College.

The pat he gave his nephew was apologetic this time, but the next instant Fairchild forgot all about his shortcomings as an uncle, for in the throng milling at the plastered and whitewashed Outer Gate, he saw a familiar grouping in mourning black. All the Ellsworths had come to deliver Master Tyrone, including the terrier Snap held in a leash by Miss Araminta, and Fairchild was quick to pick out Miss Ellsworth's light figure with Miss Beatrice in hand. He could not lie to himself: he had been hoping he might see her this day. Actually—he tended to look about him alertly whenever he stepped out of his lodgings or his office. For all he knew, Miss Ellsworth walked into town every day on some errand or other.

Of course there was no *point* in seeing Miss Ellsworth, he told himself, not for the first time.

No point at all.

"Come," he urged Paul. "Let me introduce you to someone who may be your first friend."

"A prefect?" asked the boy, his voice lifting in hope.

"No, but a junior in his third year. And living in College as you will be."

He and his nephew worked their way nearer the Ellsworths, and it was Miss Araminta who saw them first, waving eagerly and even thrusting her thumb and forefinger between her lips to give a piercing, most unladylike whistle.

At once, Miss Ellsworth knocked her younger sister's arm down and began to remonstrate, but Fairchild hurried up to them, saying loudly, "Miss Araminta! Thank you for drawing our attention. What a relief to find familiar faces in this multitude! Mr. Ellsworth, Miss Ellsworth, may I have the honor of introducing you to members of my family?"

The circle of Ellsworths swung open immediately to admit him and the Tillwoods, whom Fairchild beckoned forward. "May I present Mr. James Tillwood, my sister Mrs. Tillwood, and my nephew Paul? James, Fanny, Paul, this is the Ellsworth family." He ran through each member, and bows were exchanged.

His sister brightened on seeing he had such promising acquaintances and that one of them might prove a friend to her Paul. Her eyes went first to Master Tyrone, taking in his calm demeanor and gangling limbs, and she smiled, thinking he did not look the sort to bully poor Paul or pound him to a pulp.

But soon enough Miss Lily Ellsworth drew her gaze, and she darted a glance at Fairchild to see his opinion of the beauty. Although he was not looking at the young lady, his color was high, and he flung himself far too heartily into encouraging the two boys to speak to each other—not easy work, when one was a wide-eyed, lowly first year and the other a tall, superior third year. Moreover, without a prefect's status or even a senior inferior's, Tyrone was not about to begin the term with a puny whipster as his special charge.

Indeed, the two boys might never have willingly spoken again, after the forced acknowledgement beside the porter's lodge, if Minta hadn't said, "Ty, *Horrid Mysteries* dropped out of your pocket. I thought you finished this one."

"I did finish it, and gave it to Lily to return for me," answered her brother.

"Oh—" breathed little Paul reaching out a hand, "excuse me. That's mine."

"Yours!" laughed Minta, the only one of the Ellsworths besides Tyrone who had looked past the cover of the book. She gave it to him. "Aren't you a little young to read about coffins, cabals, and cuckolds?"

The younger boy turned scarlet. "I just like the friends and adventures. And that everything is exciting."

Unbeknownst to him, little Paul Tillwood could not have calculated a faster way to Tyrone Ellsworth's approval than to like a book he liked and to suffer his twin's scorn.

"Don't listen to her," Tyrone told Paul. "If you can't throw it, bat at it, shoot at it, or catch it, Minta doesn't think it's worth a straw."

"And if it isn't between two covers, Tyrone can't be brought to acknowledge it," his sister retorted.

"You won't have much time for reading books, I'm afraid," Tyrone said to Paul with a grimace, ignoring Minta.

"Because our studies are so difficult?" asked Paul, his brow wrinkling in dismay.

This made the older boy laugh. "Studies? No! You'll find actual learning to be a relief from all the time spent fagging. You know," he added, seeing Paul's confusion, "being ordered around by the prefects. But we get at least a Remedy and a half every week, so you can find a minute to read then, in between going on to Hills. I do."

"A Remedy is like a holiday from instruction on a Tuesday or Thursday," explained Miss Ellsworth, bending toward him kindly. "The boys mostly play games out of doors then. But on saints' days or Founder's anniversaries you have a real holiday, and you may leave school and come to visit us at Hollowgate, if you like."

Putting his thumbs in his waistcoat pockets, Tyrone radiated magnanimity. "I may accompany you myself. I have plenty of books at home you may look through. In the meantime, however, I seem to have misplaced a volume of my own, and it would be a good way for you to meet some other pupils if you were to go around and ask if anyone has found it."

"I would be glad to," replied Paul breathlessly. "What—is it called?"

"*Pempe Moron Protero*—a prodigious good read. Violet cover. Start with that fellow—Hembry." (Pointing at an ox of a boy.) "I'm almost certain I saw him with it."

"...*Pempe*," repeated Paul, stealing a look at his uncle, who merely raised one eyebrow, the corner of his mouth twisting. "All right, then."

On this mischievous note, Tyrone gave the boy a parting nod. "See you in Hall." Then he led his family onward into the courtyard.

"He tried to fool me, Uncle Robert," cried Paul, when the Ellsworths were no longer in sight. "Just like you said."

"So he did. Thank heavens your good old uncle kept your foot out of that trap. But that hoax is harmless enough, and I do think the boy is as well."

Paul nodded. "What about the invitation, sir? Do you think that was a hoax?"

To the boy's puzzlement, an expression he had never seen before dawned on his uncle's face, and the smile the man gave then was inward, not meant for him. "No. That wasn't a hoax. Miss Ellsworth's words and her kindness may be depended upon."

"How will we know Paul's chamber?" spoke up James Tillwood.

"And what did the Ellsworth boy mean about 'fagging'?" demanded Fanny.

Recalling his thoughts from Miss Ellsworth, Fairchild gave himself a shake.

"The prefects choose their chambers every half-year," he replied to his brother-in-law, "and the juniors who will be with them." Under them, he might have said. Serving them.

He had no desire to discuss what lay ahead for his nephew in front of that same nephew, for he knew Fanny would likely fear the worst and might even succumb to vapors, so he said shortly, "And fagging refers to the juniors' duties. Duties owed the prefects. A certain amount of fetching and carrying and so on. But Paul will have a fortnight before he's in Course so he can learn what is expected of him. Now, come along. You've seen the outer court, Paul, when you were here for Election Week. Did they point out to you the warden's house here on the left? And you'll remember the election chamber over the middle gate—"

"It gives me shivers," blurted Paul, his mother shivering in sympathy.

All too soon (in Paul's opinion) they were passing through the middle gate into Chamber Court, where the seven chambers housing College boys formed the ground floor of the quadrangle. And there, among the seventy scholars, the warden, the second master, choristers in brown tailcoats, and sundry porters, his family left him.

Fanny was pressing her handkerchief to her mouth by the time they regained College Street. "Oh, James, what have we done? We have abandoned him to the wolves!"

James, who had not much to say even on commonplace occasions, was completely overmastered in this instance. He patted his wife on the back, murmuring, "There, there, Fanny."

"Yes—there, there, Fanny," said Fairchild dryly. "Your dear boy will be fine. He may come to see me when he leaves out on holidays, and the Short Half will be over before you know it."

She nodded, lips pressed together. "It is only that—that—no one loves a son like his mother."

"You need a distraction, my girl," her brother announced. "What would you rather—a walk on the downs? La Croix's for coffee and a biscuit? Flight's for Sally Lunns?"

When Fanny chose La Croix's, Fairchild could at least congratulate himself that he was perfectly innocent of seeking out Miss Ellsworth. It was a matter of pure chance that he and the Tillwoods entered the establishment to find that family—minus Tyrone—gathered around two small tables shoved together, sharing a plate of biscuits and pot of coffee.

"Fairchild!" called Mr. Ellsworth, with a languid upraised hand. "Do join us!"

"Yes, do!" seconded Miss Lily, half rising to wave.

The universe could not have hit on a more effective method to stop up Fanny Tillwood's waterworks, for she was reminded at once of her earlier curiosity: might this beautiful creature have caught her brother's eye? Despite the Ellsworths' mourning black, she could see that their clothing was well-made and the material fine. And what had the tall, pale Miss Ellsworth said? That Paul might come to "Hollowgate." Whatever and wherever that was, it was big enough or important enough to warrant a name, not like poor Robert's modest lodgings in St. Thomas Street. What a good thing a wealthy bride would be for him!

She beamed at this Miss Lily while the blonde daughter—what was her name again?—darted around, collecting three more chairs, and Fanny was careful to take the middle one, that Robert might sit next to Miss Lily, which, after a hesitation, he did. James plumped down on his wife's other side, beside Miss Ellsworth.

"I see you have heard of La Croix's," ventured Fairchild, when the bustle was past and a tiny silence fell.

"Tyrone told me he would frequently send a chorister for a pint of coffee and two pennyworth of biscuits, so we thought we would try it," Miss Ellsworth replied, "because we miss him already."

"But this is a shilling's worth of biscuit," added little Miss Beatrice, "because we are so many."

"And now we are that many more," agreed Fairchild. "Therefore I will buy the next round." Turning to his sister he added, "I did not tell you when we met in College Street, Fanny, but the Ellsworths are clients of Darby and West. I am their attorney."

"Say you are our *friend*," proclaimed Mr. Ellsworth in his grandest manner. He raised his cup to Fairchild, nodding at him, and Fairchild could see Fanny was completely won by this condescension.

"Mrs. Tillwood, do you and Mr. Tillwood live near Winchester?" asked this Miss Lily.

Fanny favored her with a smile, and Fairchild could see the wheels turning in his sister's mind. "Southampton, Miss Lily. Not too far, especially with the many coaches running between home and London." Her chin rose a little. "My husband is an Improvements Commissioner there, and with the war, the town is booming, and there is much work to be done."

"We're quite humble folk," Fairchild interposed. He could sense Fanny was wanting to put the best Fairchild foot foremost, and her motivation could only be a desire to matchmake. He therefore felt a perverse desire to thwart her. "The Southampton Fairchilds consist of coal importers, sailors, teachers, and bankers cobbled together. Quite the assortment."

No sooner did the word escape him than he wished he might snatch it back. Miss Lily and Miss Araminta laughed (and quickly hushed and pinched each other); Mr. Ellsworth affected deafness; and Miss Beatrice looked at each of her family members in turn, ending with Miss Ellsworth, who seemed to shrink in her chair, the biscuit she had been dipping in her coffee floating away from her fingertips.

Fanny blinked at them, quite in the dark as to why they responded as they had, before deciding Robert must have quite put his foot in it. "All quite respectable people, the Southampton Fairchilds," she uttered quickly. "Humble, yes, but respectable. I don't know why you would use a word like 'assortment,' Robert, as if we were a box of mismatched samples at the mercer's."

"That—that was quite kind of you, Miss Ellsworth, to invite my nephew to Hollowgate," blurted Fairchild in loud desperation. "Quite kind. He's a good lad. Small for his age. I hope he will like school."

"I hope he will too," she answered, taking up the thread swiftly and berating herself for being so sensitive. Her grey eyes rose to his, and she gave a little smile that eased his tension. "A stroke of good fortune, Paul reading *Horrid Mysteries*. Tyrone cannot resist someone who will talk books with him, and there are surprisingly few bookish boys at Winchester. I hope the two of them might become friends."

"As much as an older boy and a piddling first-year junior may be friends."

Once out of the pitfall, the rest of the little gathering passed harmlessly. Mr. Ellsworth was his gracious best, asking Mr. Tillwood numerous questions about the responsibilities of an Improvements Commissioner and making comparisons to Winchester's own Paving Commissioners; Mrs. Tillwood complimented Miss Lily on a cameo she wore and asked her advice on the Winchester shops; Miss Araminta stifled fidgets and restless sighs; Miss Ellsworth and Mr. Fairchild tried not to glance at each other too often; and soon enough the parties were separating.

Fairchild accompanied the Tillwoods back to the Chequers Inn, where they would take the return coach to Southampton the following morning, and when they were closeted once more in the Tillwoods' private room, Fanny burst out with, "Robert, my dear—what a pleasant family your new clients are! You never mentioned."

"Should I have?" He dropped into the lumpy armchair beside the empty fireplace.

"They are terribly rich, I suppose?"

"Terribly." He raised an eyebrow at his brother-in-law James, who only shook his head, grinning.

Pulling the matching armchair closer to his own, Fanny sat down, tucking one leg under the other and leaning toward him. "Oh, Robert! That Miss Lily is such a beauty! Pure pleasure to look upon. And I can see how Mr. Ellsworth is already so fond of you. With approval like that, you have only to reach out your hand—you may not be wealthy yourself, but you're handsome and respectable and clearly admired—"

"Fanny, are you proposing I propose to Miss Lily Ellsworth?"

"Well, and what if I am? I know you haven't had the means to think of marriage before, and that wretched Miss Perkins of Oxford broke your heart—"

"Fanny, for pity's sake, I beg you not to resurrect that worm-eaten tale. I had a boyish liking for the girl, wrote a handful of wretched sonnets to her eyes, watched as she chose someone with better prospects (and a fine enough fellow, I do not mind admitting), and that was the end of it."

His sister placed a finger to her smiling lips. "She will never be mentioned again, then. But tell me, Robert—do you think you might try for Miss Lily? I saw how you...how you were not entirely at ease when we met them in College Street. And—and—and when we saw them again at La Croix's, I observed you hesitated to claim the seat beside her..."

She trailed off as her brother had begun to shake his head before she was half finished. "I'm sorry to tell you you're ploughing the sand there, Fanny, and you may as well save your breath."

"Because you think she might refuse you?" Fanny demanded.

"Because I think I will never ask her."

"But—but why not? Of course I only met her today," she conceded. "You, perhaps, know her better and might have discovered something to her detriment..."

"I have nothing against Miss Lily Ellsworth, other than that she appears to have a mischievous streak, as well as a flirtatious one—and those may be one and the same in her case."

"Then—why not, Robert? Do you not think her pretty?"

"She is very pretty." With an impatient gesture, he rose from his chair. "Honestly, Fanny. You had better go back to fretting over little Paul and leave off fretting about me. I may be on a better footing now, but you must not assume I am in any hurry to marry."

Fanny gave a pouting sigh. "How tiresome you are, Robert. I do not see why you would resent my interest. And the way you brought up the humbleness of our background! Not that I am ashamed of our coal importers and sailors and teachers and bankers, but one would almost imagine you *wanted* to remove yourself from Miss Lily's consideration! Yes, I am certain she will have her choice of young men, but you needn't assume you could not hold your own among them, even without money."

He said nothing to this and might have escaped the room un-scathed, had his sister not made one final chance remark: "If there will be too much competition for Miss Lily, you might try for the older sister Miss Ellsworth. I do not remember clearly what she looked like, but she seemed kindly."

"Miss Ellsworth is engaged." Innocent enough words, but they emerged brusque and low.

Fanny's head turned sharply, and what she saw on her brother's face, fleeting though it was, was enough to silence her on the subject, though it gave her much to ponder, afterwards.

CHAPTER TWELVE

Happy art Thou whom God does bless
With the full choice of thine own Happiness.
—Abraham Cowley, *Essays in Verse and Prose* (1663)

By the third governess applicant, Florence was concerned.

She had taken up her post in the drawing room for the interviews, sewing in hand and instructions given to Wilcomb and Bobbins and Boots that tea must be served three times in succession, at one o'clock, two o'clock, and three o'clock that afternoon. Snap was locked away in Minta's room, lest he take an instant dislike to any of the visitors. Lily was advised to keep her mischief to a minimum and Beatrice to—well, Beatrice hardly needed admonishment, except not to cry, and the family had learned that telling Beatrice not to cry seldom helped and often hindered.

Papa must be left to be Papa, naturally, and when he joined them Florence said a prayer of thanksgiving that he had lost his looks so long ago. Being completely bald, there was nothing to be done with the top of his head, and being in mourning confined the entire family to sober black clothing. There was, to be sure, a gleaming cravat pin peeping from the folds of his neckcloth, but that was all.

He must have decided to let Hollowgate itself speak for him, Florence thought. And she rather applauded this wisdom, for it demonstrated *some* awareness of his limitations. This morning, Florence was determined to be as optimistic as possible. Why should she not be? Mr. Fairchild had looked over the letters of these three candidates, and while he could not persuade Florence's father to choose those seeming oldest, neither had Mr. Fairchild warned her of any just out of the schoolroom.

If only they might all be plain! Hideousness was too much to ask for, but plainness would be so, so welcome.

The first to arrive was Miss Pinkerton of Romsey, and Florence's heart sank when she saw her, for Miss Pinkerton might not be just out of the schoolroom, but she didn't appear significantly older than Florence herself, and not only was she *not* hideous, she could not even be called plain. She had flaxen hair and pale blue eyes and a round little figure and reminded Florence of a Dresden bunny.

"Miss Pinkerton, you wrote that you have been in your current situation for four years?" prompted Mr. Ellsworth at his most seraphic, when Florence had given the lady her teacup.

"I have, sir."

"I see. And in this situation, you have just one charge?"

Miss Pinkerton shifted. "Just the one, yes. A girl of twelve."

"Only twelve? But surely her education is not yet complete. Will they be sending her to school?"

Florence saw her swallow as she set her teacup down with a rattle. "I—don't know. To tell the truth, I have not yet given notice."

"Well!" exclaimed Mr. Ellsworth, his complacency somewhat jarred. Florence knew he was thinking that a governess who would go in search of a new post without informing her employ- ers—leaving not only her charge but the entire household in the lurch—might do so a second time, a second time being always easier than a first.

Florence thought it only fair to the candidate to let her explain herself, and she spoke up from her corner. "Miss Pinkerton, may we ask why you seek a new situation?"

The porcelain cheeks flushed. "It is not for lack of attach- ment to Kitty—my charge. In fact, I will be very sorry to leave her—" her voice quavered, and she paused to master herself. "It is that—the...family structure is not conducive to my peace of mind."

Florence had a guess what might be robbing pretty Miss Pinker- ton of her peace of mind, and a shared glance with Lily told her Lily had the same guess. But Mr. Ellsworth stiffened at the phrase "family structure," and it was he who demanded, "Did you not know the structure of the family when you accepted the position? What do you find offensive in the 'family structure,' Miss Pinkerton?"

Miss Pinkerton looked at the tips of her boots. "The family struc- ture has changed from when I first arrived there," she replied, in barely above a whisper. "The—son has returned from university."

Hinting that she objected to attentions from her employer's family was probably enough to relegate her to the bottom of the list, but her next speech sealed her doom.

Clasping her hands together, she looked appealingly at Mr. Ellsworth and cried, "Sir, I would be so very grateful for this position! I am eminently qualified, so you would lose nothing and gain much from employing me. And—oh!—the peace I would have in this setting! So many young ladies about—and *you*, sir, a *much older* gentleman, and an honorable one, I am certain. To live without fear of—unwelcome advances—"

Mr. Ellsworth's habitual self-satisfaction crumbled under this onslaught, and Florence feared he would have a fit, so red and blotched did he turn. Miss Pinkerton could not have cornered him more neatly if she planned it. Not even to himself would Mr. Ellsworth have admitted he hoped to make advances, and to be told preemptively that any such advances would be both unwelcome and dishonorable—! Not to mention the assumption that his age disqualified him from consideration!

He could not dismiss her soon enough, and when the door shut behind her and Bobbins took away the first tea tray, Mr. Ellsworth only growled, "Too young by half. And we want her to love our Beatrice, not come to Hollowgate as a means of escape. Suppose she didn't like it here either? Objected to *our* 'family structure'? Why, she would be off to the next post before you could say Jack Robinson."

Promptly at two o'clock, Bobbins announced the arrival of Miss Patrick of Eastleigh, and Florence was grateful Snap was confined, for he surely would have barked and hurled himself at this woman, who sailed into the room solid and vast as a ship of the line. Lily was forced to affect a coughing fit and dash from the room, and Beatrice chewed anxiously on her fingertip until Florence nudged her.

Mr. Ellsworth's eyes bulged in astonishment, as if it had never occurred to him that governesses might come in so strapping a form. Miss Patrick looked like she could throw even the master of the house over her knee and spank him, if the need arose.

"As you know from my letter, I formerly ran a school," boomed Miss Patrick, when the niceties were completed. "But I had to close it, in order to take care of my mother and aunt, both of whom have since died." She pronounced this last with unflinching emphasis.

Before the Ellsworths could do more than murmur their condolences, she turned on Beatrice. "You are the proposed pupil?"

Little Bea sprang to her feet and dropped another curtsey. She had of course already done so when introduced, but something about Miss Patrick made her think the more curtsies the better.

"Mm," said that lady, scrutinizing her. "What do you know, young lady?"

"N-nothing," bleated Beatrice.

"That's not so," Florence chided. "I've taught you your alphabet and numbers, and you can write your name and recite five Bible verses."

"Oh? Let me hear one of them, child."

"O-O-O-O g-give thanks unto the Lord, for he is good: for his mercy endureth for ever," Beatrice gasped.

"And where is that found?"

"In—in—the Psalms?"

"Are you asking me? Do you not know where it is found?"

"In—the Psalms."

"Mm." Swiveling in her seat, she pinned Mr. Ellsworth with her gaze. "Very well. I approve of the child. I prefer to take pupils who have not already been ruined with imperfect teaching methods and other nonsense. You say you want French and Italian and music?"

But Mr. Ellsworth was rallying. Robust Miss Patrick was not at all what he had in mind, and she had better be sent on her way speedily. "Yes, as I said in my advertisement," he began, "but I'm afraid—"

"And the young lady I am to chaperone?" The penetrating beams turned next on Florence. "Are you she?"

"I am not," said Florence. "I am the young lady's sister and shortly to be married. No, it was the one who left a few minutes earlier. Here she comes again."

Lily glided in and resumed her place, taking up her needlework.

"Mm," grunted Miss Patrick. "I see the child will be no difficulty, but this one might."

Now it was Florence who felt a surge of indignation. "I don't know what you mean by that, Miss Patrick, but I assure you, most governesses would think accompanying Lily to an assembly or ball or two would prove a welcome variation from typical duties. I know I looked forward to such occasions with pleasure, before my stepmother died." To her dismay, her own ears caught the wistfulness in her voice. *Come now, Florence,* she urged herself. *There will still be an assembly or ball or two, even after you are married, won't there?* But she had never seen Mr. Gregory at an assembly or ball and had still not had occasion (or courage) to ask him if he even liked to dance.

"If it were you, Miss Ellsworth, that would be a different matter," rapped back Miss Patrick. "*You* seem a quiet, biddable creature. *You* did not erupt in giggles upon my appearance and find it necessary to run away to hide them. Such conduct bespeaks a sad lack of self-control."

"You are too right, Miss Patrick," Lily spoke up, to the surprise of her family. "I am humbled by your discernment. Because it's too true I am likely to cause some trouble, once I am free of these mourning restrictions. For I intend to have my fun."

"Precisely. I could see that at once. But I decided I would withhold judgment while I considered the child. You might have returned to the room repentant, apologetic, and I am not a woman to refuse grace to a fellow creature. However..."

"However, I was not suitably repentant," supplied Lily, nodding. "I see that now."

With a raised hand, Miss Patrick refused a second cup of tea, though Florence had only leaned toward the tea tray to prepare Lily's cup. She rose to her feet like a drawbridge being raised to prevent further ingress. "I am an efficient woman, Mr. Ellsworth, and I will tell you straight off that I don't think your family will suit me."

Diving for this spar like a man in a shipwreck, Mr. Ellsworth said, "What a shame. But we thank you for your candor. What a shame. Flossie, ring for Bobbins."

"If you would kindly pay my coach fare," suggested Miss Patrick, sensing weakness.

"Absolutely, absolutely."

And thus passed away the second interview.

By three o'clock, Mr. Ellsworth was not the only one wrought up and striving to hide it. What if this final candidate were unacceptable?

"Confound Fairchild," Florence heard her father muttering. "Dismissing those others, who might have been more promising!"

"Papa, what if you don't like this last one, either?" asked Beatrice timidly.

"Then I will advertise again," he pronounced. "This time as far as London. And I will not be swayed by Fairchild's arguments about lack of experience. Everyone needs to make a beginning."

The door opened, and they all straightened, but it was only Araminta with Snap in her arms. "He can't bear to be locked up any longer, and nor can I. Floss, may Aggie and I play at bowls in your garden?"

"No! You're sure to batter my flowers and plants. Go on the lawn."

"But then Snap might run at whomever comes up the drive."

"Tie a string to his collar, then."

Seeming to object to this, Snap gave a tricky writhe out of Minta's arms and bounced to the floor, barking and growling, but the true cause of his excitement appeared the next moment, as Bobbins entered the drawing room with Mrs. Whisp on his heels.

"Mrs. Whisp," he announced as impassively as he could with the dog taking hold again of his stockinged leg.

Minta rescued him, prying open Snap's little jaws and fleeing the room. (Florence could not help but notice that she passed the front entrance, which could only mean she was heading for the double doors at the end of the gallery, which opened directly on the garden gate.)

"Mr. Ellsworth, imagine seeing you here," said Mrs. Whisp, rising from her graceful curtsey. "Your daughters tell me you are oftener sequestered in your library."

"So I am, Mrs. Whisp. So I am. But this afternoon we interview governess candidates. In fact, we expect our final one any minute."

"Dear me! What bad timing on my part! I will take myself off at once."

When his daughters failed to issue polite demurrals, Mr. Ellsworth said, "Nonsense, nonsense. It won't take long, to judge by the other two applicants. Why don't you take a walk in the gardens and join us for tea in half an hour, say? Possibly less—we will send a servant to fetch you, if that is the case."

Florence's eyes widened. A *fourth* tea? But the deed was already done. Mrs. Whisp accepted with delight, taking leave of them not a minute before once more the door whisked open. "Miss Dunn," intoned Bobbins, his eyes darting around for the terrier.

If Miss Pinkerton was too young and pretty and tactless and Miss Patrick too daunting and bulwark-like, Miss Dunn was a happy medium. Florence guessed she was thirty. Smooth dark brown hair, brown eyes with promising crinkles at the corners, a pretty figure ruthlessly contained.

One peek at her father told Florence he was pleased with Miss Dunn's appearance as well. *Let us hope her personality equals her person.*

"Miss Dunn," Mr. Ellsworth addressed her, after the preliminaries were got through and they were all seated again, Florence preparing yet more tea. "Your letter states that you taught a village school in Woolston for eight years."

"Yes, for my father the curate." She had a crisp manner of speaking, though her eyes looked capable of smiling even when her mouth did not.

"But you do not wish to continue doing so...?" he prompted, his brow furrowing as he tried to remember whether her father was dead or not. Several of the applicants had dead-curate fathers, but Fairchild had made such quick work of the selection process, that Mr. Ellsworth could not remember which orphaned applicant survived the culling.

"He has remarried in recent years," Miss Dunn replied, after a hesitation, "and I have a new crop of siblings. With so many mouths to feed, rather than be a continuing burden on my family, I have decided to see what happens when I strike out on my own."

Florence could not help it. Her eyes rose from her sewing and fixed on Miss Dunn. Then Miss Dunn knew what it was like—to lose her mother and to give place to a new stepmother and several half-siblings! Florence wondered if Miss Dunn's stepmother was of the Catherine-Catchway or Mary-Fielding variety.

"I have also answered advertisements in Aldershot and Basingstoke and even one in London, but I would prefer to stay closer to home, if possible."

Florence gave her points for cleverness, knowing that, if Mr. Ellsworth thought there would be any competition, he would become eager to enter the lists.

Once more, little Beatrice was brought forward, but this time she suffered no more than natural shyness and was able to answer questions without tripping over her own tongue. Nor did Miss Dunn make any pronouncements on her, to Beatrice's great relief.

"And Miss Lily, it is you I would accompany to social occasions when your time of mourning ends?" asked Miss Dunn. "Or would it be both you and Miss Ellsworth?"

Again Florence found herself explaining that she was soon to be married, and she did so with a blush, taken with a sudden, irrepressible idea: what if she were to go out for governessing, instead of marrying Mr. Gregory?

It was ridiculous, of course. A ludicrous whim. She was not poor; she was not without alternatives. Even if she had never engaged herself to Mr. Gregory, she knew her father would forbid her to entertain the notion. The heiress to Hollowgate—a governess?

Then why did she almost envy Miss Dunn? What was there to envy in leaving all one knew and held dear to live among strangers (even kindly ones requiring light duties), neither a member of the family nor a servant? Of course, if Mr. Ellsworth married Miss Dunn, the latter would become a member of the family, but Florence could not think her father a particularly desirable husband, rich though he was.

In her distraction, she sewed the loose edge of her fabric to the center design, and it was three stitches before she caught her mistake.

If my engagement to Mr. Gregory is not all that I would wish, I must do my best to make it so, Florence told herself, as she snapped off the thread to remove the needle. *It is my duty.* Painstakingly, she poked the needle's point through the first errant stitch, to coax it out of the material. *Just because I am using my head does not mean I cannot try to please my heart. He is a good man, even though Lily doesn't like him. Honest and well-meaning. A good brother and a good parson. And I know he would endeavor to be a good husband. If I wish he...loved me, I have never said as much to him. I have never asked him. He might already! And if I wish for...demonstrations of affection, why then I must find a way to let him know that as well. For I am certain he would try to please me.*

The question was, *did* she wish for demonstrations of affections from him? She had no idea. How could she know, having never experienced more than a press of the hand and one peck on the cheek when she accepted him?

There was only one way to find out.

The final stitch removed, Florence shook out her work, and set herself to re-threading the needle. *I will send a note to him immediately when Miss Dunn is gone. I have let things go too long. I have let Lily fill me with doubt. Lily and Mr. Fair—*

Florence let out a squeak, pressing her forefinger and thumb together to prevent her pricked finger from bleeding on her cloth.

"Are you all right, my dear?" asked Mr. Ellsworth.

"Perfectly, thank you, Papa. Just carelessness."

With a bland smile he returned his attention to Miss Dunn, and Florence must have been lost in her thoughts longer than she realized because she discovered with a start that they were already discussing terms!

"Certainly before Michaelmas," Miss Dunn was saying. "Even as early as the 20th, I would hazard."

"That should do very well. I will have my attorney Mr. Fairchild settle things with you. In the meantime, you should perhaps meet my other daughter Miss Araminta—"

As if conjured, a tremendous racket erupted in the passage, comprised of yips and moans and running and tripping feet, before the drawing room door flew open yet once more and Minta and her friend Aggie tumbled in.

"Florence," panted Minta, her hair tumbled down and blood on her frock, Snap in her arms with her hand tight on his snout, "you had better come right away. Mrs. Whisp—"

"Good gracious!" exclaimed Florence, jumping up. "Did Snap bite her?"

"Well, she *would* pat him on the head after he growled at her," Minta defended the terrier.

"It was an *aggressive* pat," added Aggie loyally.

"This would not have happened, had you not been in my garden," Florence snapped. "Where I specifically told you not to go."

"Is she hurt badly?" cried Mr. Ellsworth, leaping up to follow the girls. "Poor, dear woman!"

The door slammed behind them, and gradually the ruckus receded.

"That was Araminta," explained Lily to Miss Dunn. "And her friend Agatha." As Lily had barely paused in her sewing during the interruption, she rather liked how Miss Dunn had not added to the pandemonium, nor even shrieked or risen from her seat. "And I'm afraid wherever Minta is, there is a good deal of *that*."

"Blood?"

"Blood, running, screaming," Lily answered. "You wouldn't be responsible for teaching her, of course, because she goes to school in town, but she's perfectly capable of visiting injury and chaos on us whenever she is at home."

Miss Dunn's smile appeared. "I do have younger siblings in Woolston, as I said. Injury and chaos are not unknown to me."

"That may be," Lily agreed, "but you don't have Minta. Now, would you like another cup of tea?"

CHAPTER THIRTEEN

Good Counsellors lacke no Clients.
—Shakespeare, *Measure for Measure*, I.ii.99 (c.1616)

F airchild read the contract for Miss Dunn's employment one final time. All exactly as he and Ellsworth had agreed, but he wondered if it would be null and void within the month. He had forgotten to ask Miss Ellsworth how rapidly her father married Miss Dunn's predecessors. Though Miss Ellsworth might have been too young to observe the process with her first governess-turned-step-mother, surely she remembered the second.

Curiosity consumed him, frankly. Ellsworth had sent a simple note, to the effect that he had agreed to employ Miss Dorothea Dunn of Woolston, Hants, and would Mr. Fairchild please manage all which was required, in relation to contract, salary, timing, removers, etc.?

Yes, he would, but he would also see Miss Ellsworth. For very legitimate reasons, he assured himself. It was not just to see how she took the news and what she thought of the woman. No—as the family attorney, it was his duty to learn of any concerns and offer comfort and counsel, if needed.

At least, that is what he told himself.

Donning his hat, he emerged from his office. "Hents, I'm going out to Hollowgate, if Mr. West inquires."

"Yes, sir."

But Fairchild made it no further down Parchment Street than its intersection with St. George's before he heard his name being called.

"Good morning, Mr. Fairchild! How glad I am to catch you." It was Mrs. Whisp, of all people, rosy in the crisp morning, the black ribbons on her bonnet tied in charming bows. "I ought to have sent a note first, but I was come into town to do a little shopping and thought I would just see if you were in. Do you have a few minutes, or should I come back another time?"

Biting back a grimace, he bowed and gestured back toward Darby and West.

If Hents had been addled by Miss Ellsworth's visit to the office, he was little less by Mrs. Whisp's, the stare he gave Fairchild clearly asking if every client the new man brought to the firm would be fair to look upon. The widow merely nodded in the clerk's direction, sailing past to the inner room, and when Fairchild followed she asked, "May we shut the door?"

He hesitated, debating whether to give her the confidentiality speech he had given Miss Ellsworth. But a widow was not like an unmarried young lady, he supposed.

He shut the door.

Pulling off her gloves finger by finger, Mrs. Whisp drifted into the same chair Miss Ellsworth had occupied.

"How may I assist you today, Mrs. Whisp?" He blinked at the sight of her bare hand, seeing it was lightly bandaged. "Have you been injured?"

"It is nothing. That nasty little terrier at Hollowgate, I'm afraid." Covering the bandaged hand with the other, she went on. "Mr. Fairchild, I know we are not yet well-acquainted, but you heard enough of my history at the Hollowgate dinner to understand why I might be in need of professional advice."

Taking his own chair, he waited for her to go on.

"I would like to retain you as my advisor, sir."

"I...appreciate your trust, Mrs. Whisp," he returned warily.

She folded her gloves together and lay them on his desk. "And everything I tell you will be in complete confidence, I imagine?"

"Of course." He was aware of a prickling at the back of his neck. Fairchild was not entirely certain he wanted to be in Mrs. Whisp's complete confidence. Miss Ellsworth had already mentioned the woman as a potential fourth wife to her father, so would becoming Mrs. Whisp's attorney entail a conflict of interest? On the other hand, if she did marry Ellsworth, all the business would be in the same family again.

He would hear her out, he decided. Not that he knew of an alternative.

"The matter is this, Mr. Fairchild: the Whisps wanted me to remain with the family in Weymouth, but I exiled myself."

It had not taken him long to learn that it was better for an attorney to say nothing at all than to fill silences. Thus he folded his hands on the desk and waited.

She settled back in her chair, her eyes wandering to the shelves of deed boxes. "That is to say, I did not tell the entire truth at the dinner, but who ever does tell the entire truth? It is the truth that I am widowed, and it is the truth that my husband Thomas died of the fever. What I did not explain at the time is that Thomas was not in Weymouth when he died." Mrs. Whisp paused, taking up her gloves to smooth them again. "Thomas enjoyed sailing, and I did not. Ours was not always an easy union, and sometimes he would go on little sailing expeditions—heaven knew where. His parents blamed me for his frequent absences, naturally. If I were a better wife, they said, Thomas would see no need for wandering up and down the coast. One time—just like any other time—he vanished again, but on this occasion he did not return. Not only days went by, but weeks! We were all beside ourselves. Mrs. Whisp—my mother-in-law—was certain he had drowned and would wash up on the sand at Weymouth any day."

In spite of himself, Fairchild's professional demeanor had slipped, and he was sitting forward, all attention. Mrs. Whisp noticed this, and the shadow of a smile curved her lips.

"At last," she continued, "weeks and weeks later, a letter from him arrived, posted from Southampton, saying he had been impressed and was compelled to sail with the Royal Navy for the Mediterranean. This was nonsense, of course. The Royal Navy does not conscript sons of clergymen found sailing pleasure boats! He had simply abandoned me, the rogue."

At this point she rose to pace the room, trailing a fingertip along the shelves, and raising an eyebrow at the papers spilling untidily from the blue bag West had left on his desk. Then she looked at Fairchild again, who had risen from politeness, though he remained behind his desk.

"But it turned out I was wrong, Mr. Fairchild. For after several more months, another letter came. This one written in an unfamiliar hand and from the infirmary of Greenwich Hospital. The writer claimed that one of the old pensioners claimed—shortly before he died—that Mr. Thomas Whisp had perished of the fever during the Siege of Acre! Thomas was a hero—or at least his parents chose to think so. They imagined he played some role in Commodore Smith's successful blockade."

"You sound skeptical."

"If you knew Thomas, neither would you suspect him of being a hero, Mr. Fairchild. Is it heroic to leave one's wife on the charity of one's family? Or to leave your loved ones in the dark, only to learn of one's fate through a thirdhand account?" With a toss of her head, she resumed her seat, her little foot tapping restlessly.

Fairchild sat down again. "Who sent this letter?"

"A Mr. Albert Clark. And the pensioner's name in the infirmary was Henry Johnson."

"Mrs. Whisp—are you asking me to seek these people out, that you may learn more of your husband's fate?"

Her blue eyes grew rounder. "Whatever for? Let the dead bury the dead." She dismissed her lost husband with a flourish of her arm. "I only tell you these things so you will understand why I had to leave Weymouth. When Thomas died, his family wanted to tidy up their memory of him. They wanted to pretend that Thomas and I had been happy together. Although I came into the marriage with no settlement, the Whisps said that if I remained with them, they would continue the allowance they had always given Thomas. But I could not stay in Weymouth, Mr. Fairchild. I could not."

Again, he waited.

"I would *smother* there, you understand. I asked for time to think about it, not that I needed even another moment to do so. I asked if I might go away for a time and live here. Heaven knows Mr. Whisp does not trouble himself overmuch with his clerical sinecure—why should the cottage sit empty? They agreed—reluctantly. I have been given six months to decide: either I return to Weymouth after it has elapsed, to live always with them and always with my little income from them; or I accept a pittance and make my own way in the world."

Seeing the question on his lips, she started to her feet to pace once more. And once more Fairchild courteously rose himself. He had just placed his hands on the edge of his desk when he found her beside him, the folds of her black-and-olive-striped skirts brushing him.

"Oh—pardon me." He took an awkward step away from her, striking the chair behind him with the backs of his knees.

Mrs. Whisp put a finger to her lips and leaned toward him, so close he could smell a faint floral perfume. "There is more to my story." She spoke barely above a whisper.

She took his hand in her own, ignoring his start of surprise, and pressed a small leathern purse in it. "Here is your fee."

"Mrs. Whisp—" Placing the purse on his desk, he took her firmly by her shoulders and moved her away so that he could get out from between his desk and chair.

"Ah," she breathed, when he released her. "I knew you would be a forceful person. I like that. You are almost too handsome to be one's man of business, you know."

"Mrs. Whisp," he said again, his voice cool and impersonal as he perched on the desk's outer corner. "Let me hear precisely what you are asking of me before I give you any assurances that we may work together."

"So wise and cautious as well." But she folded her hands demurely and remained where he had placed her. "Very well, it is this: I would like you to negotiate a new agreement with the Whisps. I don't need to tell you again that I would like to make my own way in the world, but, as we know, there are only so many ways a gentlewoman may do so. The paltry amount they offer me to separate myself permanently from them will not suffice. Not if I am to continue to live in the manner in which I have grown accustomed, nor if I am ever to be able to attract a second—husband."

"You will forgive me for pointing out, Mrs. Whisp, that your late husband's relations have the upper hand," Fairchild said. "If they want you to live with them, and if your husband's income derived entirely from an allowance they gave him, you have no ground from which to negotiate. Did Mr. Thomas Whisp have nothing that belonged only to him, that you could try to claim? I assume he left no will."

She brushed this off impatiently. "Nothing worth mentioning, or I would have said. You won't need anything like that."

He exhaled slowly. "While I appreciate your confidence in me, Mrs. Whisp, I think you had better save your money. The best attorney in the world would have no legal grounds to force more money from your husband's relations than they want, in kindness and charity, to give. Therefore I would advise you to use these six months to save as much as you can, and to look about you." By which he meant, *to try to secure a second husband*, and he almost groaned as he said it. Of course he didn't want her to marry Ellsworth! But from a purely objective stance, would it not be her best option? And God knew Ellsworth had shown himself willing enough to marry impoverished women with few alternatives, confound him.

Mrs. Whisp held up both hands, as if to ward off his words, and then she closed the distance between them again, so that he could only have got away from her if he scrambled, crab-like, backwards across his own desk.

"Listen to me: I do have ground from which to negotiate," she insisted, quietly. "And this is my secret, above all, that you must keep. I will reveal it only when and to whom I like."

Her blue eyes held his, and there was nothing of the charming doll in them now. "When I left Weymouth, I left my husband's relations a hostage, you see. My daughter Priscilla." Fairchild stared, but Mrs. Whisp's gaze sustained his. "I left Prissy because I knew it was her they wanted, not me. And I left her because I wanted to see if I could manage without her—and I can. I can." She stopped, rubbing the hollow of her throat. Then she clenched her fists. "Therefore, Mr. Fairchild, what I want you to offer them is that they may—keep the child—if I may have the deed to Whisp Cottage and five thousand pounds."

"I—Mrs. Whisp, have you truly given this thought?"

"I have!" she declared, her eyes blazing now. "I have, and you needn't trouble yourself to try to talk me out of it. When I am—safe—I will reconsider what can next be done, if anything. But for now I am willing to give her up to them. And—if they will not give me what I ask, I will go as low as a life-lease on the cottage and three thousand pounds. If you are not willing to help me, I must seek elsewhere, but this is what I intend to do. They will take me more seriously if I have an agent—a *man,* to be precise—to speak for me. So tell me—will you help me?"

Fairchild had thought it before, and he thought it again: the world contained all manner of people. It was no use expecting everyone to think as one thought or to do as one would have done in the same situation. And if he ever believed women were more predictable than men because they were kinder or weaker or more delicate, well—there he was likewise mistaken.

She was not asking him to do anything immoral or illegal. If he helped put her in a more stable financial position, he did not see that it would affect her chances either way with Mr. Ellsworth, so it would involve no betrayal of Miss Ellsworth. Rather, if Mrs. Whisp were financially free of her husband's relations, she might be less tempted to grasp at the first straw.

Slowly, he rose, unfolding his long limbs, and this time she retreated a step to give him space. Then he extended a hand to her.

"Let us shake on it, madam. I will help you."

CHAPTER FOURTEEN

**His kissing is as full of sanctity
as the touch of holy bread.**
—Shakespeare, *As You Like It,* III.iv.1605 (c.1599)

Florence went out to her enclosed garden a half hour before Mr. Gregory was due to come. It was a lovely, mild day, and she had discarded her shawl after some time spent weeding. With no one to see her but her intimates, Florence had wound a rose ribbon through her thick, waving dark hair. (A daring move for her, though reckless Lily had lately taken to wearing her usual clothing within the house and only donning mourning if visitors called.) At Florence's request, Barney the head gardener placed a ladder against one wall, for she thought it would help to have a task for her intended, should her courage or conversation flag.

Today was the day.

Today she would learn if her intended husband loved her, or what she could do to make him love her.

Florence had told no one, of course. Least of all Lily. If Lily had the least inkling what Florence planned, Florence did not think she could bear her sister's response. Lily would think it ridiculous, wanting to determine whether one's intended loved one. Lily would never have engaged herself in the first place, were she not already certain of it. Nor would she have engaged herself unless she herself were head over ears in love, Florence suspected. The first Mrs. Ellsworth's counsel held no special significance for her second daughter, who barely remembered her. It was a burden only Florence carried, perhaps because she was more like her mother, whereas Lily was as headstrong as Papa, in her own way.

And then there was the ticklish matter of eliciting a demonstration of Mr. Gregory's affection. Florence wanted no witnesses to her attempt, so she carefully chose a time when Minta was at school and Lily had taken Beatrice to Burden's in College Street to find her a beginning reader, with the promise of buns at Forder's afterward. Furthermore, to forestall Miss Gregory dropping in, Florence had already called upon her after breakfast.

The crunch of gravel reached her ears, and Florence stiffened with panic. Oh! Oh! Already? She should look busy. Or should she look leisurely?

Flying to her stone bench, she compromised, sitting and taking the basket of feathers she had brought out onto her lap.

Mr. Gregory, stern and puffed, unlatched the gate and let himself in.

"Good morning," said Florence, rising to answer his bow with a curtsey. "I hope you are well."

"I am." Making his way over, he took the hand she held out to him and pressed it between both his own, like a layer of mortar between bricks. "What are the feathers for?"

"Some of the garlands atop the walls have become ragged," she replied, pointing. "I thought I would replace them."

"Ah." He did not sound particularly interested, nor did he offer his assistance. "My sister tells me you have news."

"News?" she fluttered up at him. Surely she had not mentioned to Miss Gregory that she wanted to enchant her brother? She had been distracted that morning, but confessing *that* would have been another matter entirely!

"The new governess?" he prompted.

"Oh, yes," Florence recovered. "The new governess. Miss Dunn. Miss Dorothea Dunn. She will be with us before Michaelmas."

"You do not look dismayed by the prospect—not as you did when we first spoke of it."

"I—am not dismayed," she admitted. "Or perhaps I am resigned. Mr. Gregory—may we walk?"

"Certainly." He held out a stiff, formal arm, and she placed her hand upon it.

Florence hoped the contact would encourage her, but she was disappointed to find it only felt like...putting her hand on a person's arm. Mr. Gregory might as well have been her father. She remembered the mere look she and Mr. Fairchild had shared down the dining table—no touch at all, and yet she had felt connected, comforted. And then the time she had spoken to him as they stood in the drive, when all at once, with no contact at all, both of them had been struck by...something...and had retreated from it.

Mr. Fairchild has nothing to do with anything.

"I think I must be resigned to the possibility of Papa marrying again," she began anew. "I think of it as inevitable—death and taxes, as it were. And I rather liked Miss Dunn, to be honest, as did Lily and Beatrice. She was calm and intelligent and not *too* young, nor too pretty, if you know what I mean. Strangers might still mistake her for my sister, but she would be a significantly older sister, as if Papa had had a wife before Mama."

Mr. Gregory nodded thoughtfully, which made him look even more like a woodpigeon. At least he was a handsome woodpigeon. No, *no*! She had to stop thinking such things!

"And certainly I would choose Miss Dunn over Mrs. Whisp as my next stepmother any day," she blurted, simply to be saying something, and she was therefore startled when Mr. Gregory lurched to a halt.

"Mrs. Whisp?" he echoed, dumbfounded.

"Yes...I know you don't approve of her, but that does not mean Papa shares your opinion. She is pretty, you must admit, and lively." In alarm Florence noticed her intended turning scarlet. He had dropped her arm to stare at her and looked on the point of delivering another lecture on appropriate and inappropriate companions. With what she hoped to accomplish in their time together, this was the last thing Florence wanted, and indignation flared. She had sworn she would not be surly and snappish, as she had been the last time they were alone, but she did not think she deserved another lecture. Even if this time it were about her father's conduct in relation to Mrs. Whisp, there was nothing Florence could be expected to do about it. Moreover, Mr. Gregory deceived himself if he imagined his authority would extend beyond his future wife to his future wife's family.

"Now, now," she tried quickly to placate him, "I just told you I would prefer Miss Dunn to Mrs. Whisp. There is no need to fly into the boughs."

"Mrs.—Mrs. Whisp is a great deal younger than Mr. Ellsworth!" Mr. Gregory protested.

"I know that. Anyone can see that," retorted Florence, her grip on her temper slipping another notch.

"He should look upon her in a fatherly manner!"

"Mr. Gregory—you are not attending," she said through clenched teeth. "And berating me about the matter is sending owls to Athens. I just said very clearly that I would choose Miss Dunn over Mrs. Whisp, and I also acknowledged *again* that I remember your disapproval of the latter. But Papa has never consulted me over his choice of wives—not me, not anyone. As it is, one can only cross one's fingers and hope! And if he will not listen to me, sir, he will most assuredly not listen to *you*, and you would only make him angry by trying to force your opinion on him."

Her betrothed continued to hiss and sputter for another few seconds, like drops of water on a hot iron, and Florence foresaw family conflict in the years ahead. Mr. Gregory might be Mr. William

Ellsworth's parson, and he would soon be his son-in-law, but that did not mean Mr. Ellsworth would be guided by him.

She gave an inward shrug. Perhaps it was a lesson that could only be learned through repeated experience. It was not as if she herself had wholly yielded to it, after all—only look how she kept asking Mr. Fairchild to attempt this or ask that.

Stop thinking about Mr. Fairchild.

Yes.

Right.

She had lost sight of her primary goal in summoning Mr. Gregory.

Timidly, she reached to place a hand on his chest. "May we talk about something else...Clifford?" His Christian name emerged with an effort, like the time as a child when a grape lodged in her throat and her then-governess Miss Catchway pounded her between the shoulders to bring it up. The name felt unnatural to her. Disrespectful, because he was her rector and older than she was. How old was he? Wasn't his age the sort of thing she should know about him, or be able to ask?

He frowned, which did not reassure her, but then said. "Of course, my dear. Though, again, I would like to state that I do not think Mrs. Whisp at all an appropriate partner for your father."

Florence shut her eyes and wondered if the insides of her eyelids were always so red or if, in fact, she was vexed again.

But she managed to give one nod of acknowledgement, not trusting herself to reply. Her hand did drop back to her side, however.

"Come, my dear. Shall we walk again? What more pleasant subject would you like to talk about?"

It was now or never. Somehow all their talks—ever since they became engaged—seemed to end in frustration. Or in her being unhappy with him. If she wanted to mend matters, she had better lead them in the direction she hoped they would go.

Screwing her courage to the sticking place, Florence answered, "Never mind walking just now. What I would like to talk about—that is—Mr. Gregory—what I wanted to ask you today was—is—what—what led you to offer for me?"

"Led me...?" He drew himself up, mystified. This was followed by looking up at the pearly blank sky, as if it might explain the extraordinary question. Perhaps it did enlighten him because he then began to shake his head, clicking his tongue ruefully.

"My poor dear—sometimes I forget how young you are, and I am such an indifferent lover. I understand. You would perhaps welcome more assurances from me."

This was exactly what Florence would welcome, but the way he phrased it made her feel as if she were foolish and unreasonable in this desire. She took a slow breath. Heavens. If she were not careful, she thought, she would begin to hate the man.

"Yes, Mr. Gregory, perhaps 'assurances' would be...gratifying...from time to time."

"Well, then." Since she had not taken his arm, he clasped his hands behind his back and paced a few steps away, as if he had been confronted with a particularly knotty problem. Perhaps he had.

"Well, then, Miss Ellsworth. Let me supply those assurances. You are a lovely, calm—generally calm—young lady. Reasonable. A good housekeeper. You love your family. You are attentive in church. You do not seem to suffer from, say, silliness or...boisterousness or—or dreamy abstraction or—ahem!—excessive sensibility..."

Was he running through each member of the Ellsworth Assortment and explaining why he preferred her to Lily or Araminta or Tyrone or Beatrice, for goodness' sake? Because she knew that was exactly how he would characterize each of her younger siblings! When she asked him for assurances, he effectively told her he preferred her to her other family members? He might have saved himself the trouble and married Snap, in that case! Nor did it warm her heart to be called a calm housekeeper who paid attention in church.

"Thank you," she said, in a muted tone, still struggling to overcome her exasperation.

"I think you will make an ideal clergyman's wife," Mr. Gregory continued, entering into the spirit of things. "Moreover, Miranda likes you. You will fit very well in our little household."

"I like Miss Gregory, too," sighed Florence. It wasn't an untruth. She didn't *dislike* her. It was impossible to feel strongly about Miss Gregory.

She half-hoped, half-dreaded he would turn the question upon her—why did she want to marry him?—but he did not. It was just as well. Her reasons might have sounded equally lame to his ears.

This was what she had said Yes to. This was what she had expected and found satisfactory only six months earlier. Safety. Respectability. A quiet life, supplying no tittle-tattle to the county. Only look how her father chose wives! Prettiness and propinquity were all that was required. One wife would almost do as well as the next, so long as he had one. Mr. Gregory's stolidity, his utter lack of melodrama, was much to be preferred.

Only—

Why was she no longer happy with her choice? Was it because he did not seem any more attached to her than he had been in April? Nor she to him?

Fear tightened around her heart. *It is not enough*. This *is not enough. I thought it was, but I was mistaken. I am sorry, Mama.*

She wanted to love her husband, and she wanted him to love her.

She was standing as close to him as she had to Mr. Fairchild in the drive, and yet there was no sense of danger with Mr. Gregory. No sense that, all too easily, something might run away with her. That she might lose the firm hold she had on herself. Standing beside Mr. Gregory, it was all too easy to believe that temptations like those which ensnared her father were easy to withstand.

But if she could withstand temptation with Mr. Gregory, she realized, it was because Mr. Gregory posed no temptation.

Her clear eyes rose to his. She needed time alone to ponder these things. But to do so effectively, she needed to know if she and Mr. Gregory might ever be more to each other than they were at that moment. More than promised partners who did not always rub along smoothly. Could they grow into love? If they could not—well—she must think about what that would mean.

Florence did not think she could ask her betrothed to kiss her if her life depended on it. She would just have to hint, and if he did not understand the hint, she had no idea what she might try next.

"Mr. Gregory," Florence murmured, swaying closer. "What I wondered—what I wanted to ask—is whether—I wonder if we—if we might...if you might..."

The rector might be an indifferent lover, but he was a man nonetheless. A man with his promised bride. Seeing her head fall back, her lips just parting, her eyes half-closed and her color high, he stared in astonishment for a long moment, but then, faintly, his blood stirred.

Faintly, but distinctly.

And then Clifford Gregory answered the call. Taking Florence resolutely by the upper arms, Mr. Gregory did what neither one would have imagined him doing even ten minutes before: he clutched her to him, planting a firm kiss on her mouth, much as he would jam a plug of paper in a window frame to block a draft.

Florence screwed shut her eyes, waiting for sensation to sweep her away. Her arms even crept about his waist, but that was more because she feared he would overset them, he was so much larger and stockier than she. For the same reason she tried to press back as hard as she could. How long did kisses normally last?

After what seemed an eternity but was likely no more than twelve seconds, Mr. Gregory drew back, a smile spreading across his face. Florence tried to smile in return, but her lips felt numb, as if someone had taken to them with a carpet-beater.

"Ah," he said. "Ah-*ha*."

To her amazement, there was a gleam in his usually gleamless eyes. She just had time to register this before she was seized once more, her mouth crushed once more. This time her hands grasped for his lapels as he tipped her backwards.

He made a sound in his throat that might have been another ah-ha, and Florence clung on, trying to kiss him back. *This must be why all the heroines faint in books*, she thought. *Heaven knows I would like some air.*

Steps were heard on the gravel. At least, Florence heard them, and she struggled to turn her head, embarrassment and relief flooding her in an incomprehensible mix.

It was Bobbins, and Florence suspected he must have not been heard the first time he approached and had been compelled to make more noise because he was flushed and looking anywhere but at her. Mr. Gregory, finally recalled to greater awareness, released her so abruptly that she would have toppled over, had his hand not flashed out to grip her elbow and haul her back up.

"Er—miss—" croaked the footman, "Miss Lily and Miss Beatrice are come back, and Miss Lily sent me to tell you Mr. Fairchild has come as well, and won't you join them in the drawing room?"

"Oh. Yes. Yes, of course," managed Florence. She directed an apologetic half smile at her betrothed's chest (her battered mouth unable to do more), smoothed her frock and hurried after the servant, Mr. Gregory stalking in her wake.

CHAPTER FIFTEEN

**It would be unkind in me to leave her
in the distrest way she is in.**
—Mary Delaney, *The autobiography and correspon-
dence of Mary Granville, Mrs Delany* **(1754)**

S he had been kissed. That was obvious. Or else stung by two
bees.

Fairchild rose when Miss Ellsworth entered the drawing room,
shadowed by the large Mr. Gregory. He made his bow, his gaze
missing neither her swollen mouth nor Gregory's equally swollen,
smug demeanor. Well, and why shouldn't the man kiss her? They
were engaged to be married, after all. Heaven knew, if he himself
were engaged to Miss Ellsworth, he would make the most of every
opportunity. But somehow he had thought—hoped—the rector
was a different sort of person.

He had no right at all to be angry with them. None.

"Miss Ellsworth, I have come to congratulate your family on hiring Miss Dorothea Dunn as the new governess," he said, his voice sounding hard to his own ears. "And to report that all the arrangements are in order."

The young lady's mouth worked. She even touched her lips with her fingertips, and Fairchild felt another pulse of wrath.

"You must pardon me," he added dryly, "if I have called you from more important business."

The shaft hit home, for she blushed, and Fairchild was duly punished by this confirmation. To make matters worse, the insufferable Gregory chuckled. Putting a hand to the small of his intended's back, he guided her to a seat on the sofa, taking up the rest of it with his own person. Though no part of Gregory touched any part of Miss Ellsworth, the stripe of brocade sofa upholstery separating them struck Fairchild as infinitesimally narrow. The only relief to his feelings was that Miss Beatrice rushed over as soon as the couple was seated and wriggled herself between them to take hold of her sister's hand.

"Thank you for coming, Mr. Fairchild," Miss Ellsworth replied stiffly. "We look forward to Miss Dunn's arrival." She turned to Miss Lily. "Where is Papa? Does he not want to hear this?"

Her sister was scrutinizing her, and Fairchild guessed she also noticed something between Miss Ellsworth and Mr. Gregory had shifted. "He already came and went," Lily replied. "He only had time to dash in because he and Mr. Falk must see to something about the sheep."

By this point, Fairchild began to take himself in hand, and he tried to start the subject anew. "Miss Ellsworth, I know you had some concerns about the hiring of a governess. Having not met Miss Dunn myself, I am eager to hear your opinions on her."

She bent her head to catch little Miss Beatrice's eye, and he saw the rose ribbon entwined in her beautiful, lustrous hair. Was this for Gregory, too?

"Miss Dunn is perhaps thirty years of age," Miss Ellsworth began. Her voice was husky, and she stopped to clear her throat. "She is a clergyman's daughter. The daughter of his first wife, that is. He has since remarried and has several younger children. Therefore she is—determined to strike out on her own." Lifting her chin, she turned those grey eyes on him, and he felt a hot pressure at his throat, equal parts yearning and vexation. There was a question in her gaze: did he hear the similarities between herself and Miss Dunn?

He did—he did—if he could stop thinking about her kissing Gregory.

He nodded as if she had spoken. "I see. A sympathetic character. One who understands, perhaps, what it is like to be—first—part of one sort of family and then part of a very different sort."

Her lips trembled and then rewarded him by blossoming into a smile. "Yes—exactly. I felt so. Moreover, I found her to be intelligent and kind."

"I thought she seemed a little sad," put in Beatrice, to her sisters' surprise.

"So would you be," rejoined Lily soon enough, "if you had to go out for governessing. But I liked that she was calm. She didn't panic a bit when Minta came hurtling in, hollering about Snap biting Mrs. Whisp."

"Mrs. Whisp again?" Mr. Gregory straightened so abruptly he sent Miss Beatrice rolling into her sister. "Does she call very often?"

Miss Ellsworth gave an uneasy laugh and reached around her youngest sister to squeeze her beloved's shoulder. That distracted the man quite effectively! He looked over little Beatrice to regard Miss Ellsworth like a love-struck ox.

Fairchild's mouth twisted. So Gregory objected to Mrs. Whisp pursuing Ellsworth too? The parson must be more worldly-minded than Fairchild had realized, if he feared sharing his betrothed's inheritance with additional parties. Mrs. Whisp would have a time of it, if she hoped to secure Ellsworth despite the opponents arrayed against her.

Let Florence see it, he prayed, using her Christian name without even realizing. *Let her see that one of the things Gregory loves her for is her money.*

But, as the visit went on, it became clear to Fairchild that Miss Ellsworth's money was not the only thing attracting Mr. Gregory. When Beatrice sprang up at Miss Lily's request to fetch her new textbook, Mr. Gregory not only resumed his former position a hairsbreadth from Miss Ellsworth, but he closed the gap altogether, his stocky thigh falling casually against the folds of her gown. She did not edge away, but she blinked rapidly several times, and her color came and went.

Miss Ellsworth might have been the one to put Gregory on his guard about Mrs. Whisp, Fairchild realized. Perhaps she confided in her intended husband, just as she had in the family attorney. Another thing that ought to be unsurprising, yet it grated on him. The more he saw Gregory and Miss Ellsworth together, the more he wondered at the match, and not only because he admired her himself. No—he marveled at it because it was plain that a big, blustery, self-important man like Gregory would ride roughshod over his quieter bride. It would not be intentional, but he would do it. He could not help but do it.

To Fairchild's delight (and likely the delight of others in the room), Gregory rose reluctantly when the mantel clock chimed. "A meeting in town with the archdeacon, my dear," he told Miss Ellsworth. "I regret leaving you."

She murmured something appropriate and gave him her hand.

"Are you also headed back to Winchester, Fairchild?" the rector asked him.

"Not quite yet," he replied. "I thought of one more thing I would like to speak to Mr. Ellsworth about and might try my chances waiting a little longer for his return." What that discussion item might be he had no idea, but he was determined to outlast everyone else.

"Oh, but, who knows when Papa will—that is—" Miss Lily broke off and busied herself rummaging through her workbasket.

Then Mr. Gregory was gone, and the air in the room lightened accordingly.

"What you really were asking," Miss Lily said in her brisk voice, "was whether we approve of Miss Dunn as a potential third stepmother—first stepmother for you, Bea."

He looked from Miss Lily to her older sister, and when the latter gave a nod, he answered, "Indeed I was. Miss Ellsworth has let me know that any search for a governess was in actual fact a search for a new—wife—for Mr. Ellsworth. Therefore, I was anxious to know if the choice of Miss Dunn met with more than resignation and tolerance among you."

"She's better than our first stepmother and looks healthier than our second," Miss Lily shrugged.

"I like her," said little Beatrice. "She has kind eyes."

"And you, Miss Ellsworth?" he prompted.

She had taken up an embroidered cushion from the sofa and hugged it to her. "She was certainly the best of the lot. And, while not Papa's age or anywhere approaching it, she was at least some years older than I." Giving the cushion a little plumping, she set it aside. "We do thank you, Mr. Fairchild, for your guidance of Papa. Or your attempts at it."

He bowed, impatient to ask more questions but not seeing any way open to him.

"Would you like to see my new book?" asked little Beatrice, holding it out to him. When he nodded, she came to lean against his knee as he admired it, turning the pages for her and hearing the letters she could already pick out.

Lily took advantage of his preoccupation to march across the room, taking the spot on the sofa lately occupied by the rector.

"Well, Flossie? What do you think? Say Miss Dunn comes at Michaelmas and Papa proposes by Christmas. If Miss Dunn is not so bad, must you really marry the Dread—marry Mr. Gregory, rather, when spring comes?"

"I have already put it off once," Miss Ellsworth replied in a low voice. "It would not do, to do it again." She threw a glance toward Fairchild, but he turned another page of Beatrice's book and pointed something out to her.

"Did he kiss you?" hissed Miss Lily, leaning closer.

"Lily!"

"He did, didn't he?"

"Hush!"

"Because your face looks like a bruised peach."

("C is for cat," said Beatrice triumphantly. "But Lily says cat in French is *chat*. C-h-a-t. Isn't that funny?")

"I am not going to discuss it, Lily."

"Myself, I would rather kiss a donkey. Either end."

Miss Ellsworth said nothing. She flipped open her workbasket and whisked out a piece of fabric.

"You have been engaged for five months now, and he finally kisses you?" continued Miss Lily's urgent whisper. "Did it make you think you loved him?"

Fairchild strained his ears to hear Miss Ellsworth's answer, but she gave none. Beatrice turned several pages. "And here are the numbers. Miss Dunn will teach me arithmetic. Do you like arithmetic, Mr. Fairchild?"

"I—er—yes. I suppose so," he fumbled. What brought about all this kissing, if it had not happened before? Knowing her father would choose either Miss Dunn or Mrs. Whisp, was Miss Ellsworth now motivated to flee into her lover's arms prematurely?

"You—are—blind, Floss. Or else that great big man takes up so much space you can't see around him." Lily slapped her workbasket shut. "Beatrice!" She barked this last, rising and holding out an imperious hand to her little sister. "Come. Let's get you all cleaned up before dinner."

"Cleaned up?" wondered the young girl. She was clean as a new pin, as always.

"Yes. You have stickiness from the buns on your face. I can see it from here."

The pink tip of her tongue sneaking around the edges of her mouth, Beatrice obediently shut her book and went to join her sister, giving Fairchild a forlorn wave.

And then he was alone with Miss Ellsworth.

It was obvious to him that Miss Lily contrived the situation. Equally obvious was her dislike for Mr. Gregory as a husband for her sister. But why thrust her sister together with the family attorney? Had Miss Lily guessed at his feelings for Miss Ellsworth? Or did she merely hope her sister might come to prefer someone besides the rector, and he would do as well as any other?

Miss Ellsworth was pink with embarrassment or indignation or who-knew-what-all, and her needle was flashing as it whipped back and forth through her work. "Mr. Fairchild, I have seen—and I think you must have seen as well—that my family has already taken you to its heart, and therefore does not seem to—to maintain the ordinary bounds of propriety in your presence."

Carefully he chose his words. "Miss Ellsworth, believe me when I say that I...like your family very much and consider it flattering in the highest degree that they—would speak of matters that otherwise would be kept from strangers' ears."

She said nothing, but she pressed her swollen lips together (wincing), her eyes still on her sewing.

"And, if you will pardon me for saying it—you have not exempted yourself from confiding in me. From speaking of matters you might not raise in company, that is."

At this she crumpled, and a stifled sob escaped her.

"Miss Ellsworth!" Before he knew it, he was across the room, taking the seat so lately occupied by Gregory and Miss Lily. His heart sped, and he gripped the edge of the sofa with both hands to prevent himself from gripping *her*. "Miss Ellsworth, are you all right?"

Frantically she nodded, but another gulping sob broke through her control. And another.

"Should I ring for someone? Your maid? Are you ill?" he persisted, now sitting upon his hands lest they disobey him.

"I am—all right," she gasped. Whatever she had been sewing, she used it now to press to her eyes, keeping it there until she could still herself. "F-forgive me."

"There is nothing to forgive. Only, I wish I might be of service to you. Is—there something you want to say about Miss Dunn, that you did not wish to say before your sisters?"

She shook her head and took several deep breaths. "No. No." Venturing a peep in the direction of his knee, she gave a watery smile. "I may...later. But I know no harm of her now."

"Then...what is it? Can you say?" He did not dare hope she would speak of her own engagement.

Florence would have been mortified to learn that he guessed at her troubles. She only knew that the subject heaviest on her heart she could speak of to *no one*, least of all him. She was not sure she could even articulate it to herself yet. It—her tears, her distress—was a compound of everything: it was the...monster of affection she seemed to have awakened in Mr. Gregory—a huge, kissing, touching monster; it was the fact that she just referred to her betrothed as a monster; it was Lily speaking heedlessly, as if she intended Mr. Fairchild to hear; it was Bea leaning against Mr. Fairchild's knee; it was his gentleness and concern for her (another sob threatened to emerge at this); it was the awareness that she spent an inordinate amount of time either thinking of Mr. Fairchild or counseling herself not to think of Mr. Fairchild—!

No. She could not say a word of any of this. It must all be stuffed down like too many items in too small a trunk, and she must sprawl across the lid to keep everything contained.

Quietly, effortfully, she swallowed it all, all down. Then, on pretense of fetching a different color of thread from her workbasket, she edged a few inches away from him. Though no part of him had so much as brushed her, it felt as if every nerve on that side of her body was warm and vibrating.

"I don't know what to say, Mr. Fairchild. Or what you must think of me. It must be all the changes happening in our family."

"There are many, Miss Ellsworth. I am not at all surprised that you should feel...unsettled by them."

"I—am not like my father," she uttered. "I am not." Then, blushing for this *à propos de bottes* remark, she added, "That is—Papa floats along, doing as he pleases. I am not sure duty or—or concern for what other people think enters into it with him. But—both those things—duty and—and—"

"And what other people think," he supplied.

"Yes—those do matter to me."

"I know that, Miss Ellsworth," he said softly. "One need not be long in your company before that is quite clear."

She stole a timid glance at him—she could not help it—and was not reassured by the thoughtful frown on his handsome face.

Fairchild was indeed thinking hard. Very hard. He did not have a vast amount of experience with women, his abortive attachment to Miss Perkins of Oxford aside, but it did not require a genius to deduce that, if Miss Ellsworth's distress stemmed from a fear of not doing her duty, or of having other people think poorly of her, she must be troubled by some temptation that would entail both. Something that would make her think she was more similar to her father than she liked.

Could she possibly, possibly be contemplating breaking her engagement?

His pulse began leaping again in response to this conclusion, and he had to rein in his racing thoughts. What had happened before she and Gregory came in? Kissing—yes—that was obvious. Had she not liked it? And if she had not liked it, was it because she did not like kissing, or because she did not like kissing *Gregory*?

Swift as thought he looked at her, just in time to catch her looking at him. She took a hiccupping breath and sprang to her feet, her sewing falling to the floor and her thread-winder bouncing away.

"Allow me." Standing, he bent for the winder, waiting for Miss Ellsworth to gather both her wits and her sewing supplies. She seemed to be having extraordinary difficulty—dropping her work twice, knocking her sewing basket down when she went to open it—and, after the barest hesitation, he placed the lightest fingertips on the back of her bare hand to calm her.

It had the opposite effect.

On both of them.

Miss Ellsworth jumped, and Fairchild's breath stalled in his lungs as if he were a Winchester schoolboy again and had just taken a planter to the midsection. He hardly knew later if he removed his hand first or she dodged away first, but the next moment half the room separated them, and they were both breathing rapidly.

"Miss Ellsworth—I—"

"Mr. Fairchild—you—"

They both stopped and waited for the other, their eyes still locked.

It's the blasted ribbon, he thought. He wanted to unwind it from her hair and thread his own fingers through the heavy waves.

Or it was her eyes. Winter water.

Or her mouth, kissed and luscious.

He must speak, Fairchild commanded himself. Say *something*. It hardly mattered what.

He had better speak—confound it all—or he would do more than speak. He would—

But it was the mantel clock which spoke first, striking the quarter hour and rousing Miss Ellsworth from her breathless daze.

"Heavens—it is later than I thought. Minta will be home any moment, and I suspect Papa and Mr. Falk." She reached for the bell rope. "Did you still want to wait for him—Papa, I mean? You must be very busy, and you took the time to walk out to Hollowgate and must make the return walk..." Even as she babbled she was sidling toward the door. Clearly she wanted to escape his presence, and it was either let her, or endanger their relationship by making a fool of himself.

But what if the opportunity never came again?

The opportunity had already eluded him, however. Miss Ellsworth let herself out, and he heard her footsteps hurrying away.

He was alone.

Like a sleepwalker, he made his way from the house and, before he knew it, he was descending the drive again, muttering. "What would you do, then, Fairchild? Offer for her? She would refuse. She could not do otherwise, engaged as she is. Duty, duty."

How dishonorable was it, that he found himself plotting how he might persuade her to jilt Gregory? It would be sinking to a low. The rector might be stiff, bluff, loud, but he was an honored man, a respected man. He could afford to take Miss Ellsworth for his wife and not live off her fortune, as Fairchild would have had to do. *But I would love Miss Ellsworth. I would treasure her.*

And Gregory did not? He remembered the man's face that afternoon as he looked at her. He was not as immune to her charms as

Fairchild would have liked to think. And if Gregory did not want to end the engagement, she would never consider it, would she?

Duty, duty.

"Give it up, Fairchild," he said through gritted teeth. But he wished—oh, he wished he had taken hold of her and kissed the life out of her before he renounced her.

"She's not for you, you fool."

Simple enough, to say the words. To believe them was another matter entirely.

CHAPTER SIXTEEN

Alack a day, Cousin Biddy, these
Idle Romances have quite turn'd your Head.
—Richard Steele, *The tender husband: or, The accom-*
plish'd fools **(1705)**

L et's go for a walk," said Lily. "A very long walk."

Florence glanced at the clock. It was nearly the time when callers might be expected. Given the choice, she would have preferred to be alone with her thoughts, rather than facing her sister's curiosity and interference, but that would mean remaining at Hollowgate where she was too easily found.

"What about Beatrice?"

"I already told Boots to help her draw paper dolls and cut them out. Come on, then. We will walk Teg Down."

Teg Down being the highest point close to Hollowgate, the girls saved their breath for the climb, but when they stood on the modest height, surveying the surrounding downs and the town, Lily looped her arm through her sister's and rested her chin on Florence's shoulder.

"How do you think you will like living at the rectory?"

They could see Florence's future home at the base of Chapel Hill, a grey stone house with painted cream-and-blue trim, smoke rising from the chimneys.

"I don't know," said Florence. "Miss Gregory asked for my opinions on repapering the morning room and a little dressing room that will be mine."

"And what did you choose?"

Florence sighed. "I chose blue paper—scrolls and peacocks—for the dressing room and yellow roses for the morning room."

"Why—those are the colors of your dressing room and the east morning room at Hollowgate, which my grandmother chose. Did you not want something new? Something your very own?"

Hearing Lily put it that way, Florence's shoulders sagged. "You're right. They are the same colors." They were very nearly the same patterns.

"You see," said Lily, and Florence could hear the note of danger rising in her voice. "You *don't* want to leave home. At least, you don't want to leave home and marry Mr. Gregory."

"Oh, Lily, not this again."

"Not what again? I have not mentioned it for months," declared Lily. "I told myself I would keep my mouth shut and let you realize for yourself that he is not the match for you. Too old, too loud, too stuffy, too dull. No—don't pull away, Flossie. Just listen to me, for once. I thought surely he would be so disappointing as a lover that you—even you—would grow impatient with him. You're such a darling, darling Flossie that you ought to be loved by someone more...loveable!"

"I won't listen to this, Lily—"

"No—that's not right," her sister went on, determined to speak her mind. "It's not only that Mr. Gregory isn't loveable himself, it's that he doesn't even truly love you!"

"Lily!"

"He doesn't! Has he ever said he does?"

Florence's silence and compressed lips answered for her.

"I knew it," said Lily, more quiet than triumphant. "But then what about the kissing?" When Florence covered her face with her hands, Lily snorted. "It was quite obvious what you two had been doing when you came in. Mr. Fairchild even noticed."

"No!" wailed Florence into her hands.

"How could he not? Anyone with eyes could see that your mouth looked like it had been pressed in a mangle, and the self-congratulatory parson must have been the one operating the press! But never mind your embarrassment, Floss—did you like it?"

Florence's hands dropped, revealing a scarlet countenance. "Oh—I don't know. I suppose it will take some getting used to."

"Mm. Hardly an endorsement. I think he liked it, however, so you will get your opportunities to habituate yourself." Lily's chin returned to her sister's shoulder, and she gave her a squeeze around the waist for good measure. "Flossie, dear, you know how Miss Dunn comes soon. Have you thought about how, as stepmothers go, she would not be so very bad? And not only we, but all Winchester expects Papa to marry again by this point. In fact, the local gossips would be disappointed if he did not! Therefore, why need you rush into marriage? Wouldn't you like to go to balls and assemblies with me and Miss Dunn, when our mourning is finished? We never got a chance because our last stepmama was so unwell all the time, and now, just when things might improve for us—"

"I accepted Mr. Gregory's offer before I knew our last stepmama would die and Papa would want to marry again," Florence pointed out. "And I think you are premature in assuming Miss Dunn will win him. Mrs. Whisp has the lead and might prevail. But in either case, no matter whom he chooses, I'm not like you, Lily. I don't want to be the belle of the ball or anything like that. Nor do I want to marry some foolish young man I've danced two quadrilles with!"

"Did *I* say I wanted to marry some foolish young man I've danced two quadrilles with?" demanded her sister.

"No, but you know what I mean. The ordinary methods for finding husbands don't appeal to me any more than Papa's method for finding wives. How are you so certain you can find a husband whom you will love and who will love you, merely because you dance with him a few times?"

"As if that were my plan! Dancing is only a beginning. An avenue to other things. But if dancing doesn't work," continued Lily airily, "I suppose I will just marry Mr. Robert Fairchild."

"Lily!" Florence pulled away to stare at her.

"What? Isn't he a nice young man? What objection could you possibly have to him?"

"I—I—"

"He doesn't have any money, I know," Lily mock-sighed, "and his family has humble beginnings, but he is handsome and kind and intelligent and rather tactful in his handling of Papa, wouldn't you say?"

"Lily, are you in love with him?" Already a pale person, Florence Ellsworth had gone white as paper.

"Well, what if I was? What could you have against him?"

Wordlessly, Florence shook her head. She felt breathless, cold, faint. "Of course I have nothing against him. I agree with you entirely. He is a—very nice young man. So kind. Conscientious."

"Exactly." Lily studied her, noting all her sister's symptoms with the attention of a doctor. "Just what I thought. He doesn't seem particularly interested in me, however, which is frustrating. Because, as you pointed out, I want to be the belle of the ball."

"Oh, Lily, I didn't mean—"

"It's perfectly all right, Flossie. I was not the least bit offended. I admit I would very much like to be a belle, and I honestly look forward to Miss Dunn coming to Hollowgate in whatever capacity, so long as she chaperones me next summer. Do you think that's bad of me?"

"No, sweeting." Florence wrapped her arms about herself, trying not to shiver. "Then—you are saying, no matter how nice Mr. Fairchild is—you do not intend to choose him first, if that means you must forego being the Belle of Winchester?"

"The Belle of Winchester!" Lily's eyes sparkled. "I like the sound of that." With a laugh she took her sister's hands and unwound her arms. "And to answer your question, *no*, I don't want to marry Mr. Fairchild straight off. For two reasons (well, maybe three): firstly, I resent his indifference to my charms; and secondly, I don't want to marry anybody straight off because I want to have my fun."

"But would you have given up your 'fun' if Mr. Fairchild were more receptive to your charms?" persisted Florence, to which her sister responded with another laugh and a wag of her finger.

"I give up my fun for no one! But aren't you going to ask me my third reason? Hmm...I see you hesitate. Fearful Florence! I will tell you all the same, since you called me sweeting." She scrutinized her older sister again, a mischievous smile curving her lips. "It's this: marrying Mr. Fairchild would not be my first choice because I had other plans for him. You see, Floss, I hoped he might catch your eye. I was trying to interest you in him. Did it work?"

Florence stared, recoiling a step. "You mean—when you made Beatrice go out of the room with you, leaving Mr. Fairchild and me alone together?"

"Yes, and when I flirted with him at the dinner table and when I told you you were endangering his future at Darby and West."

"But why, Lily?" asked Florence faintly. "Why should you try to interest me in him?"

Lily groaned in exasperation. "Because! Isn't it obvious? I thought—and still do think—he would make a better husband for you than tiresome Mr. Gregory. Think about it: Mr. Fairchild! Not old, not loud, not stuffy, not dull."

"It was very wrong of you," Florence scolded. "Even if you do not like Mr. Gregory for me, it was very wrong to try to make me like somebody else, when I am already engaged. And you have wronged Mr. Gregory as well."

But Lily scoffed at this. "That, I deny! I have only wronged Mr. Gregory if I succeeded in luring you away. Are you telling me I have succeeded?"

Florence's hand rose to her throat, only to fall back again because her fingers were trembling, and Lily, instead of appearing dismayed by this involuntary admission, gave a shout of glee and spun in a circle. "I have! I have! I did!"

"Hush! Hush, Lily," her sister urged.

"I did succeed!" Lily obliged in a screeching whisper, still hopping about and waving delighted fists. "You like Mr. Fairchild! You cannot marry Mr. Gregory now."

"Lily—stop—you must listen to me. Please. Look, you troublesome girl—you have me at your mercy. I—I do confess that I find Mr. Fairchild a—most excellent man, and I have come to like and trust him more than I could have believed possible on such short acquaintance. But—"

"What 'but' could there possibly be?" interrupted Lily. "Unless it is, 'But I have not yet found the perfect moment in which to break my engagement.'"

"I am not going to break my engagement."

"*What?*"

"I am not going to break my engagement, Lily."

"Because—because—you want Mr. Fairchild to speak first?"

"Heaven forbid!" breathed Florence, even as her color rose. "He would never—even if he cared for me, he would never speak to me of such a matter while I am an engaged woman. It would be so...dishonorable!"

Her younger sister gave a heartfelt moan, flopping down onto the grass and putting her head in her hands. "Honor be blowed!" she uttered. "If it means you would marry someone you didn't love. Not only didn't love, but didn't even like as well as somebody else!"

"Lily," sighed Florence, thinking her sister seemed to have more in common with their father with each passing day. Each passing hour! "How could you think I would break my engagement? Mr. Gregory has done me no wrong, and I have given him my promise. If I do not yet...love him as I would like to, I must make every effort. We had not kissed before, but I think it may have changed things, and I must wait and see."

Somewhere during this speech Lily toppled over, rolling onto her back and squinting up at the sky. It was growing overcast.

"...I don't want to be like Papa," Florence was saying, "with my head turned by whomever crosses my path."

"You aren't the *least bit* like Papa," insisted Lily, "so I do not know why you waste so much time fearing you might be. Nobody who knows you, Flossie, thinks you are the tiniest iota like Papa. On the contrary! Everyone thinks you are sensible, prudent, capable..."

"Attentive in church," murmured Florence.

"...No, they think I'm the flighty one, the one who might do something foolish. But not you. Never you. Everyone knows Miss Florence Ellsworth would never be tempted by folly." With a disgusted sigh, Lily rolled up to a sitting position. "The only one who frets so much about you is *you*, but somehow I cannot convince you of that."

Florence said nothing, too busy grappling with these revelations to formulate a reply. But—even if what Lily said was true—even if Florence's fear was unfounded, was that not because, *unlike* her father, she had never indulged the whims of her heart? If she once began to, would the dreaded transformation then take place? Ah—what if, what if, what if?

"I think Mama would have regretted marrying Papa if she had allowed herself," said Florence. "But she knew regret would only lead to discontent and bitterness. She followed her heart in marrying him, but it was her head that allowed her to make the best of it."

"That may be," conceded Lily, "but she would not have had to make the best of it, had she married someone less—less *Papa*-like. If she had made a better match in the first place, she could have simply been happy, without any of the martyrdom."

"But what I am saying, Lily, is that she learned the hard way. She followed her heart and married Papa, only to discover she should have let her head rule her."

"And what I am saying, Flossie, is that it's all very well to let your head rule you, if your head can be trusted any more than your heart! But I'm not sure yours can, else why would you choose Mr. Gregory? If you don't want Mr. Fairchild, so be it, but there still exist other gentlemen whom I think would not require a lifetime of *unstinting* effort to love."

Lily made it sound as if Mr. Fairchild were there for the taking, Florence thought. As if Florence had only to decide, no, thank you, she would not marry Mr. Gregory, and there would be Mr. Fairchild to replace him. But life did not work like that! Life was not so tidy. There would be a scandal if she jilted Mr. Gregory now, and it would not be William Ellsworth's scandal, it would be her own. And, once the scandal and talk subsided sufficiently, how exactly did one then go to another gentleman and say, *Please, sir—I jilted my former betrothed in the hopes that you would marry me instead*?

"Why, bless these mourning blacks," said Lily, inspecting herself. "Grass can't stain them."

This change of subject meant Lily was washing her hands of Florence's woes for the present, her sister supposed. For the day, at least. It meant that Lily decided she had done her duty in voicing her concerns, had met with failure (again), and now could turn her attention to more fixable matters like grass stains.

As she helped her sister up, Florence thought she ought to be glad of the reprieve, but she was not. No—she was conscious of disappointment. A most un-sensible, un-prudent disappointment.

Because, would not Lily have insisted a little longer, if she thought Mr. Fairchild returned Florence's feelings? Would she not have said, "Florence, it is not only your heart and future at stake—you must think also of Mr. Fairchild. Do you care nothing about breaking *his* heart?"

Yes. She would have, if she thought Florence was indeed endangering Mr. Fairchild's heart.

Florence was certain of it.

Lily would have thought it too delicious if there were two hearts involved.

Which must mean she did not, in fact, think that.

Not that I should even be wondering such a thing, Florence reprimanded herself savagely. *It's no business of mine. Even if he took any interest in me, I just said it would be dishonorable of him to mention it because I am engaged and have no intention of breaking my engagement!*

Then why did it feel like, left unasked, the question might burn a tiny little hole in her?

CHAPTER SEVENTEEN

**She starched up her behaviour with
a double proportion of reserve.**
**—Tobias Smollett, *The Expedition of Humphry
Clinker* (1771)**

R obert Fairchild waited outside the George Inn for the
coach from Southampton to deliver the new governess Miss
Dorothea Dunn. He had debated whether he should personally
deliver Miss Dunn to Hollowgate. On the *pro* side, he had promised
as much in his letter to her; on the *contra,* nearly a week had passed
since he saw Miss Ellsworth, and the less he saw of her, the sooner
he would get over his unwise attachment.

I will send Hents, he told himself one moment. And the next:
Don't be a fool. If you cannot inure yourself to the woman, you can

hardly continue to serve the family. She will remove to the rectory soon enough.

He might not have seen Miss Ellsworth in recent days, but he had seen her surroundings, as it were, having been summoned to Whisp Cottage to discuss the draft Mrs. Whisp proposed to send her relations. Fairchild had hoped he might conduct his business with the widow entirely on the Parchment Street premises, but he could think of no polite refusal to her request to come. Thus his walk that afternoon took him past both Hollowgate and Gregory's rectory, but, like Joshua obeying the Law of Moses, Fairchild turned neither to the right nor the left.

To his relief, Mrs. Whisp did not receive him alone. She had some sort of ancient servant woman named Hubble to function as a companion and ensure the proprieties were observed, though Fairchild, after addressing the woman more than once, suspected Hubble heard and saw little that went on around her.

"This will do very well," Mrs. Whisp said with satisfaction, holding up the altered copy, after they debated her suggested emendations. "Very well indeed. And now, before you go, I insist on giving you an afternoon's nuncheon. No, no—don't refuse me! I really do desire your opinion on my cook, Mr. Fairchild, because I wish to invite guests to my little home at some point. I haven't room to give a ball, but with the Ellsworths in mourning that would be out of the question in any case. I do hope they might still play cards and hear a little music. What do you think? It is only Miss Ellsworth's opinion I fear. She might disapprove of card parties for mourners—she can be somewhat severe, don't you think?"

Fairchild only said, "I will give my opinion on your cook. Thank you."

As a bachelor accustomed to eating alone from a tray his landlady Mrs. Archibald left outside his door, he found himself enjoying the pheasant pie and the easy, undemanding company of Mrs. Whisp (and Hubble). Perhaps because of their business relationship and because she knew him to be of humble means, Mrs. Whisp smiled and laughed and chatted without (much) flirtation, and the visit relaxed him, to his surprise.

He would have walked back to town in good humor, but for one insignificant remark she made in parting: "Yes, I will think more about a card party. It might be too much of a bother. But I consider myself fortunate to have landed among such pleasant people. Good-looking, too, for the most part! I know everyone in Winchester thinks Miss Lily Ellsworth carries all before her, but a word must be said for her older sister. Miss Ellsworth may be quieter and a little daunting to a flibbertigibbet like myself, but I cannot help thinking it is those very qualities which make her sometimes blaze forth in a rare beauty. What would you say, Mr. Fairchild?"

With a muttered "you had better be the judge of that," he made a quick escape.

At exactly the appointed time, the Southampton coach passed through the West Gate and rattled up the High Street, and no sooner had the coachman pulled up before the George than a trim woman of perhaps thirty, with dark hair and eyes, descended and glanced about her. There was something about the set of her shoulders—the way she squared them—that reminded him suddenly of little Miss

Beatrice's remark, that Miss Dunn seemed sad to her. Well, who wouldn't be sad, to leave home and family and enter a life of servitude to strangers? At least she would find the family kind and cheerful, and Miss Dunn might yet live to rule them all as the fourth Mrs. Ellsworth.

Fairchild stepped forward, removing his hat. "Good day. You must be Miss Dunn. I am Robert Fairchild, the Ellsworths' attorney. Have you much baggage?"

"Not much," she replied calmly. "Woolston is not so very distant that I cannot send for my heavy winter clothing later."

"Yes, I am aware. I myself grew up in Southampton proper, on the other bank of the Itchen."

The coachman slung down two bags, one fairly light and one which might have lamed Fairchild for life, had it landed on his foot.

"Books," explained Miss Dunn, with a gleam of humor. "I can carry that one, if we are going to walk."

"Nonsense," he returned, reminded of Miss Ellsworth asking if the sacks of damsons were too much for him. Taking hold of it without allowing even a muscle of his face to twitch, he settled it on his shoulder. "It is a stroll of fifteen minutes or so, but we can easily hire a cart if you prefer."

Another gleam. "If you are certain it is not too much, I actually would prefer the exercise. We shall walk and talk of Southampton."

"She is here!" cried Beatrice, careering down the staircase from her first-floor lookout.

"Good heavens, darling, be careful," Florence tried to calm her. Removing her apron, she hung it up and began to tidy her youngest sister's hair. "Boots," she added to the maid, "please summon Mr. Ellsworth to the morning room to welcome Miss Dunn."

There was no need to call Lily, who had been practicing her music and hastened to shut the key lid on the pianoforte as soon as she heard Beatrice's announcement.

"How fortunate that she arrives while Minta is at school," Lily observed, when the three sisters took their seats in the yellow-papered morning room and ordered Snap to his bed. "We may at least begin Miss Dunn's time without bloodshed. Here, Beatrice, take your sampler, that Miss Dunn may see your sewing."

"Should we lock Snap up?" wondered Florence. "Suppose he takes one of his irrational dislikes to her?"

Lily shook her head. "If he does, it would be better to know at once, that we may determine how to deal with it."

Florence's solicitude was unnecessary, however, for Miss Dunn entered with Mr. Fairchild, whom Snap had adored from the first.

Mr. Fairchild! Why had Beatrice not mentioned that Miss Dunn was not alone? The terrier sprang up instantly to dance on his hind legs before the man, yipping in delight, and Florence realized, half in dismay and half in amusement, that she would like to do much the same thing. It seemed very long since she had last seen him.

Thankfully all attention centered on the new arrival, and Mr. Ellsworth's appearance directly behind them ensured that any awkwardness between Florence and the attorney went unnoticed.

"Miss Dunn, you are most welcome to Hollowgate," declared its lord and master with a sweep of his arm.

"Mr. Ellsworth, I am very pleased to make my home here and look forward to beginning my duties immediately," she replied with equal formality.

"Please, be seated. I hope your journey was smooth?"

"It was at least brief, sir, and Mr. Fairchild so helpful in making the preparations and seeing me the rest of the way here. Quite a pleasant walk from town." There was a little curl to the corner of her mouth, and Florence wondered what amused Miss Dunn in the latter comment. She could not have guessed that the governess was adding inwardly, *A pleasant walk, that is, if you aren't the one carrying twenty pounds of books.*

Mr. Fairchild not only hit on what Miss Dunn was thinking but grinned himself, throwing Florence into further confusion. Had something happened between the two of them, as they walked from town? Something funny? And—and secret? For neither one said anything more before Mr. Ellsworth spoke again.

"Yes, Fairchild is my right-hand man," he proclaimed, beaming upon the man as if he were a gold mine his own efforts had discovered. "But I hope you will find Hollowgate pleasing as well, Miss Dunn. For my equally capable Florence has taken measures to prepare for your arrival. Tell her, Flossie."

"Er—well, it has been some time since the little schoolroom on the first floor has been used, but Lily and I made sure it would be ready for you—clean, supplied."

"Actually," said Lily to Miss Dunn with conspiratorial mischief, "I didn't lift a finger."

"And now you have missed a second chance to serve your sister," the latter replied smoothly, "in not allowing her to make light of her efforts by giving you half the credit."

Lily's mouth made a little O, and she had not much more to say. In her desire for a chaperone to accompany her to dances, she had not given thought to what it might mean if that chaperone proved highly acute.

"I helped Flossie hang pictures in your room," whispered Beatrice at Miss Dunn's elbow. "I told her if they were crooked. And this is Snap." (She pointed at the terrier, who had returned to his cushion, but who watched the proceedings jealously.)

"Thank you, Beatrice. And, yes, I remember Snap. He bit one of your guests when I was last here."

"You needn't fear him," Mr. Ellsworth assured her. "If he takes a dislike to you, you need only kick him away."

"Papa!" protested Beatrice.

"I had better introduce myself, then," Miss Dunn said solemnly. "To see if he would prefer to be petted by me or kicked. Will you call him over, Beatrice?"

The little girl held her breath but obeyed, and, to everyone's relief, Snap merely sniffed at Miss Dunn's ankles and then trotted back to lie down.

"He is reserving judgment. Wise pup."

"Miss Dunn," Mr. Ellsworth began again from his position by the mantel. Taking hold of his lapels, he prepared to give a Speech. "It would be best to set expectations at the outset. Despite what you might assume, from the ancient splendors of our home, we

Ellsworths are an informal family. We dine together and spend our evenings together—even young Beatrice joins us. To be frank, many in your position would be expected to occupy an intermediate place, considered neither fish nor fowl. But as you are to be Lily's chaperone and, when Florence is married, Lily's companion, it seems fitting that you should mix freely with us within the house and, indeed, dine with, and spend your evenings with, the family."

"So kind of you," replied the governess. "Such an honor and indication of trust. But regretfully I must refuse. I am *not* a member of the family and would not feel comfortable behaving as if I were. Therefore I will take my food in my rooms. If I am needed in the evenings as Beatrice's governess or to accompany Miss Lily, I will of course be present. Otherwise I will keep to myself. But I thank you for the offer."

Mr. Ellsworth sputtered with surprise, and Lily and Florence could not help but gawp at each other. The effrontery! The governess had spoken with all politeness, but hers was no demurral spurred by modesty. She really did intend to refuse. As if she thought it wiser to keep both her employer and her employer's family at a distance. Was it a stratagem on Miss Dunn's part? Would keeping to herself even be possible?

Florence bit her lip. She had come so far in her attitude toward her father remarrying that she freely hoped for Miss Dunn over Mrs. Whisp. But Papa required a certain amount of flattery and eagerness to please, if he were to be won—at least, if he were to be won away from Mrs. Whisp, who already had the start of the governess.

Mr. Ellsworth required several attempts to recover his equanimity, while his daughters watched with trepidation.

"Ah, Miss Dunn," he said at last, "your humility does you credit. Credit indeed." With a magnificent effort, he hoisted his beatific smile aloft again. "But you will dine with us. And spend your evenings with us."

"Is that a command, sir?"

Miss Dunn asked this in her usual crisp voice, without a hint of defiance, but the words were bad enough, in Florence's opinion! In her alarm she glanced at Mr. Fairchild, and he raised his eyebrows in sympathy. (He had, in fact, just been thinking he might have to walk Miss Dunn straight back to town and put her on the return coach to Southampton.)

That little gesture of his—that little moment—somehow filled Florence with comfort. Yes, he knew her papa well enough by now to recognize that Miss Dunn was treading on eggs. And he knew her, Florence, well enough to guess at her panic. But it was the sympathy she treasured, the mutual understanding. If he could never be more to her than a friend, how she would value that friendship!

"Papa," she broke in, buoyed by new confidence, "we must not overwhelm Miss Dunn at the very outset. We are a new place and a new situation and a large new family. It will all take some getting used to. If she is not comfortable straight off with our informality, why do we not give her more time to become comfortable?"

Mr. Ellsworth frowned, but when he did not dismiss the idea at once, Florence pressed on. "And with so much to accustom herself to, Miss Dunn will need moments for repose. Perhaps if she dined with us on occasion—mutually convenient occasions—and spent those particular evenings with us...?"

The company waited for his verdict with bated breath. Clasping his hands behind his back, the patriarch paced the width of the room twice, the frown still marring his brow. Miss Dunn cast down her eyes but did not give any ground or betray apprehension.

At last he stopped beside the mantel again, propping an elbow upon it and turning to face them. There was no serene smile this time, but at least his brow was smooth again. "You see what good sense my Florence offers, what *consideration for the feelings of others*. Very well, Miss Dunn, we will grant you your shyness and your repose at present, with the understanding that, after a period or if the occasion calls for it, we may request your company."

She bowed her head. "Thank you, sir. Both Miss Ellsworth and you are indeed very considerate."

Her concession restored some of his satisfaction. "Ahem. Very well, then. I suppose you will want to see your rooms and settle before you begin lessons with Beatrice. As I will not see you at the dinner table, Miss Dunn, I will merely say that, if needed, I am easily found during the day in my library, whither you will excuse me now."

"I had better be going as well," said Mr. Fairchild, taking up his hat.

"And Beatrice and I will gather the servants to meet you, Miss Dunn," announced Lily. Amazed by the new governess' backbone in standing up to Mr. Ellsworth, Lily had decided she liked the woman. Therefore, if Miss Dunn thought Lily could be more helpful to

Florence, Lily wanted to show she took the recommendation to heart. Grabbing Beatrice's hand, she marched her off toward the kitchen.

When Florence and Miss Dunn followed Mr. Fairchild to the entrance, the governess thanked him again for his assistance.

"I suspect," he replied dryly, "you would have been more than capable of managing on your own."

"Oh, you had your uses, Mr. Fairchild."

Once more Florence had the feeling of the secret between them, and her spirits, which had risen, sank again.

But Mr. Fairchild turned to her, saying, "And well done, on your part, Miss Ellsworth, for handling the delicate question of Miss Dunn's personal time."

A smile blossomed on her face, accompanied by faint color. "Well, even the new boys at Winchester are allowed two weeks before they have to start fagging for the prefects, Tyrone tells me. Speaking of which, have you heard from your nephew, Mr. Fairchild? I hope he is well."

"I have not heard otherwise," he answered. "He will have a half-day at Michaelmas, and I expect I will see him then."

"Why does he not come to Hollowgate?" Florence asked impulsively. "Boys are given the whole day, if they are invited by friends in the country, and Tyrone has managed to convince the school that fifteen minutes down the Romsey Road qualifies as the country."

He chuckled but hesitated all the same. "That is very kind of you—"

"And you must come too, of course," she added, her color deepening. "I do not mean to deprive you of your nephew's company."

When he still paused, she grew further flustered. "In any event, it is a holiday, and we will have a goose for dinner, and you are both welcome, if you choose. I will tell Tyrone to invite Paul, but Paul need not—he need not—"

"I will accept on his behalf," interrupted Fairchild quietly. "Thank you, Miss Ellsworth. And good day to you both."

His acceptance of her invitation was hardly a comfort to Florence, his face had been so downcast.

"Oh, dear," she said with some embarrassment, when only she and the new governess remained in the entrance. "After successfully helping you get some time and space away from all of us Ellsworths, Miss Dunn, I seem to have done the precise opposite with Mr. Fairchild. He likely looks upon us as work. I should not have insisted—should not have forced us upon him—if he was reluctant to come."

Miss Dunn took in her companion's pretty, chagrinned countenance and nodded to herself.

"I do not think he was so reluctant to come, Miss Ellsworth," she observed.

And, indeed, that might have been the problem.

CHAPTER EIGHTEEN

Mamilius: Merry or sad shall't be?
Hermione: As merry as you will.
—Shakespeare, *The Winter's Tale*, II.i.627-8 (c.1611)

Florence sent Tyrone word that he was welcome to invite schoolmates for the Michaelmas holiday, including little Paul Tillwood, but when her brother appeared that Monday morning, having tramped along Canon Street and St. James Lane, open book in hand, he was alone.

"Did little Paul not want to come?" she asked, once he had submitted to her embrace and drawn up a chair to a heaping plate of favorite breakfast foods.

"He said was going to visit his uncle Mr. Fairchild," her brother answered through a full mouth.

"Then we will see him later, for I invited Mr. Fairchild and his nephew for our Michaelmas dinner, along with Uncle Charles and Aunt Jeanne."

"How has school been, now that you're a mighty third-year junior?" prompted Lily, when Tyrone took another ambitious bite. "Have you been beaten less?"

"Much."

"And done a little beating yourself?" asked Minta eagerly.

"Much."

"Tyrone!" Florence scolded, but her brother's grin gave him away. She tossed one of Wilcomb's light breakfast rolls at him. "Shame on you. But tell me—how has little Paul fared? Did he get a good tutor, a nice boy?"

Tyrone's face darkened, and he grunted. Chewing thoughtfully he took his time. "We-e-ell...Rayburn isn't very big or strong, at least."

"What do you mean, 'at least'?" demanded Florence.

"And he does keep *other* boys from thrashing Tillwood," he went on, observing neither Lily's warning frown, nor Minta drawing a finger across her neck to encourage him to shut up. "But that's mostly because he doesn't trust them to do the thing properly."

"You mean he beats the boy himself?" Florence cried, horrified. "He's meant to teejay him, and instead he beats poor little Paul?"

Realizing his mistake, Tyrone straightened and added hastily, "Not hard. Like I said, Rayburn isn't much. About this tall, with his hat on, mind you—" he held a hand an absurd three feet off the ground "—and ill-built. When he's not around, all the juniors call him Rawbone."

"I don't care a jot what they call him," retorted his sister, "if he uses his position of authority to torture someone smaller and younger—"

"No, really, Floss, Tillwood is *bigger* than Rawbone," Tyrone tried to stem the tide. "Younger, yes, but not smaller—"

"—Who cannot defend himself because of—of school traditions!"

Minta rolled her eyes and threw up her hands, while little Beatrice looked from Florence to Tyrone with wide eyes.

"Can he change tutors, Tyrone?" Florence pressed.

"No."

"Then could you or the other boys intervene when Rayburn bullies him?"

"*No,*" insisted Tyrone. "That is not how things work. Tillwood just has to take a pummeling now and then, and it'll all be over soon." He shoveled another bite into his mouth, in hopes that his sister would leave off, and though she made various huffing and sputtering sounds, after a pinch from Lily and a change of subject from Minta, she did. But she was not happy about it, and she determined in her mind that she would do her best to indulge little Paul when he came and ensure that his uncle knew what he was subjected to.

She had not seen Mr. Fairchild since Miss Dunn's arrival nine days earlier, and Florence felt the time had done her good. She had helped Wilcomb with preserving some of the autumn fruit and with salting the meat which had been slaughtered; with the gardener Barney's help, she had begun clearing the decaying vegetation in her garden; and she and Lily had gone for walks to town to shop or visit or attend the market. By being always in company, Florence had lately been spared Mr. Gregory's more particular attentions (though he himself was occupied with collecting tithes and planning the following year's crops), and as a result she felt more kindly toward him and could even enter the discussion of his plans for the glebe land with interest.

Not only this, but when she called at the parsonage, the dean and his wife Dr. and Mrs. Fellowes had been there, the dean to meet with Mr. Gregory and the dean's wife to pay her regular call.

"Dean Fellowes sings Mr. Gregory's praises, I must say," the dean's wife told Miss Gregory with a smile. She was a rosy woman of seventy years or so, whose round cheeks reminded Florence of Gilliflower apples. "So responsible and dependable! Not only with his parish, of course, but also in diocesan matters. Dean Fellowes says Mr. Gregory has none of the sad tendency so prevalent nowadays to neglect his duties while collecting his tithes. There are those, as you know, who refuse altogether to do their duties, while still enjoying the benefits. I refer, of course, to Mr. Edgar Whisp, who has not been in Winchester to fulfill his obligations as prebendary these many years. What does his daughter-in-law have to say for him?"

Florence and Miss Gregory glanced at each other.

"Mrs. Whisp says her mother-in-law continues to suffer from rheumatism," replied Miss Gregory, "thus keeping them in Weymouth. For the sea bathing."

"And somehow that prevents the prodigal prebendary from serving his one month per year in residence?" The dean's wife shook her head with a sigh, but soon enough her native cheerfulness returned. "Never mind. That has nothing to do with Mr. Gregory's goodness. And Miss Ellsworth, I cannot tell you how pleased I have been to hear of your engagement to him. I am sure you will make an admirable clergyman's wife."

This unexpected praise from so prominent and respected a woman struck Florence to the core, and she felt calm about her forthcoming union for the first time in months. It *was* the right decision. It *was*. Only see how she had chosen wisely and how her marriage would improve the Ellsworths' reputation! It might even wholly offset whatever damage a fourth marriage might do to her father.

Thus reassured, she had even borne with equanimity Mrs. Whisp's several calls at Hollowgate, for which Mr. Ellsworth always seemed to be present, despite otherwise being constantly with Mr. Falk, settling the quarterly accounts.

Florence had not forgotten Mr. Fairchild altogether, however. Though she saw the governess Miss Dunn only a few times in passing, each time she remembered the woman's little humorous interchanges with the family attorney and wondered about them anew. *She is older than he is. And what would they live on?* But she had to admit Miss Dunn continued pleasant, and Beatrice already loved her. It was at Beatrice's insistence that Florence invited Miss Dunn to join them for Michaelmas dinner, but she was not sorry when the governess politely declined.

"But I will join you in the evening, if I may," Miss Dunn added. "For Beatrice and I have been working on a little piece on the pianoforte she would like to present." Florence acceded to this, and there matters lay.

By the time Mr. Fairchild and his nephew arrived, the Gregorys and the Charles Ellsworths were already gathered. The two Ellsworth brothers side by side were a sight to behold. Both tall, lean, and bald, the elder William's assumed suavity of manner made him seem even older, compared to his younger brother's easy good humor. And while William Ellsworth made a perpetual show of family harmony, it was Charles Ellsworth who bounced Beatrice on his knee and teased his nieces and nephew.

"Fairchild!" Charles Ellsworth cried, when the attorney appeared in the drawing room. "We thought of calling for you at Mrs. Archibald's when we set out, but Jeanne said your nephew shouldn't be made to walk with strange grown-ups on his half holiday."

Florence's eyes had flown to Mr. Fairchild when he entered (she could not seem to help it), but at her uncle's words, her gaze traveled to Paul, trying to determine how much damage had been done to him. The small, nervous-but-happy boy she had met at the gate of the school was now thinner, hollower. But was that a result of suffering or merely adjusting to school food and not getting quite as much to eat? (Tyrone had told her first years sometimes did not have much time to eat, being rushed hither and yon in service of the prefects.) He looked glad to be there and even gave a shy nod in Tyrone's direction, and Florence wished they could stuff him with enough food at one dinner to fill him out again, poor thing. But they could make his evening as enjoyable as possible, she determined, and she absolutely, somehow, would speak to his uncle about his welfare and the horrid Rayburn.

There was no chance at dinner, however, as the conversation was often general, and Mr. Fairchild was separated from her by her aunt. Despite her concern for little Paul and the flutters she felt at seeing Mr. Fairchild again, Florence enjoyed the meal. Her aunt made an effort to converse with Mr. Gregory, asking him questions about church matters, to which he replied with a minimum of ponderousness (perhaps knowing she wasn't truly interested). The twins teased and laughed and chattered, glad to see each other again, though neither would have said so. And best of all, with neither Mrs. Whisp nor Miss Dunn present, Mr. Ellsworth had nobody with whom to play the gallant at his end of the table. He must converse like a rational man with his brother or faded Miss Gregory or his children. At one point during the meal Mr. Gregory's foot did sidle over to rest alongside Florence's own, and she left hers there a moment before leaning toward her aunt and shifting away. But it was a good sign, was it not, that she didn't mind the contact so *much*?

As soon as the women and children left the gentlemen to their port, and a servant was dispatched to request Miss Dunn's company, Lily pounced on Florence.

"Floss, may we not have dancing? It is only us, really—the family and the Gregorys, who may as well get used to us, and Mr. Fairchild."

"Oh! I don't know about—"

"What a lovely idea," Jeanne Ellsworth seconded. "I should like to dance. It has been too long. Wouldn't you like to dance, Miss Gregory?"

The rector's sister glanced at Florence. "Oh—I rarely dance. I can't think when the last time was."

"Then the last time must be tonight," pronounced Florence's aunt. "Lily is right, Florence. There is no harm in a family party. You must not overthink this. Tyrone! Minta! Help us move the furniture. Everyone can take a turn playing."

Miss Dunn entered the drawing room to find every chair, sofa and table pushed up against the walls, and everyone gathered around the pianoforte, looking through the sheet music, picking out tunes on the keys, or—in the case of Miss Araminta and Miss Beatrice—dancing.

"Miss Dunn," Florence hurried forward, her face pink. "You see we are going to have an impromptu dance. I hope you don't mind."

"On the contrary, Miss Ellsworth. It will give Beatrice an opportunity to practice," the governess replied. But there was a catch in her voice. "Nor can we have Miss Lily grow entirely rusty because of this period of mourning."

"Yes. Oh, thank you," said Florence, smiling uncertainly. "We will all take turns playing for the others. Those of us who can play an instrument, I mean. But do allow me to perform some introductions..."

When the gentlemen rejoined them, Miss Gregory and Lily were playing a duet on the pianoforte, the sound competing with Tyrone's performance of The Barley Mow, whose steps Jeanne

Ellsworth was demonstrating to little Paul, with much help from Minta, while Florence and Miss Dunn instructed Beatrice.

"Ah, dancing, dancing!" cried Mr. Ellsworth, clapping his hands. "Lily, do stop with that ruckus or else accompany Tyrone. Miss Dunn, would you do me the honor? We will need two more couples! Who will join us?"

Before Florence could think to look at Mr. Gregory, to see if he would dance, her hands were seized by her Uncle Charles, and he was pulling her into line. Her aunt Jeanne and Minta made the third couple, and then they were whirling and clapping and circling, having too much fun for Florence to be anxious.

"*I* am the boy, Minta, not you," laughed Jeanne. "You go left. *I* am the boy!"

After the romp ended and her uncle deposited by her intended's side, Florence was pink and breathless. When Mr. Gregory took her hand, she turned eagerly—he was going to dance!—but then he only said, "Charming, my dear. Charming. Will you play for the others now?"

Her face must have fallen because her aunt was beside her in the next instant. "*Mais non*, Mr. Gregory! My niece cannot play just yet because she must partner me next, and you know I myself cannot play, so I must be so selfish and dance every dance."

Florence did dance with her aunt. She danced and smiled, but inside she was aware of a rent in the fabric of her pleasure. So Mr. Gregory did not dance. Was it from disapproval, because the Ellsworths were still in mourning, or did he never dance? Mr. Fairchild was not dancing either, but she could see his foot tapping as he leaned down to his nephew and pointed things out to him. If Mr. Fairchild did not participate, it was not disapproval that restrained him. She suspected it was his position in relation to the others, and she wished ladies were allowed to ask gentlemen to dance. Then she might snatch moments to speak to him about Paul, in addition to the pleasure (for she was certain it would be a pleasure) of stepping through the figures with him.

When the second dance was ended, Florence took Lily's place at the pianoforte, and she could have kissed Aunt Jeanne when she saw her next accost Mr. Gregory! He could hardly refuse, and he did not, bowing awkwardly and stumping out to take his place.

"The Black Nag," called Aunt Jeanne, but Florence had already selected that sheet music, knowing it to be one of the easiest dances and the first she had learned as a child. Even Beatrice could trip through it with Tyrone. But if Mr. Gregory was familiar with it, he hid it well, and Florence heard "Oop! The other direction," and "No, no, Mr. Gregory—*à moi!*" To help him, Jeanne began to call out the figures, and Florence found herself staring harder and harder at the music so that she would not have to see him make wrong turns or trample feet. She was staring so hard, in fact, that she was not aware of Mr. Fairchild until he was standing beside the instrument.

"You play well, Miss Ellsworth."

"Thank you."

"And dance well," he added, almost reluctantly.

She looked up then, from the music, her expression almost defiant. "Do *you* dance, Mr. Fairchild?"

"I—rarely have occasion. But I like it very much."

Turning her eyes back to the music, she nodded to herself. *Of course* Mr. Fairchild would dance and like it very much, and Mr. Gregory would not. Not that she knew whether Mr. Fairchild danced any better than Mr. Gregory. She supposed it was possible to love dancing yet be wretched at it.

But she must put her frustration aside for the moment because she did not know if the evening would afford her another opportunity to speak with Mr. Fairchild about his nephew.

"Has little Paul enjoyed his half-holiday in town with you?" she asked, her fingers not missing a note.

"If he did not, I don't know what may be done, for we visited the booksellers, observed various animals, and stuffed ourselves at Flight's before coming here."

"I am glad of it," she replied. "For I think he appears thinner than when term began. Did—you ask him if he is happy? Because he might be having difficulties."

She did not see his grin, but she could hear the amusement in his voice. "Miss Ellsworth, when your brother Tyrone was a first-year junior and experiencing those trials you once recounted to me the day I met you, did he voluntarily tell you of such things?"

"Well—no."

"How then did you learn of them?"

"I—I suppose I pried them out of him," Florence admitted.

"Exactly. And you are an older sister whom he considers somewhat in the light of a mother. But I do not appear in that light to Paul. I am an uncle whom he—admires—and he does not want to complain to me or be thought weak."

They both glanced toward the boy in question, whom Minta was laughingly prodding and pushing, in order to teach him the steps of the dance.

"I do see," Mr. Fairchild continued, "how this time spent in a family—in a merry family such as you Ellsworths—is delightful to him."

"I hope so," she answered doubtfully.

"I know I always enjoy being with you all," he said, almost unwillingly. "Fanny and I were never especially close or lively together."

"Oh, whyever not?" asked Florence, before remembering herself. She bungled a chord and then added, "Pardon me. You need not say, of course."

"Some of the time I was away at school," he began, but there was something about Miss Ellsworth that made him want to be known by her. "But probably more tellingly, we were not a wealthy family, and there was often...strain at home."

"Ah." She had a picture of him as a little boy, younger than Paul, in a dark, cramped, silent house and felt a tug at her heart, as much for the picture as for awareness that he was confiding in her.

He gave a rueful chuckle. "Let us say it was very, very important that Paul be elected to Winchester. Very important and a very great relief."

Florence frowned at the keys, now regretful for what she had to say. "But Mr. Fairchild—I will make a full confession to you. I asked after him when Tyrone came home this morning, and my brother tells me little Paul's tutor is a brute. I am glad for his scholarship, and

I know you said they must suffer 'corrections' from their assigned prefect, but supposing it goes beyond that?"

"I concede that can be a danger, Miss Ellsworth, but I will say again that what female relatives will peacefully tolerate concerning those they love will not always accord with experience or what it behooves young men to learn."

Biting her lip, Florence shook her head. She wanted to say more, to impress upon him the perils of being subject to a bully, however small and weak the bully might be, but the dancers had gone through the figures of The Black Nag more times than usual, and Florence caught her aunt looking over. Yes—as Mr. Gregory's partner, Aunt Jeanne likely would appreciate matters drawing to a close. Obediently, Florence transitioned into the concluding bars, to spare Mr. Gregory further embarrassment and his fellow dancers further injury.

As soon as the music ended, a buzz of conversation filled the space, but she heard Mr. Fairchild all the same. "I assure you, though, that I will step outside my admired-uncle role and press him on the matter."

Her vivid smile bloomed before she could think to repress it. "Oh, thank you, Mr. Fairchild. It is all I ask! Well—perhaps I might ask one more thing: since you call us a merry family, I wish you might dance, if you like. You would find many willing partners here, and I am sure, in this friendly setting, everyone would welcome your efforts."

There was a tiny pause. Brief, but long enough for Florence to go scarlet. Heavens—he thought she was asking him herself! Hastily, she scrabbled at the loose sheet music. "I can play a favorite if you have one. Heartsease or The Queen's Jig. Or Hole in the Wall..."

Another painful silence followed which Florence thought must have been thirty seconds long but really was only a few heartbeats.

"Miss Ellsworth, if...you count yourself among the 'many' who would partner me," he began in a low voice, "I would consider it an honor."

Her already racketing pulse stumbled here and then took off again in a gallop.

He was asking her to dance!

It would not be wise to accept. Not when she had at last restored herself to something resembling contentment. But then the contentment was already dispelled, was it not? Otherwise, why should she once again be comparing Mr. Gregory to Mr. Fairchild, and why should Mr. Fairchild's nearness discomfit her?

No, it would not be wise. Moreover, there was no need. She had told herself she would mention little Paul's trials and she had done so. Dancing with Mr. Fairchild would only lead to danger and discontent and temptation.

Therefore she was about to refuse, pleading musical duties, when Miss Dunn's appearance forestalled her. "My turn, Miss Ellsworth," she announced. "And it will be a very long turn, I warn you, because I intend to play every dance Beatrice has been learning, including The Black Nag again."

"I have only played one song," protested Florence feebly.

"And played it beautifully," returned the governess, "as well as for twice its usual length. If you will permit me..."

Florence had no choice then but to slide out from the bench while Mr. Fairchild waited. Moreover, she had removed her gloves to play, but before she remembered them, Miss Dunn had taken her place and launched into a sparkling trill on the keys, and Florence did not like to lean past her.

"Come," said Mr. Fairchild, taking her hand. His own were gloved, but Florence shivered at the contact all the same and hoped he did not notice.

Miss Dunn chose Heartsease to begin, and they formed a square with Florence's uncle and Minta, which meant much of the time Florence took her uncle's hand, but there was plenty of hand-holding and arming left and right with Mr. Fairchild, and she felt her breath quicken and her cheeks flush, not only with the exercise. It was just as bad as she expected. She was fearful everyone would see and think—things. Catching Lily's eye as her sister went in hey past their aunt, she knew Lily was thinking things. And as for Mr. Gregory—!

The rector, however, was standing near the pianoforte holding forth on something to Miss Dunn as she played, the circumference of his chest gradually resuming its usual proportions.

At least, thought Florence, *if Mr. Gregory does not like to dance, he will never crush my feet or mangle my fingers or hold me too close in the turns.* Not that Mr. Fairchild was guilty of any of those transgressions—no, Florence was almost disappointed that he was so proper! Her uncle, on the other hand, took great joy in teasing his nieces, gleefully tickling Florence's fingers and wriggling his eyebrows at her when they "fell back" and giving Minta extra spins when he was called to turn her.

Florence and her partner did manage a little more talk as they danced.

"Your father and your uncle are quite different," he said.

"They are. Uncle Charles is admirably suited to his modest life, and I suppose Papa loves to play the grandee."

"What about you? Will you be sorry when you are no longer Miss Ellsworth of Hollowgate?"

"Oh! I—suppose I will miss some things and like others."

"What will you miss?"

Dancing. Though a married woman could still dance. Look at Aunt Jeanne. But would Mr. Gregory want to attend assemblies or balls in the first place?

She compromised: "I will miss evenings like this. Being with all my 'merry' family. It is one thing to live at Hollowgate and another only to visit. And too soon Tyrone and Minta will be grown, and then Bea, and they will do it all without me."

This was a dangerous subject, her future marriage. It must be because she would miss her family that she felt her throat tighten. Moreover, she was glad he did not ask her, "And what will you *like* about leaving Hollowgate?" because then she would have had to fumble and babble and think of something.

As if he read her thoughts, he changed the subject, his gaze wandering back to the pianoforte. "How is Miss Dunn doing? Is she beginning to enjoy the merry Ellsworths?"

Her gaze following his, she remembered Mr. Fairchild's moments of understanding with the governess and felt that unwelcome twinge of dismay again. Did he ask his question from curiosity or something deeper? The tiny crease that marred her brow deepened when she saw Mr. Gregory beginning to make his way toward her. Trying to keep her voice even, she replied, "Perhaps you had better ask Miss Dunn the question. This is the first time she has joined us all." But then her native sense of justice prevailed, and she added grudgingly, "Though it is also the first time I asked her."

"Well, I hope this persuades her not to hold herself apart." As the music wound to a close, Florence saw his chest rise and fall in a sigh. "Friends and companionship are not so common that we should deny them when they come within our purview. That is, not unless we absolutely must."

His dark eyes met hers briefly. Then he released her hand, bowed to her, and let the rector of St. Eadburh's lead her away.

Chapter Nineteen

It never rains, but it pours.
—Old proverb

The rains came with October, both literally and metaphorically.

"Flossie, my dearest," her father addressed her after breakfast, having called her to his library, "the other night was very pleasant, but I am sorry for more reasons than one that you did not invite Mrs. Whisp to be part of the company."

Florence blinked at him. "Oh, Papa, it was not meant as a slight. I thought the dinner was more of a family occasion."

"Indeed? And how did Mr. Fairchild and his nephew come to be considered family?"

He was not looking at her, fortunately, being occupied with lighting candles to brighten the rain-clouded gloom.

"That was the impulse of a moment, Papa," she answered. "I wanted to invite little Paul Tillwood to Hollowgate when he had a holiday—you know how Tyrone loved to come home in his first year, for those boys never have a moment of quiet to themselves at school—but Mr. Fairchild said Paul would be visiting him for Michaelmas, so I asked them both. A holiday in lodgings is hardly a holiday at all, don't you think?"

"I see, I see. Not that I minded. I am a firm believer in 'the more the merrier.' But Mrs. Whisp is such a pleasant addition to any party. To make up for our oversight, we will invite her to join us this evening for dinner. I believe she likes pork, Flossie. Do tell Wilcomb."

"Yes, sir. Is there—any occasion we are marking?" she ventured.

At that her father straightened, the candle glow lending him the phantom of youth. "It may be an occasion, Florence. I suspect it will. I have been *encouraged* to think it one. But more about that later."

"Yes, sir," she repeated faintly, reaching for the edge of the desk to steady herself. "I—will see about the pork."

It took some cajoling to persuade Lily to a walk in the rain that afternoon, but Florence could not risk the delivery of such important news within the hearing of servants.

"This had better be good," grumbled Lily, as the sisters hurried up Cock Lane, bundled and booted and huddling under a shared umbrella. "I think I deserve a cup of tea at the little place in St. George's Street for being dragged out in this mess."

"Fine," agreed Florence. "And I don't know about good news, but it's news: Mrs. Whisp is coming to dinner, and Papa intends to propose to her!"

Lily jerked to a halt to stare at her sister. "How can you be certain?"

"He as much as told me so in the library this morning." Florence tugged her into motion again, recounting the earlier scene. But if she expected Lily to be outraged or even vexed by the announcement, she was disappointed.

"Well," said Lily, when the story was told. "Is that all? I can't say I'm surprised."

"How can you say that? Lily, he has only known that woman a couple of months! A couple of months of a dinner or two and a half-dozen calls and conversations after church, and now he wants to marry her? Not to mention, Miss Dunn hasn't even had a chance—"

"Miss Dunn *has* had her chance," argued Lily, squeezing Florence close to the wall so they would not be splashed by a passing coach. "It's entirely Miss Dunn's fault that she chose to squander it and keep to herself. Had she come to dinner every evening, as Papa requested, and spent every evening with us, *as Papa requested*, Mrs. Whisp would have been forgotten. She could not have kept pace. Papa has shown himself quite capable of loving anyone under his nose, and I blame Miss Dunn that she neglected to put herself there."

Florence's sigh was lost in the noise of the weather and the traffic of the High Street. Pulling Lily into the doorway of the Black Swan, she gave the umbrella a twirl to spin off the drops. "I know Papa isn't any young lady's dream, but why do you suppose Miss Dunn was so adamant about staying away from him?"

Lily shrugged. "What would you pick? Would you rather be a poor governess in easy circumstances with a position that will last at least ten years, or would you marry the old, rich man whom you didn't especially care for?"

"When you put it like that..."

"What other way is there to put it?" insisted Lily. "Miss Dunn will likely keep her comfortable position even if Papa marries Mrs. Whisp because Mrs. Whisp is not the governessing, stepmothering sort, if you ask me. I suppose Mrs. Whisp will excuse Miss Dunn from taking me to balls and assemblies because Mrs. Whisp will want to flirt with everyone herself, but she certainly will not want to take up teaching Beatrice!"

Florence sighed again. "But Lily, do you suppose it is too late? I would rather Papa not marry again, but if I must choose, I would choose Miss Dunn."

"Well, that is the thing about marrying: one only gets to choose one's own spouse. And look what a mull you've made of that. No, Flossie, we must bear up as best we can. Here is St. Peter Street. I can't remember if Clinton's is nearer this end or the Parchment Street end."

When they turned from St. Peter Street into St. George's Street, they found the narrow passage crowded with umbrellas and pedestrians seeking to avoid the splashing vehicles of the High Street, and they were tilting their umbrella up to squint through rain at the shop signs when another pair of walkers crashed into them, sending the umbrella whirling from Florence's grip.

"I beg your pardon—" the man sprinted after it, leaving his companion to face the Ellsworth sisters.

"Why, Miss Dunn!" breathed Florence.

The governess—for it was she—gave a shaky smile, a wash of scarlet coming and going over her face. She did not look pleased to see them. "Miss Ellsworth. Miss Lily." She held her own umbrella higher, in an effort to shield them as well.

"What are you doing out in this dreadful weather?" Florence asked.

"I was—going to the post office."

"Here you are. My apologies." The man had returned, holding out the umbrella to Florence, and if encountering Miss Dunn had surprised her, to meet Mr. Fairchild rendered her speechless. For it was he, walking and sharing an umbrella with Miss Dunn!

He seemed equally taken aback. His lips parted, but no sound emerged, and his countenance reddened.

Thank heavens for Lily's presence. Lily, who was never speechless and rarely embarrassed. "Why, good afternoon, Mr. Fairchild. Isn't it a wretched day to be out? And yet here we all are! I was just going to say to Miss Dunn that she needn't go for the post in this weather. She might as easily send Bobbins the footman. He is pleased for any excuse to escape Snap's attentions, even if there should be a hurricane out."

"Thank you, Miss Lily," answered Miss Dunn, recovering herself. "But I too like to walk in all weathers, even without the excuse of

Snap disliking me." She turned to Mr. Fairchild. "And I thank you for the use of your umbrella."

"Please—take it," he uttered. "You have a longer walk."

Without another word, she nodded and went her way.

Another awkward silence would have fallen, but Lily forestalled this too. "So chivalrous, Mr. Fairchild! Clearly no lady need fear 'the lightning flash, nor the all-dreaded thunder stone' if you are about."

He gave a short bow (some water running off the brim of his hat). "It was fortunate I happened to be nearby when Miss Dunn's umbrella turned inside out. I hope all the Ellsworths are well?"

Lily threw her sister a mischievous look. "I don't know, Floss—are we?"

"Of course," murmured Florence, her eyes flicking up to Mr. Fairchild's and then away again. But then she took command of herself and looked at him again. "And you, Mr. Fairchild? And your nephew? Are you both well?"

"Thank you. Yes. We greatly enjoyed the Michaelmas dinner, and I sent him back cheerful and—more optimistic about the remainder of the term."

"I am glad to hear it," she said firmly. "And now we had better not keep you out longer in the rain. We wish you good day, Mr. Fairchild."

Bows were exchanged. Florence tucked her unhappiness in her pocket for later perusal, and they went on. The sisters had gained the doorway of the coffee house in St. George's Street, and Lily was closing and shaking out the umbrella when Mr. Fairchild dashed up to them again, his color high and both hat and hair dripping now.

"Miss—Ellsworth," he blurted. "If I might have one more word with you—about Paul—"

"Oh!" Florence, with a wide-eyed glance at Lily. "With me?"

"Yes."

"I'll be inside," said Lily promptly. "You take this." She thrust the umbrella at her sister and vanished into the coffee house.

With an uncertain smile, Florence opened the umbrella again and held it high enough that it might partially shelter them both. "Is little Paul not all right, then?" she asked.

But Mr. Fairchild was shaking his head (sending some little drops flying, if Florence had been able to take note, which she wasn't). "Forgive me, Miss Ellsworth. I just told a lie. I have nothing more to say about Paul than that he very much enjoyed his time at Hollowgate and would probably prefer to visit there than my lodgings on his next holiday."

"He is very welcome. And he need not wait for an invitation from Tyrone."

They gazed at each other, some mysterious urgency in his dark eyes and a wariness in hers. Then he said, "Miss Ellsworth—I—er—would like to say that I am not in the habit of meeting Miss Dunn in town. I—saw her in the street as I emerged from Darby and West. As I mentioned, her umbrella had failed her, and I offered mine."

Yes, he had indeed said that already, and Lily had called him chivalrous. Why did it need saying again? Not that she was sorry to learn his meeting with Miss Dunn was neither planned nor habitual, but Lily would surely have said he was protesting too much.

Florence's brow knit—if it was just a chance meeting, had he then offered to walk Miss Dunn all the way back to Hollowgate? And would he have done so, if the two parties had not collided? For that matter, would Miss Dunn have allowed him to? She, who was so strict in limiting her interactions with the Ellsworths?

Each question seemed to lead to more.

Did Mr. Fairchild's insistence on explaining himself arise from a desire to protect Miss Dunn and her reputation? Or did he tell Florence these things because he knew his activities and the company he kept mattered to her? Mortifying.

Seeing her disquiet, Fairchild cursed the fact that propriety forbade him saying right out what he wanted to say. Not just propriety. There were a hundred reasons—chief among them her engagement to Gregory. He could not come right out and say, *You must not misconstrue appearances. I care for no woman but you, pointless and hopeless as it might be.*

No, even if one were allowed to say such things, she was not free. But he had seen her surprise and dismay in finding him walking closely with Miss Dunn and could not help wanting to vindicate himself. If all he could have of Miss Ellsworth was her good opinion and her friendship, he refused to part with either.

After another pause, Florence replied, "It is like you, Mr. Fairchild, to consider Miss Dunn's reputation. I, too, think highly of her. And your explanation, though unnecessary, is appreciated. But I know that—whatever conditions or appearances might indicate, any—hints of impropriety would never be justified by those who knew your character." Only with an effort did she not roll her eyes at the end of this speech. *Florence Ellsworth! Could you sound any more pompous?*

So disgusted was she with herself that Mr. Fairchild's fleeting grimace entirely escaped her. But his annoyance was not provoked by her speech; it lay squarely with himself. In the moment, to be frank, for all that he liked the woman, Miss Dunn and her reputation were not worth a fillip.

Thus they parted, each dissatisfied and self-critical.

Florence joined her sister at a table in the corner before a brown teapot and plate of buns. Accepting her steaming cup without a word, she took a sip, but it might have been ditchwater for all her notice of it.

Lily waited with what patience she could before demanding, "Well? Was it really his nephew he wanted to discuss?"

"He wanted to say Paul really liked Hollowgate and would like to return," answered Florence, beginning to pick apart one of the buns.

"He might have said that in front of me," muttered Lily.

"And—he wanted to say he had met Miss Dunn by chance."

"Oh-ho! Now, that is interesting, since he already did say that. Do you suppose he repeated himself because he knew you were wondering?"

"Hush, Lily," hissed her sister.

"Hush, what?" Lily hissed back. "How touchy you are whenever I mention him. I confess, when I saw them together, I thought, ah-ha! So that's how it is now, is it? Not that they would have anything to live on! But if I were Miss Dunn, I would surely choose the handsome, humble attorney over the rich old man with five children. Then I thought, I wonder if our dear Mr. Fairchild aspires to become something of a dashing fellow about town. One could hardly blame him, though he would be wiser to make up to a woman with a fortune." Taking the lid off the teapot, she peered inside and then refilled her cup. "But it's curious that he should want to explain himself. I don't know about my dashing-fellow theory in that case. Could it be that he cannot help but look at you wistfully, wealthy and lovely as you are? That he would like to collect your heart, if he could? Though even I, with my suspicious and eagle eye, think you hide your feelings well. Surely *he* has not guessed, has he?"

Florence regarded the bun she had thoroughly pulled to bits.

"And," continued her sister, "if becoming a dashing fellow is indeed his ambition, why then does he not try to collect *my* heart? It's almost insulting. That's why I must comfort myself by thinking he must know he made inroads with you."

There was no use lying to Lily. Lily would have it all out of her, one way or another. "I hope he hasn't guessed my...fondness for him," Florence said slowly. "I don't mean him to guess. I have been more contented with my engagement to Mr. Gregory of late."

Lily gave a humorless laugh and slid away the wreck of Florence's bun. "And if you were any more contented, you would verge on mildly pleased. You haven't changed your mind about Mr. Fairchild, then? Because I think, with a little effort, you could attach him, and never mind Miss Dunn."

"It was the thought of Miss Dunn that made him want to explain himself," said Florence. "He did not want me—us—the

Ellsworths—to think she made a secret habit of walking out with young men. You see? He is honorable."

She sighed as she spoke, and Lily only shook her head at her. "Poor Flossie. You must admit, however, that it's nicer when he is being honorable by you, rather than by other ladies. I, for one, freely confess I will be quite put out if he marries my future chaperone before she can even chaperone me to one evening's entertainment!"

Her little joke was wasted on the downcast Florence, and the outing was not a successful one. A quarter-hour onward, Lily was glad to say, "Oh, look—the rain has stopped for the moment. Let's hurry home in between drenchings. I'll save this bun for Minta and Bea."

The first people to greet them when they were removing their wet wraps and gloves, however, were not Araminta and Beatrice, but Mr. Ellsworth and Mrs. Whisp, her arm drawn through his.

Before he even spoke, they knew. They guessed because of the radiance emanating from him, like the sunlight which had forsaken them that day.

"You must congratulate us, my darling girls," he declared, covering Mrs. Whisp's hand with his free one. "For Ernestine has agreed to be my wife."

CHAPTER TWENTY

She marking them begins a wailing note
And sings extemporally a woeful ditty;
How love makes young men thrall and old men dote;
How love is wise in folly, foolish-witty:
Her heavy anthem still concludes in woe,
And still the choir of echoes answer so.
—Shakespeare, *Venus and Adonis* (1592)

S he's coming again, sir," Hents announced, bursting into the inner office out of breath. "I saw her in the street."

"Who is coming again?" Fairchild asked, rising swiftly from behind his desk.

"The—the fair one."

"'Fair' as in pretty, or 'fair' as in light-haired?"

Fair as in light-haired.

Before Hents could untangle his tongue or his thoughts, Mrs. Whisp had opened the street door and was looking about her. It was a bright afternoon, the brighter for the torrents that fell the previous day, and it took her eyes a moment to adjust to the relative gloom.

"Ah, Mr. Fairchild. How glad I am you're in. Would it be too inconvenient if we talked privately a few minutes? I have much business to discuss..."

His heart returning from his throat to its proper position, he nodded and waved her in. No sooner did he follow her into the inner office than Mrs. Whisp tripped up behind him and shut the door herself, clapping her hands together and giving a gleeful hop. Then, to his further surprise, she laid hands on his arms and drew him toward his heavy walnut desk.

"Mrs. Whisp!"

"I know, I know—forgive my forwardness," she laughed, releasing him and demurely seating herself in the purple-upholstered chair. "It's just that I can hardly help myself! Please do sit down, Mr. Fairchild, and I will explain. I declare, though, you get handsomer each time I see you," she added, favoring him with a charming little pout as he took his seat. "It is too late for me now, but, had you been a wealthier man, I would have tried to catch you. I want you to know that."

"But I am not a wealthier man," he replied evenly. What else was there to say to such a woman, behaving in such a manner?

"Alas. That leaves me only Mr. William Ellsworth, does it not? Unless you can get me my settlement. Then I might almost marry where I please." Her lashes fluttered more expertly than Miss Lily Ellsworth's and nearly as effectively. "Have you received any word from them? About our offer?"

"Unfortunately, I have not heard anything in response to your offer." His emphasis on the word *your* was slight but perceptible. "You may be sure I would have written you in that event." He wanted to pass over her provocations but the temptation was too great. "Do you mean to say that, if you succeeded in getting your settlement, you would have no interest in Mr. Ellsworth, if you are indeed interested?"

Again her delighted laugh. "Mr. Fairchild," she said, leaning forward to rest her elbows on the desk and propping her chin on her folded hands, "as my very confidential attorney, I will reveal to you that, if Mr. Ellsworth were not lord and master of his grand, prosperous estate, I do not think you could find more than five women in England who would show any interest in him."

Fairchild made no reply.

She ventured a look at him under her lashes, her mouth curling again. "I might, of course, set my cap for Mr. Gregory. Rectors receive both small and large tithes, do they not?"

That succeeded in disturbing his unruffled surface. He sat forward abruptly, his color rising. "Mrs. Whisp! Mr. Gregory is engaged."

"Oh? Is he?" she asked in mock innocence, opening her blue eyes very wide. Though Fairchild's desk was substantial, when she leaned to mirror him, their faces were too close for his comfort, and he settled back in his chair, affecting nonchalance.

"Of course I know Mr. Gregory is engaged," she drawled. "Else why would I always see him pawing Miss Ellsworth when he thinks no one is watching?" When she saw him set his mouth, the line of his jaw standing out, she added with a sigh, "I must say, she doesn't seem terribly delighted with her prize."

That got him.

"You think not?" he blurted.

Mrs. Whisp's tinkling laugh rang out again. "You must never mind me, Mr. Fairchild. I talk and talk, and my husband Thomas used to say that I didn't know or mean half of what I said. Who knows what Miss Ellsworth really thinks of Mr. Gregory? He is handsome enough, I suppose, though older. And *such* a respected member of the community. I never go anywhere without being congratulated for being part of his flock. But does Miss Ellsworth love him?" She gave an expressive shrug. "Who can say? Of course, love does not always enter in, does it?"

Turning the conversation required a herculean effort on his part because every fiber of him wanted nothing more than to continue it. And to throttle her.

"You said you had business to discuss," he managed through his clenched jaw.

Maddeningly, her mouth twitched again. "Mm. Such marvelous, marvelous self-control. Mr. Fairchild, I really do admire you and would be in some danger—if I were a woman of means. But I am not." Pulling out her reticule, she unlaced it and removed a letter. "The Whisps did reply to *me*, you see, although my offer came through you. But I will not reply to them."

She slid the letter across the desk for Fairchild to read.

> *4 Frederick Place*
> *Weymouth*
>
> *2 October 1800*
>
> *Dear Ernestine,*
> *Mrs. Whisp and I were amazed and aggrieved to re-*
> *ceive the letter from your attorney. We did not realize*
> *things were come to such a pass that you could no longer*
> *address us directly. Have we not throughout behaved in*
> *a reasonable and loving manner? Have we not sought*
> *to keep both you and Priscilla with us, having lost our*
> *mutually beloved Thomas and thinking it the best for*
> *all involved?*
>
> *Because you have not written, we answer the question*
> *you did not ask: Priscilla is well, as healthy and frolic-*
> *some as we could wish. Every day she speaks more, but*
> *it is only to be expected that, at her tender age, she does*
> *not know to ask for the mother who is absent. Ernestine,*
> *if you return soon, your daughter is still young enough*
> *that she would not even remember you had gone, and*
> *her nature is affectionate enough that you would soon*
> *be dear to her again and she to you.*

We pass over the offer the attorney sent. To pay a fee in return for the permanent guardianship of our granddaughter smacks of the slave market, and surely that cannot be what you intend. To leave your daughter forever! Even if you thought it for the best, the exorbitant terms of your request would lay you open to charges of indifference and cold calculation. As for the deed to Whisp Cottage, how could we sign that to you without doing injury to our remaining children? No. Even were we to agree to a settlement, it could never involve real property but would be limited to monies alone, and certainly no more than a thousand pounds.

You have been at Winchester more than two months now, Ernestine. Please write to us and let us know when we may expect your return.

Edgar Whisp

"What do you think?" asked Mrs. Whisp, when Fairchild raised his head.

He thought he did not much care for either the elder Whisps or his client, but he kept this to himself.

"You see that, after his nonsense about the slave market, he did in fact counter my offer?"

"Yes, I see that. And I remember you were willing to go no lower than three thousand with a life-lease of the cottage. We might perhaps reply at forty-five hundred and the deed, in order to settle at your target."

"No, I think not," was her unexpected reply. "I have decided that I would be willing to accept less if I might have it the sooner."

"Indeed? How much less?"

"Oh, I am feeling generous. You might suggest three thousand by the end of the month, or as low as fifteen hundred by return post!"

Fairchild stared at her, unable to account for this abrupt turnabout. "I—don't understand, I'm afraid. If you would please—tell me what you're not telling me."

She pouted again at this, wanting to prolong her fun. "All business with you, Mr. Fairchild. So beastly! But if you insist on knowing, it is this: I have not much need for the money after all. For, as soon as the banns may be read in St. Eadburh's the requisite three times, Mr. William Ellsworth and I will be married!"

He should not have been staggered. It was only what Miss Ellsworth had feared and predicted, and Fairchild's first thought was for her.

"Well?" Mrs. Whisp prompted him, "aren't you going to congratulate me, Mr. Fairchild?"

"I—am amazed." The word did not begin to express it. It was not the fact of the engagement itself—though the speed of it took his breath away—it was that she would joke about her intended husband so. That she would so frankly admit she did not care for him at all, and that she would make such an admission even as she teased and flirted with another!

"There's nothing at all amazing about it," she rapped back, her jesting demeanor giving way to a grim set of her mouth. "Only men may have the luxury of amazement when a woman marries where she must. What am I to do otherwise than marry? Yes, I might crawl back to Weymouth and play the good bereaved daughter-in-law and receive an allowance for my services! Bah! I would rather throw myself into the waves than do so. Or I might stay here, taking whatever pittance the Whisps hurl at me in their desire to have me gone, and end my days eking out my bad bargain. Equally impossible. Why therefore should it be amazing that I choose instead to enchant whichever gentleman shows a willingness to be enchanted? He is free to withstand me, as you yourself prove. And if he cannot or will not—well—the more fool he, I say."

The Whisps were probably well rid of her, Fairchild thought, and if they knew what was good for them they would accept her terms. It was not that what she said did not have a thread of truth: women in her position had little autonomy without money, but he knew that, if she ever found herself in a similar situation, a young lady like Miss Ellsworth would never make the same choice. Nor would Miss Dunn, for that matter. Miss Ellsworth because she prized her honor too highly, and Miss Dunn because—

Fairchild frowned. Was it honor also that motivated the governess to avoid her employer? There was something about Miss Dunn he did not understand. He was not a vain man, but when he had come upon her in the rain outside the post office, she had been quite flustered. *Rather like Miss Ellsworth is often flustered when I see her*—But that thought had to be put down immediately.

Mrs. Whisp was observing him through narrowed eyes. "You judge me."

Fairchild gave himself an inward shake. "It is not my place to do so, Mrs. Whisp."

"Nonsense. We all judge each other, whether it is our place to do so or not. I suppose you think other women in my place might make different choices. I don't know about that. Take Miss Ellsworth and Mr. Gregory, for instance—"

"We had better keep ourselves to the matter at hand," he interrupted, taking up a sheet of foolscap.

"—Miss Ellsworth may not marry for security, being a wealthy woman herself, but she sells herself all the same. For the security of position. For respect. For the ability to say to herself she will never be a scapegrace like her father, my beloved William—"

"Mrs. Whisp," he broke in again quietly, his hand not quite steady as he dipped the pen in the inkstand, "as your attorney, you are under no obligation to explain your actions to me or to justify them. Therefore we may leave off the comparisons. Let me make sure I understand the terms you would like to offer..."

To his infinite relief, after tilting her head to consider a moment, Mrs. Whisp dropped her analysis of Miss Ellsworth, drawing her chair closer to the edge of the desk in her eagerness. "Yes! Either the three thousand at a later date or the fifteen hundred at once. And you needn't mention my marriage..."

It required several attempts and a fair amount of back-and-forth discussion to couch her proposal in appropriate contractual terms, but after a half-hour's work he sanded and blotted it, assuring her it would be posted that afternoon.

Thinking his deliverance from her company was near at hand, he made to rise from his chair. When she made no corresponding movement, however, he resumed his seat heavily. *Good heavens, what more can there be?* he wondered.

"Mr. Fairchild," she began again, ducking her chin and favoring him with the charming smile once more. "I do have another question for you."

He said nothing—of course he said nothing!—only opening his palms in invitation.

She gave a low, murmuring laugh and then flashed him with her eyes. "I know you are dear William's attorney, of course. And that Darby and West has served the Ellsworths and indeed Hollowgate since time immemorial..." She cleared her throat lightly. "...And now that I will become part and parcel of both the Ellsworths and Hollowgate before the month is out, I think it...appropriate for you to share what settlement William intends to make on me, his bride."

Fairchild only just managed to keep his chin from dropping open. Then he pressed his lips together, arranging one of the files on his desk to give himself time to think. "Mrs. Whisp—I understand your interest in the matter and acknowledge that you have every right to know Mr. Ellsworth's intentions toward you. But I'm afraid he must be the one to impart them. Until you are legally married to him, I must maintain confidentiality toward each party, as I am certain you will appreciate."

"Hmm...I thought you might say as much. Of course, of course. Silent as the grave and so forth. Indeed, I see your point. I would certainly prefer to share my own confidences in my own time."

"Exactly. Thank you."

"No, thank *you*, Mr. Fairchild." Pinning her smile back on, she rose gracefully and began to pull her gloves back on. "I will be on my way. Though—I do have another confidence for you, my dear sir."

He raised inquiring eyebrows as he slid back his chair and got to his feet.

"Two, actually." She made a slow circuit of the room, taking in again the boxes and files and blue bags before stopping directly before him. "The first is that I intend to have my fun before I marry. Are you thoroughly and completely certain you wouldn't like to join me?"

His color rose, but he said nothing.

Mrs. Whisp pressed her lips together in amusement, and she gave his chest a playful push, letting her hand linger an eyeblink there. "Very well, I understand," she sighed. "Oh, you honorable sorts! If you change your mind, do let me know."

She was about to sail through the door he opened for her when he asked, "Did you say there was one more thing?"

"There was," she answered, hardly pausing and not sparing Hents a glance as he scrambled up to get the street door.

She half turned and then threw back over her shoulder, "I'm afraid something will have to be done about that little dog."

CHAPTER TWENTY-ONE

I can no longer deceive myself.
—Ann Radcliffe, *The Romance of the Forest* (1791)

The tumultuous day Florence would remember the rest of her life began innocently enough.

"Miss, there's one other thing," the cook Wilcomb said, when the day's menu had been approved.

Seated at her desk, she looked up from the list Mrs. Whisp had made for redecorating Hollowgate: paper, paint, furnishings. "Yes?"

"I'm sorry to say I had something go missing from my room. A little canvas sack, only about this big." Wilcomb demonstrated with her hands.

"Oh, dear," said Florence, shrinking. "And—what was in the sack, if I might ask?"

Wilcomb shuffled her large, booted feet on the carpet. "Well, miss, I hope you don't mind, and maybe I should have asked beforehand, but I was in the habit of cutting things out of the periodicals, after Mr. Ellsworth finished with them. Not much, just little woodcuts and such. Leaving most of the paper for spills for the fires, o' course."

"Yes, yes," Florence replied hastily, remembering how Beatrice had been found in Wilcomb's room the day Mr. Gregory proposed. Most likely little Bea would know where Wilcomb's sack had got to because most likely Bea had walked away with it! Goodness.

"I will ask around for it, Wilcomb," she assured her. "You may depend on it. I am sorry for the nuisance. And of course you are free to do whatever you like with the papers after Papa has finished with them."

Bobbing a curtsey, Wilcomb withdrew, and Florence was debating when the best time would be to confront Beatrice when the footman appeared. "Er—miss?"

"Yes, Bobbins?"

"If I may..." He approached her, a wad of something in his hands. "My uniform, you see." Shaking the wad out, it revealed itself as a ragged stocking, and Florence saw the foot was dangling by not more than three threads. "I have more stockings, miss, but I thought you should know."

"Oh, dear," she said for the second time that morning. "I suppose...Snap?"

"Yes, miss."

"I hope he did not—do this while you were wearing it?"

"It began that way," said Bobbins with a long-suffering air. "But then I believe the—er—work was finished when he tore it off the line and dragged it away under a bush." Keeping his eyes straight ahead, if he saw Florence's apologetic grimace, he did not acknowledge it. "Under a bush," he repeated, "from whence I was obliged to crawl on all fours to untangle it."

She managed to bite back a third "oh, dear," but it was hard work. "I do apologize for your troubles, Bobbins. Very frustrating, I know. And you have borne with Snap's...antagonism...some time. I wonder if anything might be done to improve your relationship with him...? Perhaps—perhaps if you were the one to give him his food or some little treats?"

"If I must," he replied, his face a blank, and Florence was reminded of Miss Dunn asking, "Is that a command, sir?" when asked to join them at dinner. How hard it must be, to be compelled to do what you did not like to do. And harder still to try to resist it!

"Let me think more about it," she amended. "In the meantime I will purchase additional stockings when I walk into town."

He bowed and left her, Florence convinced as Lily had been that neither terrier nor footman was wholly blameless for their mutual animosity.

With a sigh she returned to her review of Mrs. Whisp's list, but it was not long before she was regarding the wallpaper of the morning room wistfully. It was a good thing after all that she had chosen yellow roses for the rectory's morning room, since Mrs. Whisp wanted Hollowgate's redone in gold stripes. Gold stripes for the morning

room, green scrolls for the main drawing room, and ornate Louis
Seize furniture to replace the simpler Hepplewhite.

"It is a good thing Papa is rich," muttered Florence, shoving the
list into a drawer of the desk. She would hate to see her childhood
home transformed, especially when her Baldric grandparents had
chosen the elements of their setting so carefully, but life was change,
she supposed. Hollowgate would not be her home much longer, and
who knew? Perhaps Miss Gregory felt the same way when Florence
chose new papers for the rectory. The thought made her pause.
"Poor Miss Gregory! She has lived there all her life, since her father
was the rector before her brother. How selfish I was not to think of
it! Why—I won't change a thing, unless she insists. And I will go
over this very afternoon and tell her."

But with the number of her tasks increasing by the minute, she
decided first she must solve the problem of Wilcomb's stolen sack.
She had better talk to Beatrice sooner, rather than later.

Marching up the front staircase, Florence continued up and up
to the second floor where the schoolroom lay. She had never before
interrupted Miss Dunn while the governess was teaching, but she
felt the urgency of confronting Beatrice demanded it.

"Why, Miss Ellsworth," said Miss Dunn, after having bid her
enter. "What a pleasant surprise." Indeed, the two of them had
hardly seen each other since the umbrella collision a week earlier,
and Florence thought that, now that her father was engaged to Mrs.
Whisp, it was unlikely he would ever require the presence of the
governess again.

Both women blushed faintly, and each mistook the reason for the other blushing. Florence blushed to think that Mr. Fairchild and Miss Dunn carried on a secret friendship, and she believed Miss Dunn blushed for the same reason. Miss Dunn had her own reason for blushing, however, which had nothing at all to do with Mr. Fairchild and everything to do with another matter she kept to herself.

"I am sorry to interrupt, but may I borrow Beatrice? In fact, may I cut short her studies today?"

"Of course. Beatrice, we will continue tomorrow. But first—" Miss Dunn stepped into the passage and pulled the door to behind her, leaving them in semi-darkness, so that she seemed a shadowy figure with only a gleam of eyes and teeth. "Miss Ellsworth, if I might have a quick word..."

Florence's heart sank. This would be the third quick word of the day, and she was beginning to dread them. What new problem could be laid at her doorstep? But she said, "Of course, Miss Dunn."

"Thank you. It is the small matter of a few items in my room having gone astray."

More missing items? What on earth was Beatrice about?

"Indeed? I am very sorry to hear it. What manner of items?"

It was hard to be certain in the gloom, but Florence thought Miss Dunn's color deepened. "Oh—little things. A pen-wiper, a pincushion, a—a letter or two from—home."

"I will ask about them," said Florence. "I am sorry you should be so inconvenienced." And then, to show she really did intend to investigate, she added, "It so happens you are not the first to be missing things."

Miss Dunn nodded and thanked her, and then Florence reached past her for the handle of the schoolroom door. "I may as well speak to Bea in here. If you will excuse me."

Beatrice had pushed aside her book and slate and was playing with a pair of paper dolls, but even these she tossed away when her sister entered, hopping up to hug Florence around the waist. "A holiday! Just like Tyrone had."

"Yes. You like your lessons, though, don't you?" asked Florence, returning the squeeze.

"Oh, yes. Miss Dunn is very clever and kind and amusing. Would you like to hear me read to you?"

"Maybe another time, sweeting. I have to ask you something first."

Beatrice looked up at her with no hesitation or anxiety, and Florence did not know whether to be reassured or dismayed. While she did not want her sister to be a thief, she had no idea what to do if Beatrice was *not* the culprit.

"Dearest, you remember that time you were in Wilcomb's room, looking at the pictures she had pasted up?"

Here Beatrice's eyes widened and color did wash over her. "Ye-e-es..."

"Have you been back there since?"

Her little sister shook her head with convincing vehemence. "I never wanted to go back after I got shut inside!"

"Then have you ever happened upon any of Wilcomb's things elsewhere in the house? In the kitchen, perhaps, or the scullery. You might have seen there a little canvas sack?" Bea was shaking her head throughout, and Florence believed her. "All right, then," she sighed. "Never mind. It will turn up. I don't suppose you've found anything of Miss Dunn's either? A pen-wiper or a pincushion or any letters?"

"No, Flossie! Why do you ask? Have all these things gone missing?"

"They have."

"Then I don't know what became of them—honestly I don't. I did once see a letter of Miss Dunn's—it fell out of her pocket, and I picked it up and gave it back to her, and I read the direction to her because I could. It said w-a-t-e-r-s waters and s-s-o-u-t-h—and I guessed Southampton!"

"That is very good reading indeed! Miss Dunn is from Woolston beside Southampton, so I imagine she receives many letters from there."

"They mean a lot to her, I think, Flossie, because she almost snatched it from me and did not put it back in her apron pocket—she stuffed it in her bosom."

But Florence was already imagining what must come next: after asking the rest of the family if they had any idea where the lost things went (a fruitless endeavor, she was sure), she must gather all the servants and do the same thing, hoping someone would step forward with a Perfectly Reasonable Explanation, since a public confession seemed too much to wish for.

Dreadful.

Well—in a few short months predicaments like these would be Mrs. Whisp's problem, and she was welcome to them.

Taking her youngest sister's hand, Florence forced a smile. "All right, then. That settles that. On to the next thing, for now. Bobbins says that Snap has chewed up one of his stockings, in addition to attacking the poor man whenever he enters the drawing room. Shall we go give our naughty pup a talking to?"

At once Beatrice's eyes filled and she began a heated defense of the terrier, which Florence tried in vain to forestall, and when the sisters entered the drawing room where Snap's bed lay, Beatrice hurled herself atop the unsuspecting, napping dog, covering him in kisses.

"Gracious, Bea, what on earth is the matter now?" drawled Lily, hardly looking up from her sewing.

"Snap is in—in tr-trouble!" Beatrice wailed, pressing her little face to the top of Snap's furry head as he tried to writhe around and lick her.

Florence was mid-explanation when the door banged open and Minta flew in, tossing her schoolbooks on the sofa and crowing, "Madame Froissart has a putrid fever, so no French today and they let us go early! Aggie and I are going to—say—what's wrong with Bea?"

Then everything must be gone through again, which only added Minta's loud protests and Lily's loud questions to Beatrice's sobs. In the uproar, Snap wriggled out from under Beatrice's effusions to dash in circles and dance on his hind legs and bark with all his strength, dodging the sisters' combined efforts to catch him and hush him, so that, when their father entered the room, he came upon a scene which taxed even his ability to see and hear only what he preferred to see and hear.

"Mercy! What is happening here?"

"Oh, Papa," breathed Florence, scrambling up from her knees, her hair in disarray. In her arms she held the terrier, who now licked her in congratulations for a game well played. "There is a little fuss today about Snap, I'm afraid. Snap and Bobbins. I may need to move Snap's bed to my room—"

"Snap will *hate* to be confined," objected Minta, "even if he could be kept there. It is all Bobbins' fault for not being kind to him. Dogs can tell if you don't like them—"

"Papa," cried Beatrice, tugging on his sleeve, tears still streaming down her red and puffy face, "can't Snap be in *my* room?"

"Of course he can't," snapped Lily. "If he would escape from Florence's room, he will certainly escape from yours, and you know you aren't fast enough to catch him."

"You're always so unkind, Lily!" Beatrice accused, her cries soon drowned by the chorus of voices (and barks) breaking out anew.

Mr. Ellsworth took one step back. Then he raised a hand for silence, which fell at once, only broken by soft hiccupping, Minta clapping a hand around Snap's snout to muffle his yips.

"My girls," he intoned, "it so happens I have an announcement to make concerning Snap." Seeing their stares, he heroically looked over all their heads and addressed the far wall. "Your new step-mother-to-be Mrs. Whisp has informed me that she has suffered bad dreams since being bitten by our mischievous little dog, and, while she knows how fond you children are of him, and while she hesitates and hates to ask—"

"She asks nevertheless," muttered Lily.

"—She asks if we might find a new home for him. As she points out, Snap himself would be happier in a home where he was not at odds with the inhabitants."

Beatrice managed to stifle her cry, but she had to flee to Florence and bury her face in her skirts to do it.

Even Minta was horrified into contradicting her earlier objection, saying, "Oh, Papa, mightn't we try him in Flossie's room first? If he was confined there and only came out on his leash..."

"You can't mean he must go *now*, Papa," urged Lily. "She does not live here yet and won't until the very end of the month, and we cannot give Snap away when poor Tyrone isn't even here to say good-bye!"

"Ah," their father beamed, "a boy and his dog." He clapped a fond hand on Florence's shoulder and then patted it once or twice. "But it had better be sooner rather than later, Floss, for my dear bride-to-be must be made happy on her visits here. A small price to pay for her pleasant company." Leaning toward the unsuspecting Snap, he tapped the terrier on the head. "'To-morrow to fresh woods, and pastures new,' Snap, my boy."

No sooner had Mr. Ellsworth delivered his bad news and left the room than Minta seized Snap from Florence. "Come on, Bea. We'll hide him where Papa and dreadful Mrs. Whisp can't find him!"

"Dreadful," murmured Florence, sinking onto the sofa beside Lily, who had thrown herself there in disgust.

"Indeed," said Lily. "Who knew anyone could eclipse Mr. Gregory in dreadfulness? But I think I may safely say I look forward to your marriage now more than Papa's. This exile of Snap is not a promising beginning."

"Lily, what do you think of Miss Gregory taking Snap? He loves her, and I think she him. And then, when I am married you all will be coming to the rectory regularly, I hope. So if he cannot be at Hollowgate, at least he could be very nearby. I will ask her, in any event. I was going to walk over there after I tried to settle the other matters."

Lily blew out a sigh. "I suppose there is no great loss without some small gain. If Snap goes to the rectory, at least our first stepmother's ugly embroidered cushion must go with him." Giving a short laugh, she jumped up and scurried across the room to pick up the fur-covered dog bed with its pattern of plum and crimson and yellow flowers.

"Florence!" she shrieked. "Look!"

Florence looked, and there, on the herringbone hardwood floor beneath where the cushion had lain, nestled amidst fur and dust and fluff, was a collection of miscellaneous items: a ball, a dusty stocking, a thimble, twine, a handkerchief—but Lily swept those aside and held up a square canvas sack in one hand and a letter in the other. "Are these what you're looking for?"

"Why, Snap, you naughty little creature," said Florence, snatching the items from her sister and clasping them to herself in joyous relief. Now she need not line up the servants for questioning, nor decide what to do if none of them confessed to the crime!

"Let me sew up the corner of that sack before you give it back," proposed Lily. "For it looks like Snap had a good chew of it."

"Oh, my. I think he had a go at the letter, too," Florence said, "but there's nothing we can do about that."

"'J. Waters,'" read Lily over her sister's shoulder. "I wonder who that could be."

"A Southampton friend, most likely. A dear one. Bea said a letter from a Waters fell out of Miss Dunn's pocket once, and Miss Dunn replaced it in her bosom."

"Ooh," Lily breathed. "A *very* dear friend, then. Let me see that."

"Lily! You can't read it!"

"I'm not going to read it," retorted Lily, holding it up to the light from the window. "I'm just going to be terribly, terribly curious. This might be the answer to the mystery, you know—of why Miss Dunn has never shown any interest in Papa."

"As if one needed a secret reason!"

"Poor, innocent Florence. Of course an impoverished governess forced to make her way in the world needs a reason, if she is to ignore such a handy means of salvation."

"Well, give it back, at any rate. It's none of our business. Now, do you see a pincushion or a pen-wiper?"

That afternoon a much-cheered Florence walked with springing step toward the rectory. What was lost had been found; her sister was not a thief, and neither were any of the servants. If Miss Gregory proved willing to shelter Snap, it would ease the family's grief and resentment considerably. And in return she would tell Miss Gregory that not a jot nor tittle of the rectory's current decorations need pass away.

Florence felt so light-hearted that she would even have borne one of Mr. Gregory's bone-crushing, face-smashing embraces with good humor.

But it was not her destiny to tolerate any more of Mr. Clifford Gregory's vehement regard. Nor was it fated for Florence to settle the question of Snap's future home on that afternoon.

When she reached the rectory doorstep and lifted a hand to knock, she heard a woman's voice carrying on the mild autumn air, though she could not distinguish the words. If Miss Gregory was in her garden, Florence thought, she would simply step around to find her there. There was no need to disturb Mr. Gregory in his study (nor to bear the brunt of her intended's affection if she need not).

Humming under her breath, she skirted the corner of the rectory, surprised not to see Miss Gregory's figure bending over her asters and ranunculus. But one of the long windows was ajar, leading, Florence knew, to the cozy back parlor, and it was through the open window the voice drifted.

Florence wondered who Miss Gregory could be talking to because she did not recall ever hearing such a purring laugh issue from the rector's retiring sister.

And indeed it did not.

When Florence reached the window, realization and perception arrived in one and the same moment.

It was not Miss Gregory she heard.

It was Mrs. Whisp.

And it was not Miss Gregory she saw within but that same Mrs. Whisp.

Mrs. Whisp, intended bride of Mr. William Ellsworth, perched on the knee of Mr. Gregory, intended husband of Florence Ellsworth, the widow's hand slipped in the bosom of his black frock coat and his about her waist, clutching her as close as ever he clutched Florence.

"Mm...mm..." purred Mrs. Whisp, when her lips were not claimed by the rector's. "So vigorous, my darling—ahhh..."

Florence must have gasped. She had no memory of it later, but clearly she made *some* noise because Mrs. Whisp detached herself effortfully from Mr. Gregory with a sound like Bobbins drawing a cork—only wetter—and then her round blue eyes met Florence's through the glass.

Time stretched.

Deprived of the widow's kiss, the rector opened his own eyes and twisted in his seat to follow her gaze. And had Florence been Medusa herself, she could not more effectively have turned him to stone.

But Mr. Gregory's petrification paradoxically released Florence from her own. She backed up a step. And another. And still another, squeezing shut her eyes briefly as if that might change what she had seen.

And then she was running, as she hadn't since she was a young girl.

Running back up the road to Hollowgate.

CHAPTER TWENTY-TWO

**I charge you, O daughters of Jerusalem, that ye
stir not up, nor awake my love, until he please.
— Song of Solomon 8:4,** *The Authorized Version*
(1611)

M r. Gregory caught up to her before she reached the lane.
"Miss Ellsworth—wait!"

They must have been a sight to behold, Florence thought later. She, pale and stunned, her heart galloping with the thousand thoughts warring for dominance in her mind, and he in his clerical frock coat, disheveled, panting, scattered.

She obeyed. Waited. And when he was facing her, they stared at each other, each at a complete loss.

"Miss Ellsworth," he said again. This seemed to be as far as he could get.

And Florence, unable to come up with anything better, replied at random with, "Mrs.—Mrs. Whisp is engaged to my father."

It helped. It gave them a place to begin.

"I know that," Mr. Gregory said in return. For once he did not use his booming pulpit voice. "And—in that context—I cannot explain what just happened."

If all was confusion and distress, at least addressing her father's engagement was easier than addressing her own. "Is she—going to jilt him?"

"I—I don't know. We didn't talk about that. We didn't talk."

"Oh." She saw again in her mind's eye Mrs. Whisp perched on his knee, their mouths and hands occupied. One part of her brain noted idly that she had never before seen the expression now on Mr. Gregory's face; nor did they understand each other well enough for her to interpret it. Was it sheepishness? Mulishness? Chagrin? Some mixture of the three?

Gradually, imperceptibly, her mind's mill race began to slow, and Florence clutched at another spar in the wreckage.

"We—had better not marry, Mr. Gregory," was the first she laid hold of.

His face fell, and his customary woodpigeon puffiness was nowhere in evidence. Perversely, she felt the urge to comfort him. This urge might have been a result of guilt—because no sooner did she voice the idea of ending their engagement than a vast, floating, sparkling, sunlit *something* flooded her. *She did not have to marry him!* She could be free again! Free to marry or not marry whom she pleased—Mr. Fairchild immediately sprang to mind, like a cork bobbing up, and she hastily kicked him away. He had nothing to do with this very moment or this very decision. Because she was not ending her engagement to the rector because she was foolish or frivolous or capricious or careless of her intended's feelings—Mr. Gregory had done all the work himself. Mr. Gregory did not want to marry *her*, and he had demonstrated his unwillingness in the starkest way possible.

It is not my fault, she whispered to herself. *I did not choose folly and dishonor. He did.*

"We had better not marry," she said again, trying not to let her joy become audible. "But—it is not so bad, sir. That is, it is better you discovered your preference now."

But he was shaking his head. Had been since her first declaration. "No, no, Miss Ellsworth—that is just it." Mr. Gregory frowned, as if the thoughts were just emerging from fog as he forced himself to look at them. "I don't think I do prefer her. When she is not directly before me. I—when I am thinking properly, I much prefer you."

"What?" Florence cried, amazed. "This is an astonishing declaration, Mr. Gregory, when but a minute ago you gave every indication of not caring for me at all."

"Yes, I know. I know it makes no sense. But I don't care for Mrs. Whisp that way. Nor do I think she cares for me—not that that is material to this discussion." He looked up, his eyes meeting hers directly. There was a light of discovery in his. "No. Now that I am myself again, I find I don't care for her that way at all. In fact—I have never said this before, Miss Ellsworth, but I—think I—love you."

Florence had often imagined what it would be like for Mr. Gregory to confess his love—the scenes had always been stilted, unnatural, possibly ludicrous—his swelling woodpigeon chest always played an outsized role—but never, never had she pictured this.

"Love me?" she breathed. "You tell me this now? After what just passed? I must say, making love to another is a remarkable way of declaring your attachment to me."

"What just passed will never happen again, Florence."

He reached for her hand, and Florence retreated, childishly putting hers behind her back. The delight which had buoyed her rapidly drained away. "What are you doing, sir?"

The rector remembered himself enough to glance up and down the lane, but, seeing no one, he lunged for her as if he would seize her. With surprise on his side, he would have succeeded, had not Florence taken another step back and landed her boot heel on a rock, thus turning her ankle and dropping in a heap on the ground.

"My dear!" he cried. "Are you hurt?"

Ignoring his extended hand, Florence scrambled up again, dusting herself off. "I am perfectly fine. But I would rather not be embraced, Mr. Gregory. I consider demonstrations of that nature to be at an end between us."

"My dear, please do not say that without first hearing my explanation—"

"What explanation could there possibly be? I find you and Mrs. Whisp—wrapped in each other's arms, and you tell me it is because you don't care for her, you care for me? Credit me with a little sense, Mr. Gregory!"

"No, no, Florence—"

"I think we had better not use each other's Christian names, sir."

"Hear me out, then, Miss Ellsworth," he insisted. "I mean only to say that—when you and I first...embraced, it—awakened—something I did not know existed in me. I could not kiss you enough. Catch you alone enough. When you were not with me, I thought about it, even. To the point that I debated urging you to move forward our wedding date."

Florence's hands flew to cover her face. She could not remember why she wished Mr. Gregory would ever speak to her of such things. It was dreadful. Embarrassing. She would give half her fortune if only he would forbear.

He tapped on her glove. "And yet, even as my ardor awakened, you drew back in maidenly modesty. I do not reproach you for it. Modesty becomes a young unmarried woman. And you must forgive me even for mentioning your reticence thus, but I hope to make myself understood. What I mean to say is, it was your love that taught me to know myself better and not think myself above the common frailties of mankind. A valuable lesson for one in my profession, you know, Miss Ellsworth."

"Mm," mumbled Florence. With an effort, she lowered her hands. "In any event, Mr. Gregory, now that you—know yourself better—"

"What I learned was that I was not above temptation," he forged ahead. "As I said, you drew back—again, for which I do not fault you—just when I found I wanted more. Mrs. Whisp had been calling on us at the rectory for weeks. Purportedly to befriend Miranda, but there was always a—a hint of something else. When Mrs. Whisp at last—presented the opportunity—I fell, I confess. I was weak. I gave way to temptation, though my heart was not in it."

If that was an example of his heart not being in it, Florence hesitated to imagine what enthusiasm would look like. "Mr. Gregory, please," she pleaded.

"Say you understand me, my darling!" He was recovering his customary volume, and she shrank from it. "Say you both understand and forgive!"

If her actions had awakened ardor in Mr. Gregory, his were awakening indignation in Florence. Did the man honestly imagine their engagement could continue under such circumstances? And did he somehow want to lay the blame for his activities on her?

"Mr. Gregory," she responded, her words clipped, "it is not that I do not understand—you found you were—subject to desires as much as the next man. Well, then. And it is not that I do not forgive you—" (Florence found it easy to forgive when she didn't love the man) "—I bear you no grudge. I say that in all honesty. But neither understanding nor forgiveness persuades me to continue an engagement I feel would be...unwise."

On this last word, her eyes widened and her voice grew soft. Wonder silenced her—to think that everything was so topsy-turvy. That marriage to Mr. Gregory now appeared folly and jilting the man wisdom! There would be talk—Florence could not very well go around proclaiming her reasons for ending the match—but it would make all the difference in the world and in her heart that she felt she was doing the right thing.

"Take time, take time," he urged. "You speak in the heat of anger. I will not accept this as your final decision on the matter."

Then she did lose her temper. "How might matters improve with further thought? Mr. Gregory, if you were tempted to—kiss—another woman—an engaged woman, at that, when you and I are not even yet married, what temptations might you face when five years or ten or twenty have taken the bloom off your regard for me? But—no, please, let me speak—it is not only the incidents of this day. If it will help you believe me, I will have you know that I have been struggling with our betrothal for some weeks and perhaps months now." Her mouth twisted wryly. "I thought, sir, that you being such an eminently good and respectable man, I would grow to love you as much as I already respected you. But, while I remain fond of you, I have learned I—do not think I can love you after all. And it is not solely the events of the day which lead me to this conclusion. In fact—I am almost grateful for them, for bringing the matter to a crisis. Who knows if I would have found the courage otherwise."

Florence was not prepared for how low her words brought him. His robust carriage sagged once more, and his crestfallen face looked suddenly years older.

"Then, Miss Ellsworth, it is my feet of clay that have lost me your esteem," he sighed.

There was no kind way to say he had lost it beforehand, so she held her tongue and stared at her boots.

"Miss Ellsworth. May I—that is—would you permit me to try again to attach you?"

"Oh, Mr. Gregory." It was her turn to sigh. "I do not think it can be done. Let us part friends and put this behind us. I wish you every happiness in future."

She held out her hand, and he moved to take it, but then he paused. "If I may ask another question...?"

Florence shifted with impatience, longing to be done and to get away. She gave a short nod.

He drew himself up again, trying and failing to regain his former stature, and stared nobly into the distance. "Miss Ellsworth, I have been plain with you that, my recent actions notwithstanding, my heart remains yours. I hope you will favor me with equal candor. You have—ahem—informed me that I failed to win your affections. May I ask if...anyone else has succeeded where I failed?"

She went scarlet, and there was Mr. Fairchild in her mind's eye to be kicked away again. He had nothing, nothing to do with this, and she was under no obligation to bring him forward. But that did not mean she could lie. Because it would be lying, would it not, to say that no one had succeeded where Mr. Gregory had failed?

Florence compromised with herself. "I am not breaking our engagement in expectation of another, sir," she replied gently. "And now good day to you."

CHAPTER
TWENTY-THREE

Most friendship is feigning, most loving mere folly.
—Shakespeare, *As You Like It,* II.vii.1071 (1599)

F lorence had not gone ten steps down the lane from her erst-
while intended before her spirits were further dampened by
the problem still confronting her. Which was, what was she to do
about her father and Mrs. Whisp? Was it her duty to tell him what
she had seen?

She had not gone many steps more before she decided it was.
Of course it was. Suppose her papa married this faithless woman,
and Mrs. Whisp then proved a faithless wife? (It was just as well
Florence knew none of the rumors that had surrounded her first

stepmother Miss Catherine Catchway—bad enough to imagine her father suffering infidelity even the once.)

Yes. She must tell him. At once. Before the excited whizzing inside her entirely faded away and second thoughts regarding her own broken engagement arose.

Not until she gained Hollowgate's drive did she remember she had originally gone to the rectory to settle Snap's fate. Well, he could hardly go to the Gregorys now, but if her papa broke it off with Mrs. Whisp, there would be no need for Snap to go anywhere. Bobbins could be appeased somehow. Nevertheless, wanting to avoid her siblings and their questions, Florence stole around to the kitchen door, that she might slip down the screens passage to her father's library.

He was there, thank heavens.

The window coverings were open to admit as much of the autumn light as possible, and he sat beside the fire with a blanket on his lap. *Like an old man,* she thought sadly. *Mrs. Whisp seems decades younger.*

Closing his book, he favored her with his usual seraphic smile. "Flossie, my dear. Come. Sit. What did the Gregorys say?"

"Say?"

"About Snap. Will Miss Gregory accept him?"

"Oh. Yes. That is, I don't know. She wasn't at home, Papa."

He clicked his tongue. "Too bad. I hope you left a note."

She made a flapping motion with her hands, too worried to treat with this lesser issue. "I couldn't. I didn't. Leave a note, that is. Papa, there is something I must tell you."

Although his smile did not slip, she sensed a stiffening in him, and she hastened on. "Papa—I don't know quite how to say what I have to say—it's a muddle—but you must brace yourself—all such a terrible shock—"

"It sounds like you would benefit from a little repose to gather your thoughts," he broke in smoothly. "I haven't much time just now, you see, for I summoned Mr. Fairchild to discuss Mrs. Whisp's marriage settlement. He should arrive any minute."

Marriage settlement!

Panic threatened to tie Florence's tongue further, but she gripped the arms of her chair until her knuckles whitened, determined to make the effort or die trying.

"No, Papa, I can express myself now—before Mr. Fairchild comes," she insisted. Taking a deep breath, she released the arms of the chair, flexed her hands and then clasped them tightly. "It is exactly Mrs. Whisp I would like to—to tell you about. You see, I am afraid she may be...rethinking her engagement to you."

The slightest narrowing of his eyes marred his calm countenance. "Oh? And she told you this, rather than telling me? Heh, heh. Most peculiar. I did not know you two were already confidantes."

"No, Papa, she did not tell me. I—saw with my eyes." Florence fixed her gaze on the fire because it was easier than looking at her father. "I went to the rectory to speak with Miss Gregory, you know, and heard a woman's voice while I was still outside. I thought I would step around and speak with her without knocking at the door—so as not to disturb Mr. Gregory if he was working—but when I went 'round the house, it was not Miss Gregory's voice

I had heard after all. It was—Mrs. Whisp's. And—and—and she was with Mr. Gregory. They were—they were—in short, they were embracing." This last emerged in a whisper, and Florence held her breath. Would he be furious? Incredulous? Would he blame the messenger?

A long silence followed, broken only by the occasional crackling of the fire. She could understand why her father chose to spend so much time in this part of the house. From the library, sounds were hushed: kitchen pots and pans banging about, children arguing, Snap barking—all was muffled or altogether muted.

When Mr. Ellsworth finally spoke, his voice was resolutely light. "I am sorry to hear your intended husband held your affections so cheaply."

"M-my intended husband?" she sputtered. What about his intended *wife*? But first things first. "Papa—after what I saw, he is no longer my intended husband. I have ended our engagement."

"Just so," he declared, patting her forearm with just the slightest, slightest tremble in his hand. "We cannot condone that sort of conduct in anyone who would win our Florence. Shameful, shameful. A dishonor to the cloth. Well, now Miss Dunn may chaperone both you and Lily, when we emerge from mourning."

"Yes, Papa—but what about Mrs. Whisp?" Florence protested. "Would you blame Mr. Gregory and yet excuse Mrs. Whisp?"

"My dear," he said, "you of all people know what a—burly and vigorous man the rector is. If he has indeed forced his attentions on my soon-to-be bride, I do not suppose she had much choice in the matter. I will speak to him. Never fear. Oh, yes, I will tell him my opinion on the matter, and I would not be surprised if the parish becomes too hot to hold him."

Her father's astounding response was not easily assimilated, and her first reaction was to doubt her own ears. Yes, Mr. Gregory was a large man, and, yes, Florence had discovered he was indeed vigorous, but was Mrs. Whisp to have *no* share of the blame? Was she to be cast as the wholly innocent victim of Mr. Gregory's irresistible assault?

Florence was on the point of asking her father if he was truly in earnest when a knock was heard. She froze in horror, thinking it must be Mr. Fairchild, when she was prepared in neither mind nor heart to see him, but when the door opened, a rumpled Bobbins announced, "Mrs. Whisp, sir, miss."

Mrs. Whisp? The woman dared to show her face here, knowing Florence must have fled homeward with her discovery?

If the library had had another exit, Florence would have fled now, but it did not, and amazement held her to her seat.

"My dearest William," cried Mrs. Whisp, rushing in without a curtsey and taking his outstretched hands. Her gazed flicked to Florence, and she nodded at her distractedly, with no hint of dismay, before returning her attention to her betrothed. "Then Florence—has told you?"

"That you were most shamefully accosted by the rector of St. Eadburh's?" he thundered, clasping her to his bosom. "She has, my love. She has told me, moreover, that all between Gregory and herself is at an end. Never again will he have an opportunity to insult those closest to me."

With her head cradled against his chest, Mrs. Whisp's flash of surprise could only be seen by Florence, and it was gone almost before Florence could register it. But there was no mistaking the widow raising her eyes and mouthing, *Thank you*.

Thanking her? *Thanking her?* As if Florence would lie to her father about such a thing! What earthly reason would Florence have, to shield Mrs. Whisp at the expense of her own father? And why would Mrs. Whisp suppose Florence would do anything, for her sake?

"Nor will that man marry us," declared Mr. Ellsworth, pressing a kiss to his chosen one's hair. "We will be married by common license in another parish. Winchester is full of clergymen. A hundred might do the job with more honor than such a person."

"My good, darling William," exclaimed Mrs. Whisp, encircling him in her arms.

"My Ernestine!"

For the second time that day Florence found herself an unwilling witness to Mrs. Whisp's demonstrations of affection, and this time she was too sick at heart to flee. For it was patent to her that her father, with his usual determination to see and believe only what he wanted to see and believe, intended to marry Mrs. Whisp, whatever Florence might have to say about it.

Mrs. Whisp for a stepmother! Even before the day's revelations Florence would have preferred Miss Dunn, and now—words could not express her dread! Peering down a vista of years, Florence foresaw more gossip, more notoriety, more additions to the Ellsworth Assortment (and these of questionable paternity). Whatever would become of them all? And now, even if she wanted to, Florence could not marry Mr. Gregory and escape her share of the infamy. Lily might dismiss ideas like family honor and the (ill) opinion of others, but Florence was not Lily, and such things mattered to her whether she wanted them to or not.

As if they had forgotten her presence, Mr. Ellsworth and Mrs. Whisp murmured and cooed, and Florence forgot herself in turn, only staring at them blindly, nearly as close to them as she had been to Mr. Gregory and Mrs. Whisp not a half hour earlier.

How long this scene went on no one could say, and only Bobbins' reappearance recalled the couple to themselves.

"Mr. Fairchild," he intoned.

The name snapped Florence from her trance. While her father and his intended decorously drew farther apart, Florence rose shakily to her feet to make her curtsey, her color high. She had to grip the back of the chair to stay upright.

Mr. Fairchild had paused on the threshold in surprise, evidently not expecting to find his client accompanied by either woman. "Sir—is this still a good time?"

"Yes, yes. Yes, indeed. If my dear Ernestine and Florence will excuse us...?"

Like a sleepwalker, Florence took one wobbling step toward the door, only to have her elbow caught by the attorney.

"Miss Ellsworth, are you well?"

Her eyes, wide and lost, flew to his concerned ones, and she felt his grip tighten on her arm. From that grip she felt strength and comfort flow. Reassurance. Yes, he was her friend. Whatever might be the situation between him and Miss Dunn, the look in his eyes told her he was nevertheless her friend. If only the warmth of his hand on her elbow did not make her want to turn altogether into his arms.

"She's perfectly fine," Mr. Ellsworth assured Fairchild, coming over to put his arm about Florence's shoulders. Fairchild reluctantly dropped his hold. "Just a stimulating morning for my girl. More on that later. Off you go, Flossie."

"Yes," she agreed, barely audible. "If you will pardon me—tasks—see where Lily has got to—" She hurried past him from the room.

Not fast enough to elude Mrs. Whisp, however.

"Miss Ellsworth," the latter called, "do stop a moment before I take my leave."

Reluctantly, Florence obeyed, and the two women faced each other in the entrance hall.

"So you have ended it with Mr. Gregory."

A nod.

"Poor man. I do sincerely pity him, Miss Ellsworth. For I think he was fond of you."

What was there to say to this? If Mrs. Whisp were as sincere as she claimed, why would she then be kissing the man? Because she loved him herself? Or because she did not care whom she hurt?

Again Florence said nothing, and Mrs. Whisp regarded her with curiosity. "Such a reserved young lady. But you must answer one question for me, if you please—did you tell your papa what you saw? It seems you did not."

"You had better ask him," Florence murmured, turning away. "I am sure you will want him to know more of what—'befell' you."

"Mm." Mrs. Whisp dropped a light hand on Florence's forearm, from which Florence forced herself not to squirm away. "I praise your discretion, in any case, Miss Ellsworth. We ladies must stick together, you know, to survive in this world. And if ever I have a chance to serve you a good turn, you may depend on my doing so. I would like to be your friend."

This declaration was more than Florence could understand. She only knew she had no desire for friendship in this form. If she could have given voice to what lay heaviest on her heart, she would have cried, "You might leave my father alone, if you wish to do me a good turn!"

Outwardly, however, she only nodded again, not trusting herself to speak. Then she got away as fast as she could.

"I'm sorry, sir, could you say that again?" Fairchild asked, his hands clutching the arms of the very chair Florence occupied minutes before.

"I said, Fairchild, that you may tear up the papers for Miss Ellsworth's marriage settlement. The match with Gregory is off."

A thousand questions flew to the end of his tongue, and Fairchild had to remind himself that he was merely the family attorney and did not have the right to ask them. But holding them in might bring on apoplexy at this rate, if the heat washing over him and the speeding of his heart were any indication.

He allowed himself: "I don't understand."

Ellsworth sat back in his own chair, tenting his fingers, his usual bland smile uncharacteristically strained. "It's simple enough, Fairchild. My daughter decided Gregory was not the man for her. Not the man she thought. So she has ended it. Just today."

"Ended it," repeated Fairchild. The temptation to abandon Ellsworth on the spot and go in search of the man's daughter had to be wrestled into submission. Fairchild only managed it by swearing to himself that he would pursue her and offer for her as soon as he decently might, man of modest means though he was. The worst she could say was No, but she was a kind and true young lady and did not seem to think about money as much as other people did, and Fairchild thought she liked him well enough not to dismiss the idea out of hand. At any rate, the game was well worth the hazard.

How long was a decent interval after a broken engagement? A month? A fortnight? An hour?

"I see the news has taken you quite by surprise, Fairchild, and I suppose it will cause a little stir," Ellsworth went on. "But as the match had already been postponed several months and was not to take place until the spring, I imagine its dissolution will not occupy our neighbors overlong."

"Yes, sir."

"Now, as to what will be settled on my Ernestine," he resumed, rising to stand before the fire with his back to Fairchild. "I would like to execute a new will. One that reverts to the terms laid out for my previous wife Mary."

Fairchild gave his head a shake to clear it. Good heavens—the man didn't know the half about his new bride, and he wanted to load her down with gifts already? Not that Fairchild could enlighten him. The existence of Mrs. Whisp's daughter was protected by client confidentiality, drat the woman.

He opened the leathern portfolio he had brought with him and withdrew copies of the current and penultimate wills. "As you have it in your current will, if you were to marry again and your wife survived you, she would receive five thousand pounds in a lump sum. Do you mean to say, sir, that in the event of your pre-deceasing Mrs. Whisp, you intend to settle twenty thousand pounds and a life-lease on Hollowgate on her?"

That restored Ellsworth's beam of complacency to full bright-ness. "Precisely, Fairchild. Twenty thousand pounds and a life-lease on Hollowgate. Just as Mary had. In the event of my death, my Ernestine will be the only parent remaining to however many of my children continue at home. Therefore she cannot be expected to decamp from Hollowgate with them, in order to make way for Florence."

"But, sir," objected Fairchild, "supposing all the children are grown by the time you are unhappily taken from them? What need would Mrs. Whisp have of so vast an estate, all by herself as she would be?"

Instead of appearing surprised by this observation, Ellsworth only looked even more smug. "Ah, Fairchild, there you see I have thought of an outcome you have not: Mrs. Whisp is yet a young woman, and it is not at all unlikely she and I will be blessed with more, mutual, children."

Further additions to the Ellsworth Assortment—of course. Fairchild bowed his head briefly in acknowledgement and to hide his grimace of pity for Miss Ellsworth. Surplus infant siblings, at her age? All the more reason he should persuade her to marry him. At least then, God willing, she would be spared the responsibility of their care.

But he must not think of Miss Ellsworth now. The sooner he finished her father's business—however foolish and inadvisable Fairchild deemed that business—the sooner he could devote his energies to more important matters, like how he could engineer an encounter with her and make his feelings known.

Retrieving a pencil from his same portfolio, Fairchild lay a blank sheet of notepaper on the library desk. "Let me get this down, sir. I assume the twenty thousand pounds would be taken from each of your existing children's inheritances equally? Thus four thousand each if the number remains at five..."

CHAPTER TWENTY-FOUR

**"Horrible!" exclaimed Cecilia, "I believed
not such guilt and perfidy possible!"**
—Fanny Burney, *Cecelia* (1782)

On this occasion, to Fairchild's disappointment, William
Ellsworth did not invite him to stay for dinner, and Fairchild
had no choice but to depart Hollowgate when their meeting ended,
though he dawdled in the entry hall, looking and listening with all
his might in vain for Miss Ellsworth.

But he was not halfway back to Parchment Street before he decided it was for the best that he not speak yet. It was one thing to
throw himself at Miss Ellsworth's feet, trusting to her kindness and
her indifference to wealth, and quite another to be the kind of man
who could do so without distaste. Yes, if she learned to care for him

beyond friendship, his comparative poverty would not matter to her, but it would matter to *him*.

He would speak to Mr. West. If Fairchild was to take over for Mr. Darby in earnest, that ought to involve a partnership, and a partnership would bring a welcome increase in his future earnings. Men like William Ellsworth might be content to live off a wealthy wife, gradually coming to consider her money as entirely his own, but Fairchild had no desire to be a William Ellsworth.

Finding a time to speak with Mr. West was easier said than done, however, for the quarter sessions were upon them, and West had been appointed deputy of the court by the clerk of the peace. Which meant, while Mr. West was away dealing with road repairs and rates, licenses and larceny, militia and maintenance, petty offenders and poor laws, Fairchild was left to handle Darby and West's ordinary business. Moreover, the firm's clerk Hents was out, tending his mother who had broken her leg in a fall.

Which was how it came to be that Fairchild was entirely alone that afternoon when he heard the street door open and shut, followed by tentative footsteps in the outer office.

"May I help you?" he called, giving the blue bag he held a twirl to shut it and emerging from the inner office. "Why—Miss Dunn!"

The governess stood pale and shaking, her bonnet askew and something crumpled in her gloved fist.

"Are you all right?" he asked when she did not speak. A fear stabbed him, that something had happened to Miss Ellsworth, though it would make no sense at all for Miss Dunn to seek him out in that event. But perhaps the gossip of the broken engagement had proved too much, and Miss Ellsworth sent Miss Dunn as a messenger? "Is everything all right at Hollowgate?" he pressed.

"Hollowgate?" She shook her head, regarding the crumpled ball in her hand. A letter. "It is not Hollowgate. It is—something else. Mr. Fairchild, you are a attorney. I hope you can advise me."

If it was nothing to do with Hollowgate, Fairchild could and did relax, enough to wonder with bemusement if every unmarried woman in Winchester would eventually seek him out for legal advice. He must certainly point out this tendency to Mr. West, when he asked for an increase in wages.

To Miss Dunn he said gently, "I will try, if I can. Can you tell me about the matter?"

To his renewed alarm, her eyes filled, and he hastily looked about for somewhere for her to sit that was not his inner office. He had no intention of being found in a compromising position with her again, on the remote chance that Miss Ellsworth should appear again unexpectedly.

When he fetched the purple-upholstered chair from before his desk, she accepted it gratefully, dabbing her eyes with her handkerchief, while he climbed onto Hents' stool. Then, as with Mrs. Whisp, Fairchild practiced the discipline of silence and waiting.

Soon enough she gathered herself. Taking the crumpled letter, she smoothed it upon her knee and folded her hands atop it.

"As you know, Mr. Fairchild, I have been in the habit of walking to the post office regularly. It—was not only for the exercise. I have been expecting—a letter for some time. Since I arrived in Winchester, to be precise."

When she broke off, he waited a few moments, averting his gaze so he would not see her throat work.

"That letter—came today." Lifting her hands from atop it, she smoothed it again. And then—again—crushed it into a ball. Her voice, usually so firm and crisp, shook a little when she spoke again. "I trust, as a attorney, you will keep things in confidence—"

"Excuse me, Miss Dunn." He held up his hand. The very last thing he needed was another secret he must keep from the Ellsworths. Miss Dunn might say her distress had nothing to do with Hollowgate, but he could not be too careful. "While I would be only too glad to be of assistance to you, you are well aware that William Ellsworth is a longtime client of Darby and West. Therefore, if whatever you have to tell me will in any way infringe on my duties to—that family, I must beg not to be involved."

Ridiculous, really. He thought of the magnitude of the secret he kept for Mrs. Whisp from her betrothed, despite Ellsworth being such a longtime client, and was certain Miss Dunn's was probably child's play in comparison.

The governess faltered, uncertain at this rebuff, but then her chin came up. "As a matter of fact, after what I learned today, my business will have no bearing on the Ellsworths or my situation there whatsoever."

"I am relieved to hear it." He let out a slow breath and indicated with an open hand that she should continue.

Once more she smoothed the letter across her lap. "I have been at Hollowgate a fortnight now, Mr. Fairchild, but I had not heard from—my correspondent—for some time. Even before leaving

Woolston. In fact, the long silence—Jem's silence—was one of the primary reasons I went out for governessing. I had no thought of it beforehand. Rather, I had first thought I would…escape being a burden on my family by the time-honored route of marriage."

Fairchild had a guess where this explanation was going.

Miss Dunn paused, swallowed. "The details don't matter now. That route of marriage is now closed to me." An echo of the usual crispness in her voice returned. "So my question for you, Mr. Fairchild, is how exactly does one sue for breach of promise?"

In an instant Fairchild was on his feet. "Breach of promise, Miss Dunn!"

"That is the term, I believe. When a man promises marriage and then cries off?"

He strode up and down the room before stopping at Hents' desk again. The clerk's pens were in sorry condition.

"Miss Dunn. I understand the painful nature of your position, but I must tell you that a suit of that nature would not only subject you to unpleasant gossip and notoriety, but it most certainly would have a bearing on your employment with the Ellsworth family."

"How so, unless you exposed me?" she demanded, rising herself.

"I would not need to, madam. The publicity itself would answer. These things are not tried in secret. And it is not only my reluctance to represent interests counter to my clients' interests which motivates me to say this. Unless you have suffered—damages that could be recovered—you would gain nothing by such an action and lose much."

The hint was delicate. If the damage was invisible and irrecoverable—if Miss Dunn had foolishly parted with her virtue—well, the least said about that the better.

Passionately Miss Dunn brought her fist down on Hents' desk. "There was no damage of that nature, sir. It is the principle of the matter. He cannot be allowed to do this! To make me promises—to require my secrecy and force me to subterfuge, only to vanish. And now—at last—to write and say I will never see him again? He cannot be allowed!"

"You say he required your secrecy?" asked Fairchild.

"...He did."

"Then no one knew of your engagement but the two of you?"

"No one." Her passion ebbed, and now she raised worried eyes to him. "Is that material?"

He sighed. "I'm afraid it is. If no one but the parties involved knew or acknowledged the engagement, there would be no occasion to claim damages based on your lost 'expectations,' as it were. And your decision to take a governess position would tell against you. It could be seen as an admission that there was no engagement, or you did not think it binding because you saw the need to support yourself."

"I took the position for spite!" declared Miss Dunn, firing up again. "To show him I was not pining at home, waiting and hoping."

Fairchild said nothing. What was there possibly to be said?

After a time, Miss Dunn spoke again. "But—but—is there no recourse, then, for his perfidy?"

With another sigh, Fairchild ran a hand through his dark hair. "Miss Dunn. You may of course seek another legal opinion, but I cannot say strongly enough that I recommend against pursuing a suit. I fear you would gain nothing from it but ill fame and criticism."

The corner of her mouth pulled down wryly. "Well, then I would be all the better fit for my employer's family, would I not? I venture to say my own *petit scandale* would be a mere drop of the bucket to those Ellsworths! I don't know if the whispers have reached you, sequestered here as you are, but the rumor-spreaders have been busy multiplying the fame of Miss Ellsworth's broken engagement."

"What do they say?" was his unwilling question.

"That Mr. Gregory objected to Mr. Ellsworth marrying a fourth time and disdained to form so disgraceful a connection, lest it ruin his chances of future promotion in the cathedral close." She waved this off. "But if you think my little woes would endanger my position with *such* a family, I must learn to bear them as best I can and leave my revenge to heaven."

Although Fairchild understood she was bitter, he was aware of liking her less than formerly. But perhaps, like Miss Araminta Ellsworth's archery, he was missing the true target of his anger. That would be the injustice of the gossip itself, that Gregory would come out of the broken engagement smelling like roses, while more mud was slung upon the Ellsworths. Fairchild did not yet know the reason Miss Ellsworth broke it off, but if she had indeed been the instigator as her father claimed, then Rumor was wrong. And if the gossip was as false and loud as Miss Dunn claimed, Fairchild knew Miss Ellsworth must be tortured by it.

I will see her soon, he vowed, *even if I have to leave half my work here undone and trump up some implausible excuse to call at Hollow-gate.*

Meanwhile, Miss Dunn had tucked away the much-abused letter in her reticule and was tying her bonnet again. She seemed to be recovering her usual calm, but when she offered a hand to shake his own, he could feel she was still stiff with outrage.

"Miss Dunn," he said, "I apologize again that I could not give you an answer you liked, and I wish you all the best."

She brought up her other hand to clasp his between, her shoulders drooping briefly. "I know it, Mr. Fairchild. I am not angry with you. I'm angry with—" She broke off with a sharp shake of her head. "In any event, there is no need to apologize for talking sense to me. I—knew you would. It was why I came. You, at least, are a man of honor."

It might have been a satisfactory conclusion to a difficult scene, but it was not to be. For just then an unexpected and all-too-familiar voice interrupted their *tête-à-tête*: "Oh, my, my!"

In the intensity of their talk, neither Fairchild nor Miss Dunn had heard the street door open, and—to be fair to them—the instant Mrs. Whisp had seen the two of them hand in hand through the crack, she took care that they wouldn't.

"I'm so sorry to interrupt. I'm here without an appointment again, Mr. Fairchild."

Miss Dunn only regarded her with cool aplomb, neither jumping in alarm nor snatching her hands from Fairchild's. "Mrs. Whisp. You are not interrupting. I came seeking Mr. Fairchild's legal counsel, and he has given it to me. I bid you both good afternoon." With a curtsey, she marched from Darby and West as if she visited attorneys' offices and held the hands of those within every day of her life.

Fairchild could not hide his dismay with equal ease, and his color darkened. The day could not arrive too soon when he was rid of Mrs. Whisp's "business." Would that he had never agreed to help the woman!

He thought the widow would brim with questions regarding the governess' presence, but she only shut the door behind Miss Dunn and dashed back to seize the very hand Miss Dunn had released. "What demand you are in!" she cried. "Soon I *shall* have to make appointments, if I mean to catch you at liberty. But I have been your client longer than Miss Dunn, sir, so I insist on my share of your time and attention." She glanced carelessly about the room. "But where is your poor, awkward clerk today?"

"Tending his mother, who is unwell."

"Ah." (He did not like the sound of that "ah.") "And Mr. West?"

"...At the quarter sessions."

"Ahh..." A broad smile spread across her face, and she sidled nearer. "Then you were alone with Miss Dunn, just as you are now alone with me. Mr. Fairchild, how very, very improper!"

The woman tried his patience in the best of circumstances, and Fairchild was in no mood for her now. He pointed at the purple chair. "Won't you be seated and tell me what brings you today?"

Ignoring his invitation, Mrs. Whisp danced in a circle. "I come to celebrate!" she sang. "And I insist you rejoice with me because we have done it!"

"You have heard from the Whisps?"

She sank into an exaggerated curtsey and then rose, her eyes triumphant. "You have guessed it. I have heard from the Whisps."

"And they agreed to your terms."

Without answering, she turned her back on him, still humming to herself as she opened her reticule. Then she spun to face him again, holding up a paper for his inspection. It was a draft drawn on Wilson Brothers for £1500.

"Good heavens," he said, taking it from her to study more closely. Not only had he never seen such a sum before, but he marveled at what it represented: the sale of a child, essentially. And poor Priscilla Whisp's mother was gleeful!

"Yes, the heavens have been good," she said archly, gliding closer. "And you, Mr. Fairchild, have been my angel."

He wondered later if he could have prevented what happened next but decided he could not have, because how could he have foreseen it? He was studying the check, and Mrs. Ernestine Whisp behaved as no other woman of his acquaintance.

"I have everything I want," she murmured. "Save one last, little, tiny, harmless thing, and I have promised that thing to myself as a reward."

And then she pitched herself at him, flinging her arms about his neck and pressing her mouth to his.

And, of course, that is when the street door opened yet once more that day, this time to reveal in one lightning-struck tableau the very last people he would have chosen for witnesses: his employer Mr.

West, his young nephew Paul Tillwood, Miss Lily Ellsworth, and his beloved, beloved Miss Ellsworth.

CHAPTER TWENTY-FIVE

The Tempter, or the Tempted, who sins most?
—Shakespeare, *Measure for Measure,* II.ii.169
(c.1616)

To understand how the Ellsworth sisters and little Paul came to be in the doorway of Darby and West, it is necessary to retrace our steps somewhat.

If the day Florence ended her engagement to Mr. Gregory was a series of distresses, the week that followed was little better. It was not that regret overtook her—she was spared that at least, not missing her former lover once.

It was that—even keeping largely to Hollowgate as she did—she could not but be aware that Winchester was once more afire with gossip about the Ellsworths.

She knew it because she overheard the servants more than once discussing the matter. They hushed the instant they were aware of her nearness, and Florence affected not to hear, but she could not help blushing, even more so because she wondered if this was how her father acquired his habit of pretending not to hear what he did not like to hear.

She knew it because Minta came home unexpectedly from school and reported, "Jane Liddell said her brother said there is a pool made up at one of the coffee houses, wagering whether you or Papa will remarry first, and the odds favor you!"

"Me?" cried Florence. "How could it be me, when Papa is engaged, and I am not?"

"Because they think you jilted Mr. Gregory in preference for someone else. Don't worry, Floss—I boxed the ears of both Jane and the girl she was telling it to. That's why I was sent home early."

And she knew it because the one day she ventured into town with Lily, their path crossed that of the dean's wife Mrs. Fellowes, and Mrs. Fellowes gave her the sternest of looks and most audible of tut-tuts, before whisking away into a shop to avoid encountering her.

"The presumption of that woman!" growled Lily, seeing how Florence looked near tears. "Why does she not ask Mr. Gregory why you won't marry him? He would not dare lie! I have half a mind to march right in there and tell her the truth."

But Florence seized her arm, muttering, "Leave it, Lily. It will only make matters worse. It is nobody's business but mine and Mr.

Gregory's, and the more shame to Mrs. Fellowes for listening to gossip."

"Oh, I don't blame her for listening to gossip," said Lily contrarily. "I adore gossip myself. But in this instance the gossip is so horribly wrong that I resent her not knowing better. Anyone who knows you can see you're no heartless jilt—why, you wouldn't even jilt Mr. Gregory when I *begged* you to!"

"Hush," hissed her sister, hurrying her along.

Only moderately less unpleasant than the gossip was the rejoicing some of her family members did not trouble to hide from her.

"Isn't it splendid, Aunt Jeanne?" Lily demanded when they called in St. Thomas Street. "Florence running off Mr. Gregory? Although I almost like him better now, now that he did something so unconscionable."

"I do not," declared their aunt, serving the tea with her neat precision. "We are well rid of a man who would treat our Florence so. Weak. Weak and foolish!"

"But Aunt Jeanne," Florence objected, "if you call Mr. Gregory weak and foolish for succumbing to Mrs. Whisp's wiles, what must you think of Papa?"

A shake of the head sent her black curls bouncing. "Ah, your papa. He is unique, *Dieu merci*. Your uncle Charles says that, after William marries this woman, he might come to long for the easy days of his previous wives..." Reaching out, she tucked a strand of Florence's waving dark hair behind her ear. "But never mind your papa. You, *ma chère*, you have made the right decision. I said nothing when you were promised to him, but now...*en quelques mots, j'en suis ravie!*"

"Me too!" chorused Lily. "I'm delighted too, Aunt Jeanne!"

"I will miss his sister Miss Gregory, however," Lily added presently. "Which I did not expect. So colorless a creature. I suppose this explains why she looked embarrassed whenever I mentioned Mrs. Whisp to her. That woman must have been calling at the rectory as often as she called at Hollowgate, playing Papa and Mr. Gregory against each other, but Miss Gregory could not tell us. How I wish I could have seen Mrs. Whisp's maneuvers! Papa falls so easily that she had hardly to lift a finger, so it was tiresome to observe, rather than interesting. But Mr. Gregory must have required a great deal of effort to seduce. Why should she put in all that work, when he could never have married her? Do you think she did it for amusement?"

"You yourself say it would have been amusing to see," her aunt pointed out.

Aunt and niece giggled conspiratorially, and Florence smothered a sigh and tried to redirect the conversation away from mocking her former intended. "I wonder what we will do about church. Papa says he will not set foot in St. Eadburh's again as long as Mr. Gregory is there, but we can't never go to church again, can we?"

"I don't see why not," said Lily, incorrigible. "I rejoice to think I will never, never sit through another one of Mr. Gregory's sermons, though I might have liked to go just one more Sunday, to stare him out of countenance: *I know you betrayed my sister!*"

"It would be easier to stare Mr. Gregory out of countenance than Mrs. Whisp, to be sure," Florence said. "As far as I can see, she is not the least bit embarrassed."

"That is because you're embarrassed enough for the both of you," retorted Lily, taking another biscuit. "What a stepmama she will make! Suppose she tries to steal my beaux!"

"You haven't any beaux."

"Not yet, but I will!" Lily soon grinned, however. "Let her try! Look at the men who fall for the likes of Mrs. Whisp: Papa, who as I said falls for nearly anyone, and Mr. Gregory, who fell because he thought himself incapable of falling! If Mrs. Whisp steals such beaux as Papa and Mr. Gregory represent, I think I will be able to bear their loss."

"You will have many more besides," Jeanne assured her with a fond smile.

"Yes, indeed," agreed Lily simply. "In fact, Mrs. Whisp's chaperonage may save me a great deal of time, by weeding out the fools and leaving behind only the wise, admirable ones." She stole a sly sidewise look at Florence. "Ones of Mr. Fairchild's ilk, say. *He* would never be taken in by such a one as our dear stepmother."

"Oh, Mr. Fairchild," beamed their aunt, putting a hand to her chest. "*Je l'adore!* So gentlemanly and sensible. So kind to poor old Mrs. Archibald, his landlady. And so very handsome."

"Aunt Jeanne," whispered Lily, leaning closer and putting her back to Florence, "I will tell you a secret. I want Florence to marry Mr. Fairchild."

"Stop it, Lily," snapped Florence, but her aunt had to set her teacup down quickly, lest she spill it as she clapped her hands in delight.

"Yes! *En voilà une bonne idée!*"

"Now that she's free," Lily went on. "I know he hasn't any money, but Florence has plenty."

"Money—bah!" their aunt scoffed. "Has money made your papa happy? No. He is not a tithe as happy as Charles and I. What do you say, Florence? Would you like to marry Mr. Fairchild?"

Florence vowed to herself that she would call on her aunt and uncle *without* Lily in future—or at least until they had something new to occupy them. Her face was hot, but it was half vexation.

"In the first place, he hasn't asked me," she said shortly, "and in the second it's most unkind of you both to be so flippant with matters so personal to me. I think I will go home now."

"Ah, you must forgive us!" her aunt declared, seizing Florence and kissing her hand impulsively. "You understand it is so easy to arrange other people's lives. Of course you need not marry Mr. Fairchild, even if he asks. I only hope you will choose a fine, honorable man *like* our neighbor. You like him, do you not?"

"She does," said Lily. But seeing the mulish set to her sister's face, she grimaced and got to her own feet. "But we won't talk about it, if it displeases you, Floss."

"Thank you," answered Florence, still unbending. But she returned her aunt's kiss.

It was a silent walk home, Lily knowing better than to needle her sister further and Florence lost in her own thoughts. For she did like Mr. Fairchild, despite not wanting her family to trumpet the matter. Did like him and did agree that he was gentlemanly and sensible and handsome and fine and honorable as her aunt declared. And if Mr. Fairchild ever gave her any opportunity or indication that he would like to be more than friends, or more than attorney and client's daughter, Florence intended to encourage him. But it did not mean she wanted everyone or anyone talking about it. Was not her ill-fated engagement to Mr. Gregory and its aftermath painful enough? If ever, ever heaven favored her enough that Mr. Fairchild favored *her*, Florence might still beg him to keep it quiet for a time, so that Fame did not paint her as both a Jilt and a Flirt. In the meantime, she did not think she would walk into town again for some time, till the whole affair had blown over.

Unfortunately for Florence's new resolution, Fate would ordain that she return to town the very next afternoon.

The early October day was fair but chilly, and Florence pinned herself in a wool shawl, determined to clear out the dead annuals from her garden and pick some of the pippins. The work brought not only color to her cheeks but a measure of peace. In her garden there were no gossips, and anyone who might have sought her there in earlier days would not disturb her now—Mrs. Whisp now went straight to her father's library when she called, and the Gregorys—well, Florence wondered when she might ever see them again.

She weeded and uprooted her way along the wall, standing to loosen her wrap and admire her progress. Then she took up an empty basket for the apples and smiled up at the tree hung with rosy fruit.

A face smiled back.

Florence shrieked, dropping the basket and nearly falling over as she stumbled back.

"Don't be afraid, miss!" called a voice. "It's just me."

"Just who?" she demanded, a hand to her hammering heart. But she was reassured by the higher pitch of the voice.

There was a rustling and several pippins bounced to the ground before a boot appeared, and then a leg, and then—with a whoosh and a thump—little Paul Tillwood dropped down before her.

"P-Paul?" Florence squeaked. "Whatever are you doing here?"

"You said I might come anytime."

"So I did, but I thought you might restrict those visits to holidays and half-holidays," she replied, amused. "It *isn't* a holiday or half-holiday today, is it?"

He traced a line in the soil with the toe of his boot and then flashed a grin at her. "Well...no."

"Paul—are you playing truant?" Her clear brow clouded. "Has there been...trouble?" He looked well enough. In fact, Florence thought he was neither so pale nor so thin as he had been just a week earlier.

"What do you mean 'trouble'?"

"Oh...I mean—with your schoolmates or—your tutor—or anything. Else why would you run away?"

"I haven't run away," the boy declared stoutly. "I've gone Continent."

By racking her brain, Florence recalled Tyrone using the phrase. "But Paul, you haven't gone Continent. If you had, you would be sitting in the infirmary right now, not eating apples at Hollowgate. Not to mention, you can't be unwell, if you walked all the way here and climbed my apple tree."

"You wouldn't send me back to school, would you, Miss Ellsworth?" he wheedled. "I'll get in fearful trouble if they discover I'm not in sick-house and I've given myself a holiday. They'll likely give me a tunding on top of Hall."

Florence had no idea what that was, but, knowing Winchester, it likely involved a beating. She frowned at him, aware for the first time that little Paul had a gleam of mischief in his eye. Why, he *knew* she was soft! That she worried over the hardships of school, and he was using that knowledge to his own advantage!

Folding her arms across her chest, she replied carefully, "I wouldn't be surprised. And in this instance, you might actually deserve your punishment. But don't worry—Tyrone says if you pad yourself well, it hardly hurts a bit."

Paul sputtered at this, amazed that the tender-hearted Miss Ellsworth would sell him so. But then he saw the gleam in her own eye, and he smiled. "What will you do with me then, miss?"

"I haven't any idea," she admitted with a laugh. "But I do know that you had better go back before you are missed, so I will leave you in your uncle's hands. But first Wilcomb our cook will wrap you up a little luncheon of bread and cheese and a few more of these pippins."

Within the half hour Florence had enlisted Lily to accompany them, and they were walking up Cock Lane past the barracks and through the West Gate, Florence's heart secretly dancing as she thought of seeing Mr. Fairchild again and for the first time as a free woman.

She repeated the words to herself: Gentlemanly. Sensible. Kind. Handsome. Fine. Honorable. Everything she had thought Mr. Gregory was, and he had turned out not to be. She wondered if her mama would have approved of Mr. Fairchild. He was not a rich man, true, but Henrietta Baldric had disdained marrying for money. And Mr. Fairchild had all the qualities Florence's mama likely had once imagined she would find in William Ellsworth.

A hundred different things could happen, of course, she told herself, trying to dampen her expectations. He might only and ever feel friendship for her. He might be in love with Miss Dunn (though Florence would guess that Miss Dunn did not return his feelings). Her papa might disapprove the match. Her papa might dismiss Mr. Fairchild in dudgeon.

But her heart danced in anticipation, nevertheless. She could not help it.

"Isn't that Miss Dunn again?" asked Lily, when they passed the Guildhall.

Florence glanced and just saw the governess darting down St. Peter Street. "The post office again, I suppose," she murmured, aware of a twitch of unease. At least Mr. Fairchild did not accompany her this time.

"And look there," Lily nudged little Paul to a halt at the foot of the Market Cross. "A statue of William of Wykeham. I do believe he is turning a disapproving eye on you for trigging it this afternoon."

Though she winked at him as she teased, Paul was starting to look uneasy himself. His luncheon devoured and his uncle's office drawing nearer, the day's adventure was taking on a new light.

"Why, Miss Ellsworth and Miss Lily," came a voice behind them. "What an unlooked-for pleasure to see you in town."

The young ladies turned to find Mr. West making his bow.

"Good afternoon, Mr. West," said Florence. "We are even now going to Darby and West."

"Then let me accompany you," he replied in the hissy manner that made Lily squirm. "I have a brief recess from the quarter sessions, where I am serving as deputy, and require something from my office." He regarded Paul with one eyebrow lifted until Florence said, "This is Paul Tillwood. Paul, this is Mr. West, your uncle's employer."

The boy colored, gulping and making a clumsy bob of a bow as they walked.

"If I recall," drawled Mr. West, "you are now a first-year at Winchester?"

"Yes, sir."

"How do you come to be in the town today?"

"Er—"

"You would not be playing truant, would you, young sir?"

"Er—"

"Well, Paul has something he must discuss with Mr. Fairchild," Florence interjected. It was not precisely a falsehood; Mr. Fairchild would indeed have something to say about the day's activities.

"Hm." Mr. West's skepticism showed, and he decided a lecture was in order. "I hope you will grow to be a well-conducted, honorable young man, Tillwood, like your uncle."

"Yes, sir," gulped Paul.

"But you will never make prefect if your demeanor fails to meet the highest standards. And being made prefect is often the path to a fellowship at New College. You want to go to New College like your uncle, do you not?"

Another gulp. "Yes, sir."

"Then model your behavior on his, child. And remember William of Wykeham's motto: 'Manners maketh man.' He does not refer merely to courtesy, but rather to one's overall comportment, moral, physical, and spiritual."

"Yes, sir," said Paul.

While Florence was warmed to hear Mr. West's good opinion of Mr. Fairchild, she still pitied poor Paul having to be bludgeoned about the head figuratively with his uncle's goodness before he returned to school, where another more literal pummeling from his tutor likely awaited him. She tried to give him an encouraging smile, but he was staring droopingly at his feet by this point, quite cast down.

But they reached Darby and West at last, and Mr. West courteously flung wide the door.

Therefore the scene that met them was visible to the entire party, like the stage in a jewel box of a theatre where there were no bad seats.

The scene of Mr. Fairchild in Mrs. Whisp's arms, her lips locked with his.

Chapter Twenty-Six

Yet send me back my heart and eyes,

That I may know, and see thy lies,

And may laugh and joy, when thou

Art in anguish

And dost languish

For some one

That will none,

Or prove as false as thou art now.

—John Donne, *"The Message"* (c.1590s)

How Florence got through the minutes that followed she never knew. At first there was an explosion of sorts within her. Incredulity, hurt, anger, confusion. It burst altogether and all at once, and she felt something fragile shatter with the blow. Then came a slow, sick feeling. A mist before her eyes, through which she dimly saw Mrs. Whisp release Mr. Fairchild. And an awareness of Mr. Fairchild looking at her, but she could not, would not meet his eyes.

"Ahem! By heavens, Fairchild," said Mr. West, the first to fumble toward recovery. "Where is Hents?"

"His mother." Fairchild's throat seemed equally obstructed. "Mrs. Hents broke her leg. He is home with her. Why—why, Paul, whatever are you doing out of school?"

Paul opened his mouth, but nothing emerged. Lily looked at Florence, but Florence was pale and dazed, and Lily did not want anyone to notice her pain, so she blurted, "He came to visit us at Hollowgate, and we have brought him here. And now he is yours." Mercilessly she gave little Paul a push toward his uncle. "Good afternoon, Mrs. Whisp," she added. "What brings you here?"

"Business," replied their soon-to-be stepmother, much more experienced with exciting situations and therefore trying to hide the thrill the danger gave her.

"Well, then," Lily said crisply. "We'll be on our way and let you...carry on. Good-bye." Thrusting her arm through Florence's, she marched her away.

Lily waited until they were out of town and past the barracks before she ventured a word. "Flossie, dearest—"

Florence shook her head, pressing her lips together, and Lily knew that meant she did not trust herself to speak.

Lily sighed. "Flossie, dearest, you needn't talk. But I must. You know I must." When her sister said nothing, Lily pressed on. "The timing was most unfortunate, was it not? I begin to think Mrs. Whisp plans to seduce every man we know. I suppose next we shall find her with Tyrone."

Even for her sister's sake, Florence could not muster a smile. *You must rally, Florence Ellsworth! What will become of your family if you do not? What is your excuse for this weakness? That you thought you might love him?*

"Will you...tell Papa about what we saw?" asked Lily. Really, at the moment, she didn't care a fig for her papa, but it was easier to begin there than with Mr. Fairchild.

"I don't know," said Florence in a low voice. "If I did, I suppose he would blame Mr. Fairchild, just as he blamed Mr. Gregory."

"Then—you don't blame Mr. Fairchild?"

"Of course I do," she breathed, a hand to her midsection as if she felt a pain there. "I—cannot think how he would come to be in such a situation unless he invited it. But still—I think Papa would dismiss him, and it would not be fair that only Mr.—Fairchild should bear all the blame."

Lily absorbed this. She herself was angry with Mr. Fairchild. How dare he prove as great a fool for that woman as Mr. Gregory and her own papa seemed to be! She had thought him worthy of Florence, but he was not. Fine and honorable and kind! *Bah! as Aunt Jeanne would say.*

"I wonder if I ought to try talking to *her*," murmured Florence, clinging to her father's peril to avoid looking into the abyss of unhappiness yawning beneath her.

"To Mrs. Whisp?" marveled Lily. "What would you say, and what could you gain by it? If you accuse her of being a seductress, how would that change anything?" They had reached the gateposts, but they paused there. "You could not even threaten to expose her behavior to Papa because we know, and she would know, that he would find some means to excuse it or ignore it. Like you said—he would throw the blame on Mr. Fairchild, which I don't particularly mind at the moment, but you seem to."

"Ah," said Florence tightly, "but that is because you would prefer to put the blame all on Mrs. Whisp. Would that not be equally unfair? When I found her—and Mr. Gregory—together, he admitted that they were both in the wrong. She for pursuing and he for giving way to temptation."

Lily stamped her foot. "I am not excusing Mr. Fairchild! I think him as guilty as Mr. Gregory, if only for the same weakness in the face of temptation. Men!" she scoffed. "Fools, all of them! I shall become the belle of Winchester, if only to kick them all in the face!"

"Lily..."

"Oh, don't reprove me, Flossie—don't you see I am indignant on your behalf? I wanted you to marry Mr. Fairchild. I've made no secret of it. And now he has turned out to be as weak and folly-prone as the rest. Wherefore I abhor myself and repent in dust and ashes, as Job would say. Promise me you won't die of a broken heart, Floss."

"Nonsense. Of course I won't die," Florence said, managing some of her usual firmness. "No words had been spoken between Mr. Fairchild and me. I hadn't even settled for myself whether he preferred me to Miss Dunn. Mrs. Whisp, at least, has answered that question. For, while I too think Mr. Fairchild...weak...I still think enough of him to suppose he acted on his greatest preference. Unlike Mrs. Whisp, I don't think he has gone around kissing whomever he could." Pulling on Lily, she started them up the drive to Hollowgate. "No. Mr. Fairchild made me no promises. Neither one of us had promised the other anything. Therefore neither one of us would have the right to die of a broken heart, even if such silliness were permitted."

Of course she wouldn't die, Florence told herself again.

She would just, for a little time perhaps, be very, very, exceedingly miserable.

Quite a different scene played out in the office of Darby and West.

Mr. West took up the blue bags he had come for, merely raising an eyebrow at Fairchild before he departed again, which expressed plainly enough, *We will have much to discuss when I return.*

"Paul," said Fairchild, "I will deal with you presently. For the moment, will you wait for me within, so that I may speak to this client privately."

"Yes, sir," Paul muttered. He had always thought of being an attorney as stuffy sort of work—papers and proceedings and making copies of things. It had never occurred to him that it might involve kissing attractive women. Perhaps he might like to be articled to his uncle later, when he was finished with Oxford. But, to be finished with Oxford, one had to go to Oxford. And to go to Oxford, Paul would have to secure one of the New College fellowships, which likely meant studying hard and limiting these self-appointed holidays and trying with all his might to become a prefect. Well, if he must, he must. At least he might make a better prefect than Rawbone. Pathetic Rawbone! (It had not taken Paul long to see his tutor's bullying nature arose from self-doubt, and Paul—out of a pitying impulse—always did his best to look fearful and wounded when Rawbone undertook to beat him.)

In the outer office, Mrs. Whisp gave a rueful chuckle. "Dear me! I believe I have given my embryo stepdaughters another shock. Not to mention your colleague." Reaching out, she lay a hand on his sleeve, inviting him to join in her amusement, but Fairchild jerked from her touch as if it were the strike of an adder. His face was dark and furious, and she saw he had only a tenuous hold over himself.

In fact, Fairchild was fighting a desire to kick over every piece of furniture in the place.

Not offended by his sudden movement, Mrs. Whisp studied him. "Ah. I see you worry you have jeopardized your law career."

"Confound my law career!" burst out Fairchild.

Cocking her head to one side, she continued to observe him, pieces of the puzzle falling into place. "If it's Miss Ellsworth you're concerned about, then, why not simply go and explain yourself?"

"Explain myself?" he echoed in disbelief.

"It's what Mr. Gregory did, when she caught him with me," she answered mildly, still half amused.

His eyes snapped to hers, comprehension dawning in them. "She—Miss Ellsworth—'caught you' with him?"

"Mm-hm."

He gave a scornful laugh, beginning to pace the length of the room. "You tell me to go and explain myself, as Gregory did, yet you see what he got for his pains. She refused to marry him."

"Well, Mr. Fairchild, I trust you're a cleverer man than Mr. Gregory. You're certainly a more charming one. And we charming people can get away with more than the uncharming ones."

Heedless of the courtesies, he threw himself down in the purple-upholstered chair, running his hands through his hair. "And what would you have me tell her?" he demanded.

"That I threw myself at you. Which I did."

"And you think she would regain her respect for me, when I purchased it at the expense of a lady's reputation?"

"Oh, the bubble reputation," quoted Mrs. Whisp dismissively.

He was on his feet again. "Reputation may mean nothing to you," he replied, "but it means a great deal to her. If I went to her and declared your sins as scarlet, and my own as white as snow, it would not serve me at all. She would think the less of me for sacrificing you."

"Then for heaven's sake, paint me as light crimson, if it would be more helpful, and yourself as faintly, faintly pink! The proportion of blame may be whatever you like. Truly, Mr. Fairchild, you have been a friend to me, and I didn't mean to do you an ill turn. Only let me know what you do say to her, so my story might accord with yours. I can lie low at Whisp Cottage until I hear from you."

But he shuddered at the thought of a confederacy with Mrs. Whisp. It was bad enough, wretched enough, that he had lost Miss Ellsworth's good opinion—the only part of her he thought he could boast of possessing. No—there would be no collusion between himself and the widow. He would sooner elope with Mrs. Whisp altogether than strike any more bargains with her.

"No," he said at last, still too angry to mince his words. "I do not know what I can say to Miss Ellsworth, if I will not tell her the truth. Nothing, perhaps. But you and I must fend for ourselves, it appears. Even our business together is now ended: you wanted money to give up your daughter, and you have got it."

This struck home, and her round blue eyes narrowed. "Well, well, for all your veneer of the kind gentleman, Mr. Fairchild, I see you have your savage streak."

His own eyes were cold. "If I cannot be honest at all times, when the opportunity to do so presents itself, I must tell all the truth I can. But call it savage, if it pleases you."

He might have made an enemy, but he could not bring himself to care. Mrs. Whisp glared at him a moment longer, but when he did not relent, did not apologize, she drew herself up. With an icy "Good day to you," she flounced from the office.

Fairchild turned the key, locking the door behind her.

No more surprises.

Then he sank to the floor, leaning his back against it, his thoughts feverish. So much for Mrs. Whisp. Heaven only knew what she would tell people, and yet it could hardly do more damage. At least where Miss Ellsworth was concerned.

Could anything be done about Miss Ellsworth? What could he do, if he could not explain himself? But how could he *not* explain himself? He had explained himself when she discovered him sharing an umbrella with Miss Dunn, but that had been the right thing to do in that instance. Not to explain would have jeopardized Miss Dunn's character. But in this instance, to explain would tear a woman's character down, and that was inexcusable.

He had never yet had the chance to tell Miss Ellsworth his feelings, and now the chance was taken from him. No woman on earth would want to receive the attentions of a man she had just seen making love to another, and that her own incipient stepmother! She had ended her engagement to Gregory for that very reason, and discovering the identical failings in Fairchild would be intolerable. He, Fairchild, would be punished doubly hard, precisely because he *was* the second incident.

"Uh—Uncle Robert?"

Fairchild had entirely forgotten his nephew, and he looked up to see the boy's head poking through from the inner office.

"Sorry to be a nuisance, sir. As Miss Lily Ellsworth said, I gave myself a little unauthorized holiday and visited Hollowgate."

"How—did you get away from school?"

"I went Continent this morning. But, instead of going to sick-house, I slipped out to Kingsgate Street."

With a struggle, Fairchild rose to his feet again and tried to focus his wandering brain. "Why—what made you want a holiday? Were things...bad at school?"

Paul shrugged. "Not particularly, but I was thinking of the Michaelmas dinner. Little Beatrice Ellsworth was telling me that the pippins were nearly ripe and that their cook Wilcomb liked to make them into tarts, but she preferred them right off the tree. So

I thought I would pick some, but no sooner had I climbed the tree than Miss Ellsworth came out to work in the garden, and I was stuck! I sat up there a good hour, not daring to come down, until even I had eaten my fill. But she found me, eventually, because she wanted pippins herself, you see. Found me and brought me here."

"I see."

Paul half hoped his uncle would call it all good fun and offer to take him for tea and buns before returning him to school, but the man looked preoccupied and almost ill. No buns today, clearly.

But the boy must indeed have been absorbing some of the lessons his superiors had been thumping into him since August, for he now recognized that his escapade, while fun for him, had interrupted and upset his uncle.

He blew out a breath, determined to show he was learning and growing. "Uncle Robert—as you seem—quite busy with work and—er—other things, I want you to know I'm perfectly capable of taking myself back, sir. I'll go straight to sick-house for a night and come Abroad tomorrow morning. No one will be any the wiser."

This must have got through because Fairchild's mouth twisted in an approximation of a smile. "But what if I don't want you to get away with your crime? You've told a lie, a serious offense. One for which boys like you are often made to stand up under the nail when they're caught."

Paul blanched, remembering Digger, only a fortnight earlier, being made to stand up on Junior Row during the whole of school time before receiving a "Bibler" at the conclusion. "I'll never do it again!" he declared, his voice cracking in his distress. "Uncle Robert, I swear—I'll never do it again. Only let me go back this time—"

Fairchild said nothing, but, after another minute (an excruciating one for his nephew), he moved aside and lifted his fingers in dismissal.

That was enough for Paul. He fumbled with the key and latch but finally got the door open, and then he too was gone without a backward glance.

With a heavy sigh, Fairchild carried the purple chair back to the inner office and sank into it.

Ironic, really, trying to instil honor into the boy. Where had honor got *him*?

But even if he threw honor to the winds—even if he lay Mrs. Whisp open to every ounce of censure she deserved, what would he gain? He would be vindicated of the taint of rakishness in Miss Ellsworth's eyes, only to be tarred by the dishonor of sacrificing another—and that a woman—to make himself look better.

"Blast," he said aloud.

It did not suffice.

Heavier curses followed, and, when even they were not enough, he ceased altogether and sat motionless for a very long time, until the autumn dusk swallowed him in shadow.

CHAPTER TWENTY-SEVEN

**Let us al turne over the leafe, and take another course.
—Thomas Bluet, *Important considerations, which
ought to moue all true and sound Catholikes* (1601)**

I
t's odd, isn't it," said Florence the following morning to Lily at
breakfast, once Beatrice had gone to her lessons and Araminta
to school, "that Mrs. Whisp should be the one who did something
shameful, and yet *I* am fearful and embarrassed of seeing her again?"

"I'm surprised she didn't dash home ahead of us, to tell Papa her
version of the story before we could," her sister answered, tapping at
the shell of her boiled egg.

"She knew she didn't need to," said Florence thoughtfully, her
eyes wandering to the window, where fog obscured the view of the

lawns. "She must have come to the same conclusion we did: that Papa would believe her and blame Mr. Fairchild. Still, I wonder when we will see her."

"Any time would be too soon."

The first caller that day, however, was not the widow.

"Miss Gregory," announced Bobbins, when the sisters had adjourned to the morning room. Snap gave a faint growl, but it was half-hearted at best, now that the footman was in charge of his treats. (Having to declare a truce with the servant was only one of the new indignities in the terrier's life. He also must put up with a daily "sweep" being made under his bed.)

"Oh!" cried Florence, torn between pleasure and disquiet. Surely Miss Gregory had not come to plead on her brother's behalf. Might he have sent her?

Lily had leapt up, prepared to flee and don her mourning clothes, but when she heard the name she resumed her seat. Miss Gregory might disapprove, but not for the world would Lily miss a moment of this.

In came the rector's pallid sister, but on this occasion her color was high with the awkwardness of it all, and Florence realized she would not be considered an unattractive woman, if she might take more care with herself and step out from her brother's large and opaque shadow.

"Miss Ellsworth, Miss Lily." Miss Gregory blinked in surprise at Lily's *bleu-mourant* wool gown, but she said nothing and took the seat Florence indicated for her. Snap was immediately off his cushion to put his front paws on her knees, whimpering until she lifted him into her lap.

"Miss Gregory," said Florence, clutching her embroidery hoop. "I hope you are well."

"Thank you, yes. And you?"

Trivialities followed, rarely to be dispensed with in polite society, but Miss Gregory must have been as impatient with them as Lily because she soon said with uncharacteristic abruptness, "Miss Ellsworth, surely you wonder why I call today."

"I—did not know when I would have the pleasure of seeing you again," admitted Florence.

"No." That little word contained multitudes. Awareness. Apology. Anxiety.

They were silent for a moment, each thinking of Mr. Gregory. In her distraction, Miss Gregory ceased to rub Snap's head and instead absently tugged on his fur in handfuls until the dog wriggled away to the floor in protest.

"Miss Ellsworth, my purpose in coming is this: to tell you that we are going away."

"Going away?"

"Yes. Clifford intends to hire a curate for St. Eadburh's." She gave a faltering smile. "Both the bishop and the dean and—well—nearly everyone has candidates to suggest, so I do not think the process will take long. The new parson may be read in by All Saints' Day."

"So soon?" Florence breathed. "But—where will you and—Mr. Gregory go?"

"We cannot go very far, you know, since Clifford is still a prebendary of the cathedral, but he thinks we might remove to town. There is a little house for rent beside St. John in the Soke, and Clifford might assist there from time to time because the vicar is rather elderly."

"Oh," said Florence. "Indeed. St. John's is all the way on the other side of town. Quite a distance from the rectory and Hollowgate. I myself have never been there. How—do you think you will like it?"

To the sisters' alarm, Miss Gregory's eyes filled, and she had to swallow twice before she could answer. "It—will be better than leaving Winchester altogether. Any change will be distressing, of course. I grew up in the rectory. But—I am certain—with the passage of time—"

She broke off, and just in time, for an incongruous, cheerful whistling reached their ears, and soon enough the door opened to admit Mr. Ellsworth.

"Ah, my bonny ones," he greeted his daughters, "and you, uh, Miss Gregory." If he was a little stiff with the rector's sister, she merely bowed her head and turned slightly away. It gave her an opportunity to draw out her handkerchief and quietly dab at her eyes.

"Good morning, Papa," his girls greeted him, Florence adding, "Miss Gregory was just telling us that she and—Mr. Gregory—will likely be removing to a new home in town because a curate will be taking St. Eadburh's."

"Indeed?"

It was plain to Florence that her father took this news as tantamount to an admission of guilt on the rector's part, and if the rector was guilty, that meant his dear Mrs. Whisp was innocent. He looked toward Miss Gregory again, willing now to include her in the sunshine of his favor.

"Indeed," he repeated, heartily this time. "Well, turning over a new leaf requires courage, and I commend you for your willingness to begin anew. But we will miss your visits, Miss Gregory. You have ever been a good neighbor." (The lightest of emphases on "you.")

"Thank you, sir," she said softly. She raised her eyes, still shining with her recent tears, her cheeks still pink with embarrassment, and both Ellsworth girls were again startled by her hitherto hidden vividness. Mr. Ellsworth must have noticed as well, for his brows rose in both surprise and thoughtfulness, and if he had come to the morning room for some specific purpose, it slipped his mind as he claimed the chair beside their visitor.

"Have I ever told you, Miss Gregory, that I remember you when you were a wee little thing in a white frock and blue sash, your hair tucked up under a cap?"

"Y-you do?" marveled Miss Gregory.

"Certainly. Even as a child you liked flowers," he mused. "I remember I—like a foolish young man—wanted to present my sweetheart Miss Baldric—later the first Mrs. Ellsworth, you understand—with a bouquet, and when I passed the rectory garden, the blooms were too tempting. I picked violets, narcissus, freesias. And you came running up to me, crying, 'Don't, sir! Those belong to my mother, and I am fond of them too!'" He chuckled, shaking his head, while his daughters stared, to have him dredge up this reminiscence. They could not remember the last time he willingly mentioned their mother—and to call her his "sweetheart"!

Florence felt her throat constrict. How different her life would have been, had her mother lived.

Miss Gregory was equally nonplussed, for different reasons. She remembered the moment referred to because later she did not know how she had the spirit to accost such a handsome young man. He had laughed at her that day, given her a roguish smile and a tap on the head—and taken the flowers all the same. It was hard—if not impossible—to recognize that dashing gentleman in the bald and spotted and wizened man before her, but, she supposed, he likely found it similarly impossible to find the indignant young girl in the faded spinster who sat beside him.

Before the emotions evoked by Mr. Ellsworth's reminiscence subsided, the terrier shot up from his bed to bark at the door.

"Oh, heavens, I thought he was past this," grumbled Lily, rising to grab him before he could lunge at Bobbins' stockinged ankles. But it was not Bobbins' reappearance that set Snap off—it was Mrs. Whisp in the footman's wake, and even Lily could not hide her dismay when she found herself face to face with the woman.

"Why, good morning, Mrs. Whisp."

"Good morning, Miss Lily." Head held high, the widow swept into the room with only the barest hesitation at the sight of Miss Gregory. "Ah. Miranda. Miss Ellsworth. My heart. I hope I am not intruding?"

Mr. Ellsworth gave her a courtly bow, flicking his fingers Lily's direction. "Not at all. We are your family now—or will be soon. That said, the dog had better be locked up, Lily."

"No, no, William," was Mrs. Whisp's surprising demurral. "I have repented of thinking he and I cannot live together. I have decided this little creature and I must learn to love each other, and I have brought him a titbit or two as a peace offering. Bring him here, Lily."

With remarkable bravery, considering her earlier experience with Snap's sharp little teeth, Mrs. Whisp offered him a cube of cheese from her fingertips. And, to Florence and Lily's mutual disgust, Snap took it gently and wagged his tail, giving no more than a perfunctory growl when Mrs. Whisp then proceeded to pat him on the head.

It was a sop, Florence supposed. If the sisters would not try to prevent her marriage to their father, she would allow them to keep their dog. She glanced at Lily, who raised an eyebrow and gave a shrug. *We weren't going to bother to tell him anyway, so why not keep Snap?*

"I had better be going," said Miss Gregory, redder than ever. "Miss Ellsworth, if you might see me out...?"

Oh, dear, thought Florence, *here it comes.*

When they were in the entrance hall, the rector's sister pressed Florence's hand, whispering, "I am so, so sorry, my dear Miss Ellsworth, for what has lately occurred."

"Please—it will be for the best, ultimately."

"For you, perhaps," said Miss Gregory ruefully. "My brother has been quite despondent. He has not deputized me to ask, but Miss Ellsworth, if there were *any* chance—any chance at all—"

Even as the picture of Mrs. Whisp and Mr. Fairchild sprang once again, intense and painful, to Florence's mind, she shook her head. "No. I'm sorry. I'm afraid not. I may—never marry, Miss Gregory, but nor will I marry your brother."

Miss Gregory bowed her head in submission. "I understand. Thank you for your honesty. I hope you can forgive him—forgive us."

Again Florence felt the cheapness of her forgiveness. How easy to say she forgave Mr. Gregory! But if Mr. Fairchild were to come, asking Florence to forgive *him*...well, that would be a much costlier undertaking.

Trying her best, however, to appear as if she struggled with the request, she squeezed Miss Gregory's hands in return and said in a halting voice, "I—hope so as well. It is just a matter of time. But I wish you both well in your new home."

With this Miss Gregory must be content, and she took her leave.

Several minutes later, Florence was still dawdling in the entrance hall, reluctant to return to the morning room. But when she heard approaching footsteps and the voices of the maids Boots and Monk, she snatched up Lily's cloak from the hat stand, threw it about herself, pulling up the hood, and darted outside.

It was still foggy and damp, the moisture drifting and curling across the lawn and the drive. Florence wished she had Lily with her, rather than just Lily's cloak—then they might walk and walk. As it was, she must content herself with going only so far as the gate or perhaps just a little way down the Romsey Road. But when she reached the pair of brick columns flanking the entrance to the drive, a figure emerged, also cloaked, hat pulled low.

"Ernestine."

Florence gasped, choking back a squeak. "No," she said curtly. "I am not she. Who are you?"

"Don't pretend," he snapped, reaching out fast as lightning to snatch Florence's wrist. "I saw you go in."

A bubble of panic flew from her stomach to her throat, and she writhed, trying to tug away. "Let me go this instant!"

In her struggle, the cloak's hood fell back, revealing her dark hair.

Abruptly he released her. "My mistake," he growled.

He turned on his heel, his sudden withdrawal restoring some of Florence's courage. "Who are you?" she demanded again. "And why are you waiting outside Hollowgate?"

"Saw her go in," he threw back over his shoulder. "I'm a creditor. She owes me money. A lot of money."

"Then you would do better to call at Whisp Cottage," she called after him sternly, "and not lurk about here."

In answer, he merely lifted a hand, not even turning back to look at her, and the fog soon hid him from view.

Florence required a moment to catch her breath, waiting for her heartbeat to slow. A creditor! How much debt was Mrs. Whisp in? Did her father know?

It had not required finding Mrs. Whisp in compromising situations with Mr. Gregory and Mr. Fairchild to guess that the widow did not marry William Ellsworth for love, but this bald proof that she wanted only her intended's money grieved Florence, nonetheless. *Poor Papa. He seems halfway in love with her already, while she doesn't care a straw for him! She must owe a great deal, for that man to follow her and behave so outrageously. Papa can have no idea of it.*

She heaved a sigh, her gaze following the road toward Whisp Cottage and town. Why did every last thing about Mrs. Whisp entail Florence wrestling with herself, trying to determine her duty toward her father? If she went running to him now, tattling about his future wife's debts, what would it gain her? He would likely brush that off just as he brushed off the tale of her amorous entanglement.

No. Blabbing to her father would achieve nothing.

What Florence needed was sound, reasonable, objective advice.

Mr. Fairchild.

He popped into her head unbidden, as he always did. And the mere thought of him was enough to make her stiffen and brace herself. For she both longed to see him and never wanted to see him again.

"He could not give me objective advice," she whispered, arguing with herself. "Not if he is...attached to her."

But what if he had only been dallying with Mrs. Whisp, tempted by folly as Mr. Gregory had been?

He was able to advise me earlier, though what I asked for was against what Papa, his client, might like. Even if Mr. Fairchild—prefers Mrs. Whisp now, might he not still be able to offer sound, helpful counsel?

Some part of Florence was afraid she was so willing to think so because she could not resist seeing him again, however much it might hurt. And another part of her wanted to upbraid him for proving so vulnerable to the charms of such a woman. *After what he knew I thought of her!*

She hadn't any right to upbraid him, of course. None at all.

But she wished she might all the same.

CHAPTER TWENTY-EIGHT

My beloved is gone down into his garden, to the beds of spices, to feed in the gardens, and to gather lilies.
—Song of Solomon 6:2, *The Authorized Version* (1611)

The first problem Florence met, in wanting to consult Mr. Fairchild, was where to do it. She could not bear to visit Darby and West; nor could she summon him to Hollowgate without her father knowing (and possibly Mrs. Whisp). The home of her aunt and uncle would have been convenient, but with Aunt Jeanne already wanting to matchmake, Florence did not think she could bear it—nor did she want her aunt to know about Mr. Fairchild and Mrs. Whisp because she did not want her aunt to think poorly of him! It was all so confusing.

That left one place, and Florence sent a note before she could change her mind.

Hents did not deliver the note straight off because his employers Mr. West and Mr. Fairchild were closeted in the inner office, and Mr. West had commanded they not be disturbed.

"I assure you, sir," Fairchild said, not for the first or second time, "It will never happen again. I am not in the habit of using the office—or indeed any place—for assignations. The client Mrs. Whisp came with a business purpose."

"And what business purpose did the embrace serve?"

But Fairchild was still determined not to vindicate himself at a woman's expense, and he had to content himself with saying only: "A valid question, Mr. West. But it will not happen again."

West shrugged, swinging his leg as he sat on the corner of his desk. "You understand, Fairchild, that I know you're a young man and attractive to the ladies. I'm not complaining. It's good for business, if anything. But if you want to be able to keep all the female clients happy, it wouldn't be prudent to show any one of them special attentions."

"Sir."

"And if the reputation of Darby and West is to maintain its sterling quality, there must be no rumors of that nature attached to us."

"Of course, sir."

"What you ought to do, Fairchild, is marry. I don't imagine it would discourage anyone, male or female, from doing business with us, and it would protect the firm's reputation." The leg swung again.

"Now that you've taken over Darby's clients, there's no reason you can't take over Darby's share of the fees. It won't make you a rich man, any more than it's made me one, but you'll certainly be well-off enough to afford a wife and modest house in town and perhaps under half a dozen children."

Instead of appearing elated, Fairchild's mouth twisted in a self-mocking grin. "Thank you, sir. I'll keep it in mind." Ironic, really. Just when the means to marry Miss Ellsworth without sacrifice of self-respect landed in his lap, she lay further out of reach than ever. While she might agree to marry a poor man, she would never, never choose a dishonorable one.

"That's that, then," said West, returning behind his desk and taking up one of the files. "Now to dig myself out of the pile of accumulated work...What did you say was the state of the Codswell affairs...?"

By the time West departed to consume a chop and pint at the King's Head, two hours had passed. Hents distributed the few notes and items from the post to either partner's desk, singling out the note from Hollowgate for Fairchild's attention. "I think this one wants an answer, sir."

"Very well."

While he did not recognize the hand, the direction of Hollowgate was enough to make his fingers unsteady as he unfolded it.

Hollowgate

8 October 1800

Dear Mr. Fairchild:

I hope you will pardon me for requesting your assistance again in a busy season. I have one matter I would like to ask your advice on, in regard to my father's upcoming marriage, which will take place Sunday at St. Maurice's. If you would be so kind as to come to Hollowgate, you will find me in the walled garden each morning between ten o'clock and noon, where we will not be disturbed. If, for whatever reason, this is not amenable to you, you need not send word.

Your obliged friend,
Miss Ellsworth

Fairchild gave an incredulous laugh when he read this missive. Not come? Not come, when he thought he had forfeited her friendship and trust forever? It might kill him to go and speak with her, without being able to excuse or explain himself back into her favor, but that would not be half as unbearable as *not* going to her aid. And perhaps, by the grace of God, they might begin again to establish some semblance of their former relationship.

It rained early the next morning, but by the time Florence pinned on her shawl and donned her boots after breakfast, it had cleared. The leaves and autumn fruits and remaining flowers were jeweled with raindrops, and the shining gravel crunched beneath her heels.

"Did you want my help, miss, picking the Margils?" asked Barney the gardener.

"No, thank you," she said quickly. "The trees are small, and I will manage myself. Snap will keep me company." Snap would also warn her of anyone approaching.

Promptly at ten o'clock, the terrier gave a happy bark, dashing to the closed lower door to stand on his hind legs and scrabble at it.

It could be anyone, Florence reminded herself, feeling her pulse begin to fly. After all, now that Mrs. Whisp fed him titbits, the perfidious dog had decided she was not so bad, and he even preferred her to Bobbins, the other titbit supplier.

But it was neither Mrs. Whisp nor Bobbins who appeared, but Mr. Fairchild, removing his hat and looking apprehensive. "May I...?"

When she nodded, he reached over to unlatch the door and let himself in.

Each was too self-conscious to register the other's discomfiture, but an objective observer would have thought both stiff and proper and uneasy. Fairchild nearly stumbled over Snap, and the corner of Florence's apron slithered from her fingertips, sending Margil apples rolling hither and yon.

Chasing apples gave them something to do, at least, instead of looking at each other or not looking at each other, but once the fruits were safely in the basket and Florence untangled from her apron, she had no choice but to address him.

"Mr. Fairchild, thank you for coming," she murmured. "I don't mean to be peremptory in my requests. That is, I hope you don't think of them as summons—"

He cleared his throat. "Miss Ellsworth, I am always willing—nay—*eager* to assist you." And though he felt a fool for saying it, considering how she had last found him, he added, "I hope you will always rely on my friendship."

She gave a trembling smile (also remembering how she had last found him), wishing she could believe in his friendship. Did he say the same words to Mrs. Whisp? To Miss Dunn? If he, in his "friendship" had kissed Mrs. Whisp, had he also kissed Miss Dunn? And if he had, why had he never, never kissed her, Florence?

The kissing was a mystery to her. How, truly, did men operate? Mr. Gregory had confessed he was a man like any other, "subject to desires" like any other, vulnerable to temptation when it presented itself in the form of a willing Mrs. Whisp. Apparently, if that was how all men behaved, Mr. Fairchild was not exempt.

Moreover, Mr. Gregory seemed to think it not only possible that Florence would overlook his lapse but altogether probable and reasonable that she would do so, once she understood the nature of human (or at least *manly*) frailty.

Am I at fault here? she wondered. Was her father's example not one to be shunned but one to be tolerated as simply the way of the world? A man loved you as long no other opportunity presented itself. And if a man yielded to temptation, it did not necessarily follow that he did not care for you—just that he couldn't help...being a man.

Florence's eyes fell to Mr. Fairchild's handsome, well-cut mouth. And he felt the look down to the soles of his boots.

"I—thank you all the same for coming," she breathed. Somehow—she couldn't say where she found the strength—she tore her gaze away and fixed it on the basket of apples at her feet. For his sake—their friendship's sake—Florence thought she should make certain of one thing before she consulted him. To the Margils, therefore, she said, "I would not, in my selfish desire for your counsel, want to cause you pain, sir. That is—if it is...painful to you, to think of Mrs. Whisp marrying my father, I need not trouble you with this."

"Let me be perfectly plain, Miss Ellsworth," he replied swiftly, his voice taut, "apart from concern for the effect the marriage might have on your...family's well-being, I care not a straw whether the woman lives or dies."

Her eyes flew to his in confusion. If he could speak of Mrs. Whisp so callously, then it was true! What men did with their lips and their bodies had no connection to what they felt in their hearts. A disappointing thing to learn about the other sex, yet, at the very same time, she could not help but be glad that Mr. Fairchild did not care for the woman.

Fairchild could read her astonishment, but he could not regret his words. Let her think him heartless. If he could not reveal how Mrs. Whisp threw herself at him, he could at least make clear there was no love lost between them.

Without either of them knowing how it happened, the space between them narrowed a step.

In a few words, she told him about the creditor at the gate.

"So you see, Mr. Fairchild," Florence concluded, "I find myself in another dilemma."

He frowned, wondering what else Mrs. Whisp had neglected to share with him. Was the £1500 she extracted from her late husband's family meant to pay her creditors off, or did she mean to keep the sum to herself and present Ellsworth the debts, once she married him? If she had not dismissed him, Fairchild, from her service, he could have asked her himself (once he got over his anger at her), but as it was he could only shake his head at the woman's opacity. Layers upon layers...

"You wonder if you should tell your father?" he prompted.

"Yes." She glanced up at him. Looked back down. "Only—when I have told him things before which he did not like to hear, he...did not listen."

He wished he might press her on this. He wondered if ending her engagement fell in this category. If they had been on their previous footing, he might have asked whatever he wanted, but as it was—

"Miss Ellsworth, you asked me before to speak to your father about the wisdom of remarrying, and we saw how little success I met with—"

She was already shaking her head. "Oh, no, Mr. Fairchild, I am not asking you to put yourself and your position at Darby and West in jeopardy again! I have learnt my lesson there. I am sure you have already done what you could to advise him as to the...marriage settlement, and I know he would not look kindly on you saying anything to make Mrs. Whisp look bad." Her voice sunk as she said this, and Fairchild suspected she spoke from experience. "I only wanted to speak with you to ask if there was anything we—I—you might suggest."

Not for the first time did Fairchild curse the day he ever accepted Mrs. Whisp as a client. She might have dismissed him now, but that did not mean he could spill her secrets. Debts and a daughter! Fairchild did not envy William Ellsworth his post-marital discoveries. But who knew? Perhaps Ellsworth would shrug and overlook them as he did other unpleasant things.

"Perhaps I am worrying too much," Florence hurried on, when he didn't answer. "If the debts are not entirely crippling, the estate can absorb them—and Papa will have my—my marriage portion for ready money, if necessary. I was a little panicked when I wrote to you, I'm afraid. I am not accustomed to being accosted by tradesmen or creditors—and at the very entrance to Hollowgate! But paying the debt or debts will get rid of such persons. And—and—and I am sure there can be nothing worse ahead than—what has gone before—" She broke off suddenly, feeling her throat close. But indeed, what could possibly be worse than catching Mrs. Whisp embracing first her former intended husband and then the man Florence admired most in all the world? If such caresses did not mean anything to the gentlemen, they certainly meant something to Florence. A little debt could not compare to such things. Given the choice, Florence would willingly have handed Mrs. Whisp her entire inheritance, if it could have undone what she saw at Darby and West.

But alas.

What was done, was done.

"I understand your concern," Fairchild answered carefully. He studied the shadow of her dark lashes on her cheeks. *Start over,* he reminded himself. *Begin again. Mrs. Whisp will marry Ellsworth, but even if she did not, she will never catch me out again. In time, God willing, Miss Ellsworth will have better memories of me to weigh in the balance.*

He must be patient.

Florence was not looking at him, but that did not mean she could not feel his steady gaze. Slowly, her color rose, and he watched, fascinated.

"I agree that any attempt to—prevent—the marriage would prove fruitless," Fairchild said. "And, unless Mrs. Whisp has been as profligate as the Prince of Wales, you are right in thinking the estate should be able to meet her financial obligations. So, yes, surely the worst is past, where she is concerned, and what—lies ahead can only be an improvement."

She hardly heard him. Her heart was beating so loudly it filled her head. Because an idea had caught hold of her: if men were men, and if they could not, in their frailty, resist temptation, why should Mrs. Whisp be the only one to be kissed?

Here they stood in her beloved walled garden. Utterly alone.

Yes.

Yes. If men succumbed so readily to temptation, then could Mr. Fairchild be brought to yield again? Because, if men could succumb to temptation, why, so could she! She could, if it meant he would kiss her too.

But how had it worked with Mr. Gregory? Surely her breath had not been so short and her heart so riotous on the former occasion. She had managed it then, trusting instinct.

Slowly, Florence lifted her eyes to his, eyes of winter water. Slowly, slowly she drifted an inch nearer. Her lips parted.

Fairchild's head jerked back, his own heart thundering. What was happening? She could not know the danger she flirted with, drawing so close to him, her beautiful, beloved face turned up like a blossoming flower, her innocence almost a fragrance.

If I kiss her, I am lost forever.

But it was not this which stopped him.

It was Mrs. Whisp. Or the thought of her. It was the thought of giving Miss Ellsworth what he had unwillingly given the other woman only a few days earlier. Though every atom of him wanted to crush his mouth to hers, he knew Miss Ellsworth would consider it a cheap thing from him—something given easily to any woman who fell his way. And that was the last—the *very last*—thing he wanted.

Just as she was the very first.

With a wrench, he scraped back a step on the gravel, his breathing ragged.

He would wait.

He would wait for as long as it took, blast and confound it all.

And when he kissed her, he vowed, *if* he ever kissed her, he would repay himself abundantly the sacrifice he made now.

Florence was only aware of a stirring of disappointment. Embarrassment. The cold feeling of coming to her senses.

Oh, she was a fool! A fool, and he did not want her.

She swallowed and retreated a step herself, too humiliated to disguise the movement as anything else.

"Thank you again for coming," she uttered stiffly. "You are too kind."

The hurt she could not hide easily overwhelmed his tenuous control, and Fairchild would have taken hold of her then, had not Snap that moment burst between them, knocking over the apple basket and barking wildly as a vole skittered across the corner of an empty flowerbed.

The enchantment was broken. And the visit ended much as it had begun, with the two of them chasing apples and returning them to the basket. Once the task was accomplished, neither one of them could think of a way to return to the elusive moment, and Florence soon excused herself, leaving Fairchild to walk slowly back to town, wondering whether he had succeeded in laying the beginnings of a new foundation or merely squandered what might be his one and only, his sole, chance.

CHAPTER TWENTY-NINE

... The imperfection and sinne which is adjacent and concomitant to the vertuous actions of just men.
—Francis White, *A replie to Iesuit Fishers answere to certain questions propounded by his most gratious Matie: King James* **(1624)**

S t. Maurice's by the High Street was a larger church than St. Eadburh's, and the rector Mr. Newbolt led a larger congregation, but such was the fame of the Ellsworth family that many of that congregants lingered after the morning service to witness Mr. William Ellsworth of Hollowgate be joined to Mrs. Thomas Whisp, lately of Weymouth. Not only congregants, but also a few townspeople were present, for who could resist seeing the entire Ellsworth Assortment, handsome and still clothed in mourning, trailing after the happy couple as they walked into town? Miss Dunn accompanied them as well, since someone must take charge of Beatrice while Florence and Lily served as bridesmaids. The bride wore lavender wool, the only hint of her less recent loss being the black ribbons trimming her bonnet and sleeves, and she carried a bouquet of ranunculus, yellow and pink. A transparent white veil hung from the brim of her bonnet, secured to it with more flowers.

Though they had often passed the church, Florence had never been inside. After the falling-out with Mr. Gregory, the Ellsworths had not attended church, but once Mr. Newbolt issued the common license, Mr. Ellsworth began to talk of favoring St. Maurice with their presence. Florence shivered throughout the service in the dank medieval space and told herself she would wear both a cloak and a redingote in future, but Lily was amused by the brass plate inscribed to "Frideswide, first wife to Charles Newboulte," the both of them lying by their daughter Dulcabella Johnson.

By the time the service ended most of the pews had people in them, and only a few shuffled out to speak to Mr. Newbolt and get on with their day. Others threw the Ellsworths looks ranging from sheepish to curious to supercilious, and a bold few changed their seats for pews more forward, the better to see the ceremony to come. It was just such a group that abandoned the very last pew, leaving one man in sole possession of it.

Florence, who had been pinning one of Mrs. Whisp's veil flowers more securely, caught sight of him from the corner of her eye, and her breath hitched sharply.

"Careful with those pins!" sang Mrs. Whisp. "We can't have my bridesmaid poking herself and bleeding."

In answer Florence only managed a gurgle in her throat because the man turned directly to look their way, and she was certain, absolutely certain, it was the creditor who had lurked at the end of the drive! Oh, heavens, was he going to insist on payment the very day his quarry came into funds?

There was no one she could turn to for sympathy or assistance, Mr. Fairchild being the only person she had confided in, but Florence scanned the pews nevertheless. Perhaps he might have come?

"What is it, Floss?" hissed Lily.

Florence shook her head, pressing her lips together.

A brief silence fell, everyone who wanted to leave having made his way out, and those who remained behind were turning their attention back to the front of the church when, in that tiny pause: "Jem!" gasped Miss Dunn. Or it might have been more of a shriek.

The man in the last pew stiffened as if he had been struck by lightning, his eyes suddenly so wide Florence could see the whites all around them. For an instant she thought he might take to his heels. Heads turned; necks craned; a questioning buzz broke out. And then everything happened at once. Florence saw the man rush for the end of the pew, even as Miss Dunn began to climb over the back of their own, crying, "Stop him!" But before Florence could respond in any way, she was knocked over herself by the weight of Mrs. Whisp, who had collapsed in a faint. Mrs. Whisp fell against Florence, who then took out Lily, who then careened into Tyrone, who himself knocked down Araminta, who narrowly avoided landing atop little Beatrice. Only the Ellsworth patriarch remained on his feet, staring to see the rest of his party sprawled on the cold stone floor.

It was his brother Charles Ellsworth who had the presence of mind to fling himself out of the penultimate pew, just managing to lay hold of a corner of the mysterious man's cloak, slowing his flight until Jeanne Ellsworth could seize another handful, while a few more parishioners, recovering from their surprise, blocked the way to the west-end door.

"What is it?"

"Who is he?"

"Who shouted?"

"Call the constable!"

"*I'm* the constable, Darwent, you moonling!" This last was said indignantly by a stocky man who squeezed his way through the growing press.

Those who could not get nearer were beginning to climb onto the pew benches for a better view, and someone even ran up the steps leading to the vestry to peer down.

Unceremoniously, Florence heaved Mrs. Whisp off herself and thrust her at her dazed father. Without a glance back at her siblings, who were themselves struggling up and trying to straighten and dust off their clothing, she pushed past them to follow Miss Dunn.

The governess politely but firmly begged people's pardons as she wriggled and nudged and outright shoved her way through them to get at the pinioned man, Florence darting in her wake, and when she reached him there was a wave of violent shushing throughout St. Maurice's, so that almost complete silence fell.

"Well, Jemmy," Miss Dunn declared, arms folded over her mid-section, her strong voice giving only the slightest quaver, "if you repented of how you treated me and have come back, why did you try to run now?"

"Miss Dunn, you know this man?" whispered Florence. She took hold of the woman's forearm and pressed it, hoping to recall her to herself. Honestly, did it only take living with the Ellsworths to transform any respectable person into a scandal magnet?

"I do," replied Miss Dunn coolly (but not especially quietly). "He is my intended husband Jemini Waters."

"I'm not!" cried the man.

"You are," she insisted, "and I have the letters to prove it. I pass over the last one, in which you attempted to break your promise. And there *was* a promise. How dare you deny it!"

Now, in nine cases out of ten, if a poor woman in respectable circumstances accuses a man of promising to marry her and then wronging her, she would find immediate and unquestioning sympathy among her listeners. The man would be scorned and abuse hurled; the women would shake their heads and tut-tut and prepare to turn the circumstance into a cautionary tale. But there was something so daunting and self-possessed about Miss Dunn that no one condescended to sympathize with her. They only waited with breath held to have the matter further explained.

"You made me promises, Jem Waters. Promises I relied on. And then you vanished! I wrote and wrote and never heard from you until ten days ago, when you finally answered me and said it was all over between us."

"At least," interjected a high, clear voice, "he did not tell you he was dead."

There was a collective intake of breath as every head swiveled to see the bride herself forcing her way into the circle.

Mrs. Whisp threw back her veil, her normally round blue eyes narrow and sparking. She hurled her bouquet at Jem Waters, the individual ranunculus blossoms flying apart on impact to scatter at his feet. "Jem Waters, indeed! I could murder you with my bare hands!"

"You know this man?" Miss Dunn asked in an echo of Florence's earlier question. Her countenance drained of color, and her arms fell to her sides.

"Of course I know this man," snapped Mrs. Whisp. "He is my *late* husband, Mr. Thomas Whisp."

It was a scandal to surpass all scandals, and though, strictly speaking, none of the blame for it could be laid at the Ellsworths' doorstep, both Miss Dunn and Mrs. Whisp were intimate enough with that family for all the disgrace to land there when it was later recalled.

"Your husband, my dear?" came Mr. William Ellsworth's faint wonder. If the day's marvels could be crowned with a duel or bout of fisticuffs, the people of Winchester might weep in gratitude; therefore the subset of them represented at St. Maurice's eagerly parted to allow Ellsworth access to the main combatants. Slowly he approached, trailed by the remainder of his Assortment, and he seemed to have aged a decade in the last minute.

"My husband," repeated Mrs. Whisp ruthlessly. "The same husband who abandoned me some time past and who wrote to me claiming he had been pressed into naval service. The same husband who purported to serve at the Siege of Acre under Commodore

Smith. The same husband, on whose behalf, another person wrote to me from the Greenwich Hospital infirmary, declaring his death by fever."

Thomas Whisp's fists curled and his jaw set. No shame sat on his brow, but rather pugnacity. "And I suppose you're blameless? You stand here to get married again—"

"I thought you were *dead!*"

"You plunder my parent's savings—"

"They got what they wanted, and how dare you accuse me of wronging your parents when you were the one who broke their hearts!"

"I was going to come back—"

"Back from the dead?" screeched Mrs. Whisp. "You walk away from everything—home, wife, child—"

"Child?" echoed Mr. Ellsworth and Florence and Lily and Miss Dunn.

"—And deceive some other woman, and you say you were going to come back?"

"And you?" Thomas Whisp countered, sensing his wife was winning the crowd. "I wasn't the only one to walk away from Priscilla, and I didn't sell her for £1500!"

Uproar met this, and a woman wholly unrelated to anyone or anything swooned and had to be helped outside.

"That's it, isn't it," Mrs. Whisp said, her voice now low and cutting. "This is about the money. You returned from the dead—the prodigal son resurrected in Weymouth—only to find your parents had given me—a sum—and you are here to recover it."

"Money," he grunted. "It's my money, all right, but it's also yours. I'm here to take you home, Ernestine."

Florence startled. Of course. The mysterious creditor outside Hollowgate had called her "Ernestine" when he stopped her. Not "Mrs. Whisp," but "Ernestine." She should have known he was more than he appeared.

"And what makes you think I will go with you?" retorted Mrs. Whisp. "After your abandonment and selfishness and lies! After you have been making up to some trollop under an assumed name!"

"Trollop?" yelled Miss Dunn, but her voice choked with furious tears. "I have done nothing to earn such an epithet. I am guilty of nothing beyond being deceived by the appearance of goodness and believing an offer made to me was given in good faith. I too was lied to and abandoned! But I have no regrets now." She sprang forward, shoving the unprepared Thomas Whisp in the chest, and then whirled to point her finger at Mrs. Whisp. "You both deserve each other. Liars, both. Seducers, both. I never want to see or hear of either of you again!"

Gulping and sobbing and hiccupping, she turned next to the Ellsworths. "F-forgive me. I resign. Today. This moment. F-forgive me, Beatrice." And then her emotions overcame her, and she dashed from the church, onlookers spinning out of her path as if she were on fire.

For the first time that morning, a glint of humor appeared in Mrs. Whisp's eye, and, to Florence's bewilderment, she saw it answered by a quirk of Mr. Whisp's mouth.

"*That* one, Thomas?" asked Mrs. Whisp dryly.

He jerked his chin the direction of William Ellsworth. "*That* one, Ernestine?"

"At least mine has money."

"And mine has looks and youth."

"*Had* looks and youth. If I'm not mistaken, she's left you forever."

"No more than you've been left," he replied equably. "No one can marry a married woman."

"I still might kill you, you know, Thomas."

"Not if I don't kill you first."

And with that, he extended an arm to her, and she placed her hand on it.

As if turned to stone, the witnesses watched the outrageous, reunited husband and wife make their way to the door, where the rector Mr. Newbolt still stood, thunderstruck by such a scene in his church. At the entrance, Mrs. Whisp glanced back at her own abandoned bridegroom.

"William, I do apologize. I was fond of you, in my way." Her gaze flicked to Florence, and her head tilted thoughtfully a moment. Then she shrugged, turning away and calling over her shoulder. "The dog, however—"

And that was the last that was seen of Mr. and Mrs. Thomas Whisp.

CHAPTER THIRTY

**The simple inherit folly: but the
prudent are crowned with knowledge.
—Proverbs 14:18,** *The Authorized Version* **(1611)**

T he—the cat doth play, and after slay." Beatrice traced her finger under each line as she leaned against Florence's knee. "A dog will bite a-a th-thief at night. Flossie, will Miss Dunn ever return?"

"I don't think so, sweeting."

"That man broke her heart, didn't he?"

Florence sighed, pulling on one of Bea's ringlets. "I suspect so. But I think the manner in which he treated her will help her to mend. He lied to her, you know."

"Like Mrs. Whisp lied to Papa."

"Yes."

"Do you think Papa will get better soon?" Beatrice asked, her eyes enormous. Their father had spent the past fortnight abed, even his capacity for stubborn optimism overcome. Though Florence herself had got up every day and gone about her daily activities, in her heart she understood his despondence. She too would love to lie abed and shut the world out. She too would prefer never to show her face again until all Winchester had forgotten the latest nine-days' wonder and moved on.

"I know so," she answered. "Papa is so rarely unwell." The more interesting question in Florence's mind was whether this embarrassing rumpus might cure him of his desire to marry again. Surely enough was enough. Would he rise from his bed a wiser man?

She tapped the page. "Here now—read this sentence to me."

Reluctantly the pupil returned her attention to the primer, but she was not forced to continue long before Boots looked into the schoolroom. "Post for you, miss."

"For me?" For a second Florence's heart rose to her throat—was it possibly from Mr. Fairchild? She had neither seen nor heard of him since their meeting in the garden, though she had both hoped and dreaded that her father would call him out to Hollowgate, if only to cancel Mrs. Whisp's marriage settlement and execute yet another will. What must *he* think, of all that had passed?

It was not from Mr. Fairchild. This hand was unfamiliar.

Florence carried the letter to the window to unfold.

4 Cliff Street
Ramsgate

1 November 1800

Dear Miss Ellsworth,
I imagine you little expected to hear from me again,
and I have been so happy of late that it surprised me as
well that you lingered in my thoughts. My dear spouse
and I are entirely reconciled and have agreed to let
the past rest, and we make a new beginning now, in a
new setting, far, far from the rest of his family. Perhaps
it is my vast contentment that restores my forgiving
nature. Not that I have anything to forgive of you, Miss
Ellsworth. I am sure you read this and say, "Indeed!
Ernestine Whisp ought to beg my pardon, for interfer-
ing with my engagement and jilting my father!" but
I do not apologize for either of those things. As to the
first, you would not have been happy with such a person
as the rector, and one day you might even think with
gratitude of my part in ending your engagement. And
as to the second, your father seems like the sort of man
easily comforted.

No, I write to you because I have forgiven someone else.
To be plain, I have forgiven Mr. Fairchild. When you
discovered the two of us in flagrante delicto *at Darby*
and West, he was quite angry and spoke cutting words
I thought I would not soon forget. But now that I am

happy and have all that I want, I no longer begrudge the poor man the impulses of the moment and do remember his services to me. Nor have I forgotten that I also thought myself somewhat in your debt, for not trying (or for trying and failing) to turn your father against me.

Therefore, what I have to tell you is this: Mr. Fairchild was my attorney, as well as the Ellsworths'. I met with him several times concerning a legal matter, and he assisted me. When you found me at Darby and West that day, it was the final occasion. And being quite delighted with the outcome of our mutual efforts (and finding Mr. Fairchild quite irresistibly handsome, as I am sure you understand), I took him by surprise and kissed him. Which was exactly when you all appeared at the door.

As I wrote above, he was very, very upset on that occasion, believing it would be dishonorable for him to vindicate himself to you at the expense of my reputation. Therefore, I am certain, he has made no explanation at all, continuing to leave you with the misapprehension that he enjoyed, and possibly sought, my affections. I am still insulted to admit it, but Mr. Fairchild was indifferent to me from the beginning. But I solace myself that the main cause of his indifference was that his heart was already given elsewhere.

I leave you to make your own deductions, Miss Ellsworth, and hope you will not prove as great a fool as others of our mutual acquaintance.

Yours very faithfully,
Ernestine Whisp

A letter like this was not easily recovered from. The initial shock, occasioned by Mrs. Whisp's utter lack of remorse, was forgotten the instant the woman referenced Mr. Fairchild. She had been his client, secretly? And the two of them had worked together to bring about some satisfying conclusion? What could that conclusion have been, if not to engineer her marriage to William Ellsworth? But would Mr. Fairchild not have thought it unethical, to pit one client against another?

But that puzzle was set aside with equal rapidity when Mrs. Whisp confessed that she had kissed Mr. Fairchild, and not he her. And he had been angry afterward!

"Can it be," Florence whispered to herself, "that she is right? That Mr. Fairchild was angry because he cares for me?"

But he had not kissed her in the garden when she tried to allure him. Was his refusal from honor or pity? Affection or indifference?

"That's enough for today," she announced, springing up from the window seat. "Go and find Lily and tell her to listen to your music, dearest."

When Beatrice had obeyed, Florence darted along the passage and flew down the stairs. She did not know what to do or where to go, but she could not be still. It was raining out, so she dismissed the idea of pacing in her garden, but she had to move.

She would walk the gallery, she decided. It would be cold and drafty with no fires lit, but she was certain she could walk long enough and fast enough to be warm. She was warm already. But she would fetch another shawl—she had left one in the morning room.

Flitting down the dimly lit screens passage, she emerged from it outside the library, where she slid to an amazed halt, for the door was ajar and voices drifted out. *Papa is out of bed?*

"Come in, come in," called her father, sounding like his old, contented self. "We are ready for you."

We? Bemused, Florence pushed the door farther open. "It's me, Papa."

William Ellsworth sat in his favorite chair, miraculously restored to health, his face beaming with its wonted serenity, and his hand clasping—that of Miss Gregory.

Florence's mouth dropped open.

There were no words.

Both she and Miss Gregory turned scarlet, the latter in embarrassment and Florence in shock, but if Mr. Ellsworth was similarly discomfited, he gave no sign. "Why, my darling Florence! I thought you were Fairchild. But this is perfect. You must be the first to congratulate us. Dear Miss Gregory has consented to become my wife."

Consented? Consented? How had he even offered, bed-ridden as he had been? Would William Ellsworth indeed marry anyone of the female sex who came within his orbit? Did her father merely make a list, and tick off each prospective spouse as she became available or unavailable?

For a little, little eternity, Florence stood there, her head spinning. Miss Gregory, who was to have been her sister-in-law, was now to be her stepmother? Faded, quiet, homey Miss Gregory? And this marriage would happen. Make no mistake: Miss Miranda Gregory was not the sort to have secret husbands or other scandalous impedimenta.

"I—I—I wish you every happiness." With a jerk, Florence forced herself to enter the room.

Miss Gregory rose just as stiffly, and the two of them embraced.

"You are surprised, my dear Flossie." Her father beckoned her over and placed a benedictory kiss upon her forehead.

"I am, Papa." But already her amazement was beginning to ebb, perhaps because she had been William Ellsworth's daughter for three-and-twenty years. Really—of the three possibilities for a third stepmother, Miss Gregory would serve admirably. Apart from her relation to Mr. Gregory (which would only grow less awkward for Florence with time), what objection could there be to her? She was kind, she was respectable. Tongues might wag, saying she married William Ellsworth for his fortune and his home, but those same tongues would also understand and praise her prudence.

"You feared that, because we were betrayed by a heartless one, we would never again find happiness," Florence's father was saying.

She stifled an unexpected urge to giggle. Because she wondered if he spoke using the royal 'we,' or if he meant Florence too must have felt betrayed and feared for the impossibility of future happiness.

"I am glad you have found happiness again, at any rate, sir," she answered. And then, making an effort, she looked steadily at Miss Gregory until the latter lifted her rueful countenance. "Miss Gregory, I am happy you won't be leaving us for faraway St. John in the Soke and that you and I—will be family after all."

Then Miss Gregory embraced her again, and while they were still holding each other, Bobbins appeared to usher Mr. Fairchild in.

He positively started on seeing Florence there, but then he quickly gathered himself to make the appropriate bows and greetings. For her part, she had had the minute's warning that her father expected him, and she met his glance with comparative composure, all the while hearing Mrs. Whisp's voice: "...his heart was already given elsewhere."

"You'll stay for dinner, won't you, Fairchild?" asked Mr. Ellsworth. "We can't work you hard and then send you back out in the rain on an empty stomach. No, no, I'll even have the coach brought 'round afterward and see both you and Miss Gregory home myself."

"Thank you, sir, but I'm afraid I can't today. The Charles Ellsworths have invited me to join them." His dark eyes glanced Florence's direction again, and she felt a shiver run up the length of her back. His heart was already given elsewhere.

"I'll leave you all to your business," she said abruptly. "But—perhaps—Mr. Fairchild, before you go, I might send something with you for my aunt...? They will have eaten the Margils I sent earlier, and I would like to give them more."

"I...welcome any service I might do you."

Florence had no idea how long Mr. Fairchild's meeting with her father would last. Nor did she know what she would say to Mr. Fairchild when he came to her, but she knew she would say something. Too much was at stake to say nothing. Why should only those who dared, who threw caution (and common sense) to the winds, succeed in love? (If her father's and Mrs. Whisp's fates could be called "succeeding"—but they seemed satisfied with their results.)

If Mrs. Whisp were mistaken—if Florence did not hold and could not win Mr. Fairchild's affections—she would at least know where she stood with him, once all silences and misunderstandings were swept away. Thus she told herself, as she selected a dozen apples for her aunt, cushioning them in some rags and stowing them in a sack.

Still she waited, her anxiety creeping back and her courage draining. Soon Lily would come looking for her, or Beatrice, or both. Soon Minta would return from school. Soon a servant would seek her out to answer a question or settle a matter. Wilcomb was already eyeing her for lingering in the kitchen. Then she remembered her earlier desire to walk in the long gallery. It would do as well as any other place to wait, and its very draftiness would ensure her solitude. With a word to the cook, in case Mr. Fairchild sought Florence in the kitchens, she took up the Margils and hastened away.

It was an hour later, as Florence stood staring up at the portrait of her great-uncle Cleveland Baldric, that she heard steps at the far end of the gallery. She began to tremble, taking a swift inventory of herself in the spotted mirror, and seeing her paleness give way to a feverish glow.

She should walk to meet him. Give him the apples. Where were the apples? The apples were the whole purported reason she was detaining him, and what had she done with them? She looked around her in a panic—without any apples, Mr. Fairchild would know it was just an excuse, a ploy to get him alone, and then Florence would be so dreadfully embarrassed it would tie her tongue. He would think she was trying to corner him again, to woo him again. Ah—she was no better than Mrs. Whisp, throwing herself at the man! What a foolish idea this had been! Stupid, foolish girl. Why had she pinned her hopes on Mrs. Whisp's stray remark?

"Miss Ellsworth?" Too soon he was beside her, and she had not moved a step and did not think she could, to save her life. "I hope you have not been waiting long."

She shook her head, further addled by his nearness. How very handsome he was! How firm and upright his person and how intense his dark eyes.

"Are you all right? I know this must be a blow to you, your father and Miss Gregory. A blow after so many blows. I have been...thinking of you."

Florence made an indeterminate sound in her throat, part gulp and part croak.

"...But given Mr. Ellsworth's determination to wed and the possibilities before him, I think he has made more than the best of a bad lot."

She managed a nod.

There was a pause. He seemed uncertain what to say next.

Florence pinched one hand with the other in vexation at herself, and this had its salutary effect because she blurted, "I don't know where the apples went."

"Oh—the apples?"

"For my aunt."

"Yes, I remember." Another pause.

Florence gave herself another vicious pinch. Speak, you ninny!

"Did you want me to help you look for them?" he asked.

"No," she barked, feeling perspiration break out beneath her arms, despite the chill of the gallery. "I mean—never mind them for now. I have—something else for you." With that she thrust her hand in her pocket, withdrew Mrs. Whisp's letter, and almost hurled it at him.

Fairchild, who at once recognized the hand that wrote the address, felt his stomach sink somewhere about the level of his knees. Oh, heaven—what has the woman said or done now?

Taking the letter gingerly to the window, as if it contained the outcome of his entire future, he read it. Read it and experienced his own whirlwind of emotions, ranging from renewed anger—she forgave him?—to relief that Miss Ellsworth finally understood the nature of his relationship with Mrs. Whisp, to a mixture of embarrassment and hope. He might despise Ernestine Whisp; he might resent her; he might think her a horror of unnaturalness, but she had done for him the one thing he could not do for himself. Mrs. Whisp, of all people, had finally laid bare Fairchild's heart.

It took him a minute to master himself. He read the letter twice. He folded it carefully. He returned it to Miss Ellsworth.

"What she says is true," he muttered, leaving Florence to wonder wildly if Mr. Fairchild were referring to his business relationship with Mrs. Whisp, or to who initiated the kiss between them, or to his own feelings for Florence. But she was not left to flounder long. He went on. "Mrs. Whisp came to me of her own accord, asking for help in dealing with her—husband's family. The nature of Thomas Whisp's disappearance and—supposed death—left matters unclear. Working together, we were able to...settle things to her satisfaction. Even if I could disclose more on the matter, it might no longer pertain, Thomas Whisp having risen from the dead, so to speak."

"I understand," murmured Florence, wishing he would continue.

After another hesitation, he did. "She also told the truth about what happened that day in the office when you and your sister brought Paul. I would not have you think what you saw was...typical of me, but I did not see how I could vindicate myself without casting aspersions on her. And I thought you would think the less of me for trying to place the blame for my conduct on a lady."

"I understand," said Florence, more faintly than before. "Truly I do."

They inclined a fraction toward each other, though neither one was aware of moving.

"And...she told the truth, Miss Ellsworth—Florence—about—my heart. About it already being given elsewhere."

She said nothing, but she began to tremble.

He was hardly steady himself. "I mean to say—I have long wanted to say—that my heart belongs to you. And only you."

"Ah."

At last, slowly, her eyes lifted to his. And in hers shone incredulity. Joy. She still could not speak, but then, no words were needed.

She loved him.

She loved him? He was staggered. Disbelief and exultation flooded him almost equally. And it was a flood, picking him up and sweeping him away, spinning. She loved him!

Then there would be no years of waiting, after all, no need for patient rebuilding. Because she loved him. And, in spite of everything, he had not managed to lose that love.

Gently, as if she were a soap bubble, a dream too delicate to handle roughly, Fairchild took her face in his hands and touched his mouth to hers.

At the brush of his lips, Florence thought she would dissolve. Melt into a golden shimmer of love. Within and without, all was warmth and sunshine and summer. And then he was kissing her harder, her lips and her face and her hair, murmuring her name. Her frame would no longer hold her up, but his arms did. She tried to say his name, but his kiss stole her breath.

It was long—very long—before they finally drew back to an arm's length under Cleveland and Silas Baldric's disapproving stares.

"I thought you might not care," said Florence softly, "when you would not kiss me in the garden."

He gave her a little shake. "I wanted to. Of course I wanted to. And I very nearly did. But I thought, I'll be shot, if I let her think I go around kissing anyone who offers."

"But Robert, that might have been one occasion when I wouldn't have minded you being just a hair less honorable."

"Careful what you wish for, love—for I am tempted this moment to treat you with all manner of dishonor and scandal."

(Cleveland and Silas Baldric were here obliged to witness proofs of Mr. Fairchild's assertions.)

"I don't know when I began to love you," Fairchild said presently, his arm wound about her and his cheek resting against her hair as they stood at the window. The rain had stopped, and the sun was making a valiant attempt to pierce the clouds. "It was either the first visit you paid me at Darby and West, when I outraged you by thinking you were worried about your inheritance, or else it was the first time I met you, when I outraged you by dismissing the horrors of Winchester."

Laughing, she turned her face into his shoulder. "And I don't know when I began to love you because I did not dare admit it to myself. But I was jealous of Miss Dunn."

"Miss Dunn?" he echoed, his puzzlement obvious. "Because of the umbrella incident? That one I did explain."

"No, no—well, yes, actually, but before that, even. When you walked her to Hollowgate from town, and you two were laughing about something."

"Were we?" Fairchild frowned, trying to remember, and this in itself comforted Florence. Then he shrugged and gave the tip of her ear a playful nibble. "Well—whatever it was, it was not important enough to lodge in my memory, or for her to give up her doomed engagement."

"Poor, poor Miss Dunn." Florence could afford to be generous now. "How very wrong of Mr. Whisp to mislead her so. At least Mrs. Whisp thought herself a widow when she engaged herself to Papa and went around kissing—" she broke off abruptly, thinking that Mr. Fairchild did not know about Mrs. Whisp and Mr. Gregory. It seemed wrong to tell him now, when Mrs. Whisp had been generous to her and when Mr. Fairchild himself had gone to some lengths to shield the woman.

But he wanted no more secrets. Holding her away from him so he could meet her eyes, he said, "Mrs. Whisp told me that you found her kissing Mr. Gregory as well. That was why you ended your engagement, was it not?"

Florence hung her head. "It was. And, from what I could see, he returned her kiss. But I should have had the courage to end it sooner, when I knew I did not love him and never would. In that, at least—in pursuing her heart's desires—Mrs. Whisp is a bolder woman than I."

He grinned. "I don't know. You Ellsworths are a reckless bunch. And if you have boldness enough now to take me, a relatively poor man, and to give the town even more to talk about, that will make a second scandal that is entirely your own."

"Oh, Robert, let them talk," she cried, throwing her arms about his neck.

"You mean it? You'll marry me, and soon?"

"I've never meant anything more. I will, Robert. I will."

Drawing her back to him, he made a low sound in his throat. "Then seal your promise, my love."

In later years, if either Robert or Florence remembered Mrs. Ernestine Whisp and her career of destruction through their small set in Winchester, they did so entirely without anger, resentment or accusation. In fact, the best word to describe their feelings toward Mrs. Whisp would be gratitude, for the part she played in bringing about their loving, and lasting, happiness.

The adventures of the Ellsworth Assortment continue with Lily's story in *The Belle of Winchester.*

THE HAPGOODS OF BRAMLEIGH

The Naturalist
A Very Plain Young Man
School for Love
Matchless Margaret
The Purloined Portrait
A Fickle Fortune

THE ELLSWORTH ASSORTMENT

Tempted by Folly
The Belle of Winchester
Minta in Spite of Herself
A Scholarly Pursuit
Miranda at Heart
A Capital Arrangement

PRIDE AND PRESTON LIN

www.christinadudley.com

Printed in the USA
CPSIA information can be obtained
at www.ICGtesting.com
LVHW041320261024
794892LV00041B/619